A SPY ABOVE THE
CLOUDS

A NOVEL OF WW II

Enjoy!

NEW YORK TIMES & USA TODAY BESTSELLING AUTHOR
CIJI WARE

A Spy Above the Clouds
Copyright © 2021 by Ciji Ware

All rights reserved under international and Pan-American copyright conventions. By payment of the required fees, you have been granted the non-exclusive, non-transferable right to access and read the text of this book, whether on screen or in print. No part of this text may be reproduced, transmitted, downloaded, decompiled, reverse engineered, or stored in or introduced into any information storage and retrieval system, in any form or by any means, whether electronic or mechanical, now known or hereinafter invented, without the express written permission of Lion's Paw Publishing / Life Events Media LLC. Please respect this intellectual property of the author, cover artist, book designer, and photographer.

A Spy Above the Clouds is a work of fiction. All characters—both historical figures and fictional creations—along with events, real locations, and real persons portrayed in this book are fictitious or are portrayed fictitiously. Any similarities to current or past events or locales, or to living or deceased persons, are not intended and solely a product of the author's imagination.

Cover design 2021 by BespokeBookCovers.com
Cover designer: Peter O'Connor
Book Design and Formatting: Author E.M.S.
Proofreader: Tamara Kaupp
Photo credit: Woman Skier/Getty Images
Maps: Lion's Paw Publishing

Print edition ISBN: 978-0-9990773-4-4
e-Book edition ISBN: 978-0-9990773-3-7

Additional Library of Congress Cataloging-in-Publication Data available upon request.

1. Fiction, 2. World War 2—Fiction, 3. American women secret agents—Fiction, 4. Women spies in WW2—Fiction, 5. British spies—Fiction, 6. American spies—Fiction, 7. OSS, SOE, CIA, MI6 intelligence agencies—Fiction, 8. Female secret agent, 9. Spy schools and spy-craft training in WW2, 10. 20th century fiction, 11. Washington D.C. in WW2, 12. French Alps in WW2, 13. 20th century OSS, SOE, CIA, MI6 intelligence agencies,14. Female spies in WW2, 15. Churchill's Secret Agents, 16. Battle of the Plateau des Glières, 17. Lake Annecy in WW2, 18. Spies in WW2, 19. France in WW2, 20. French Resistance, 21. 1936, 1940 Winter Olympics

e-Book Edition © 2021; Print Edition © 2021

Published by Lion's Paw Publishing, a division of Life Events Media LLC, 1001 Bridgeway, Ste. J-224, Sausalito, CA 94965.

Life Events Library and the Lion's Paw Publishing colophon are registered trademarks of Life Events Media LLC. All rights reserved. For information contact: www.cijiware.com

PRAISE FOR CIJI WARE'S FICTION

"Ware once again proves she can weave fact and fiction to create an entertaining and harmonious whole." *Publishers Weekly*

"This novel is a magical combination of brilliant plotting, achingly real protagonists, and an emotional roller-coaster of danger and courage...all set during a chapter of World War II that is little known. *A Spy Above the Clouds* is one of the best books I've read in years! I've been haunted by it for days ever since..." CYNTHIA WRIGHT, *New York Times & USAToday* bestselling author

"Vibrant and exciting..." *Literary Times*

"A story so fascinating it should come with a warning—do not start unless you want to be up all night." *Romantic Times*

"*A Spy Above the Clouds* is a mesmerizing tale of courage and redemption with characters so compelling they will remain with you long after you read the last page. This epic tale of World War II will leave you breathless, the people and places so real, you'll feel the snow striking your face, as brave Viv challenges Hitler's invading forces. KIMBERLY CATES – *USA Today* bestselling author

"A mesmerizing blend of sizzling romance, love, and honor... Ciji Ware has written an unforgettable tale." *The Burton Report*

"Ingenious, entertaining, and utterly romantic... A terrific read." JANE HELLER, *New York Times & USA Today* bestselling author

"Oozes magic and romance... I loved it!" BARBARA FREETHY, #1 *New York Times* bestselling author

"Fiction at its finest. Beautifully written." *Libby's Library News*

"Thoroughly engaging." *Booklist*

"As Ragtime set the gold standard for historical novels, [*Landing by Moonlight*] includes real life characters and events co-mingled with the author's well-researched imagination to lend a verisimilitude of intrigue, romance, and history." RICK FRIEDBERG, TV/Film Director, *Friedberg Productions/Hollywood Pictures*

"[*Landing by Moonlight*]…has excitement, betrayal, romance…what more can you ask for! I highly recommend this book." Mary Kay, verified purchase, *5-Star Amazon Review*

"From the first chapter, I was caught up in [*Landing by Moonlight*]… I recommend this novel to anyone who is interested in [WW II] and loves spy stories." *5-star BookBub Review*

ALSO BY CIJI WARE

Find all of Ciji Ware's books at all online retailers, at bookstores via the Ingram catalogue, and listed on www.cijiware.com.

DEDICATION

To the handful of heroic American women secret agents who joined British and French intelligence agencies—some prior to the United States entering World War II—and most especially:

Elizabeth Devereaux Rochester Reynolds

American secret agent in WW II's British Special Operations Executive/French section, ambulance driver, courier-on-skis, explosives saboteur, and recipient of the *Légion d'Honneur*

and to

21st century American ambulance drivers, EMTs, nurses, doctors, immunologists, virologists, healthcare scientists, hospital administrators and support staff on the front line of the war against the Covid-19 virus—all heroes that deserve our collective gratitude.

WWII: France Under Wartime Occupation

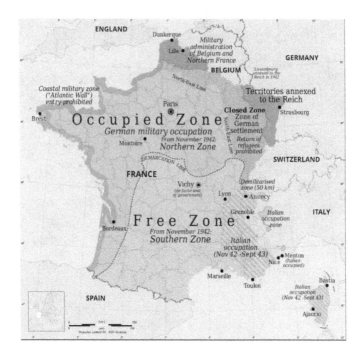

Haute-Savoie / French Alps 1944

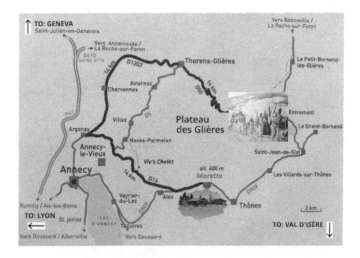

LIST OF CHARACTERS

Note: Check out the author's research photos on Pinterest at https://www.pinterest.com/cijiware/a-spy-above-the-clouds-a-novel-of-ww-ii/

FICTIONAL CHARACTERS

Constance "Viv" Vivier-Clarke – "Violette Charbonnet" – volunteer American ambulance driver at the American Hospital in Paris; later secret agent in the British SOE (Special Operations Executive); she has British and American dual citizenship

Marcel Delonge – "Victor Fernique" – former French Foreign Legionnaire; later a colonel in the defeated French Army. During WW II, he becomes an intelligence officer leading a Resistance network behind enemy lines as a deputy of Charles de Gaulle

Roger Gianakos – Greek-American embassy attaché in Athens

Pamela Bradford – Viv's British-born mother; widow of Charles Vivier-Clarke; currently married to Karl Bradford

Charles Vivier-Clarke – Viv's deceased late father; an American of French-Alsatian descent; a pilot killed in WW I

Karl Bradford – (birth name Braunheim); Viv's stepfather; German-American steel ball-bearing magnate

Adrienne Vaud – Swiss-born school friend of Viv's; driver in the Ambulance Corps, American Hospital, Paris

Gaston Dupuis – Adrienne Vaud's friend working in the Swiss Embassy in Paris

Colonel Wilhelm Gerhardt – German SS officer in occupied Paris

Lawrence Cupperman – Jewish-Canadian escapee hidden at the American Hospital

Jasmine Bernard – *passeur* guiding escapees from Paris to Switzerland

Renée Reynolds – Swiss-American escapee to Switzerland

Erik Thoman – Renée Reynolds' colleague working in the Swiss Foreign Office, Geneva

"Kurt" – Swiss intelligence officer assigned to the border with France

Lucien Barteau –"Gilbert"– French air circus stunt pilot; later SOE's Air Operations Officer

Dr. Jean-Paul Morand – Alsatian-born physician practicing orthopedics and family medicine in the alpine ski resort of Val d'Isère; member of the French Resistance

Dominique Morand – Dr. Morand's widowed sister

Claire Morand – Dr. Morand's widowed mother

Marian Moraski Bardet– a teenager hiding from the SS in Val d'Isère

Colonel Helmut Seitzer – German Commandant in Val d'Isère

Valentin Hervé – a bicycle manufacturer in the Haute-Savoie

Clément Grenelle – gravedigger and member of the Resistance in Chaumont

John Merrick – "Pierre" – British Major and SOE leader of the Resistance network Mountaineer

Paul Malloy –"Fingers" – an American SOE wireless operator

Anton La Salle – café owner in the alpine town of Annecy

Olivia La Salle – his wife and cook at their café in Annecy

Julien Paquet – leader of the *maquis* on the Plateau des Glières above Lake Annecy in the Haute-Savoie

Jacques, Gaspard, Yves – young partisan saboteurs trained in explosives

"Piggy" – a mid-level member of the SS assigned to 84 Avenue Foch, Paris

Major Johann Ziegler – *Wehrmacht* Officer and judge advocate in Paris

HISTORICAL FIGURES (DEPICTED FICTIONALLY)

Dr. Sumner Jackson, M.D. – American surgeon from Maine; resident Physician in Charge and Chief Administrator of the American Hospital, Neuilly-sur-Seine, a suburb of Paris

Toquette Barrelet De Ricou Jackson – Dr. Jackson's Swiss-born wife of 21 years; a nurse in WW I; member of the French Resistance in WW II

Phillip "Pete" Jackson – the Jacksons' only child

Elizabeth Comte – nurse at the American Hospital in Paris

Colonel Maurice Buckmaster – Head of French Section, SOE (Special Operations Executive) in London, a secret British WW II intelligence organization founded in July 1940 at the behest of Winston Churchill; the unit specialized in espionage, reconnaissance, and "irregular warfare," including sabotage behind enemy lines

Vera Atkins – Buckmaster's Deputy, SOE in London; "mother hen" for female secret agents

Peter Churchill – "Raoul" – British SOE network leader in Provence and Haute-Savoie

Odette Samson – "Lise" – French-born SOE secret agent and courier for Peter Churchill

Lieutenant Tom Morel – former French Army; established the Haute-Savoie *maquis*, a large military organization on the Plateau des Glières

Captain Maurice Anjot – former French Army; leading member of the *maquis* on the Plateau des Glières

Jean Moulin – a de Gaulle deputy and organizer of the Free French partisans

Hans Josef Kieffer – Gestapo, Head of Counterintelligence, 84 Avenue Foch, Paris

Group Captain Hugh Verity – flight commander No. 161 Squadron, RAF

Winston Churchill – Prime Minister of Great Britain

Charles de Gaulle – led Free French Resistance against Nazi Germany primarily from London during WW II; later President of France

General Dwight D. Eisenhower – Supreme Allied Commander, WW II; later President of the United States

Franklin D. Roosevelt – President of the United States

PROLOGUE

December 29, 1943

A slender figure, clad in stark white camouflage from hood to ski boots, slammed to a halt in a shower of snow at the crest of a gorge overlooking the tiny French alpine village of Le Crêt. The ridge was a short run to another small hamlet, Val d'Isère, an up-and-coming ski resort until the war began, encircled by crystalline mountain peaks soaring twelve thousand feet above the valley floor.

A thick woolen scarf covered the lower half of her face and grazed her lips as she inhaled the stinging cold air. She stared down at her wide, wooden skis that she'd painted white, now hidden by fresh-fallen flurries. Her body trembled from the harrowing descent in deep powder, barely remaining upright as she hit treacherous patches of ice exposed at unexpected intervals. Digging her ski poles into the side of the slope, she shifted her knapsack to a more comfortable position on her back, its canvas interior plump with a change of clothes, a few cherished cosmetics, and half a dozen hand grenades. Strapped around her calf under her ski pants, her service revolver felt like a slab of ice.

She drank in another frigid breath that seared her throat, giving silent thanks that she would arrive at her destination before dark. Mere meters from the Italian border, the granite crags above her head were wreathed in thick, boiling clouds portending a coming storm. Below her, too, a blanket of fog filled the deep ravine as biting winter wind stabbed through her leather gloves and penetrated to her toes and thick-soled boots trapped in her skis' cable bindings.

Her lower extremities were completely numb, now, despite the two pairs of heavy woolen socks that Marcel had bestowed upon her prior to yet another dangerous journey through sleet and snow. She thought of that nightmarish crossing of the Pyrenees from France into Spain eighteen months earlier, only hours ahead of a posse of Nazi pursuers. She was grateful that this time, her mission involved far less drama.

Marcel... God only knows where you are...

No skiing assignments like hers for *that* former vintner. She could only pray that at this very moment, Marcel Delonge was drinking a *kir royale* at some bistro in Paris.

"Here's to you, Miss America," she remembered him saying as he raised a glass filled with his own vintage and tilted it toward a window where the Pyrenees rose in all their terrifying splendor. "If anyone can cross that snow-packed track up there, ill as you are, it will be *you*."

The red wine had tasted of summer black and red berries, soft and ripe on the palate. That day at Marcel's vineyard in the South of France, she'd only spared him an angry nod, set aside the glass, and pulled the bedclothes up to her chin.

Pushing aside such distracting recollections, Constance Vivier-Clarke squinted down the snowy track that would ultimately lead her to the safe house. Hopefully, a warm meal and a glass of *vin ordinaire* would be her reward for delivering a memorized message to Jean-Paul Morand from Major "Pierre," head of their secret alpine network aptly dubbed Mountaineer. She and her British boss had become great admirers of the local French resistance leader Morand who doubled as the village doctor, setting skiers' broken bones and hiding downed Allied pilots and Jewish escapees in the attic of his chalet.

Viv was startled out of her reverie by the guttural sounds of conversation echoing up the gorge and bouncing off the sheer cliff on her right. Seconds later, two tall figures appeared around the bend less than twenty feet in front of her, trudging up the narrow track she had been about to ski down. They, too, were wearing white camouflage jumpsuits, their skis, like hers, also disguised with white paint. Unlike her, their skis were poised on one shoulder with menacing rifles slung over the other. The insignias on their upper arms warned Viv that the two appeared to be members of one of the German *Wehrmacht*'s elite mountain brigades.

"*Merde, merde, merde!*" she swore quietly, her breath visible in puffs that fogged her goggles for a few seconds. Her mind racing, she realized there was no time to reach beneath her ski suit for her gun. Her gloved hands fumbled to find the outside pocket of her knapsack from which she pulled out a pear-shaped object, palming it into her right hand while her finger sought to locate the safety lever secured by a linchpin.

Catching sight of her, the lead soldier shouted, "Halt!" his comrade bumping into his back as they two stopped advancing up the hill.

The soldier's German-accented French, along with his harsh command, echoed throughout the ravine at a pitch Viv feared could trigger an avalanche in a region notorious for its dramatic flows of snow and ice. He slapped one hand to the strap attached to his long gun as his skis slid to the ground. "Make one more move down the mountain and I shoot!"

Viv silently cursed not choosing the longer path along the lower ridgeline that would also have led to her desired destination and provided a few straggly trees for cover. Here, there was nothing to shield her from her adversaries a few meters away on the steep incline. A different kind of cold skittered down her spine as the soldier took aim.

Waving her small weapon, she shouted back, "Make one more move and I'll throw this *grenade!*"

The miniscule missile nearly disappeared in her gloved hand and Viv wondered if the soldier had even seen it.

"Put your hands above your head!" demanded the soldier, although she took note of the unsteady barrel that shifted between her neck and chest.

Viv, at age twenty-eight, wondered if her attackers had even reached their nineteenth birthdays. She obediently raised her hands as ordered, fanning the fingers of one hand as best she could to reveal the grenade.

"What do you think you're doing on this trail...and dressed like *that*?" he demanded.

German mountain troops operating in the French Alps used

white-painted skis and wore white jumpsuits over their clothing—
just as she did—to avoid being readily seen against the snow in this
time of war. As Viv had no identifying patch on her arm, they would
correctly assume she must be one of the clandestine enemy operators
who had plotted against them these three years since their Führer
had invaded France in May of 1940. Lately, the war had been going
poorly for them, and the Germans were now more prone than ever
before to shoot first and ask questions later.

Viv wedged the edge of her skis more deeply into the snow, bent
her knees slightly—and for a second—considered hurtling herself
downhill to knock the two backwards off the cliff. The boy with
the rifle moved his finger to the trigger, so she made a different
decision.

She gently waved her two raised hands above her head, as if in
surrender. At the same time, she again inserted her index finger and
thumb into the grenade's detonator device and informed her
adversaries, "This is a hand grenade with my finger on the pin, so
you put *your* hands up!"

The young men's eyes widened in terror, at last recognizing the
weapon she held. She briefly wondered if the *Boche* would notice
her French pronunciation—tinged with the tiniest New York twang.

"Drop that rifle!" she ordered with a nod to the soldier holding
the long gun, "or I'll throw this *live* grenade directly at your feet.
Even if you shoot me, I still have time to hit you and we'll all be
blown to bits…*see*?"

She continued to wave her small armament with her finger in the
pin in an arc over her head.

"*Mein Gott!*" exclaimed the man standing behind his comrade.

The Germans were beginning to sink knee-deep into the drifts
that swirled around them like frosting on a wedding cake. Viv could
see that both young soldiers were startled to hear a female voice
emanating from beneath the face covering of the tall figure now
threatening them. The soldier pointing his gun at her lowered it,
staring bug-eyed, his mouth slightly ajar, his gaze fixated on the
contents held in her raised hand.

"You are a *woman*? You have—"

"Yes, I do! I have a *live* grenade in my hand and I'm ready to
use it, so toss your gun over the cliff, now!" she insisted sharply.

Without hesitation, the soldier heaved the weapon over the ridge, where it disappeared beneath the crisp crust of snow. "And you, too," she directed the other soldier whose rifle had remained slung over his shoulder. "Toss your gun where he did!"

With his face now as white as his ski suit, he complied. His long gun sailed far beyond the trail and landed in the deep snow without a sound.

"B-*Bitte, mein fraulein*," the soldier who had first accosted her began to blather in German, a language Viv had picked up, along with serviceable French, during her boarding school days in Lausanne and Berlin a decade earlier. Tears were now streaking the boy's wind-reddened cheeks. "*Bitte, bitte—*"

His companion remained stoic and silent as if, somehow, he knew his young life would end badly in this war of Hitler's choosing. Viv pointed in the direction the two had been traveling up the trail, a route, she knew, wound to higher ground through the towering gorge, presumably to a far German outpost somewhere above the clouds.

Viv gestured uphill. "Now, I'll just stand here and watch you both scissor yourself up to that next ridge and to wherever you're bivouacked," she directed. "And, if you're smart, you won't even mention our encounter and will invent a story how you lost your rifles," she added pointedly. She could only hope they'd come up with some excuse that didn't reveal how a solitary woman on their trail had bested them. And once she'd shed her skis, snowsuit, goggles and scarf, chances were good they couldn't identify her to their superiors, should they make a search of the nearby villages, as they certainly might.

With a sharp intake of breath, she wondered suddenly if there might be other German soldiers from their unit nearby. She prayed she could quickly make her escape down to Val d'Isère before they could alert their Nazi brethren. If only they'd thought about it— which Viv had gambled they wouldn't—an exploding grenade in the current weather conditions would have surely brought down an avalanche on their heads and killed everyone in its path, including the villagers—at the bottom of the valley.

Viv watched as the two soldiers, obeying her command, drew nearer with each labored, uphill step, telescoping the short distance that had separated them.

"Now, you run along, won't you?" she urged pleasantly, although she felt her stomach clench. "I'll just hold this grenade in my hand with my finger on the pin until you're out of my sight."

Viv angled the edges of her skis to be able to move off the trail so the two young men could make crosshatched markings with their heavy boots puncturing the soft snow as they hastily toiled up the angled ascent. As they passed by within inches of her, she gestured with the small weapon that had just saved her life.

Once they'd passed, she called cheerily, "*Auf Wiedersehen*," and waited until they'd disappeared around a bend.

This trip had become the deadly Pyrenees all over again.

Viv checked to make sure the grenade's pin was still secure and then swiftly stowed it with its mates in her rucksack. She seized her poles and edged her skis back onto the trail once again. Glancing over her shoulder, she pushed off down the mountain as if she were the Olympic skier she'd once hoped to be...and the devil was after her.

Ultimately, it turned out—he was.

PART I
CHAPTER 1

Four Years Earlier…
September 3, 1939

"Miss…uh… Clarke, is it? I can see you now."

"*Vivier*-Clarke," Viv corrected the harassed attaché with pomaded hair parted down the middle. He peered at her through rimless glasses as she sat sanding her nails with a silver-handled file. She could feel the stares from a gaggle of petitioners anxiously milling about in the sweltering lobby of the Athens U.S. Embassy. Given she'd only just arrived, Viv was aware that the others waiting nearby were obviously wondering why she was getting the attention from the authorities ahead of them.

The temperature in the crowded anteroom had grown oppressive for the throngs that had hastily arrived in hopes of getting their travel documents in order. Their worried, pinched expressions revealed their desperation to return to America now that Germany had invaded Poland two days earlier. The fetid air was filled with the fear that most of Europe was now teetering on the brink of all-out war.

For her part, Viv realized that by comparison, she probably appeared cool and collected, dressed in her crisp, white linen trousers, a matching linen shirt, and an expensive-looking blue blazer with white piping edging its collar and cuffs.

A member of the upper crust elite, they think…and just because my stepfather is rich.

She assumed those surrounding her probably thought she looked like some displaced Hollywood starlet with her curtain of burgundy hair obscuring her left eye.

The embassy official waved a piece of paper in his hand, informing her, "I've just received a cable from your father, Karl Bradford."

Viv bristled at the mere mention of his name.

"My *step*father," she insisted tersely. "Bradford is *his* name. If you'd taken the time to examine my passport, you'd see that my last name is hyphenated. It's Vivier-Clarke—the same as my late birth father."

As soon as the words were out of her mouth, she could hear how snotty she sounded, but she couldn't help it. She absolutely despised Karl Bradford and the way he threw his money and weight around, along with other complaints too numerous to mention.

The attaché glanced at the sheaf of papers in his hand, including her passport stamped with the seal of the United States and indicating she'd turn twenty-five in a month. He opened it. "Yes, I see, now. 'Miss Constance Vivier-Clarke.'" He gestured toward a corridor. "Come this way, please."

Viv slipped her nail file into her handbag and followed him down a hallway off the reception room. At an inch-and-a-half shy of six feet, she felt her usual sense of awkwardness at being nearly a head taller than the man about to interview her.

In a small, stuffy room, she was settled in a seat opposite a desk piled high with files relating to scores of dislocated Americans and aspiring refugees. A fan slowly revolved overhead, rustling the paperwork on the cluttered surface. The slight breeze offered welcome relief from the blistering September heat enveloping this ancient city perched on the edge of the sapphire Aegean Sea.

The attaché frowned, glancing down at the young woman's passport. "Hmmm…

'Vivier.' Your birth father was French, I take it?"

"*No,*" she informed him, making an effort not to sound as annoyed as that question always made her. "My father was French-*American,* but he flew for France and Britain in the Great War." She paused ever so slightly for effect. "In the spring of 1918, he bailed out of a downed fighter over the English Channel, but his parachute failed to open."

"I'm so sorry," mumbled the functionary in charge of granting proper departure documents.

Viv fought to push away the image of her father plummeting three thousand feet into the churning sea. She struggled to keep her voice steady as she always did when the subject of his death was mentioned.

"His name was Charles Vivier-Clarke, so after my mother's second marriage, I kept Vivier-Clarke as *my* legal name. My mother uses her current husband's name—Bradford—but I do *not*," she reiterated.

The attaché frowned again and pointed to a document in her file.

"I see that you have dual citizenship. American *and* British. Were you in Athens studying?"

"Oh heavens, no," she said with a short laugh. "I skied all last winter at Chamonix and Verbier in the Alps, training for an Olympic tryout."

"Goodness," the embassy official replied absently, focusing his attention on the top paper in the file.

Viv breathed a sigh of relief that her interrogator didn't inquire if she'd made either the British or the American Olympic teams—which she hadn't. There had been days when she had been just a wee bit hung over and hadn't shown up to practice. She adored skiing and the wonderful freedom of schussing down hills no other girl she knew would dare attempt. Then, the damning words "wash-out" rang in her head, along with the scowling visage of the veteran ski coach she'd hired.

"You're a waste of my time," the coach had told her bluntly. "You have the talent, but no discipline. I train winners, eager to learn, but you are merely an over-indulged amateur. A party-girl who gets by on her looks and money, but not with *me*, my dear."

That morning when she'd turned up an hour late and the coach had flung such insulting words at her, Viv had stormed off the lift platform and never saw the former Olympic alpine ski champ again. Meanwhile, in the back of her mind, she knew she deserved his dressing-down. But instead of apologizing and asking for a second chance, she'd booked herself on the Simplon Orient Express and headed for Greece.

"So, what have you been *doing* since the spring?" the embassy official inquired with a steady gaze.

"Since spring?" She glanced at the ceiling to give herself a moment to think, knowing that the answer she would have to give was beyond embarrassing. She affected a nonchalance that had long been her shield. "I've just been swanning around the Greek Islands with some friends, living the 'good life,' I'd guess you'd call it."

"No job needed to pay the bills?"

She inhaled a breath to buy another moment's thought. For the life of her, she had no notion of what she might be fit to do to earn money to pay bills in the real world.

She summoned a breezy reply. "Fortunately, in my case there's no need for gainful employment," realizing what an entitled twit she must seem to this man.

"So, your parents pay for your…uh…travels, I take it?"

"I'm given a monthly allowance, and the major bills go to my stepfather." She offered a jaunty smile. "At least I learned a couple of languages at my various boarding schools while my parents hop-scotched around the major capitals of Europe selling Bradford's Ball-Bearings to whatever military-industrial complex would buy them."

Her American questioner arched an eyebrow.

"I see. Well, all that has probably come to an end," he declared, "and your father—I-I mean your parents—want you on the next boat back to New York." He glanced at a cable Viv could see lay before him on his desk. "It says here that Mr. Bradford has already departed for America; your mother is closing up their apartment in Paris and will soon follow." He pushed an envelope in her direction. "Karl Bradford has kindly provided funds for your upcoming journey, part of which have already been used to secure your passage on a boat from Athens to Marseille. From there you'll board an ocean liner eventually bound for America."

"With German U-boats patrolling the Atlantic?" she protested. "No, thank you!"

It was the attaché's turn to inhale, pursing his thin lips.

"You may not have yet heard the news, Miss Vivier-Clarke," he informed her in even tones. "Germany invaded Poland two days ago."

"Of course, I know that!" she retorted and instantly wished her response had sounded more polite.

The attaché continued with steely patience, "Britain and some of the Commonwealth countries, as well as France, declared war on Germany earlier *today*."

He paused, and Viv sought to quiet her hands trembling as they strayed toward the desk to retrieve her all-important passport.

"I-I hadn't heard *that*," she stammered.

France…officially at war…for sure there would be no Winter Olympics…

The attaché noted brusquely, "Thank goodness America has no intention of embroiling herself in this mess. Since you'll be traveling on your *American* passport this trip," he said with deliberate emphasis, "you'll be perfectly safe on your journey home."

"Sorry," she retorted, "but I do not consider America my home."

His lips grew thinner. "Nevertheless, that *is* your next destination." He pushed the envelope with the rest of her travel documents and a half-inch pile of large denomination French francs closer to her side of the desk. "Your…uh…*step*father has arranged for one of our embassy colleagues to escort you from Athens to Marseilles and then see you aboard your ship sailing for the United States. Most likely, it'll be the last one departing from there for the duration."

"Of the *war*?" Viv asked, her tone revealing her dismay at this news.

"Yes," was his crisp reply, pointing to her exit documents. "You're all set, now."

Before Viv could voice any possible protest, the embassy official rose from his chair, indicating their interview was over.

"I fear, Miss Vivier-Clarke, that I must bid you adieu. As you can see, many of your fellow citizens have far more serious problems than you do, and I must try to solve them starting today."

CHAPTER 2

On the first day of Viv's journey from Athens back to France, she quickly realized that the embassy escort assigned to her was nothing more than a lowly clerk. Roger Gianakos turned out to be a nervous Greek American who normally toiled in the blazing hot basement of the chancery's archives.

Viv knew her behavior was deplorable, but she took great pleasure in giving the hapless young fellow the slip every chance she could as their small passenger boat made its six-day cruise through the Aegean and Mediterranean seas from Athens to Marseilles.

Tall, dark, skinny, and decidedly not handsome, Gianakos insisted, like the minder he was, on their dining together three times a day—only to have her consistently claim a fraudulent case of *mal-de-mer*. Viv delighted in abandoning him abruptly mid-meal, as if feeling ill, and then making her way into the bar to sip champagne with anyone only too happy to let her buy a round of drinks.

On the sixth day of the voyage, minutes after their ship pulled into the chaotic southern French port, Viv discovered the perspiring Mr. Gianakos, clad in his ubiquitous rumpled tan suit, standing outside her cabin. She could tell by his stern look that he was anxious to get her off his hands. In a way, she couldn't blame him, perfectly aware she'd behaved like a total bitch the entire trip.

"Your next ship is berthed just a few piers from ours," he announced, his relief only too obvious at such convenient proximity. "It sails tonight, heading west around Spain and then out across the Atlantic to America. You'll make one stop in the Bahamas."

She saw that he was peering past her shoulder at her large

traveling trunk with the distinct markings of luggage maker Louis Vuitton that stood open in her cabin. Various items of clothing were draped carelessly over its top, and a matching cosmetic case was perched on her bunk.

"Steward!" Gianakos called to a uniformed member of the crew at the end of the passageway. "Please assist Miss Vivier-Clarke closing her trunk and fetch a porter *immediately.* The young lady and her luggage must disembark within the hour."

Viv leaned against the doorframe to her stateroom. Hearing Roger's insistent orders, a plan began to take shape in her mind.

After five years splitting her time between France and Switzerland—along with a half year picking up a rudimentary grasp of German in Berlin—the last thing Viv wanted or intended was to sail home and live with her parents in Hickory, North Carolina, three miles from her stepfather Karl's boring manufacturing plant.

Smiling sweetly, she announced, to Roger, "I'm afraid I'll need to pick up a few personal items from the pharmacy before I board the other ship." She bestowed her brightest smile. "Why don't you see to the luggage and I'll meet you at the other dock."

Gianakos vehemently shook his head. "I'm afraid I cannot allow that. My instructions from the embassy and your father—"

"My *step*father!" she interrupted, her attempt at a friendlier approach evaporating. "I *am* over twenty-one, you know, and I'm not his child."

"Be that as it may," he countered stiffly, "my instructions are to *personally* see you safely on board the ship to America."

"And I imagine that Mr. Bradford paid you minions working at the U.S. Embassy in Athens a pile of his filthy Nazi money to see you *do* that."

Roger flinched but remained stoically silent.

"Crossing people's palms with silver has always been the way Karl Bradford—born *Braunheim*—by the way," she informed him, "has managed to get whatever he wanted."

Again, Gianakos made no reply.

Viv felt herself seething inside. Her stepfather simply paid out-and-out bribes masquerading as donations, presents, or "old-fashioned American goodwill"—as he liked to describe his corrupting payoffs. That his most recent fortune had been gained from selling his ball bearings to Hitler's growing war machine was beyond disgusting to her, but it was pointless to protest the iron hand that her stepfather had always employed in personal as well as business matters. Since the time Viv had been twelve, she, the rebellious stepdaughter, typically found an equally underhanded way around his authoritarian decrees.

Facing her 'minder,' Viv composed her expression into one reflecting deep embarrassment.

"Honestly, Roger, I-I don't want to cause any trouble for you," she said gently, as if she'd finally given in to his demands. She knew how to feign obedience when it was called for. "The steward can tidy up here and close my trunk. We might as well go now," she added, sounding resigned.

She turned to seize the handle of her alligator handbag and retrieve her handsome cosmetic case with shiny brass fittings framing each corner. Matching her traveling trunk, it was also made by the famous French firm of Louis Vuitton. It had room for a change of clothing beneath the upper tray filled with expensive face powder, eye makeup, and a collection of Chanel lipsticks and rouge. There was also a concealed compartment for her valuable jewelry, along with space for the contraceptive diaphragm her mother had bestowed Viv on her seventeenth birthday, obtained from a doctor at the American Hospital in Paris. She'd lived out of the small bag before, and she could do it again.

Now, if I could just figure out a way to get away from Gianakos...

With her germ of an idea coming into full bloom, she offered him a look of supplication.

"I know you're in a hurry, Roger, but surely you'll allow me to stop to buy a supply of...ah...sanitary napkins? I face a long journey at sea and, well..." She allowed her voice to trail off, then added meekly, "My monthly will come while I'm on board—"

Roger held up his hand as if to stop her from speaking another word about her embarrassing "predicament." It amused her no end to watch his face flush nearly purple.

"Uh...well...of...of course," he mumbled. "I'll just inquire of our driver where the nearest pharmacy might be."

"Thank you, Roger," she murmured. "That's so kind of you."

———◇———

Less than an hour later, Viv watched while Roger Gianakos climbed out of the back seat of their hired car and stood in front of one of the few locations near the harbor in Marseille where certain female unmentionable items could—hopefully—be purchased.

Viv, too, then stepped from the vehicle, hiked the strap of her handbag over her left shoulder, and made a grab for her cosmetic case.

"You can leave that in the car," Roger said, his eyes alert while his cheeks began to burn once more for being privy to such an embarrassing errand.

"Surely you don't want me to carry a month's supply of…well, *you* know…in my hands as I board the ship," she said.

"Oh! Well, right. No, of course not," Gianakos replied, staring down at his wing-tipped shoes, the leather toes covered with grime and dust from the docks. He finally looked up and met her gaze, telling her, "I'll just wait here, then, but try to be quick about it, will you? I need to get you settled onboard your ship, and then I'm due to take our boat back to Athens in two hours' time."

"Well, it may take me a little while to find what I need, but I'll go as fast as I can," she assured him with what she hoped was a submissive smile. "Be right back."

Viv felt Gianakos's gaze as she entered the pharmacy. As soon as she was inside, she quickly walked the length of the building, barged past a sign in French that indicated "Employees Only," and exited the back door. From there she hailed a passing taxi, leaning forward to give the driver instructions.

"Take me to the railway station. I'll pay you double if you get me there in ten minutes!"

She was struck by the thought that her escaping Roger Gianakos' clutches like this would probably get him fired—and felt a moment's remorse. Even so, she could only pray there was a train departing for Paris before her Greek shadow figured out what direction she'd used to escape. Viv patted her cosmetic case beside her on the seat and then opened her handbag to count the plump packet of French francs and American dollars provided by Karl Bradford to see her across the Atlantic, and then by train from New

York City to North Carolina. It was a generous travel fund. At least the S.O.B. was good for *something*.

The driver, taking his passenger at her word, stomped his foot on the Citroën's accelerator and careened around the corner with tires squealing.

"*Adieu Marseille, bonjour, Paris,*" she mused, her spirits rising.

Her fresh plan was to get to France's capital city in time to prevent her mother from closing up their apartment on Avenue Kléber. It was a flat that Viv's late father had purchased for his young wife years before, situated a few streets away from the very fashionable Avenue Foch.

Her thoughts drifted to Paris's broad boulevards, jewel-like parks, and wonderful beaux-arts architecture that she loved so well. Viv pictured herself sipping coffee at Café Les Deux-Magots or strolling with an as-yet-unknown beau beneath the Eiffel Tower when the purple wisteria was in bloom.

Leave France for an empty, aimless life in Hickory, North Carolina, sharing a house with a stepfather she *despised*? No way!

Of course, Viv admitted to herself, she had absolutely no idea what she'd do to pay her own way if her mother had already left for America and Karl Bradford's pin money ran out. After all, France had just declared war on Hitler's Germany.

A wave of uncertainty washed over her. She had to admit that no one had ever paid her to do *anything*. Once her mother married Karl, her parents had basically abandoned her to various boarding schools in Switzerland, but had salved their conscience, she realized now, with a lavish allowance. Viv had always been the one in her crowd to blithely hand over francs to pay for a round of drinks or purchase a pair of skis during an impromptu trip to an alpine resort.

Recalling her ski instructor's harsh opinion of her, a tiny voice in her head would occasionally whisper the truth: She'd behaved as a spoiled, pampered, over-indulged American more often than she cared to admit. But could she learn to be anything else, she wondered? Could she *do* anything else, other than be the person everyone her age considered the wild one in their crowd, living off her unpleasant stepfather's wealth?

A war had just started with German fascists poised to invade France, and here she was, trained for nothing practical. She'd frittered away the time since her schooling had ended, peevishly delighting in the many ways in which she'd annoyed her parents as she bounced around the playgrounds of Europe. Despite her expensive education, she couldn't even *type*. She had failed too many of her academic classes out of sheer indolence ever to be someone's secretary or serve as a child's governess, let alone an infant's nanny—the types of employment she imagined open to women.

So, what had all her rebelliousness gotten her, she wondered? She'd had a growing awareness, lately, that her anger at the way her parents had palmed her off on others had fueled her devil-may-care behavior, but how hard a habit would it be to break? Her half-hearted training regimen with her Olympic ski coach had been a total bust, despite her love of the sport. Some perverse willfulness to meet the low expectations of others had gotten the upper hand over her long-buried desire to succeed like her brave airman father had—until a faulty parachute had cut his life short.

So, she wondered, how capable *was* she of actually buckling down to something serious and earning her own way? She pondered the aimless, sybaritic lifestyle she'd indulged in, even as the dark shadow of war had started to spread across Europe. She recalled the fevered crowds screaming "Heil Hitler!" when Karl had insisted she study the German language in Berlin. She'd been given failing marks on the written tests at the *schule* he'd chosen, but she'd easily acquired enough German vocabulary chatting with other students in bars and cafés to understand the thundering cheers of the Führer's adoring throngs. By the end of her stay, she comprehended every word of the poison screeched through a loudspeaker by the all-powerful leader of the Nazi Party.

And what had been her reaction to witnessing this rising tide of fascist authoritarianism, Viv asked herself, facing some hard truths, perhaps for the first time? She'd whiled away hours lounging in Berlin's chocolate shops, drinking cocoa laced with schnapps and flirting with strapping blond Aryan boys who soon elected to wear the uniform of the Third Reich.

Fiddling while Rome burned—that's what *she'd* done, Viv concluded as the taxi drew up in front of the Marseille-Saint-Charles train station. But now that France—the country for whom her

Franco-American birthfather had given his life—was threatened with domination by Germany, what could she do even to *survive* the hard times sure to come?

Very little, she admitted, as she handed over double the fare to the driver, who set her small piece of luggage next to her feet. She stood, rooted to the ground as the taxi pulled away from the curb. Adjusting the leather strap of her alligator handbag, she gazed at the crowds bustling into the station. Her cosmetic cased weighed heavily in one hand. She took a step, about to hail a porter, but then held back. She would carry it herself, she thought suddenly, and save a few francs.

She absolutely *had* to learn to be more frugal and disciplined, she scolded herself. She could make a start by conserving the funds tucked inside her outrageously expensive purse she'd bought on a whim because its deep red shade matched the color of her hair. What was truly important *now*, however, was figuring out her next move.

Viv sensed a startling, unfamiliar, and fledgling sense of determination to shed her feckless behavior—and marveled at how strange it felt.

For pity's sake, I'm not a lightweight imbecile! I can figure this out!

She squared her shoulders, marching into the train station to buy a one-way ticket to Paris. She was a healthy, able-bodied young woman. Surely, she'd think of something to keep body and soul together…perhaps even find a way to be useful during France's darkest hour. The question, of course, was: How?

CHAPTER 3

To Viv's amazement, not only was her mother still in Paris, but she had not packed a single trunk by the time her daughter turned up at the front door of her family's elegant flat on Avenue Kléber. The widow, Mrs. Vivier-Clarke—now, the admired hostess known as Pamela Bradford among Paris's chic expatriate crowd—stood at the door to the first-floor apartment with a look of astonishment at the sight of her only child standing in the hallway.

As always, Viv's forty-four-year-old mother was impeccably dressed, this day clad in a pair of bias-cut black silk trousers and cream-colored silk blouse. Her blond hair was pulled back in its customary, stylish chignon fastened at the nape of her slender neck. Lustrous teardrop earrings and two ropes of creamy pearls completed her ensemble.

For the first time in years, industrialist Karl Bradford's head-turning wife threw her arms around her daughter and clung to her shoulders for several long moments. When Pamela finally released Viv, she led the way without preamble through the foyer where the crystal chandelier hanging overhead threw ribbons of multi-colored light across the polished marble floor.

"After Karl left Europe so abruptly and France declared war, I couldn't imagine *where* you were exactly," she said as they entered the sitting room, her high heels tapping a staccato tattoo on the polished parquet.

Following in her mother's wake Viv responded, "And *I* worried that you'd be long gone to America by now."

Pamela whirled in place, her well-manicured hands perched on silken hips.

"You can be assured that I was certainly *not* about to board a ship to cross the Atlantic with the British navy shooting at everything that moves and all those German U-boats sinking passenger ships like the poor *S.S. Athenia* last year," she declared.

"But, what about Karl?" Viv asked. "The cable he sent to Greece said he'd already left for New York and that you were closing up this flat."

Her mother's lips flattened into a straight line.

"He apparently had early warning about the planned invasion of Poland last week and took one of the last commercial flights from Berlin to Iceland. Then he flew to somewhere in Canada. From there, I expect he took trains back to North Carolina."

"Well, of *course,* he'd have early warning of the butchery in store for poor Poland, having just sold all those ball-bearings of his to the Nazi munitions factories," Viv retorted. "Really, Mother, how can you—"

"Now, let's not quarrel about your father, again—"

"He's not my father! And I'm not here to quarrel. I'm here to tell you I don't want to sail back to the States, either. I want to stay in this apartment in Paris and see what I can do to...well...to try to help France in some way. It's bound to get pretty grim."

By this time, they both had taken seats on the Louis XVI furniture with its plump, peach silk upholstery. Nearby, the fourteen-foot windows offered a stunning view of Paris and the treetops lining Avenue Foch, a few blocks away.

"Ah..." Pamela said, her eyes narrowing. "You obviously didn't make it on any ski team, so now you're ready to call a halt to that endless vacation of yours, are you? Skiing in the Alps all last winter...and then sunbathing on every beach in the Mediterranean? How were Chamonix and Verbier, by the way? Full of those ex-pat playboys you're usually so chummy with?"

Viv ignored her mother's questions delivered with her customary sarcasm when it came to her daughter's recent and constant traveling. They both were perfectly aware that these activities provided a way for Viv to keep her distance from a stepfather she'd actively come to detest after realizing that the principal source of Karl Bradford's wealth these days came from Nazi coffers. Even so, Viv shrugged, affecting indifference.

"And, Mother, don't forget the beaches in Greece. I spent at least a month lounging on Corfu and Skiathos."

Despite her successful struggle to maintain her cool, Viv was stung by the swift transition her mother often made between overtures as a concerned parent and her automatic defense of her wealthy second husband whose alliances with German industrialists were an anathema to anyone following current politics.

"Yes, of course, the Greek Islands" her mother replied, her tone laced with its usual acid accusations. "Karl showed me the bills before he left for Berlin, my dear, so I was able to keep up with your breath-taking touring schedule. Do tell me who your traveling companions were that you treated to all those rounds of drinks at hotel bars."

"I expect those young men you speak of are soon to be cannon fodder in this war Karl and Hitler have started."

"Oh, do *stop!*" snapped her mother.

Viv could see Pamela was tired of sparring, now that her daughter was skilled at summoning stinging reposts of her own. With breathtaking speed, her mother's deliberate archness suddenly evaporated.

With hands clasped tightly in her lap, she demanded, "You haven't come home because you're *pregnant*, have you? Because that would be the absolute limit! Especially now."

Viv's head reared back as if she'd been slapped. She felt a rush of white-hot anger, followed by a steely determination not to give her mother the satisfaction of knowing she'd landed a blow after all. The supreme irony was that Pamela had been the one to explain how women could avoid "doing something stupid" and had persuaded Dr. Jackson at the American Hospital in Paris to fit her daughter for a diaphragm. Her mother's fear of the complications of out-of-wedlock pregnancy had little to do with *Viv's* welfare, her daughter well knew; only what an inconvenience and embarrassment such an unwanted situation with her rebellious daughter would cause *her*.

At length Viv replied in a calm, neutral tone, "No, Mother. I'm not pregnant."

Pamela shifted her glance and stared, unseeing, out the tall window on her right, framed by its silk drapery the color of ripe peaches.

"Well, *that's* a relief, at least" Returning her gaze to Viv, she added, "And, may I remind you that the lovely lifestyle you've enjoyed since you finished school in Switzerland has been paid for by the profits of Karl Bradford and that ball-bearing company you so disparage."

"I *don't* disparage what he manufactures...just to *whom* he sells his wares," Viv countered. "Even *you* can't forget those last trips to Berlin we three took together. Those rallies we witnessed, with Hitler shouting through the microphone to huge crowds of his manic followers, swastika flags snapping in the breeze." She barely suppressed a shudder just recalling once again those frightening scenes. Her mother made no comment. "And you can't have ignored the horrible stories coming from refugees pouring out of Eastern Europe," Viv declared, unable to disguise her outrage. "I have heard on good authority that the Nazis are beginning to euthanize *children* who have chronic illnesses or disabilities, to say nothing of their treatment of Jews and—"

"*Stop* it!" Pamela hissed. "Those are just rumors, and even if they're true, Karl has nothing to do with any of that."

"Or so you hope," Viv retorted. "May I remind *you* that *your* lovely lifestyle depends on keeping the peace with him, doesn't it? Even so, you don't seem any more anxious to return to North Carolina than *I* do, otherwise you would have boarded that flight with him from Germany to Canada. Lucky for you, though," Viv added, "now it's too late—although as a British subject with war now declared between Hitler and England, things won't be so nice for you if the Germans do invade France."

Pamela frowned, dismissing Viv's warning. "Everyone says the French and British troops will stop Hitler cold at the Maginot Line."

Viv's mother was parroting the conventional wisdom about the impregnability of concrete fortifications and weapon installations built along France's eastern border with Germany and the Italian frontier. Constructed in the 1930s following the Great War, this French line of defense was designed to defer any threatened invasion by the *Boche*, the disparaging slang the French used to label German foot soldiers. But Viv wondered if a line of concrete would actually be a match for Hitler's mighty war machine that had already crushed so much of Europe?

During the prolonged silence that followed, Viv became aware of rhythmic ticking sounds from the gold-plated clock on the mantel, its Sèvres porcelain face painted with a milkmaid amidst gamboling lambs. At length, it was Viv who spoke first, extending a tentative cease-fire.

"As it turns out, Mother, you are right about one thing. Given what's going on in Europe right now, I think I should start doing something useful and try to find a better path for myself."

"And what could *that* possibly be?" her mother retorted.

Viv met her gaze. "Frankly, I don't know…yet."

On the long train trip from Marseille to Paris, she'd had time to acknowledge a peculiar sense of free-floating guilt she'd been feeling these last months about living off the funds supplied by a stepfather whose politics and business practices she disparaged every chance she got. By the time she'd stepped into the bustling

Gare de Lyon, she had been filled with a sudden desire to be a different sort of person than her mother and stepfather. She was certain if her *real* father were alive, he wouldn't be pleased with a daughter who had deliberately sloughed off her studies and failed even to show up at high-level ski lessons for a sport she supposedly adored. It had certainly occurred to her that the new-found resolve to find a way to help France fight fascism might be rooted in the deep feelings she had nurtured all these years for an idealized parent who had died trying to protect his family's country of origin. Looking back at it all, she desperately wished, now, she'd been the kind of daughter to have made the late Charles Vivier-Clarke proud—but knew she had not.

Maybe I'm a late bloomer, Viv thought with a rueful glance at her mother. Perhaps her recent act of striking out on her own for Paris had set her on a bumpy road to something akin to growing up? It certainly had appeal.

Viv's gaze drifted to Pamela's hands that were tightly clasped in her lap once more.

"Well, I must say," Pamela murmured, "seeking a better path than the one you've been on is certainly a change in tone."

Viv plastered a smile on her face and asked pleasantly, "You're right, it is. And what about you, Mother? What's *your* plan?"

"My plan is simply to continue carrying on," Pamela replied with a shrug of her silk-clad shoulders.

Unwilling to mount another challenge, Viv rose from her chair.

"Well," she replied, "we can only pray you're also right about the Allies stopping Hitler from overrunning France." She glanced at the ornate clock on the marble mantelpiece. "It's just gone four. Shall I make us a pot of tea?"

CHAPTER 4

May 1940

It had taken months of fruitless effort on Viv's part—declaring her American citizenship and ignoring her British—before she finally landed an actual job during the days France was first in tumult. In the intervening time, she'd managed to find a volunteer spot rolling bandages and serving tea to patients at the American Hospital in the fashionable Paris suburb of Neuilly-sur-Seine. Thanks to the BBC wireless reports, she and her mother had already learned the Germans had bombed a Scottish naval base in March, followed by the Nazi invasion of Denmark and Norway in the first week of April.

By May tenth, the worst news of all arrived: German Panzer tanks had crossed the border into France from Belgium. Quickly, Viv was given emergency medical training and abruptly promoted to ambulance driver. And now, during this second week of her new position, she and other volunteers, including her mother, had assembled for a meeting hastily announced by the head of the hospital.

Viv had barely taken her place on the veranda outside the chief physician's office when the imposing Dr. Sumner Jackson, himself, walked in. In the restricted screened-in space, the longtime ex-pat physician's physical presence at six-feet-one-inches was commanding, as were his massive shoulders and arms, his thatch of dark hair, and startling blue eyes framed by an awning of bushy eyebrows. Dr. Jack, as he was known around the hospital, was a former resident of

Maine, now in his mid-fifties. He swept into the veranda trailed by several other staff doctors, all of whom wore crisply starched white coats, along with expressions creased with worry.

Viv, dressed like the other ambulance drivers in her newly issued military attire and Red Cross armband, sat next to her mother in the first row of hospital volunteers. Adrienne Vaud, a Swiss school friend and fellow medical attendant-driver, sat on Viv's left. When Viv had heard about the need for new recruits, she'd told Adrienne, and the two women had signed up on the same day.

As morning sun slanted across the veranda, the battles being fought within a hundred miles of France's capital city seemed hard to even imagine. Parisians and Americans living abroad, like Viv, were still drinking coffee in the cafés during the day. In the balmy evenings, the city's residents met with the few friends who had not yet been conscripted into the military or some other form of national service.

The shock to French citizens and ex-pats alike finally registered when the Germans made swift work of the Maginot Line's two-hundred-mile stretch of concrete fortifications on the border with Germany. This shocking collapse, Viv figured, had to be the reason she and the others had been swiftly recruited and were now being summoned to this quickly called meeting.

She and Adrienne, as well as Pamela, had managed to pass an intensive week of first-aid training, along with their driving test, piloting the lumbering Chevrolet ambulance assigned to them without mishap. Within days of qualifying, they'd made their first run to pick up wounded French and British soldiers in the wake of a particularly ferocious German onslaught that descended on France May eighteenth.

The first group of men they'd loaded into the back of the ambulance were soaked in blood and crying out in agony. One even had his severed arm wrapped in his jacket and placed next to him on the stretcher. It had been a grisly and harrowing experience, and Viv's mother, especially, had appeared visibly repulsed by their mission.

After that first run, Adrienne had commented with an exhausted sigh, "Well, I rather sympathize with your mum. Wouldn't you say that being a medical attendant and ambulance driver have forever erased the romantic notion of 'doing one's duty?'"

Viv had grimaced. "But Mother seemed mortally offended to have been given such a repugnant assignment at an institution to which she'd donated so much money."

As for Viv herself, she had been glad her latest assignment had turned out to be so challenging. Yes, she was exhausted but felt more alive than she ever had in her entire life. The soldiers that had survived the agonizing, bumpy journeys from the battlefield near Amiens to the doors of the hospital had touched her deeply. They shared ardent expressions of gratitude for having their lives saved when so many had perished.

Viv gazed around the hospital's veranda, now nearly filled to capacity with staff. She imagined that the meeting concerned their ambulance unit's recent journey to the battlefields that had very nearly met with complete disaster. All along the route back to Paris, swooping German aircraft had shot directly at their vehicles.

What kind of savages behave like that? she wondered.

Having witnessed the German assault on their medical convoy, she wasn't surprised to learn that was the very reason they had all been assembled outside Dr. Jackson's office on the fourth floor.

"Before a single hospital ambulance is sent out in the field again," the head doctor declared, his index finger stabbing into the air, "your individual teams will be responsible for *painting over* each and every red cross decaled on the vehicles you drive."

Dr. Jackson paused and then added, "Targeting neutral entities like the Red Cross is part of the terror campaign Hitler relishes. I'm afraid I must alert you that the German pilots are making special efforts to fire on your vehicles. You must complete the task of removing the red symbols *today*. We have been informed on good authority that it may be only days before German ground troops arrive in Paris."

Alarmed reactions in the doctor's audience ricocheted on all sides while Viv heard her own sharp intake of breath.

"As a result, we can soon expect to receive many more casualties," Dr. Jackson announced. "The order of *all* British and French troops to evacuate to Dunkirk has already been issued. Those that are too wounded to travel to the port will be brought here and to other Paris hospitals."

Everyone on the veranda appeared in virtual shellshock. Allied soldiers had been forced to seek any way possible to retreat toward the English Channel—or suffer the annihilation of the entire British Expeditionary Force.

Viv wondered, suddenly, if the Germans would take over the American Hospital if or when they invaded Paris itself. It would be a violation of International Law if they did, of course, since the United States remained, technically at least, a neutral player in the conflict—as was Switzerland.

Viv's thoughts spun in various directions as Dr. Jackson continued to speak. Her American passport would offer protection, she speculated, but for how long? Her mother was British. What would happen to *her,* an enemy alien, if the entire country fell to the Germans in the next few days? And what of the French friends Viv had made since coming to work here, to say nothing of members of the hospital staff that were known to be Jewish? Viv had witnessed with her own eyes the rampant German anti-Semitism when she'd been a student in Berlin in '37. Plenty of French were also anti-Semites, Viv was loath to admit. The horrifying ramifications of a German occupation of France were too many and too appalling to contemplate.

Just at that moment, Dr. Jackson's wife, a Swiss citizen like Viv's friend Adrienne Vaud, appeared at the threshold of the veranda without notice or fanfare.

"This must be an important meeting if Toquette is here," whispered Viv's mother.

Like Sumner Jackson, his wife was also in her fifties. The couple, along with their only child, Phillip, lived at Number 11 Avenue Foch, not far from Viv and her mother's flat on Avenue Kléber. In fact, the Bradfords' longtime financial support of the American Hospital and their resulting social acquaintance had been the path Viv had eventually trod to secure the position she now filled.

Dr. Jackson offered a welcoming nod as he spotted his wife's entrance and smiled faintly as she took a seat against the back wall.

"Next to your ambulances parked in the main garage," the chief physician announced, "you'll find cans of dull green paint that should easily obliterate the red crosses on all your vehicles. You'll also find the brushes you'll need to complete the work."

Someone in the back row spoke up in a voice laced with undisguised concern.

"And what about the crosses on the hospital's roof?"

Dr. Jackson offered a brusque nod. "Never fear, the red crosses painted on the roofs of all our buildings are being removed this afternoon." He inhaled deeply once again, and Viv could almost picture the weight of the world pressing down on oversized shoulders that could have belonged to a footballer. "Given the likelihood Paris falls to the Germans after a period of bombing or on-the-ground fighting, we will also be sand-bagging the perimeter of the buildings tomorrow, and all the windows will be taped." He allowed the shocked silence to fill the veranda. Then he nodded his dismissal, saying, "So, again, thank you all for your work as medical attendants, ambulance drivers, mechanics, and the entire hospital staff…and for volunteering today to make this needed correction regarding our physical plant and the medical vehicles."

Pamela leaned toward Viv. "You and Adrienne go along and get started with the painting, dear. I'm just going to have a quick word with Toquette."

Viv nodded and turned to follow her coworkers off the veranda. She didn't initiate conversation with Adrienne until they were well out of Pamela's earshot.

"After hearing all that, what do you bet my mother calls a halt to her short-lived ambulance driving career and ends up head of the 4 p.m. tea service delivery in the wards every afternoon?" she muttered as the two younger women moved through Dr. Jackson's office and into a long corridor of the doctors' wing.

Adrienne politely ignored Viv's pointed comment as the pair walked down the hall with the staff. As Viv's best friend at their Swiss boarding school, she was only too familiar with tales of Pamela Bradford's legendary vanity.

Shifting to a safer topic, she teased, "Viv, I dearly hope you are handier than *I* am with a paintbrush. I don't recall painting vehicles was one of the skills taught to us at Le Manoir, do you?" she joked, referring to their posh school in Lausanne where they'd been taught to lay an elegant table, prepare a pheasant for roasting, and recite poetry in French and Italian. "Actually, I've never painted even a fence post in my entire life!"

Only half joking herself, Viv replied, "After that last trip from Amiens driving through enemy tracer fire, I cannot *wait* to paint out those Red Cross targets."

Despite the skepticism of the battle-axe, Beverly Benedict, who'd supervised their Red Cross medical training and reprimanded them at every juncture, Viv had learned to drive a hulking ambulance with reasonable skill and endurance. Surely it wouldn't be too hard to obliterate the markings that made her a sitting target of the God-damned Jerries?

CHAPTER 5

May 25, 1940

Inside the hospital's garage, Adrienne pointed a rubber hose at their Chevrolet ambulance, now smothered in a thick layer of mud and dust. As hissing sprays of water peppered the vehicle's sides and hood, Viv noted that the recent coat of green paint blotting out the former bold red crosses didn't quite match the original olive color covering the rest of the ambulance's chassis. As streams of water spewed from the nozzle, Viv followed along behind her friend with a large rag, endeavoring to remove any dirt left behind after the rigorous dousing.

A young man in a white coat suddenly appeared in the broad doorway.

"Viv!" he called out. The male hospital orderly, whose name she didn't know, obviously knew hers. "Dr. J wants to see you in his office on the double."

She exchanged a startled glance with Adrienne and dropped her filthy rag on the vehicle's running board. Viv couldn't imagine why she would be summoned to the chief medical officer's quarters and wracked her brain for any infringement their imperious supervisor, Beverly Benedict, might have declared Viv had committed in the few weeks she'd been a medical attendant/ambulance driver.

She was aware that the Jacksons and her late father had known each other during the Great War when Wing Commander Charles Vivier-Clark had flown battle sorties and his fellow American had served as a field doctor—the latter somehow surviving the carnage of trench warfare. Viv had been so busy that she wasn't even sure if Dr. Jackson knew that she and her friend Adrienne had been promoted from rolling bandages to driving for the American Hospital's ambulance corps.

Adrienne offered a wave of farewell with the end of her hose as Viv dutifully followed along behind the messenger who had come to fetch her.

"Come in, come in," urged the harried physician the instant he spotted Viv at the threshold to his inner office. "Close the door, will you please?"

Viv took the seat Dr. Jackson indicated on the other side of his broad desk. The doctor's piercing blue eyes stared inquiringly at Viv as he folded his skillful surgeon's hands on top of the papers that sat upon his desk.

He pointed to one of two files.

"I see by the reports of Head Nurse Elizabeth Comte and Ambulance Supervisor Benedict that you and Miss Vaud have done an excellent job in the short time you've been in our ambulance corps."

Surprised to learn she wasn't in some kind of trouble, Viv felt herself relax against the back of her wooden chair. Even cranky old Beverly Benedict must not have written too damning a report about her. Sumner Jackson, his drawn face reflecting the intense stress of recent days, inclined his head and lowered his voice.

"I knew your father, of course," he said with an air of melancholy that warmed Viv's heart. "How old were you when you lost him?"

"Five-and-a-half. Even so, I do remember him quite clearly…."

"A very brave man who met his fate far too soon." He regarded her for a moment and then added, "From all I know of you, Viv, I believe I can trust you. Would you agree on that score?"

Startled by his question, Viv was at a loss as to what she should reply. At length she decided a light-hearted answer was best.

Cracking a smile, she asked, "Trust me to drive the ambulance without crashing into anything?" She nodded. "Yes, I think you can.

At least, so far, so good, with no thanks to the Jerries shooting at us, even *without* the red cross painted on our hood."

"What I'm referring to is…can I trust you to keep a *confidence*? A secret that would be dangerous if known in certain circles—even here at the hospital."

Viv paused, wondering what possible disclosures the august Sumner Jackson might be about to make in her presence.

Before she could answer he said, "I'm not sure if you've noticed, but some of our patients here are actually perfectly healthy downed Allied flyers, along with a handful of French and British soldiers who are escaped prisoners-of-war."

Viv had heard the whispered rumors, but she and Adrienne routinely delivered their wounded charges to the emergency department and rarely even entered the wards. Thus far, she'd had no real proof if any of the hospital scuttlebutt was true. With the Nazis poised to invade the city, she hadn't had a moment to dwell on the subject of what else might be going on around her during the frantic pace at the American-run hospital.

The institution had been founded in 1909 to take care of both wealthy ex-pats and not-so-wealthy Paris-loving Americans like Earnest Hemingway, Gertrude Stein, and the occasional member of an embassy staff who'd taken ill, or a visiting dignitary with an emergency appendectomy. During the previous war, Germans had come within the outskirts of Paris but had never threatened the medical establishment now directed by Dr. Jackson. How the place would survive in *this* war was anybody's guess.

Sumner Jackson's gaze returned to the other file on his desk. Pointing to it, he said, "There's a man in our wards who is of particular value to both French and British forces and therefore must be among the *first* to be evacuated from Dunkirk."

The tattered remnants of the defeated French Army, along with the battered survivors of the British Expeditionary Forces that had come to France's support in the fight against Germany, had kept the ambulance corps busy night and day. But to drive someone to Dunkirk *now*? It seemed pretty far-fetched.

Viv immediately found herself speculating whether there were *any* safe routes north out of Paris to the seaport where the defeated British Army was fast retreating in the face of the German advance.

She could only imagine the air power the Krauts would order into the skies to shoot anything on the ground that was heading in that direction.

"The passenger I speak of that must be transported to Dunkirk has recently recovered from some serious flesh wounds on one side of his face and left shoulder that he received in the fighting in Amiens." Dr. Jackson frowned, adding, "I've just been given an urgent summons about him. He claims he's fit enough to leave the hospital and is determined to get back to London, but I won't release him to go on his own."

"So he's a Brit?" she asked, wondering exactly *who* had notified Dr. Jackson that this mysterious patient was urgently needed in London.

"No, he's very definitely *not* British," corrected Dr. Jackson with a trace of the first smile Viv had ever seen on the face of the rather forbidding chief physician. "As you will quickly find out if you accept this assignment, he is *very* French and hates the Nazis as much as Toquette and I do…maybe even more."

Viv knew from what her mother had told her that Dr. Jackson and his wife Toquette had met each other while performing heroic medical service near the front during the terrible trench warfare of the late 'teens. Both the nurse and the medical officer had seen the results of German brutality in that conflagration: incendiary bombs, land mines, and the mustard gas that was so lethal. No wonder the Jacksons would be ready to fight them again, Viv thought.

"You'd actually like *me* to be the one to take this patient by ambulance to Dunkirk?"

"It will be very dangerous," Jackson warned, "but as a woman driver—and with the cover story I've invented—you probably have the best chance of anyone on the staff getting through to the coast."

Viv wished her mother could hear the confidence Dr. J was expressing in her daughter's abilities as an ambulance driver, and before the hospital's director could change his mind, Viv hastened to assure him. "I gladly accept the assignment."

"And what about your teammate?"

"Adrienne Vaud? She'll do it," Viv replied with confidence, "but if for some reason she says no, or can't, I can handle it all myself. You've said the patient is ambulatory and doesn't need major medical care." She glanced down at the file on Jackson's desk that she assumed was the Frenchman's. "Am I permitted to know the gentleman's name?"

"He goes by Victor Fernique...but even *I* don't know if that's his true name."

"In the hush-hush trade, is he?" Viv asked, her interest more than piqued. "Those are the people I've heard who have numerous code names and aliases." She felt buoyed by the relief she saw reflected in Dr. Jackson's expression that she'd agreed to his request. "Victor is an easy enough name to remember. When should I leave?"

"As soon as you have gathered the necessary supplies for a few days travel. Tonight, at the latest," he urged. "I want you to set out immediately in order to avoid as many German roadblocks as you can, should they get to *Dunkerque* before you," he added giving the port city its proper French pronunciation. "Victor will pose as a gravely disabled farmer who received his injuries in a threshing accident and was brought here because of our reputation for plastic surgery and healing flesh wounds. This will explain why he supposedly needed to be transported back to his fictional farm—which just happens to be near the port of departure." Jackson gave her a steady look. "If you are still sure that you're willing to take on this assignment, my assistant will provide you with a map and several suggested alternative itineraries."

"I'm willing and able to do this," she assured him, her heart racing with excitement, along with a *frisson* of fear at how daunting a task it would likely be.

The corners of Dr. Jackson's mouth suppressed a smile. "Just as I thought. You *are* your father's daughter."

Viv beamed at Jackson, warmed by his words. But then she wondered if she were in any way as brave and reckless as her mother had often complained that her father had been. In all the years her family had lived in France, Viv had never been to Dunkirk or even the adjacent region north of Amiens. Would she actually be able to get this Victor Fernique person safely to his destination? What if he were exposed as a spy—

Dr. Jackson interrupted her swirling concerns.

"The hospital commissary will have prepared food for you to take on the journey, so stop there before you leave."

Viv mentally pushed away the debilitating doubts that had suddenly assailed her in the guise of her mother's voice.

Really, Constance...you're not fit for anything remotely useful. And just be warned: the champagne will soon run dry, so I suggest you cease being such a party girl and find some sensible man to pay your bills...

Viv leaned forward in her chair and mentally shook herself. This *was* her chance to finally do something really useful and prove her mother wrong. Prove *Karl Bradford* wrong.

Dr. Jackson pushed an envelope with the hospital's identifying letterhead across his desk.

"Here are some documents that identify you as the civilian member of our hospital's staff—which you actually are—along with a file with Victor's medical records, altered as to the reasons for his injuries. If you get stopped, you can show them your American passport and everything I've given you to convince authorities our cover story is true."

Viv took the envelope he offered. "Thank you for your confidence in me."

"I do have confidence in you, Viv, but for you, it may be more of a case of 'no good deed goes unpunished,'" Dr. Jackson replied in a wry tone. "Even so, it's an urgent task that must be done, and the reports on you have been stellar." He rose from his chair and extended his hand to her as she stood up. "I only hope to God you make it safely to Dunkirk...and back." His demeanor had resumed its usual sobriety. "Godspeed, Viv, but be prepared for the worst. By the time you return to Paris, the Germans might very well be in charge here at the hospital."

CHAPTER 6

"We're lost, aren't we?" demanded a voice from the back of the ambulance. "You have absolutely no idea where you are—or where we're going."

Viv glanced over her shoulder at the long, lean figure with half of his haggard face swathed in bandages. The other half, with one eye visible that was the color of dark chocolate, was glaring at her accusingly.

Victor Fernique had been a total pain in the neck from the moment the orderlies brought him from his hospital ward on a gurney to the curb where her ambulance was idling in preparation for the journey to Dunkirk.

At first, she'd felt genuine sympathy for her passenger. She'd assumed that the wound on his cheek masked by a mass of gauze and white tape, along with poultices on his shoulder, were fiercely paining him after having been lifted off his hospital bed and transported to her ambulance at the curb. However, even before she'd climbed into the driver seat, his arrogant, irascible personality had made itself known.

"Where's the driver?" he'd demanded when he saw her standing beside the vehicle's back door where she and Adrienne were waiting to help the orderlies load him inside.

"You're looking at her," Viv said calmly, although her pulse jumped at his implied disdain for her gender.

"My God!" he'd exclaimed to the orderly nearest him. "I need an experienced driver for this trip. We're not embarking on some holiday, here! These women are all volunteers. One nearly *killed* me bringing me back from Amiens."

"You made it alive to the hospital, though, didn't you?" Viv retorted, wondering what unlucky female driver picked up the wounded man from the battlefield. When Viv had peeked at his file, she'd learned he'd once been a member of the French Foreign Legion and later joined the regular French Army when France declared war on Germany. Much to her surprise, buried on the fifth page of his file was his real name: Marcel Delonge. Some clerk typist somewhere must have slipped up. Gazing on his unruly mass of dark hair and scowling face, handsome despite the bandage, the 'real' Marcel was not likely to be a pleasant passenger.

The file she'd skimmed noted that during the battle to defend against the German troops storming into France from poor, overrun Belgium, Delonge had been hit by a shower of shrapnel in his left cheek and shoulders. Viv knew he would have bled to death, but for the quick aid administered by the attendant-drivers "that nearly killed" their patient.

Staring down at him stretched out on the gurney, Viv had met his unfriendly stare.

"Perhaps you couldn't *hear* the Jerries' bullets raining down on all of us during those journeys from Amiens back to Paris. Or perhaps the noise over your head disturbed your naptime that day," she added sweetly. To the orderlies she barked, "Load him in! We've got to get going."

Viv stomped toward the driver's side with Adrienne in her wake.

"Golly, Viv," her teammate said. "Are you going to be all right with this fellow? I feel terrible not going with you, but without your mother driving anymore, they're awfully shorthanded and—"

"Don't worry," Viv interrupted. "I am going to give this Legionnaire the ride of his life and put him on the first boat I spot off the shores of *Dunkerque*," she declared with a flourish, giving the evacuation port the French pronunciation Dr. Jackson had.

Of course, she'd had no idea if she and this tough customer would even make it to the coast. As dusk was falling, they'd set off to the north of Paris. Viv prayed to a God she had no faith in that the route Dr. Jackson's assistant picked was the best one to take.

Her cranky and demanding traveling companion was supposed to be lying prone on a canvas stretcher attached with metal clips to the left interior side of the vehicle. Suspended from the stretcher's outside corners were two-inch woven canvas straps affixed to the ambulance's ceiling. Instead of remaining horizontal and resting, Marcel was now leaning on one elbow, peering over her shoulder at the road ahead and squinting through the ambulance's dark windshield.

It was a hot spring night. Viv glanced in her rearview mirror just as her passenger ripped the bandage off his face. Even in the gloom, she could make out a narrow, five-inch scar with barely healed surgeon's stitches. The slashing wound ran, like a miniature railroad track, at an angle from just below his eye, across a very high cheekbone, to within a quarter inch from the corner of his mouth. Olive-skinned and looking more like a Spaniard than a Frenchman, Marcel Delonge's prominent nose had a slight bump near its bridge as if it had once suffered a stinging blow. From what Viv could see of the unscathed side of his face, he was a startlingly good-looking—but distinctly intimidating—specimen of irritated manhood. When the scar healed, she could imagine he'd have the looks and swagger of an eighteenth-century pirate—and be just as dangerous to know.

For a few minutes more, they rode along without speaking. Special agent "Victor Fernique's" pronouncement a few minutes earlier about their being lost had been an outright statement, not a question. Unfortunately, Viv knew, it was also a true one. Silently admitting this fact to herself, she grabbed the steering wheel more tightly and watched her knuckles turn white. Eyes glued to the road, she avoided looking at him in the rearview mirror, but could feel his gaze boring into the back of her head.

Finally, she shouted above the grinding of shifting gears, "By the way, you were very foolish to remove your bandage. This monster kicks up a lot of dust and your wound could get re-infected."

"It's insufferably hot back here!" he shouted over the din. "I've been damn well suffocating in this mummy costume they wrapped me in."

Fortunately, the ambulance's engine rumbled loudly enough so she could pretend that she couldn't hear his ongoing barrage of caustic comments. His complaints included concerns over the direction they were taking, along with criticisms of her driving skills, and the disgust he felt having been fed by the hospital staff a single potato and cooked cabbage for lunch.

Less than a mile after this exchange, and without warning, he reached a long arm over the front seat and made a lunge for the map that lay open beside her. Viv slammed on the brakes and tried to grab it out of his hand, succeeding only in tearing off a corner.

"God dammit!" she seethed through clenched teeth. "What do you think you're doing, you great dolt!"

In French, her use of slang was a much more insulting version of "idiot."

"What I'm doing, Miss America," he said with a jibe at the faint New York-ese sadly detectable in her French, "is trying to get us on some sort of route that might actually end up in *Dunkerque*—or at least close enough so that you and I can avoid being shot by some stinking *Boche*. In case you wondered, my goal is to stay alive and find myself a boat that will get me to England."

"Believe me," she shot back, "I am in total support of your doing that!"

Viv watched in shock as her supposed charge then slithered, scarred head leading the way, over the back of the passenger seat where he managed to unfold his lanky frame beside her. He snatched the part of the map out of her hands that she'd torn in their struggle. Then he laid both sections in his lap, his long legs bent at sharp angles in the seat where Adrienne customarily sat.

"Have you a torch, *chérie*?" he inquired in dulcet tones, almost as if they were lovers.

Recognizing sarcasm when she heard it, Viv replied, tight-lipped, "A flashlight is under the seat on the floor next to the medical kit…behind your fat feet."

With a snort of laughter, he retrieved the battery light, focused its beam on the map, and studied it for a long moment.

"Back there, we went through the town of Aras, correct?" he demanded.

"Yes," Viv spat.

"Well, if we keep driving in this same direction, we will run into a road jammed with thousands of Tommies trying to make for the coast like we are—and I'll be stuck just like those poor sods are going to be. And if we go this way…" he pointed, staring at the map at a road heading northeast, "I'll bet you a hundred francs, the Krauts will be launching aerial raids, taking off from captured Belgian airfields. They'll be flying low with tail gunners ready to mow down anyone they see…like sitting ducks on a pond."

Viv watched as her passenger's scarred, slender forefinger traced a thin line due north of Aras that ultimately bent toward Dunkirk a few miles from the north coast.

"So you think we should go *that* way?" she asked, worried by the isolated route he'd indicated. "The line on the map is awfully narrow, isn't it? Doesn't that indicate it's not a very good road?"

"It's not a road at all," he declared as if *she* were the dolt. "It's a sheepherders' trail."

"A *sheep*herders' trail?" she repeated, aghast. "You want us to take this heavy ambulance over hill-and-dale on a narrow dirt *track*? Talk about getting stuck! If it's rained at all up there, we could get mired in muck and never make it to Dunkirk in time."

He cast her a steady glance across the space that separated them. "How good are the axles on this thing?"

"This 'thing,'" she retorted, "is built on a truck's chassis and it's made by the Chevrolet automobile company in America. I'll bet the shafts are a lot stronger than any Citroën's," she challenged, tilting her chin, expecting him to dispute her claim. "But even so, driving this monster up a mere trail carved by a bunch of *sheep*..."

"Well, we'll just have to see if I'm a better navigator than you are, won't we?" the infuriating man added with a smirk that ended in a wince when it obviously began to pull at the stitches on his injured cheek.

"Look..." Viv insisted with exasperation, "before we go any farther, let me re-bandage your face, will you?"

Ignoring her offer, he pointed at the map once more. "And since it hasn't rained in a couple of days, if you take that turning a hundred yards on your right, we'll soon learn just how good a driver *you* think you are."

CHAPTER 7

Marcel Delonge's words of doubt regarding Viv's driving skills began to echo in her ears after ten miles of piloting the ambulance along the bumpy sheep's track in the dark of night. Several times she was forced to slow to a crawl, uncertain if she were even still following any sort of path at all. Twice, with her irascible passenger casting furrowed glances from the seat beside her, she'd come to a complete stop and gotten out of the vehicle to open a gate marking an enclosed field. She'd hopped back in to drive through into the next pasture, and then, once past it, exited the ambulance a second time to close the gate.

"At this rate, we must be barely traveling ten kilometers an hour," she muttered under her breath.

Her passenger, slouched next to her, opened one eye.

"*Eight* kilometers an hour according to that speedometer of yours."

Viv slammed on the brake and turned to face him.

"Do you think you're in any condition to drive? Because if you think you can get to Dunkirk any faster, please, be my guest!"

Viv figured that if he wrote up any after-action report on her, she'd be court-martialed for her insolence—or whatever they'd do to an insubordinate ambulance driver like her—but she didn't care. She was thoroughly fed up with her passenger and wanted to scream. He reached for the light, pulling himself upright to study the map.

Gesturing toward his side of the windshield, he instructed her, "Drive on just a bit. See that shepherd's hut there on the right? We'll stop there so we can have a piss and eat some of that food you brought."

Viv squinted in the dim light and steered her vehicle across an area with ruts half a foot deep. Looming toward them was a battered wooden structure with a stone chimney, a solitary window, and a door hanging by a single hinge.

"Park near that tree over there, he directed.

He got out and shone the flashlight's beam to illuminate his path, leaving Viv in the dark to fumble in the back of the vehicle for the food hamper. She took hold of the heavy container and plodded in his wake toward the small, tumbled-down building.

The evening air was still warm from the heat of the previous day, and the atmosphere was even hotter once they got inside the decrepit hut. Soon, they were both standing on a dirt floor in a deserted space, but for a cot pushed against one wall and a table and a solitary chair standing in the middle of the stuffy one-room structure.

"Open the window, will you?" he growled, "and where's the food?"

"*Merde, monsieur!* Will you give me a minute?" she demanded. She pointed to the hut's front door with a lower slat missing. "Go outside, have your piss, and then open the damn window yourself!"

"*Quelle insubordination!*" Marcel retorted with mock indignation. "Woman, do you dare address a colonel with such disrespect?"

"You're a *colonel?*" Viv replied, taken aback. "It didn't say that in your file."

"No… I expect it didn't."

"But it did say your real name, Marcel Delonge."

Ha! That stopped him in his tracks!

Marcel scowled, again hissing at her, "*Merde!* Keep that to yourself or I'll have to have you killed."

A guy like him probably isn't joking.

She turned her back to open the wicker food hamper that one of the hospital cooks had prepared for them.

Over her shoulder she retorted, "Henceforth, I shall certainly address you as 'Colonel Hush-Hush.'"

As she struck a match and lit the candle she always carried in her attendant's supplies, he replied, "At least, *chérie*, it's a step toward showing me the respect I so greatly deserve."

Without further elaboration, Marcel exited the hut, apparently to relieve himself outside.

"*Quel idiot exaspérant!*" she muttered at his retreating back, her best translation of "What an exasperating jerk!" When he returned, she pointed to the table and slapped down in front of him a hunk of bread and some cheese that was wrapped in parchment paper. "Here, eat this," she ordered, with a glance at the scar on Marcel's left cheek. "After we finish, I'll clean and re-bandage your wound."

She dug into the hamper once more and brought out a bottle of red wine and left it for him on the table. She took her portion of their meager repast over to the cot and sat down on a torn, threadbare blanket. For the next ten minutes, the two ate in silence.

———◇———

Viv's candle illuminated her first-aid kit that sat open on the table next to the nearly empty bottle of red wine they'd both consumed. Drinking the burgundy clearly had improved their mood as Marcel had finally consented to her cleaning and re-bandaging his scarred cheek.

"This will sting for a bit," she warned as she applied a swab saturated in alcohol to the closed incision slicing diagonally across Marcel's left cheek.

Her patient sucked in a breath but kept his head steady while she endeavored to clean the wound of its thin layer of road dust. Next, she fashioned a narrow strip of gauze and surgical tape that covered the track of stitches flanking the red line on his cheek. She imagined that the lighter-weight bandage would be less bothersome and more comfortable than his previous post-surgical dressings.

"Done?" he demanded as she began to pack up her supplies.

"Done," she repeated. "Do try to keep it on your face, will you?" she added, arching an eyebrow as she'd seen some of the credentialed nurses do at the hospital.

"It should do well enough until I can see a proper surgeon in London," he replied, his faint smile laced with a hint of mockery. "My thanks, Miss America." He settled back in the hut's only chair. "Where did you acquire such skills, and how in the world did a rich Yank like you end up driving an ambulance to Dunkirk with a man like me in your charge?"

Viv snapped her first-aid kit shut. How did he know her stepfather was rich, she wondered?

"That, my dear colonel-if-you-are-one, is a long story that would take from here to your destination to relate. And, of course, I'd have to ask the same of you, which would be a waste of time, wouldn't it?" She glanced at the narrow cot positioned against the wall. "Now, are we to sleep a few hours, or get back on the road?"

The fact was, her patient looked pale, despite his tanned complexion, and she could tell the wine had had its effect. In fact, she was eager for an hour's sleep herself after so many spent behind the wheel.

Marcel glanced over at the bed. "I suppose the gallant thing to do is offer my lady driver the bed."

"Yes, actually, it is, but you are the one who looks as if he could use some shut-eye even more than I do." She gestured toward the cot. "Be my guest."

Viv pronounced the words "shut-eye" in English, as she had no idea how to translate the American slang into French. Marcel, it appeared, knew what she meant.

"No, you take the cot," he said, rising from the chair where he'd allowed her to clean his wound. "I'll sleep on the stretcher in the ambulance and will wake you when I think we should continue on."

Viv cocked her head to one side, placing the food hamper on the table next to her first-aid kit.

"Glory-of-glories," she said. "I do believe you and I have finally *agreed* on something! Do you feel strong enough to take these with you and store the hamper in the back and my medical gear under the front seat?"

Without reply, he grasped an article in each hand and headed for the door that stood half open on its one hinge. By the slope of his shoulders, Viv could tell he was feeling the same weight of fatigue, as was she.

———◇———

A harsh whisper and Marcel's wine-laced breath burst against her ear.

"Get up! *Now!*"

"W-What...?" she replied with a groan. For a few moments she was not even sure where she was.

"Planes overhead! It's nearly daybreak, and they'll be able to spot the ambulance parked outside."

Viv, still clad in her uniform minus its jacket, sat bolt upright on the narrow cot in the dim light of the shepherd's hut.

"You're sure it's Germans?"

"Who else rules the skies these days?" he snapped, grabbing her arm. "Come *on!*" He tossed her jacket at her that he'd grabbed from the bottom of the cot. "The back of the ambulance can be seen near the tree. They'll spot the vehicle—figure someone's sleeping in here—and blast this place to dust."

Viv leapt off the cot, glanced around the room for anything else she might have left, and followed Marcel, who was already out the door and running toward their vehicle in the light of early dawn. The roar of airplane engines had become deafening by the time she reached the side of the ambulance and fumbled in her leather handbag for her keys.

"No, no, NO!" Marcel shouted in the uproar. "Get down! Under the running board for cover!" He was already in a crouch. "Slide under the chassis, like this!" he ordered and then disappeared. Several planes to their right had already passed over them, but one appeared to have veered out of formation and was heading directly toward the hut at a very low altitude.

Viv dropped to the ground, stretched out on her stomach, and inched her way like a crab between the wheels' two axles. Marcel roughly pulled the length of her body against his and covered her head and shoulders with his arms.

The noise of the single engine screamed overhead. The next thing she heard was the staccato sound of gunnery fire, the bullets pock-marking the dirt along a path to the door of the shepherd's hut. Then, a loud whistling sound was spiraling toward them and Viv felt Marcel's entire body stiffen as they both braced for the impact of whatever weapon was hurtling to earth.

All Viv could think of was, *I'm going to* die *in the arms of this insufferable—*

A loud explosion obliterated any further considerations as pieces of the wooden hut slammed against the ambulance's rear door and sides. Soon Viv could hear the crackle of fire and feel a blast of heat assaulting their hiding place beneath the ambulance.

"A direct hit…" murmured Marcel.

Viv could only assume that their former night's shelter had been incinerated by the bomb dropped directly on the roof from a plane whose engine's roar grew faint and then faded into the distance.

Marcel's wine-laced breath was again brushing against her ear.

"You still with me, *chérie*?" he murmured.

"Yes," she replied, her voice smothered by his arms still wrapped around her shoulders and head. "But barely. There so much smoke, I can't breathe."

Marcel relaxed his grip. "I think you'll have to re-bandage my face. It's hurting like hell."

"Then let me roll out from under here," she said on a strangled breath, her nose and mouth filled with the dust kicked up by the attack they'd just survived.

She worked her way sideways until she emerged from under the running board and could pull herself to her feet. She made a grab for the passenger-side door handle to steady herself but pulled her hand back instantly. It was hot as a stovetop.

Glancing over her shoulder, she gasped audibly at the sight of the collapsed and burning heap of wood and stone that had once been a shepherd's hut. There was a pile of ash where, only moments before, she'd been asleep on the cot pushed against the wall.

Marcel emerged from under the ambulance. Viv reached out to steady herself against his forearm in hopes that the trembling that had suddenly begun to wrack her frame would subside. She slowly met his glance and then looked back at the burning hut. If he hadn't awakened her, she, too, would have been a pile of ash at the dawn of this May morning.

She could feel Marcel studying her face, which she imagined had gone white beneath the dust that covered them both. Before she knew what was happening, he pulled her against his frame, pressing her cheek to his chest.

"Yes, I saved your life, Miss America," he whispered in his distinctive, gruff accent. The gravel in his tone hinted of the world of war he had inhabited long before she had joined the fight against the Nazis.

"I would have been dead," she whispered, bumping the top of her head against the bottom of his chin. "You slept in the ambulance on guard duty, right?"

"Right. Which means you owe me... Viv, isn't it?" He grasped her shoulders and pulled away to gaze at her with dark eyes that revealed nothing.

She willed her body to stop shaking.

"Yes, Viv. As in my last name, Vivier-Clarke, and I'll pay you back by getting you safely to Dunkirk," she declared, meeting his gaze. "Then we'll be even."

"*Only* if I make it to England, *chérie*. And if I don't, I promise I'll come back as a ghost to haunt you—and won't you be pleased?" he added with a satisfied smirk.

He puts the gall in Gallic! she thought, although for some reason she found herself smiling. To Marcel she merely said, "Sit here on the running board and I'll dress your wound. Again."

CHAPTER 8

Viv cleaned and neatly bandaged Marcel's incision for a second time. Before they set off along the rutted dirt track, she sat behind the driver's wheel while Marcel made an inspection of their vehicle.

"Just a few bullet holes in the ambulance's carcass," he reported, settling into the seat beside her, "plus patches of bark blown off the tree where you parked this monster."

"We're beyond lucky they didn't do any more serious damage," Viv said as she shifted into a lower gear.

Marcel served as lookout for any other German war planes flying along the shepherds' trail, but the rest of the day passed without incident as they made their way northeast until the track suddenly ended. He peered through the windshield and then with a glance at the map, declared that they were on the outskirts of a village with the odd name of Le Pont de Spycker.

Viv brought the vehicle to a rolling stop and rejoiced at the sight of a nearby canal that was clearly headed toward the sea. On the map it also indicated that there was some sort of forest that bordered on a Fort-Mardyck. Next to it there was another hamlet, Saint-Pol-sur-Mer, and nearby, Dunkirk itself with its expanse of beaches that looked to extend both east and west.

"Your shepherds' trail actually got us here," she marveled on a long breath, squinting through the windshield, now nearly opaque with dust.

"I've done this trip before," Marcel revealed.

Viv looked at him with surprise.

She'd heard rumors that British secret agents were sometimes picked up on the English Channel by Royal Navy submarines...but surely the Brits didn't routinely rescue random Frenchmen?

"*When* were you here 'before?'" she demanded.

"There's no time, now, to tell you, but maybe I will one day."

"I doubt that," she replied. "You hush-hush types never do."

With a shrug, Marcel gestured to the stand of trees just ahead. "Can you drive a little further to the edge of the woods overlooking the shoreline? You can let me off and I'll make my way from there."

Viv put the ambulance in gear and drove the short distance to the beginning of a small forest. A hundred yards beyond, they walked to a ridge with a view below of lines of uniformed men stretching from the water's edge, far into the town of *Dunkerque* itself—all waiting anxiously for an armada of rescue craft that might never arrive.

Marcel glanced over his shoulder. "I just thought of something. Any more food in that hamper that you could spare? I may have a long wait down there."

Viv nodded. "I'll divide what's left between the two of us," she said, adding, "I have a long journey back myself to Paris, remember? Just wait here."

Within minutes, she'd wrapped some cheese and a chunk of bread in a silk Hermès scarf—one among several from headier days that she kept stowed in her knapsack—and returned to the ridge, handing the bundle to Marcel.

"Ah...silk," he said, stroking the fabric between his thumb and fingers. "What a very pretty package you've made for me." He inhaled a breath. "You wear Chanel Number Five, yes? Lovely."

"I'm surprised you detected the scent over the smell of the cheese."

Marcel's smile was annoyingly cocky. "I'm quite familiar with it. Chanel Number Five, I mean. It's a wonderful fragrance, isn't it?"

Incorrigible!

"Bon voyage, Colonel H-H," she said pointedly.

He offered a mock salute. "Farewell to you, too, Miss America... until next time."

She squinted at him through the bright May sunshine, her hands on her hips. She thought of the German *Luftwaffe*, its planes poised to harass the departing troops as they lined up on the beach. Then, she considered her long drive back to Paris. Alone. At least Marcel Delonge had kept her on her toes—and he *had* saved her life, after all. She hated to admit it, but she would almost miss his company.

As he prepared to leave, she blurted, "So! You, *Monsieur* Frenchman, have got to talk your way onto a British navy boat, don't you, and get yourself across the Channel in one piece, while *I... I* have to find my way back on a sheep's trail to Paris with the German tail gunners shooting at my ambulance."

Marcel turned to face her as Viv felt a shiver of apprehension about her upcoming journey. By the time she arrived at the capital—if she ever did—the Germans might have already gotten there first.

"Yes, we both have some difficult moments ahead," he said, his expression now somber. "I wish you good luck, *chérie*."

He actually sounded sincere, she thought.

Viv nodded. "Thanks. And by the way, *merci beaucoup* for saving my life." She sucked in a breath at the memory of how close she'd come to meeting her end this very day. Wondering out loud, she asked, "What do you suppose the odds actually *are*, Marcel, that either of us will make it back alive?"

Marcel leaned toward her and brushed his lips against each cheek in turn. Then he took a step back. The corner of his mouth not marred by recent surgery arched faintly.

"Ah...as the priests say: let us *never* rule out miracles." The brief amusement in his eyes faded and he added quietly, "And may I thank you for your excellent chauffeuring and medical care? Let's not say *au revoir,* but rather *à bientôt, chérie*."

"Not goodbye," Viv murmured in English, "but until next time?"

Marcel nodded. *"Oui, bien sûr.* Or a better translation, 'see you soon, darling.'"

Before she could blink, Marcel Delonge bolted over the ridge and began to slide down the steep slope toward the vast beaches that stretched in both directions. She watched his boots mark his progress, carving deep ruts in the sandy hillside. Viv shaded her eyes with her right hand in a kind of salute of her own, bidding a final farewell to the mysterious figure clutching her colorful scarf bulging with bread and cheese. Soon, she lost sight of him as he melded into the thousands of men swarming the beach in hopes of rescue.

She looked up and gazed out to sea. On the far horizon, she could just make out a flotilla of boats—both large and small—steaming in their direction.

"Oh, thank *God*," she murmured. The British had come to retrieve their defeated soldiers, along with a few fellow fighters hailing from all over Europe.

What day is this? She counted back from when she and Marcel had departed Paris. To her surprise, she determined that it was a Sunday, May 26, 1940, and the massive evacuation of Allied troops from Dunkirk back to Britain was about to begin.

———◇———

To Viv, it truly *was* a miracle that she made the trip from Dunkirk to Paris without a loss of life or limb. When she passed the burnt-out shepherd's hut, she forced her eyes away from it and stuck faithfully to the sheep trail that Marcel had chosen until she came upon the town of Aras once again. From there, it was slow going on circuitous back roads as thousands of escapees were fleeing out of Paris on the main highways. She assumed they had departed on the news that German troops were expected to invade within the week.

As soon as she'd driven onto the grounds of the American Hospital, it was obvious that big changes were already underway. Hospital staff and deliverymen were streaming in and out of every door in sight, carrying packages and pushing equipment to and fro. The moment Viv emerged from the driver's side of the ambulance, Adrienne was waiting in the garage by the side of the driver's door and threw her arms around her friend.

"Thank God you made it!" Adrienne cried. "I was so frightened for you because we heard the damn Germans were shooting everything that moved on the roads in and out of Paris. I honestly didn't think you'd get through without being killed."

"The trip to Dunkirk was worse than coming back, but yes," Viv nodded, "it's not a junket I'd like to repeat."

Viv's friend gestured toward the hospital buildings outlined by the garages' open doors. "Basically, we've suddenly become a French auxiliary war hospital."

"Is Dr. Jack still in charge?" Viv asked anxiously.

"Oh, yes. He's even set up a temporary dressing station at Fontainebleau to treat the most seriously wounded coming back from the final battle. It's basically head, bone, and gunshot cases." Viv felt her friend's gaze take in her dusty face and rumpled uniform. "You better sneak off, clean up, and grab some rest. They've got us driving back and forth from Fontainebleau night and day." She lowered her voice, adding, "It's sickening to see the roads choked with fleeing Parisians and frightened troops. The damn German Suka dive-bombers shriek out of nowhere and shoot up civilians who are running for their lives! We've got one ward with just wounded women and children."

Viv shuddered at the memory of the bomb that had fallen directly on the shepherd's hut only moments after she and Marcel had scrambled under the ambulance.

Meanwhile, Adrienne flung her arms around Viv a second time and gave her another hug. "What a relief you made it through! I can't believe you were saddled with that rude man who had all those bandages on his face. I bet he was a rough customer."

Viv inhaled a deep breath and tried to appear calmer than she felt.

"Just another soldier," she said. "Hopefully, by now, he's being miserably seasick half-way across the Channel."

She was too exhausted to relate how that "just another soldier" had saved her life. Viv found herself hoping he'd have as good luck as she had making it to his ultimate destination.

———◇———

Viv couldn't believe the transformation that had taken place in the few days since she'd driven to Dunkirk and back. As battle after battle had been lost in the German onslaught launched from Belgium, Allied casualties had begun to arrive at the hospital in massive waves. On the first of June, Dr. Jackson was officially named "Resident Physician in Charge" of emergency efforts, while the entire staff began to work long hours of physically and emotionally exhausting shifts. Even Toquette Jackson donned her nursing whites for the first time since the end of the Great War. She pitched in with all the other "Florence Nightingales" attempting to keep a semblance of order and best medical practices within the wards.

On the third of June, German bombers let loose on the outskirts of Paris as a warning of the invasion of the city that was likely to occur very soon. Adrienne pointed to a recent copy of the international edition of the *Herald Tribune*, the English language 'Bible' of American expatriates living in France.

"The front-page article says that now, the *Luftwaffe* has no more British troops to harass at Dunkirk as they've all boarded the ships sent from England."

Viv suppressed a shudder, once again recalling the low-flying plane that had bombed the shepherd's hut to cinders. A surge of hot anger infused her reply.

"Yes, and now the German flyers can concentrate on killing the fleeing civilians on the roads leading from the city. What kind of monsters *do* things like that?"

———◇———

A few days later, each woman had driven her own ambulance with no co-pilot due to the mobile unit being seriously shorthanded.

"Wasn't your last trip back just like being in a shooting gallery?" Adrienne exclaimed to Viv when they'd both finally returned to the hospital after five harrowing hours behind the wheel.

Viv nodded, taking off her uniform's cap and mopping her brow that glistened with perspiration in the heat of the day. "On my run, it looked as if the Jerries were mowing us down for sheer sport of it all," she said, shaking her head in disgust. She pointed at some recent holes puncturing the fender of her vehicle. "Look! The bullets went right through the metal, next to the ones I got driving to Dunkirk."

Adrienne sighed. "We should be grateful for such small favors. At least, they didn't blow us up today."

———◇———

By the second week in June inside the hospital's Memorial Building, the wounded lay on stretchers in the corridors, waiting for someone to die to free up a bed.

That same week, Adrienne sat in the front seat once more when Viv halted their ambulance at the entrance to the emergency ward. They'd been sent on a special mission to bring back four downed flyers, a job that required two people to handle it.

"Please tell Nurse Comte that these are Royal Air Force boys in the back," Viv directed the orderlies who had appeared at her driver's side window. "They were shot down two weeks ago and somehow made their way to Fontainebleau."

Viv knew, but said nothing to Adrienne, that Dr. Jack had given her a separate message to deliver to his wife, Toquette.

"Tell her, please," the doctor had requested of Viv, "that anyone ambulatory from this latest group should attempt to get up from their beds as soon as they are healthy enough to make their way dressed as civilian Frenchmen to the South of France."

Meanwhile, Adrienne glanced at a second set of orderlies approaching the ambulance, a worried frown creasing her brow.

"The Germans are bound to do a search of the hospital once they take over Paris," she whispered. With a nod toward the back she added, "These Brits probably don't speak a word of French. Won't they be spotted right away as enemy soldiers by the Nazis?"

With a sigh, Viv opened the driver's side door.

"I doubt we're supposed to ask questions like that," she answered in a low voice, wondering how the men would ever travel south and then over the Pyrenees into neutral Spain. "I imagine you and I had better play dumb that they're even here in the hospital."

Adrienne nodded. "I'd rather *not* know any details, if you take my meaning...neutral Swiss that am I, and all that," she added with an attempt at a smile.

"Yes," Viv agreed, as she stood next to their mud-spattered vehicle. "I agree. The less we both know what's going on around here, the better."

Except the truth was, Viv actually craved information as to how these brave boys could be gotten to safety so they could return to fight the Nazis on another day. It gave her a secret thrill to recall the way she and Marcel had dodged dangers stalking them on the way to Dunkirk and how she'd somehow managed to return safely back to Paris all on her own. And despite the bone-chilling sight of what one German bomb had done to the cot she'd slept in, it had been such a rewarding feeling to have kept Marcel out of the enemy's clutches by ferrying him safely to Dunkirk, both of them thumbing their noses at the German bastards who'd tried to kill them. How different those few days with him had been from the dull routine of washing fenders and windshields after each trip to the front. It had truly transformed her idea of what it meant to fight the enemy, and she wondered how she would fare merely serving as an ambulance driver again.

Viv strode toward the rear of the vehicle and prepared to greet the quartet of orderlies now waiting to remove her British passengers. She gave the signal for the staff to lift the stretchers out from the ambulance's stuffy interior. Viv smiled encouragingly at the flyers' drawn faces filled with apprehension and memories of the frightening events they'd just endured. She placed her hand lightly on the shoulder of each man and silently vowed that she would do whatever she could to fight the expected onslaught of German invaders who were about to descend on the City of Light.

CHAPTER 9

By the tenth of June, Paris was declared "an open city" with no government authority truly in charge. The Gendarmerie in their dark blue tunics and sky-blue trousers disappeared from most street corners and an eerie silence even infiltrated the sidewalk cafés. All Paris appeared frozen in place waiting for the monsters to storm the gates.

Fighting a tide of her own anxiety, Viv commented to Adrienne, "Can you believe how the French have simply given up even though the barbarians are about to breach the barricades?" The two friends sat cross-legged on their cots in the nurses' wing. Adrienne inhaled a deep breath and shook her head in agreement.

"Act Two of a German play the elder generation has already seen."

A few days later, Viv's disquiet doubled over on itself when the vaunted *Herald Tribune* didn't appear on Paris news kiosks. The previous evening, Adrienne, who had met up with a male friend who worked at the Swiss Embassy, repeated some alarming news when she and Viv met for breakfast in the staff mess.

"Gaston Dupuis told me that Panzer tanks will soon be rattling down the road a half-mile from the hospital!" Viv groaned, but before she could reply, Adrienne continued, "And he said that General de Gaulle has resigned from the French Army! He broke with Pétain and he's been whisked to London to join Winston Churchill in opposing the German invasion of all Europe."

And just as they'd feared for so long, on the fourteenth of June, Nazi tanks rolled in from the countryside, past the city limits. After their morning meal, the two women were walking toward the hospital garage when they exchanged looks of alarm at the sudden, rhythmic clanking sounds of tank tracks on the road nearby.

"The Panzers?" Adrienne said, her head cocked to one side.

Viv didn't reply, but angrily stomped into the garage, grabbed a hose, and began the daily chore of cleaning their vehicle to prepare for their next assignment.

As the hours went by, no new orders were given. Meanwhile, the two women could hear blaring loudspeakers mounted on vehicles roaming along avenues adjacent to the hospital grounds.

German-accented voices announced in ear-splitting French, "All citizens should remain calm and stay inside your buildings!"—a message that was repeated endlessly until the sound drifted away.

"I want to see for myself what's going on!" Viv announced, a now-familiar surge of anger rising in her chest. Adrienne didn't reply, but surprised Viv by hurrying to keep up with her as she made a dash for the driver's side of their ambulance.

"Okay, if you're going to come," she directed, "sign us out for a food delivery run."

Adrienne did as Viv directed and then jumped into the passenger seat.

"We'll be sacked if they ever find out we're doing this," Adrienne said, breathless from her exertions. "And what if the Germans attack our ambulance?"

"I don't *care*," Viv said grimly. Taking backstreets, she pulled up on a side road near the Arc de Triomphe as the sounds of jackboots on the pavement grew louder. "I'm an American and you're Swiss. *We're* not the conquered!"

"Not yet," Adrienne replied.

Small knots of Parisians who, for various reasons had remained in the city, stood in stricken silence as phalanxes of goose-stepping German soldiers surged down the Champs-Élysées in the warm spring air of June 14.

Viv and Adrienne could only watch in tearful stillness as the Paris they knew was transformed in a day. They gazed skyward as an enormous Nazi flag with its bold, black swastika in the center descended from the highest parapet of the arch. Viv felt sick to her stomach at the thought her father had died in the battle to defeat Germany in the previous war, and yet, here they were again, rolling into Paris with their tanks and guns. How many innocent people would perish this time around, she wondered?

Staring at two red cloth corners of the flag flapping in the breeze, Viv murmured, "De Gaulle, at least, escaped to London."

But did Marcel Delonge make it across the Channel, she wondered?

As the rows of invaders passed by, even the women's small show of grim-faced resistance to the German takeover of the country held no glimmer of cheer for the two ambulance volunteers. Viv vainly fought the tears that finally spilled over and ran down her cheek.

"I've seen enough," Adrienne said in a low voice. "Can we go, now?"

Nodding, Viv climbed into the driver's seat and cautiously drove their lumbering vehicle along back streets, returning, unnoticed, to the hospital garage. By the end of that same day, Nazi swastikas were flying from Paris landmarks throughout the city. As an additional show of force, with the arrival of every new battalion of soldiers, the German occupiers held a succession of parades down several other main thoroughfares.

"I heard the troops marched right past Dr. and Mrs. Jacksons' home at Number 11 Avenue Foch," Adrienne declared as she and Viv brushed their teeth in the nurses' lavatory, preparing for bed.

Viv nodded, tucking her toothbrush into her cosmetic case. "Dr. J said that most of the buildings on his street have already been commandeered by the Nazis for their private use and the owners turned out on the streets." She met Adrienne's glance in the mirror they shared and saw the alarm flaring in her own brown eyes.

Nazis were neighbors of the Jacksons, now?

Given that Dr. J had allowed escaping British and French soldiers to occupy beds in the American Hospital, she was certain that the secrets some of the staff were keeping now spelled danger for them all. How long before there was a Nazi takeover of the institution, itself?

———◇———

On June 23, Hitler himself toured Paris and posed proudly beneath the Eiffel Tower now flying a Nazi insignia. Most of the traces of the France that Viv had known and loved were gone in a fortnight and a national nightmare had truly begun. Dr. Jackson had thus far pushed back when German authorities inquired about the availability of hospital beds for the invaders. He underscored that it was an American institution, run by an American doctor—and the United States was not at war with the German occupiers. Viv whispered to Adrienne entering the wards with their wounded charges, "So far, so good."

For Viv and Adrienne, the succeeding days and weeks of the summer of 1940 were a blur of transporting the remaining wounded from battlefields to the makeshift field hospital established inside a casino at Fontainebleau, forty miles south of Paris. From there, if the soldiers hadn't died, they were transported to the American Hospital on the outskirts of Paris.

As autumn gave way to winter, the Nazi occupiers forbade listening to the BBC on penalty of arrest—or worse. The only bright news, as far as Viv was concerned, was Dr. Jackson's announcement in their staff meeting in early November that Franklin Roosevelt was re-elected to an unprecedented third term as President of the United States.

"Maybe now," Viv confided to Adrienne, "he can override all those right-wing 'American First-ers' like Charles Lindberg, who's been so cozy with the damn fascists, and give Churchill the support he so desperately needs."

Every time she even said the word 'fascists' aloud, she recalled with a shudder the rallies she had witnessed in Berlin in the mid-1930's. Viv remembered on one occasion, when her mother and Karl had been in the city on business, she'd been so upset by the sea of raised arms and screaming youth who'd been close to her in age, that she'd demanded to know why Karl would sell an American product in a country like Nazi Germany. Her mother had rebuked her "insolence," prompting Viv to bolt from her parents' hotel room and refuse to speak to either of them for the rest of the day. They'd left her in her Berlin school learning German without saying goodbye.

Recalling those dark days, Viv said under her breath, "God, I *hate* those cruel bastard Krauts"

Adrienne offered her customary defeated shrug. "Well, it certainly looks as if they're here to stay, so you'd better not say that too loudly."

———◇———

As the weeks ground on, Viv stopped by her mother's flat only sporadically. However, on one visit in the first week of December, Pamela opened the door and immediately waved a pile of American dollars she'd grabbed out of her handbag.

"Look what Karl arranged," she said, smiling happily. "He wired funds to the American Embassy in Vichy. The ambassador had someone bring them to us in Paris."

"Does Karl want you to use the money to try to return to America?" Viv asked, the pulse in her head throbbing at the mention of her stepfather.

"I suppose, but the embassy attaché who called here said that soon, even Americans won't be able to leave, let alone British citizens like I am. But here I will stay," Pamela declared, her face serene as she poured herself a drink. "The Paris spring collections will be available soon, so I have no more interest in returning to North Carolina than you do."

Viv looked questioningly at her mother. "Why can't someone

with an American passport make plans to leave France if they want to? The U.S. isn't at war—yet."

Pamela shrugged with disinterest. "I have no idea, but that's what the young man told me when he dropped off the packet. Apparently, Karl asked why you hadn't left France last September. I told the attaché to tell him that you've been playing Florence Nightingale with all those young men at the American Hospital." With a pleased smile, she returned the money to her handbag. "But at least I can keep my larder filled. That was dear of Karl, don't you think?"

Viv thought darkly, the words "dear" and "Karl" didn't belong in the same sentence.

CHAPTER 10

By Christmas week, 1940, all armed resistance by the nation in continental Europe ceased. France's sham government—led by the elderly General Pétain in the spa town of Vichy—carried on a power-sharing charade with their German overlords. But it was clear to Viv and everyone at the American Hospital that it was the occupiers who were now calling the shots.

Meanwhile, members of the ambulance corps found themselves delivering Red Cross packages to a new brand of detainees: "Enemies of the Reich."

Viv gazed through her windshield at one of the barbed-wire camps for political prisoners—and Jews in particular—that were now scattered throughout France's occupied zone. The inmates, in fact, were random persons the Nazis considered "suspect" and could be incarcerated without anything or anyone to stop them.

Just before Christmas Day itself, Viv and her mother returned from the hospital where they encountered several German soldiers standing guard at the entrance to their apartment building on Avenue Kléber.

"Halt!" barked one of them in guttural French. With a flourish the officer brandished his weapon in their faces. "No admittance!"

Pamela drew herself to her greatest height and barked back, "Excuse me, but I *live* here!" She began digging in her handbag for documents to prove her assertion.

"Not anymore, you don't," he snapped. "By orders of the—"

Ignoring him, Pamela marched passed the German guard, stormed through the lobby of their building, and pounded on her own front door. Viv trailed behind her, praying the guard on the street wouldn't shoot them in the back.

In the next instant, an SS officer opened the carved wooden portal of their flat. Viv's immediate impression of him, with the menacing skull insignia imbedded above the brim of his hat, was that, clearly, she and her mother were not welcome arrivals. He stared in shock and displeasure as Pamela pushed past his shoulder and strode into the middle of her ornate drawing room. She turned to confront the soldier clad in his gray-green uniform with a line of beribboned medals on his chest.

"Sir, you have obviously made a dreadful mistake!" she declared in her most aristocratic British manner. "I am dear friends with General Albert de Chambrun whose son is married to the daughter of the distinguished Vichy official, Pierre Laval—second only to General Pétain, himself! He would never allow someone to take over my home!"

Viv remained in the foyer, wondering who would win this *contretemps*. As for the Nazi officer, he looked at Pamela Bradford for a long moment, put his head back, and laughed.

His luggage lay on the floor just inside the flat's entrance as he raised the glass of fine Bordeaux he had obviously liberated from Karl Bradford's excellent cellar and declared, "I am sorry, madam, but mentioning those swine will do you no good. *Sturmbannführer* Hans Kieffer, himself, assigned me these quarters." The intruder was an imposing officer with slicked-back blond hair, and he took a sip of his wine before adding, "As you may know, he runs the SS counter-intelligence services at Number 84 Avenue Foch, not far from here." He took a second sip. "Herr Kieffer delights in arresting those enemies here in Paris who dishonor the Fatherland when they disobey the rules we have established for everyone's well-being."

Viv repressed a shudder, as she had heard the rumors of what happened to anyone unlucky enough to be taken to Number 84 Avenue Foch to face Herr Kieffer.

"What you are saying is of absolutely *no* consequence to *me*!" Pamela sputtered. "I'll have you know—"

"And *I* will see your papers, please!" he interrupted.

The officer's lips had hardened into a straight line, and Viv knew instinctively that her mother would not win this battle.

"Please," Viv said urgently under her breath, "just show him your—"

But before she could grab her mother's arm, the officer took a step closer to them both.

"You are British, ya?" he demanded of Pamela, taking in the sight of her cashmere coat and the smooth, blond chignon that bestowed on her such an elegant air.

"I most certainly *am* British!" Pamela retorted.

"And therefore, our enemy." The officer's startlingly blue eyes narrowed. "And you, *fraulein*?" he asked of Viv.

"American," Viv replied before her mother could speak for her. She was relieved she had her U.S. passport in her handbag, and not her British one.

"May I see?" he asked as Viv dug to retrieve the document with the American seal on the front. The soldier compared the photo in its first pages to Viv's face where she was standing two feet away from him and handed it back to her. Her mother reluctantly opened her purse and drew out her British passport.

"You are both living in Paris?" he said, inspecting Pamela's document.

"Yes," Pamela snapped, "and we were in this flat long before you arrived."

The SS officer laughed without amusement and replied, waving her passport in front of her, "Well, Pamela Bradford, we will be rounding up *your* lot—all the ex-pats from England—any day now." He stared at her outstretched hand and after a long moment, handed her back her identity document.

To Viv he conceded, "I am pleased there is so little enthusiasm for America to join the so-called Allies who are destined to lose this war. However, I suggest you and this woman you're with leave the premises immediately if you don't wish me to have you removed by some of my colleagues from Gestapo headquarters just around the corner."

Pamela's gaze swept over her peach silk furniture and drapes, the chandelier winking above their heads. To Viv's utter amazement, her mother suddenly assumed an air that could only be described as kittenish.

"But what about all my beautiful clothes in the closets here, officer?" wheedled Pamela. She offered her most seductive gaze. "Surely you'll let me take them with me? My gowns...my silk stockings. Won't you need the space for your handsome uniforms?"

Viv felt like slapping her.

This German is a Nazi pig! Men were bleeding to death in the hospital corridors where both she and her mother served as volunteers. Yet, here was Pamela bargaining for *silk stockings* with the enemy who'd blatantly requisitioned their family's apartment!

Viv's heart began to pound as she watched Pamela point to the glass of wine the officer held in his hand.

"I see you've found one of my husband's favorite reds," she said, her smile ingratiating. "There are many other lovely ones in his collection downstairs I can show you. Even some outstanding German whites," she mewed. "My husband owns Bradford Steel Ball Bearings, an important manufacturer in America, you know, and he's done much business in your country. Surely you can..."

She allowed her sentence to linger in the air, full of promise.

The officer nodded, as if he completely understood the code in which Pamela Bradford was signaling him. Although several years younger than her mother, the officer smiled faintly and allowed, "You may come tomorrow—shall we say four o'clock, *fraulein*—to pack your trunks and transport them to wherever you will be living." He inclined his head. "I am Colonel Wilhelm Gerhardt." He clicked his heels. "Perhaps, Pamela, we can review the inventory of your husband's wine cellar at that time?"

He'd noted even her first name from her passport, the swine!

Viv looked on, transfixed, at her mother smiling contentedly as if she'd won a skirmish worth savoring.

Her daughter, in disgust, could only whirl toward the door and march across its threshold. Behind her, she heard the new occupant of her father's Avenue Kléber flat click his heels together once more and declare "*Heil Hitler!*" in farewell.

————◇————

The moment Viv and Pamela emerged from the apartment building's lobby, Viv turned abruptly in the street, hands clenched by her sides.

"So, you're willing to sleep with that creep just to get—"

"For God's sake, *hush!*" Pamela hissed. She glanced around the street to see if the SS guard outside might be within earshot. "I promised him nothing but a dose of charm," she declared, but Viv heard the note of defiance. "You don't expect me to give up my beautiful things without a fight? How *dare* they take my apartment as well!"

"*Our* apartment," Viv shot back. "That deed is in my name, too, remember?" She shook her head in disbelief. "But now, you're only too happy to consort with an enemy who killed my *father?*"

Pamela's slap to Viv's cheek landed so fast and hard, Viv was nearly knocked to her knees. Before she could even respond, her mother strode down the boulevard, hailed a rare passing taxi, sidled into its back seat, and disappeared down the street. Viv rubbed her throbbing cheek while speculating that Pamela would check into a posh hotel without seeming to care that scores of Germans were probably already staying there.

As for Viv herself, that night she wound up on the sofa in Adrienne's fifth floor *chambre de bonne,* the former maid's room atop a private home on rue de Beaune.

"Stay as long as you like," Adrienne said generously. "It's nice to have your company day or night."

————◇————

As days passed after her argument with her mother, Viv invented clever ways to avoid seeing Pamela at the hospital. Even so, she couldn't manage to shake her anger about the way her mother had behaved toward the German officer. It certainly wasn't because she was particularly shocked Pamela might be unfaithful to her stepfather to get her possessions back. It was something that struck a nerve far deeper, a peculiar sense that almost felt like *grief.* The woman who had given her birth had no loyalty to her first husband's memory or to anyone but herself and her own welfare.

Viv described the unhappy scene to Adrienne late one night as they sat on the floor of her friend's flat, sipping cheap wine after another grueling day at the hospital.

"She actually slapped you that hard?"

"She has a very swift right hook," was Viv's sardonic reply.

Adrienne remained silent for a moment, and then commented, "Well, as the saying goes: the truth always hurts."

"That's for sure," Viv acknowledged glumly. "But it always seems to injure *me*...never her."

CHAPTER 11

A few days later, Viv arrived at the hospital ten minutes late signing in for her upcoming shift. To her great discomfort, she nearly collided with her mother, who stood just inside the front entrance. Pamela smiled as if nothing were amiss between them.

"My goodness, you certainly are in a hurry."

Viv made no reply. Her mother waited a moment and then spoke again.

"I think you should have the grace to congratulate me," she said airily. "I've just taken possession of a new flat on rue des Canettes near the church of St. Sulpice, a block off Saint Germain, if you please!"

Viv was amazed to hear her mother had found a place in such an attractive neighborhood. The Germans had requisitioned nearly all decent living quarters in Paris for their own use. The fact that the Jacksons still had possession of their fine address at 11 Avenue Foch in the posh Sixteenth was a kind of miracle.

"How in the world did you manage to find an apartment?" demanded Viv. "And in St. Germain, no less?"

Her mother bestowed a Mona Lisa smile and waved as she turned and strode down the corridor in the direction of the commissary. A few yards further down the hall, she glanced over her shoulder and called out, "I'll fill in the details another time. I'm late for helping with the tea service. Do come by rue des Canettes and see my new home where there's room for you, if you like. It's Number 20."

The next day, curious in spite of herself, Viv arrived at the address that turned out to be charming, but decidedly smaller than their previous flat, and on the third floor. Climbing the limestone stairs, she was greeted by the sight of her mother surrounded by furniture, clothing, and housewares from their former home. Viv slowly turned around in the compact sitting room, surveying the many articles her mother had managed to secure from her erstwhile life on Avenue Kléber.

"So," Viv said after a long pause, "the officer who took over our apartment obtained *this* one for you and released many of your belongings?"

Pamela nodded, avoiding her daughter's direct gaze while pouring herself a glass of champagne. "Colonel Gerhardt was surprisingly accommodating."

Viv felt her pulse begin to quicken.

"Are you happy, now, Mother, that you've officially become a collaborator?"

Instead of reacting angrily, as Viv fully expected, given their last exchange on the subject of consorting with Germans, Pamela merely took a slow sip of champagne from her crystal glass transferred from their former flat.

At length she said, "Please, Viv, let me enjoy what I have. No more quarrels. Really, darling, it's *so* tiresome. I merely claimed what was mine."

"And exactly *how* did you claim it?" Viv asked, sweeping her arm in an arc at the collection of gowns, glassware, silver, and even a tiger's head rug waiting to be unfurled on the parquet floors of Pamela's new living quarters.

"Actually, I explained to Wilhelm that Germany considered the American whose flat he'd commandeered a *friend* of the Fatherland. I informed him about all those ball-bearings Karl had sold them and that I was not someone to be treated cavalierly."

"Oh, *Wilhelm*, is it now?"

Ignoring her daughter's acid tone, Pamela continued to take delicate sips of her champagne as she surveyed the newly transported possessions with a pleased expression. The opened bottle of bubbly rested in a handsome silver bucket with an ornate "V-C" engraved on its side—another artifact from Pamela's marriage to Charles Vivier-Clarke.

Viv found herself wondering if beautiful women like Pamela Bradford felt they were simply entitled to secure whatever they wanted from the opposite sex—be they gentlemen or scoundrels—simply by virtue of their good looks and sexual appeal?

The simple truth was that when the widow, Mrs. Pamela Vivier-Clarke, married Karl Bradford-born-Braunheim, she had betrayed everything Viv's birth father had believed in, fought for, and had even given his life in service of. "Mr. Ball-Bearing," as Viv had always labelled her stepfather Karl Bradford, was a grasping, vulgar, greedy, under-educated bully. He was also a dynamic force of nature—and very rich. *That,* Viv had always supposed, was his primary attraction as far as Pamela was concerned.

Truth was Viv's mother had ignored the fact that her second husband had browbeaten his spirited stepdaughter from the moment they'd met. To put an end to the constant battles with Karl, Viv had been sent to boarding school at the age of twelve. She rarely saw her parents, but for a few holidays or during Karl's business trips to Germany. Ruefully, she wondered, now, if some of her rebellious behavior was simply part of the defensive shell she'd erected around herself for protection.

Musing about her youthful years leading up to the war, Viv was startled from her meandering thoughts when her mother waved a hand studded with her best jewelry.

"Yoo-hoo… Viv!" Pamela exclaimed, irritation etching the lines that had begun to bloom around her mother's exceptionally blue eyes. "You're a million miles away. Can't you see that I've managed to make lemonade out of lemons by acquiring a three-year lease on this delightful *pièd-a-terre*?"

Viv gave a slight shrug, her mind devoid of a reply.

Her mother refilled her own glass with more champagne and flashed the smile of an accomplished coquette. "I liberated some of *your* things, you should know. Your Louis Vuitton cosmetic case is next to the front door. I thought you might like to take it to the hospital with you to freshen up if you plan a date with one of the doctors."

"Thank you," was all Viv could manage, a hollowness she couldn't explain expanding in her chest.

Pamela pointed to a slender wine bottle on her sideboard. "Now, look, darling, if you don't fancy any Veuve Clicquot," she said, waving her flute, "have a glass from one of the few bottles of this wonderful Gewurztraminer I have left—"

Viv was shocked to feel a knot of pure rage gripping her gut and she began to pace up and down in front of the fireplace at the end of the room.

"I bet you gave that Nazi the *rest* of Daddy's collection of Alsace wines, didn't you? For God's sake, Mother, his Vivier family *fled* from Alsace to America when the Germans invaded and raped their region in the *last* damn war. How *could* you make Daddy's wine from there part of your bargain with that colonel?"

"Oh, please, it's just wine!" Pamela snapped. "Pull yourself together, Constance!"

But Viv knew she was way past the point of being able to do that.

"You were paid in furniture and probably traded every *case* of my dead father's Gewurztraminer for your favors, didn't you?" she blurted. "You let that man bed you, even though you know better than most people what these Nazi fiends are visiting on innocent people still living on Vivier family land!"

"Oh, for pity's sake," her mother scoffed. "The French themselves are finding all kinds of ways to accommodate to this new reality."

"Not *all* French people!" Viv countered, doing her best to try to rein in her anger. "Surely not the Alsatians."

Pamela's tone hardened. "Your father was mental on the subject of Alsace, if you ask me. I thought he was crazy when he, *American* born, mind you, joined the French and British in the last war—and died doing it, more's the fool!"

A familiar vision passed before Viv's eyes of her father leaping from his flaming cockpit into the void, his unopened parachute streaming lifelessly above his downward trajectory. She struggled to keep her voice even.

"You know as well as I do that Alsace was given *back* to France in the Peace Treaty twenty years ago, and now the damn Krauts have overrun it *again,* stealing all the wine—*again*! You've seen those horribly wounded British and French soldiers Adrienne and I brought in from the battlefront last spring. Hundreds were volunteers from Alsace."

"German soldiers were 'horribly wounded,' *too*," Pamela replied, sarcasm now appearing to be her best defense. "Haven't you noticed? Everybody gets hurt in war. Don't you think you're being a bit over-dramatic about a few cases of wine?"

"It's more than the wine, and you know it!" Viv retorted.

Somewhere in the back of her brain she realized her fury was linked to far more than just that her mother had played *collaborateur* with the hated Germans, or that the woman who had given her birth didn't honor the ultimate sacrifice Charles Vivier-Clarke had made for Alsace and for France.

No, Viv knew in the place where she couldn't lie to herself that her rage was also about a little girl who'd been told to be quiet and not make a fuss when she felt like crying every day for months after her father was reported killed in action. It was about a lonely teenager packed off to a Swiss boarding school with no loving adult to confide in when she wondered if boys would always ignore her because she towered over so many of them. With a flash of insight, Viv acknowledged silently that she'd been virtually *abandoned* by this woman who was so nonchalantly trading the last of the Vivier family's Alsace wine to a nasty Nazi. As a child, she'd always wondered secretly if there must not be a good reason that her mother didn't care to keep her own daughter near her.

Viv leaned one hand against the carved wooden mantel trying to cool her emotions. After a few deep breaths, she looked across the room at her mother and said quietly, "I suppose I shouldn't be surprised that you wouldn't think twice about trading Daddy's wine in exchange for all your possessions, then fucking a Nazi to seal the deal."

Pamela stood across the room absorbing Viv's verbal attack, surrounded by her treasured peach-colored Louis XVI silk furniture.

Viv's hands fell to her side. "I am done here," she murmured, passing her mother on her way to the foyer.

Near the front door she spotted her Louis Vuitton cosmetic case sitting on a chair. It had been a gift one Christmas sent to her boarding school when Pamela cancelled plans to have her daughter rendezvous with Karl and her in Paris. It had been a classic Pamela and Karl Bradford *quid pro quo*. Viv had received an expensive bribe in return for not making a fuss about remaining at her Swiss school over the holidays.

She recalled that when the winter term resumed that the luxurious present had been the envy of all her schoolmates, including her best friend Adrienne. Its shining brass corners and distinctive cream-and-brown colored covering had soothed Viv's wounded heart a little, for she'd taken it to mean that, somehow, her mother did care.

Viv would never assume that again.

Even so, she couldn't quite leave it behind. She seized the case's leather strap with her left hand, and with her right, yanked open the front door of Pamela's new flat, slamming it hard as she left.

Viv had barely taken a step before she nearly ran into the erect figure of Colonel Wilhelm Gerhardt. Resplendent in his Nazi uniform, he'd just arrived on the third-floor landing. Viv froze, her cosmetic case in one hand, her feet unable to move.

"Good evening, *fraulein*," the colonel said politely in English. "Just leaving?"

Viv inhaled deeply before answering between clenched teeth, "You betcha!"

Gerhardt cast her a puzzled look, apparently unable to translate her vehement reply. As he stepped aside, Viv lurched toward the first flight of stone steps, her footfalls echoing in the stairwell.

She'd head for Adrienne's place. Where else could she go?

CHAPTER 12

The following day, Pamela Bradford sent a letter on her embossed personal stationery. In it she asked Dr. and Mrs. Sumner Jackson for their understanding, explaining that she was finding it was too risky to travel from St. Germain to Neuilly-sur-Seine each day and could therefore no longer volunteer at the hospital.

When Viv learned of her mother's resignation, she swiftly petitioned Dr. Jack for permission to sleep most nights in the nurses' quarters at the hospital. For far different reasons than Pamela, Viv pointed out that it would be best for her to avoid having to go from Paris to the suburb by underground metro with irregularly running routes.

When Dr. Jackson agreed, Adrienne, too, asked to be assigned a bed in the nurses' quarters, given their expanding duties as part of the Medical and Ambulance Corps. Both women stashed their few possessions, along with Viv's cosmetic case, under their beds lined up next to twenty others along a wall.

As the weeks rolled by, Christmas 1940 was hardly noticed, except for the sad fact that the Germans appeared one day to arrest the hospital's gardener, a British subject named Burgess. Viv asked nurse Elizabeth Comte why the hospital board of directors had taken no action to try to get the poor man released.

"The Germans aren't likely to comply with our request, even made by neutral Americans," she replied. "I'm guessing the hospital board is holding its fire to protect any American or French staff whom the Germans might arrest in the future."

Especially if they knew we are harboring British and French soldiers masquerading as ill patients... Viv thought, although neither she nor Elizabeth would be foolish enough to say such a thing.

———◇———

Each day of the New Year of 1941, life in Paris became even grimmer with petrol rationing growing dire, along with numerous roundups of Jews, mysterious disappearances of familiar faces, and an onslaught of severe food rationing which made feeding the hospital's staff and patients increasingly difficult.

"How do you think your mother is doing with all the extra rationing now?" Adrienne asked one frigid February day when the vegetable garden they'd been asked to help with the previous autumn was now covered with a few inches of snow.

"Pamela?" Viv responded, sensing a familiar ball of anger forming spontaneously in her stomach. She affected a shrug while pushing away thoughts of the officer living in her father's flat on Avenue Kléber—except for the nights Viv assumed he spent with Pamela on rue des Canettes. "You know Mother. You can bet she's doing just fine."

In addition to their worries about shortages of food and medical supplies necessary to keep the institution running, Viv, Dr. Jackson, and the entire staff of the American Hospital now lived in constant dread of a German takeover of the facility.

During one of the head physician's regular closed-door meetings with trusted staff, Dr. Jackson announced, "Any *non*-German who has the slightest physical complaint is welcome in these wards, very few questions asked. We'll also now take industrial accidents, victims of bombings, and other non-German unfortunates...but *fill* those beds, please! Packing our wards is our only hope to remain independent of the Nazis."

Few staff knew, besides Viv and Adrienne, that downed airmen and even escaping Jews were beginning to fill a new ward set up in the basement. These particular patients would remain there with sheets drawn up to their chins until a certain group from outside the hospital could speed them on well-trod escape paths to Switzerland or across southern France to the Pyrenees and over the mountains into Spain.

"As long as our beds are occupied by people who do not wish us harm," Jackson emphasized to Viv one day, "I can say oh, so politely to the Gestapo in that building they've requisitioned across the street, 'Sorry, Herr Fritz. There isn't a hospital bed to be had. '" He flashed one of his rare smiles and winked.

Viv smiled back, but silently wondered if it were only a matter of time before the Nazi occupiers' iron fist descended on and put an end to Jackson's clandestine activities.

———◇———

When spring came, and Viv and Adrienne weren't delivering food and supplies loaded in their ambulances by the Red Cross to POW camps, they were helping Toquette Jackson with one of her never-ending "projects." She and an army of volunteers had begun to dig up the beautiful rose gardens on the hospital grounds to plant much-needed rows of additional vegetables to augment their dwindling stores.

Toquette often invited Viv for a meager supper at the Jackson home at 11 Avenue Foch, mere blocks from where the feared Hans Kieffer—apparently with the help of Wilhelm Gerhardt—had established the Nazi anti-Resistance counterintelligence headquarters at Number 84.

In March, Viv had rejoiced to hear that President Roosevelt signed the Lend-Lease Act despite tremendous opposition from the "America First" contingent led by aviator hero, Charles Lindberg.

"I'm totally amazed," Viv said to Adrienne. "Dr. Jack said eighty percent of Americans are still opposed to the U.S. joining the war. Somehow FDR got Lend-Lease passed in Congress. American destroyers are now on their way across the Atlantic."

"I'm Swiss," Adrienne responded dryly, "so Congress approving the Lend-Lease of warships doesn't sound very 'neutral' to me. I suppose that your country will join with the Allies soon?"

Viv sighed. "Only if we're attacked, or so FDR promised running for re-election."

———◇———

One evening in early May, Viv was startled to hear Toquette bid her husband, young son, and her guests to gather around the wireless to listen to a forbidden broadcast from the BBC. Keeping the volume low, they all strained to hear the news of what was happening in Britain now that a German *blitzkrieg* had decimated blocks of London and other British cities, killing some 32,000 civilians.

As Viv listened to the illicit news confirming such a frightful death toll across the Channel, she had a sudden vision of Marcel Delonge. She couldn't help wondering: did he ever make it across the Channel to England? Where was he now? What assignment would de Gaulle's Free French spies have him doing these days—if he were still alive?

Viv's meandering thoughts about the man who had saved her life were interrupted by the radio announcer's alarming warning that *all* British citizens still living in occupied France were likely to "be interned very soon by the Nazis into camps that generally do not adhere to the rules of International Law."

Viv's pulse pounded. What would happen to her mother? In the next instant, a familiar, leaden feeling weighed on her chest. She imagined Pamela raising a glass of her father's Alsatian wine in toast with Colonel Gerhardt.

Mother is a survivor...any daughter of hers need not be concerned.

Toquette reached over and patted Viv's forearm.

"Didn't Doctor Jack tell me you have dual citizenship, Viv? British and American?" Viv nodded. Toquette paused for a long moment and then said, "You *do* travel in Europe on your American passport, yes?"

Viv nodded again. "My British one is locked in my family's safe in the States. My stepfather told me to leave it there. I think he guessed what was coming."

"For now, it's wise you only carry your American one," agreed Toquette with a look of relief. She sought Viv's gaze. "However, I do fear it's time for your mother to think about leaving the country while she still can."

Viv raised her hands in a gesture of feigned helplessness.

"Pamela Bradford has long been convinced she wouldn't be subject to mistreatment by the Nazis."

Dr. Jackson looked up from having just turned off the wireless and changed the dial to a station broadcasting German propaganda, thereby confounding any snoops that might be monitoring their house.

"That's a very unfounded supposition," he said. "Tell your mother I said so."

"I will if I see her," Viv replied diplomatically, "but her view is that she knows people high up in Vichy...and others...who would move swiftly to prevent any arrest."

"A foolhardy view in my opinion," he replied.

Viv exchanged a look with her hostess and managed a small shrug as if to say, "You're both wasting your breath. My mother *always* thinks she'll get her way..."

———◇———

For the remainder of 1941, Dr. Jackson somehow managed to hold on to control over who was admitted to the American Hospital. Miraculously, it didn't include a single German—either ill or healthy.

Gasoline had become so scarce, twenty of the ambulances were converted to run on *gazogene,* a concoction of carbonized wood chips. Viv found the retrofitted vehicles nerve-wracking to drive, but she knew mastering their operation was vital, not only for transporting patients, but also for bringing food from farms around Paris to the hospital to feed some five hundred people each day.

Viv and Adrienne spent most of their working hours these days delivering Red Cross packages to the increasing number of Nazi-run internment camps being built all over the occupied zone of northern France.

"It's disgusting, the conditions in those camps!" Adrienne declared as she and Viv were washing down their ambulance after a long day on the rutted roads outside Paris. "And the poor Jews! They're held in the worst conditions of all."

"Hordes of them are suddenly not even there anymore," Viv replied, depression settling in as she recalled the pinched, frightened faces of the people they witnessed each time their assignment took them into the camps. She turned off the hose and joined Adrienne in toweling off the sides of the vehicle. "You rarely see the same prisoners twice in those wretched pens."

Viv thought back to the person she had been when she had behaved like such a spoiled child in front of the embassy official in Athens seeking the official documents she needed as war broke out. She was certainly glad she had come to France because, for the first time ever, she finally felt that she had a purpose in life. But what an ignorant dope she'd been then, with no idea what it was like to be someone the German enemy could just dispose of at will. Embarrassed it had taken her this long to grow up, she honestly didn't care what her mother or Karl thought of her anymore. And maybe, even, what she was doing *now* would have made her father proud.

———◇———

With most of 1941 going badly for Britain, there was finally some good news: the sinking of the battleship *Bismark* by the British Navy. That was followed by a declaration that the Unites States had frozen all German and Italian assets in America.

"Good!" Viv exclaimed when she heard.

"Another act of non-neutrality," warned Adrienne. "What do you bet the Germans will do something in retaliation to drag America into actual combat?"

In recent months, Viv had become well aware that an increasing number of patients admitted personally by Dr. Jackson into the basement ward were, like certain inmates in the Nazi camps, "suddenly not there anymore." The odd empty hospital bed signaled that its former resident had mysteriously been sent on his way before the SS was any the wiser. Within hours, another admittee would settle in. Viv could only hope that these Allied prisoners-of-war, downed airmen, and prominent Jews who came and went ultimately made it over the borders into Switzerland or Spain.

She couldn't help wondering who Dr. Jack and Toquette had recruited to spirit them out of the hospital and on their way to safety—and would their SS neighbors find out?

Chapter 13

December 1941

December 7 marked the memorable day when the Americans working at the hospital received a rare Sunday summons to assemble in Dr. Jackson's office. With Toquette standing by his side, he greeted them with a wave to be seated.

"We have just received a cable from Washington D.C. that eighteen American ships were sunk by the Japanese in a surprise assault on Pearl Harbor, Hawaii."

Gasps filled the air. To Viv and everyone's shock and surprise, it was the Japanese, not the Germans, whose actions resulted in America losing five battleships and some 2400 military and civilian personnel killed in a single day of attack.

"I just want you all to be prepared," Jackson said. "I have no doubt America will soon officially be at war, and that should alter things considerably here in Paris."

The doctor's predictions were "spot on," as Viv's mother said. Within twenty-four hours, the U.S. and Britain jointly declared war on Japan. By December 11, Hitler had declared war on the United States.

"So much for America's staying out of the conflict in Europe," Adrienne commented.

"What would Switzerland have done if the center of Geneva had been obliterated by German bombs and twenty-four hundred Swiss citizens were killed?" Viv demanded.

Adrienne paused and then replied, "The Germans wouldn't do that. Their money is locked up in our vaults in Geneva."

"Of *course* Germany wouldn't bomb you," Viv snapped. "All that stolen gold in the Swiss vaults is the only thing that *allows* you to be neutral…it's what keeps Hitler and his SS goons from calling the tune in Bern or Geneva."

"True enough, "Adrienne agreed amiably. "Where I grew up, money is at the root of…everything. Even so, at least our young men don't become cannon fodder in these global wars as regularly as yours do."

Cannon fodder. Was that all Viv and her fellow Americans were, regardless of their commitments to a democratic ideal—just like the poor Brits in the blitz?

Viv realized with a start that because she carried an American passport, she was now in just as much danger of being picked up as an enemy alien and put into one of those camps as her British-born mother was. So far, however, it appeared that Pamela's liaison with Wilhelm had held that off—for her, anyway.

With an unsettling sense of foreboding, it struck Viv that *she* had no protector. With the bombing of Pearl Harbor, there would be no one able to intervene on her behalf if the Nazis stormed the nurses' quarters and arrested her. The island of safety she'd thought she'd always inhabit did not exist for her in France anymore. Her ambulance driver's uniform with its Red Cross patch on her arm was her only hope to remain incognito and—God willing—unnoticed by the authorities.

———◇———

On the first warm spring night in the new year of 1942, Viv was included in a small gathering for supper at the Jackson home at Number 11 Avenue Foch. She was seated at a table in the back garden beside an earnest, dark-haired young man from Canada. With a start, she recognized she'd recently fetched the very same person from a POW internment camp in Compiègne. His medical chart had said he'd developed a disorder involving his pancreas, and the SS released him to receive care at the American Hospital. Viv had delivered Lawrence Cupperman to the basement ward, but here he was this May evening, looking remarkably fit, sitting at the outdoor dining table on Toquette's right. She leaned toward him, patting his arm and murmuring something that prompted a slight nod.

In the hour that followed, a late arrival slipped through the garden's rear entrance. Their hostess quietly rose from her chair, as did Lawrence Cupperman. Without fanfare or farewell, Toquette escorted the two men out the same gate that the latecomer had just walked through from a back alley—but only she returned to her guests at the table.

The next day, Viv was curious to know more about the young man she'd seen leave the party. She invented a reason to visit the hospital's basement ward and stood at the doorway, her mouth slightly ajar.

Someone else now occupied the bed she'd seen Lawrence Cupperman tucked into by the nurses less than a week earlier. Viv could only conclude that the Jacksons were not merely shielding downed airmen and perhaps Jewish escapees in the hospital, but also directly connecting them with *passeurs*, the guides who could lead them out of France to safety. For several long moments, Viv stared at the empty bed.

Neutral? Oh, no, Adrienne... Swiss-born Toquette Jackson is no more neutral in this struggle against the Nazis than her husband, Dr. J...or than I...

———◇———

Everyone at the hospital was shaken by disturbing reports of German air raids against Britain's many cathedral cities. Meanwhile, Dr. Jack passed along to his closest staff reports of fierce fighting in the Crimea, Poland, Russia, and in far-away Egypt where British General Bernard Montgomery had now taken command.

A few days after the dinner party in the Jacksons' back garden, Viv and Adrienne were sent to fetch a supply of crutches made by a woodworker nearby. When they returned to the hospital garage and unloaded their haul for the day, one of the mechanics hailed Viv and Adrienne en route to grab supper in the mess hall.

"Somebody came by earlier, Viv, and said you should report to Dr. Jackson's office as soon as you return."

Adrienne looked at her quizzically, but Viv merely shrugged.

"Thanks," she replied to the messenger, then turned to her

teammate. "You go on ahead to dinner. I'll catch up with you as soon as I can."

When she reached the fourth floor, Toquette Jackson, dressed as she was most days now in her nurse's garb, hailed her in the hallway.

"Viv, dear," she said, nodding in the direction of the double doors behind them, "Doctor Jack had to go into emergency surgery. An appendectomy," she explained. "He said...well..." she hesitated, gently nudging Viv's arm so they could step out of the hallway into a vacant supply closet. She closed the door. "He wanted to tell you himself, but we both thought you need to know right away, so he asked *me*, if I saw you, to—"

Toquette hesitated a second time.

"*What?*" Viv demanded with a laugh, her stomach actually growling with hunger after an afternoon behind the wheel of her lumbering ambulance.

"Your mother was picked up this morning at her flat and interned by the Nazis."

"She's been *arrested?*" Viv was stunned. So much for her mother's Nazi 'protector,' she thought, as disbelief, shock and alarm collided, to say nothing of the possible repercussions for her in the wake of this news.

"The SS swooped in at six o'clock this morning and took her away."

Viv leaned against one of the storeroom shelves, trying to catch her breath, her elbow brushing the pile of sterile linen behind her. Part of her was incredulous, given her mother's apparent cozy relationship with at least one officer of the Third Reich. On the other hand, perhaps the peers of Pamela's SS "friend" on Avenue Foch had been pressuring him? Why—Colonel Wilhelm Gerhardt's colleagues might wonder—was a prominent citizen of the United Kingdom like Pamela Bradford not yet apprehended as were so many other British-born "enemies of the Fatherland?"

Realizing, now, that everything had changed in her world, Viv fought off a wave of panic that began in the pit of her solar plexus. Her mother was in a prison! The two hadn't spoken in months, and Viv's mind was filled with the obvious questions mixed with a soupçon of guilt as to what she should do next.

"How did you even know my mother was taken away?" she asked.

Toquette lowered her voice to speak without fear of being overheard outside the supply room.

"A neighbor who...ah...keeps us informed of such things called at our home and spoke to our housekeeper. She sent our son on his bicycle from Avenue Foch to tell Doctor Jack so he could warn you right away *not* to go near your mother's flat."

"That was kind...but, to tell the truth, I haven't been there in quite a while," murmured Viv, pushing away the memory of their final argument.

"Well, I must admit, Viv dear, considering the situation, that's a big blessing."

Viv was sure, now, that not only were the Jacksons full-fledged members of the growing French Resistance efforts in Paris, but that Toquette must have a network of sympathetic people that kept her apprised of latest developments.

"Oh, God," Viv groaned, wondering what the scene must have been like when the German SS called at Pamela's residence. "I *warned* Mother about flaunting her fancy clothes and lavish lifestyle." Viv paused, stopping short of disclosing her mother's connection to the SS officer now living in the family's flat on Avenue Kléber. Wilhelm Gerhardt obviously hadn't prevented her arrest and perhaps even caused it! Reluctant to speculate about the role the colonel may have played, Viv said, "Do you suppose that someone in her neighborhood ratted on her, telling authorities she was British? Is it known where they've taken her?"

"My sources say Vittel," Toquette replied. "You've delivered Red Cross bundles there, haven't you? It's the spa town not too far from Vichy." Viv nodded. Toquette said, "That's where most of the female British enemy aliens have been locked up."

"Well, at least it's still a *spa*, which is better than what I saw at Compiègne. Maybe I could be assigned to take more Red Cross packages there and try to—"

"That's exactly what Dr. J and I advise you *not* to do!" Toquette exclaimed. She lowered her voice again. "The SS are picking up people right and left these days. Frankly, Viv, your height makes you stick out like a sore thumb as an American, and your rosy complexion broadcasts to the world your English heritage. You mustn't even *think* of doing anything foolhardy like that—or you'll end up behind barbed wire like she is!"

Viv fought against another stab of guilt at how relieved she felt being urged by the Jacksons *not* to play rescuing angel for a woman who would risk very little if she'd learned her daughter was the one arrested. It was strange, Viv thought, how the words of a therapist she'd sought in a moment of teenage desperation came back to her now.

That's what narcissists do, *Viv...they are incapable of thinking about anyone's welfare above their own. To expect otherwise just gives birth to future resentments...*

Recollecting the psychologist's warning, Viv felt Toquette's gaze seeking confirmation that she'd take to heart her advice not trying to rescue her mother.

"You're right, I know," Viv agreed with an audible sigh. "It'd be the height of stupidity to think I could do anything to free her, but still..." Viv searched Toquette's face and asked bleakly, "What should *I* do now, do you suppose?"

"You told me that you only travel with an American passport these days, yes?" Toquette asked. "You said your British one is at your home in New York?" Viv nodded. "Well, don't let anyone see it," Toquette urged. "The American one, I mean. The security men are sure to be watching your mother's flat. If they stopped you and found it on you, you could be in deep jeopardy. I'll see if I can locate for you some...ah...different identification for now." She placed her hand on Viv's arm. "Apparently, yesterday when your mother was arrested, she was quite..."

Her sentence dangled in the air between them.

"Outraged? Offended?" Viv supplied. "She behaved like a slighted queen?"

"Something like that."

"But how do you know all this?"

Toquette raised an eyebrow and appeared reluctant to answer such a direct question. Finally, she said, "Oh, you know how neighbors love to gossip. And there are others, close and trusted confidents, who are kind enough to keep us informed."

"So in front of those goons, Mother behaved like she was royalty?"

"More like an avenging angel, from what I've been told. She raised Cain in German, English, and French because the Gestapo officials were not going to transport her trunk."

"Oh, dear Lord!" Viv exclaimed. "Not *that* again. She tried to take a *trunk* with her?"

"Observers on rue des Canettes said the SS corralled two German soldiers innocently wandering down the street and ordered them to somehow wedge the trunk into a Citroën. Into the back seat went your mother and the two Gestapo agents. Her neighbors hung out of windows gaping at it all. Even passers-by stopped to watch, I was told."

Viv heaved another sigh. She found it hard to fathom that here she and Toquette were, standing in a supply closet at the hospital, and across the street was a Gestapo outpost where people less fortunate than Pamela Bradford were rumored to be tortured each and every day. At least her mother had been sent to one of the better camps, Viv thought—and then she wondered if that were actually true.

Toquette leaned forward and sought Viv's gaze.

"As much as Sumner greatly appreciates everything you've done as a member of the Ambulance Corps, he thinks, given the information we have about your mother's arrest, that it's time for *you* to head for the unoccupied zone and then to Switzerland."

Viv stared at Toquette, dumbfounded.

"Me? Leave Paris?"

Toquette looked at her sadly. "It would be best for you to leave France altogether." She paused and added, "Immediately."

"But I'm needed here at the hospital!" Viv exclaimed, fighting a sense of pure panic. Beyond the boundaries of the American Hospital was an Enemy Aliens No-Man's Land, *her* status now, she thought with a jolt. And even if she had some magic means of departing from France, what in the world would she *do* with herself? The sense of purpose and validation she'd experienced in her work had been new to her—and affirming. She couldn't leave *now*!

Toquette hastened to assure her, "Your excellent skills and judgment are very definitely needed as an ambulance driver, but I fear that you are now in rather grave danger. I learned that your mother loudly demanded of the SS that they contact you so you could come fetch her from Vittel when certain people, she claimed, would see that she would be released." Toquette leaned closer. "Viv, dear, they know who you are, and perhaps even your associations with us and the hospital. That, alone, will put you on their list of people to watch—or arrest."

"And it could also endanger everyone here," Viv murmured, her life suddenly turned upside down.

CHAPTER 14

Adrienne walked into the nurses' wing and stared at the sight of Viv packing a small duffle bag and a knapsack. Viv then pointed to her cot, bidding Adrienne to sit down so she could disclose some of the conversation she'd just had with Dr. Jackson's wife.

"So *now* what are you going to do?" Adrienne asked, distressed to hear of Pamela Bradford's arrest and Viv's stated plan to leave.

"Head for Switzerland. I'll be traveling light, so I'm giving you my cosmetic case for safekeeping, along with the keys to Mother's flat on rue des Canettes." Viv dug into her handbag. Toquette had kindly sent someone to fetch the keys from the concierge, and miraculously, the woman had handed them over, proving to Viv that Toquette had strings to pull all over Paris.

"You don't have to do this," Adrienne protested. "Give me access to her flat."

Viv shook her head, putting the keys in her friend's palm. "Look, Adrienne, Switzerland is unlikely to forego its neutrality, but still, you gave up your place when we moved to the nurses' wing, so you might need somewhere to stay if the Germans ever take over the hospital. Mother's new place is pretty modest, and she's paid three years' rent, so let's hope the Krauts don't commandeer it, too. *Do* check about that before you move in," she added with a grim smile. "So it looks like my only alternative is to head for Geneva. I'm leaving with a *passeur* at Gare de Lyon at eleven tonight."

Adrienne tucked the keys in her pocket. "I'll write down the names of some people in Geneva in case you stay there for the duration." Viv's friend glanced down at the Louis Vuitton cosmetic case. "And I promise to take good care of this beauty if I can use it once in a while," she added with a sly grin.

"Of course," Viv replied. "Let's just say I've given it to you on a *permanent* loan." Adrienne cast her friend a stricken expression. Viv returned a steady gaze. "Look, Adrienne, if we don't ever see each other again, the case is yours." Her eyes narrowed with amusement, "If I eventually return to Paris, you have to give it back *and* promise me that you'll let me into the rue des Canettes flat if I knock on the door, agreed?"

Adrienne, no longer smiling, nodded solemnly.

Viv reached into her bedside table's drawer and pulled out her American passport.

"I've wrapped this in oilcloth. Will you help me bury it in the hospital vegetable garden and memorize where we put it? Toquette said that once I leave here, I don't dare get caught with it if I'm picked up or interrogated."

"But, with no identification—"

"She somehow obtained phony papers for me that say I'm neutral Swiss!"

Adrienne shook her head. "I guess that was the best she could do, but your height makes you look so American—or even British, with those pink cheeks!"

"How many times have I heard that?" Viv intoned. "At least, I yodel really well."

Adrienne shot her a look and then grabbed a used envelope. She swiftly scribbled down several names and addresses in Geneva and one in Bern and handed it to Viv to tuck into her knapsack. As they'd talked, it had grown dark outdoors. The two young women stealthily made their way from the nurses' wing to the hospital vegetable garden.

Viv feared she was going to break down in tears as she clutched her passport in the name of *Constance Vivier-Clarke*, wrapped in its oilcloth protection, the interior pages marked with dozens of exotic stamps and visas from previous travels. She watched Adrienne take her turn digging to a depth of three feet below the carrot patch.

"Well," Adrienne said, attempting to jest, "given that your hair is sort of a burgundy color, and the carrots planted here are deep orange, this patch can be a reminder for us where we're burying the damn thing." She gestured in the direction of a row of carrots on her right and then looked up at Viv. "Do you want to do the honors, or shall I?"

Her voice tight, Viv knelt and said, "I'll do it." She leaned in and gently placed the treasured document at the bottom of the hole. "It almost feels as if I'm burying part of myself."

Adrienne began shoveling dirt back in the hole and then replacing a half-grown carrot into its spot in the row. She pulled off her gardening gloves. "At least this way, we'll remember where we've put it when the war is over."

When the war is over...

Whenever will *that* be? And who will win? Viv wondered, but she tried to cheer them both by joking, "Let's just hope they don't plant potatoes here next spring."

Adrienne didn't laugh, but replied with grim regret, "I wish I knew someone I could truly trust in Bern. It's called 'The City of Spies,' you know."

Viv had heard Bern had earned that nickname during the Great War. "I'll try to give that city a miss, then. I'll go straight to Geneva, once I get across the border."

"You might not be able to avoid Bern," Adrienne warned, "because an American Mission is there. That's the address I wrote down for you. Gaston, my friend at the Swiss Embassy here in Paris, once mentioned to me an American named Allen Dulles is assigned there. I'm thinking he might be someone who could confirm to local authorities who you are...and that you're a genuine American—which of course, anyone who's not blind and heard you speak French with your New York twang would guess."

"Gee, thanks." Then Viv brightened. "Maybe this Dulles character can produce some documents for me and get me to England," she said excitedly. "I could volunteer for war work as a French or German-speaker in London."

"But first you have to get out of France," Adrienne reminded her with a worried frown. She shook her head, referring to the details of the recent plan of escape that Viv had disclosed when she was packing. "Really, Viv, why don't you just find your *own* way to the

Swiss border? I know you admire the Jacksons a lot, but helping some *passeur* you've never met to escort *eight* escaping Jews is just asking for trouble."

By this time, the pair was heading for a side entrance to re-enter the nurses' wing.

"Two birds with one stone," Viv declared blithely, although her heart gave a lurch at how dangerous it was likely to be to make her way south with this large a group into southern France's supposed 'Free Zone'—a journey that was no mean feat in itself. Then they'd travel east to the heavily guarded border with Switzerland. "The plan is to get myself to your 'land of neutrality' while saving a few poor souls from those dirty camps you and I have visited more often than we like to remember."

"Just save *yourself*, Viv," Adrienne urged. She seemed about to say something else, but instead, merely hugged the woman with whom she'd shared so many treacherous miles as ambulance drivers. "Take good care," Adrienne cautioned, her voice catching.

"You be safe, too," Viv replied, unsteadily. She forced a smile and gestured toward her knapsack that stood beside the door of the nurses' wing. It was packed with a change of clothes, a few precious cosmetics, some food she'd liberated from the commissary, and her phony Swiss documents.

"Here's where we part. *Adieu, mon amie.*"

"*Au revoir, Mademoiselle* America," Adrienne murmured. "*À bientôt.*"

"See you soon—I hope," Viv repeated in English, throwing the knapsack over her shoulder. *Would* she and Adrienne ever see each other again, she wondered?

A sudden memory flashed through her mind of her abrupt parting with Marcel Delonge overlooking the beaches of Dunkirk. She smiled at the recollection that, like Adrienne, he had also called her "Miss America" and he preferred *à bientôt* to *au revoir*. She waved to Adrienne in a final gesture of farewell, seized her duffle bag, and turned to go. Viv knew she'd feel a lot safer if someone like that quick-witted, irascible man with the scar on his left cheek could be her traveling companion and protector on the perilous journey ahead.

But, for now, she'd have to depend on her own wits to make it to Switzerland.

PART II
CHAPTER 15

Spring-Summer 1942

For hours, Viv had sat opposite an elderly man and his stout, overdressed wife in a first-class compartment on the overnight train from Paris. They'd rolled through the night with a stop in Lyon, finally pulling into the station nearest the Swiss border.

Their *passeur*, a paid guide, turned out to be a former middle-aged schoolteacher named Jasmine. She was to shepherd a group of eight Jews scattered throughout the five cars, along with Viv and a Swiss-American girl with a thick, blond braid down her back named Renée Reynolds. Jasmine had advised them to move onto the platform and blend into the milling crowd until they could spot their leader outside the station. She'd promised to take them through the dark, deserted streets of the alpine town of Annemasse located a few kilometers from the border with Switzerland.

Viv, acutely conscious of her inordinate height and dark crimson hair, cautiously stepped off the train fingering her phony Swiss identity card that had been mysteriously procured by Toquette. Jasmine had slipped it to her at the Gare de Lyon station in Paris when the two had pretended to be delighted at their supposed unexpected encounter.

"When you have a chance, rough it up with your shoe," Jasmine had whispered. "It looks too new."

Glancing at it now, Viv felt it looked as phony as *she* appeared as a twenty-eight-year-old American attempting to pass as Swiss.

She hung back from the others, watching the Jewish Dutch

couple that had been in her compartment struggling with numerous parcels and two bulky, battered suitcases they never should have brought with them.

Suddenly, she heard *"Contrôle!"* shouted down the line.

"They've caught someone," gasped the elderly man. His wife grabbed his arm in panic, resulting in his dropping one of their suitcases.

Viv heard a shriek, followed by hysterical crying. Two Vichy French soldiers pushed their way through the disembarking throng of travelers, thrusting people aside to make way for an Italian officer and a very blond plain-clothes man who definitely looked German. They were dragging a dark-haired woman who appeared to be in her fifties.

Renée, the other young woman in their group who held both American and Swiss passports, appeared by Viv's side.

"Merde! Now what the hell do we do?" she whispered. "I thought I'd be safer in Switzerland, now that the Nazis occupy so much of France."

"Why don't you just cross normally with your Swiss passport?" Viv murmured.

"I still have my American passport on me," Renée explained under her breath, "and I don't want to give it up. If the guards on the French side stop and search me, they might arrest me as an American enemy alien if I tried to cross through the normal route."

"It's Russian roulette, no matter how a person tries to cross the border," Viv whispered, thinking of her own ID document buried beneath the carrots at the American Hospital. Now she wished she'd done the same as Renée, taken the risk, and kept her American passport with her.

"We want to get into Switzerland tonight," Renée insisted, *sotte voce*, "so you and I had better stick together."

Viv surveyed the rail yard. On her left was the station house. On her right was the train with a few shadowy figures moving through it. She surmised that they were soldiers checking for stragglers that might be trying to hide from authorities. The town of Annemasse, after all, was the 'gateway' to an escape to Switzerland from eastern France. It was still supposed to be demilitarized. Rumors were rife, however, that the Germans had already started moving in to take over such sensitive border areas as this French township where their journey by rail had ended.

"Oh, God," moaned Renée, "there *is* a checkpoint set up here."

Viv glanced at the line of passengers that was shuffling toward the officers examining identity documents.

"If they see your American passport, we're toast. Let's edge back," Viv murmured to Renée, creeping closer to the protection of the station house where she saw a low white fence a few yards beyond with a flowerbed planted in front of it.

At a signal from Viv, both women bounded over the fence but weren't quick enough to escape the notice of two soldiers who had been checking for stragglers on the train. From the platform of the last car, they shouted at the women and gave chase.

Viv, with Renée a few feet behind her, bolted into a courtyard where she saw a large open doorway. A half-minute ahead of their pursuers, Viv raced inside what she could only guess was an old livery stable. She and Renée barely had enough time to hide behind the large door before the soldiers rushed into the darkness. With their backs to a wooden wall, Viv pulled the door tight against the front of their two bodies. She struggled to swallow her rising panic when she recognized in the dim light filtering from the courtyard the dreaded gray-green of German military soldiers.

So the damn Boche are *infiltrating the eastern frontier of the Free Zone...*

Renée grabbed Viv's hand, their stiffened arms keeping them still as statues. Meanwhile, the uniformed twosome began to curse each other for losing sight of their prey.

"*Kommen sie,*" barked one of them. "We've missed them. Let's go, and keep your mouth shut about all this. It's better if we get back before we're figured for fools."

Viv, who periodically suffered from allergies, felt the tickle of a sneeze coming on. She squeezed her eyes shut and held her breath to tamp it down just as the pair left without ever looking behind the wooden door. A second after their footsteps faded in the courtyard, she plunged her nose into the crook of her arm, stifling her "Ah-choo!"

"Thank God they left," Renée said hoarsely, "or we would have been done for."

"Well, we'd better get our bearings and figure out which way to the border," Viv replied. "It looks as if there might be Germans all over this town."

"God only knows what happened to all those Jews that Jasmine was shepherding," Renée said, "although they can't have gone far."

The two women peered into the now empty courtyard, ventured outside, and walked down a narrow alley that branched off to their right.

"Another wooden door," murmured Viv, pointing ahead.

"It must be the back entrance to that large house there," replied Renée, gesturing to a broad roof above their heads.

Next to the door that they confirmed was locked, Viv spotted an open window that they could scale and crawl through. One at a time, they landed in a stone-flagged storeroom with shelves and the floor filled with all manner of household castoffs. Viv squinted at a young man leaning against the wall beside yet another thick wooden door; he had been smoking and looked suddenly panic-stricken at the sight of them.

"Wasn't he in our group on the train?" Viv murmured. "Golly, what luck! Hello, there," she called out softly. "You made it through the checkpoint, I see." She pointed to Renée and said to him, "Do you recognize us? On the train with you. Did Jasmine and the others make it through all right?"

The young man heaved a sigh of relief and stamped out his cigarette.

"They're all inside," he said. "We thought you were gone for good."

By this time, Viv could hear voices on the other side of the door speaking in low murmurs. The young man knocked softly to grain readmittance.

After a loud metallic click the door opened. Jasmine, their *passeur*, stood at the threshold, the group of escaping Jews clustered behind her.

"Well, *there* you two are! Your scampering away caused the perfect diversion. No one was left at the *contrôle* when they gave chase after you. The rest of us walked straight into the street, around the corner, and into this safe house. Come in, come in!"

Viv and Renée soon found themselves in a bedroom jam-packed

with their fellow travelers. "Find a spot to lie down," advised Jasmine, "and take this chance to sleep. We can't set out until later when the streets will be crowded for market day."

Viv cast a glance at the motley assortment of escapees and wondered at their chances they could all make it into Switzerland.

But at least they were safe. For now.

———◇———

Viv barely remembered falling asleep, but a few hours later, Renée tapped her on the shoulder urging her to wake up and gather her belongings.

"Come along," the *passeur* ordered briskly.

Jasmine took Viv and Renée into the courtyard. There, she presented them each with a well-ridden bicycle loaded down with provisions stuffed into the saddlebags. An additional wicker basket was attached to the handlebars.

"Oh, dear Lord," murmured Renée.

The cargo in each basket included a squawking chicken in a cage.

"Follow me," Jasmine ordered, "and keep up. The others will be taken in a covered cart. We three need to appear as if we do this route every day."

Viv's alarm grew at the sight of uniformed soldiers patrolling streets crowded with villagers on this market day. Head down, she and her companions peddled steadily through the town and eventually picked up the main thoroughfare that led to the entrance to a farmhouse a few miles beyond. They turned onto a dirt road in the direction of a small barn. There, they delivered the provisions and thrust the hens into a small chicken coop while the farmer's wife hoed her vegetable garden without giving them a glance.

Once their bicycles were unloaded and stored in the barn, Jasmine led Viv and Renée into a small grove of trees behind the farmyard and commanded, "Stay here out of sight until nightfall. And don't make *any* noise. Even though they're not supposed to be, Germans are all over this region now. Once it's dark, take the path through these trees until you come to a railroad track. Follow it to the first farm shed you see. It's a few meters from the border, and two men will come to guide you over the line."

"*What?*" Viv protested. "I thought *you* were leading us into Switzerland.

"I was engaged to get you *to* the border...not across it." Jasmine then turned on her heel and vanished into the gloom.

CHAPTER 16

It was past midnight when they closed in on a decrepit farm building Viv could see silhouetted against the night sky. As they approached, a wooden door slowly opened.

"Ah...hello," greeted the elderly Dutch gentleman Viv had met in the train compartment as they'd left Paris. "You, again. We thought you'd gone on without us."

If only, Viv thought, her gaze drifting to each of the eight refugees huddled around the hay cart that must have been the vehicle that brought them to this spot. To Viv, the notion of getting past the heavily guarded border with ten people seemed not only impossible, but ridiculous—yet, here they all were! The young man they'd seen smoking earlier among the group of fleeing Jews held out a quarter of a loaf of bread.

"We still have some provisions. Are you hungry?"

Viv nodded as he broke off a piece from the baguette and handed her a jug of water. Chewing on the tough crust of bread, Viv said to Renée, "You speak French with more of an American accent than I do."

Renée offered a rueful laugh. "That's because I barely learned enough French to gain entrance into the Sorbonne to study art history."

"But you say you're Swiss."

"Swiss-American with an emphasis on the Yank, so it was time for me to flee France. As I told you, I was afraid they'd find my U.S. passport and confiscate it, so I decided to sneak across the border. I didn't think it would be this hard, though."

Viv licked her fingers of the last crumbs, wishing that she, too, could make it through the Swiss checkpoint with her identity ensured as American.

Viv asked, "Did you ever meet a Swiss woman I knew in Paris? Adrienne Vaud?"

Renée gazed at her in amazement. "We both liked the same young man at the Swiss embassy in Paris," she said with a laugh, "but Adrienne was too busy driving ambulances around France, so she got him as a friend and I, a boyfriend."

"Gaston Dupuis, right? And you left him behind?" Viv teased.

"Gaston was neutral about everything," Renée said with a shrug. "I found him pretty dull after a while. And then the Nazis invaded Paris. Once America joined the war, I started trying to figure out how to leave France without getting arrested."

"Same story here," Viv said with a nod. She settled her head against her knapsack. "Let's try to get some sleep."

Viv was just dozing off when she heard the shed door open, and three men stomped in. One with a dark beard and a pistol tucked into his belt pointed at Viv and Renée.

"You two. Come with me."

"But what about the others?" Viv demanded.

"You're young. Fit. You're the only ones we're willing to risk it for."

"But Jasmine promised!" said the young man who'd given Viv bread.

"Jasmine didn't give us enough money," he replied, "or she took more than her share for herself."

"You've already been paid! You're just trying to extort these people because they're Jews. Aren't you?" Viv accused, her eyes narrowing in anger.

It would be far less risky for the *passeurs* if only Renée and she were to head out with these men, but suddenly Viv felt to do that would be totally callous and wrong.

She glanced at the others and then proposed to the scowling leader, "We'll discuss a...a bonus for you and your men once you've taken *all* of us to the border—*or* we'll take our chances and head there ourselves and you won't get a centime!"

"You don't even know where you are, much less where to cross the border," the leader scoffed.

"I have a Guide Michelin map, went to school in Switzerland, and I can sure as hell get us there," Viv retorted, offering the biggest bluff of her life.

There was dead silence among the thirteen people gathered within a few kilometers of the Swiss border.

"All right," he growled. "Gather your belongings," he said, eyeing the elderly couple whose arms were already loaded down with their possessions. "But I'm warning you, we won't wait for any stragglers."

Within minutes, their guides led them out a back door, and soon the group found themselves walking through a small, deserted village. At the corner of a church, the head *passeur* made a sharp left turn. He seemed to acknowledge Viv was now the leader of those trying to escape. Pointing in the direction of weed-strewn railroad tracks that stood beside the dirt road they'd been on, he ordered, "Follow those tracks to a crossing-keeper's house. Go in the door and wait for us there."

The small house was, as described, at the end of the tracks, and a man stood waiting in the doorway.

"We were told to expect you," he declared and beckoned them to file inside the door. "We're crossing tonight, too."

The living room was full of people. Shocked by the sight, Viv asked, "How many of you *are* there?"

"Seven...including a child and a baby."

By this time Renée had caught up, heard the man, and let out a low groan.

"This is insane," she murmured. "We'll never make it in this crowd."

Viv could only nod a greeting to five more adults, a little girl holding a small doll, and a baby nestled in its mother's arms.

Around three a.m., two of the three *passeurs* appeared suddenly in the doorway, harshly demanding everyone prepare to leave. "You're to walk out the door here and turn to your right," announced their bearded guide. "A hundred yards from here is a ditch. At the top is the border. You'll have ten minutes before the next patrol comes by. After you get across, be sure to *separate* when you run through the adjacent field," he emphasized. "That field ends at a road on the other side. The open area is a kind of no-man's-land that

French police, German soldiers, and Swiss guards patrol at different times, so cross quickly. And by the way, the Swiss are getting fed up with you refugees, so don't expect a warm welcome if they catch you. Now give me the money," he demanded.

Viv had collected a small sum from each in her original group of ten and handed it to the leader. Scowling, he snatched the wad of bills from her and held his free hand out to the members of the other group where, one by one, they gave him his fee. A second later, he and his henchmen marched out the door and disappeared into the gloom.

"So much for guiding us across the border," Viv murmured. She then addressed the eight in her group, plus Renée. "C'mon. Let's go."

She wanted her party to get a head start so they wouldn't all attempt to cross the border in a big bunch. The older couple began to argue about which one of them was to carry particular parcels.

Viv whirled around, scolding them in a harsh whisper, "And *no* talking, any of you!"

CHAPTER 17

Despite the early summer season, the night's plunging alpine temperature stung Viv's cheeks and seemed to work their way down her spine despite her heavy woolen coat. Within yards of leaving the crossing-station, Viv almost tumbled down an incline that proved to be the ditch that the *passeur* had described. Once she'd regained her balance, she led the way to the bottom of the hillock and up the other side. A menacing twelve-foot-high barrier of barbed wire stretched in both directions as far as the eye could see.

Bingo! The border. Just like that...

By this time, the other group of seven had reached the edge of the ditch farthest from the fence and was chattering far too loudly for safety.

"Be quiet over there, for God's sake!" Viv called to them in a hoarse whisper. To her group she said, "Our group goes first and be sure you stay *separate* from each other—even family groups—so we don't create undue attention crossing the open field." She pointed above their heads. "The moon's very bright and it's a clear night, remember." Then she added, "So don't talk! Voices carry in conditions like this."

Viv and Renée laid their coats across the two center strings of barbed wire. Viv held up the higher one with two hands clutching the fabric of her coat while Renée pushed down the lower wire with the arch of her booted right foot.

"All right," Viv whispered harshly to the first in line. "Go, go... GO!"

The first of the original escapees climbed through the opening their ad hoc leaders had provided. Within minutes, the second group passed through, with Viv offering a smile of encouragement to the little girl clutching her doll as she easily slipped through the space between the two lengths of barbed wire.

Next in line was the girl's mother. "Let me hold your baby while you go through," Viv murmured. "Renée, can you spread both wires open for her to get past?"

Viv clasped the infant in her arms while its mother struggled to make her way through the treacherously sharp spikes that Renée managed to keep apart.

"Here you go," Viv said, passing baby between the wires.

With only a nod of thanks, the woman, her newborn, and her daughter, who looked to be about six, set off across the field. To Viv's alarm and frustration, the rest of the second group had ignored her advice and waited for one another, gathering in a noisy bunch until all the refugees were through the razor-sharp barrier.

Viv gave Renée a push. "Now *you*!'

Renée had bolted toward the others when Viv looked up and pleaded, "Wait! You've got to hold it for *me*!"

"Sorry," Renée whispered, turning around. "I'm so scared, I can't think."

Once Viv made it through, the pair gingerly lifted their clothing off the barrier, only to see that the entire group was thundering away from the fence like a small herd of cattle. Clearly visible in the moonlight, the large knot of refugees sprinted across the wide, open field, most of them burdened by their heavy belongings, their voices ringing out in the cold air.

"Let's head in that other direction," Viv commanded *sotto voce*, pointing to the far left, away from the group, "and be sure to stay a few meters apart from me."

They'd only traversed a short distance when, far to their right, two soldiers, bayonets fixed, began yelling in German, as they sprinted after the scurrying clump of fugitives.

"Get down!" Viv whispered harshly and dove for the grass covering the field.

Shrieks and cries rent the air. Viv felt physically sick, certain that they'd all be caught and would soon find themselves in a Swiss jail—or worse, pushed back over the border into the arms of the Gestapo. She lay, face down, her hands covering her ears to block out the cries of the children, the screams of the women, and the harsh, guttural shouts of the soldiers ordering everyone to put their hands in the air.

By this time, the moon had risen high in the sky, enormous and revealing. Viv had no idea how long she and Renée lay shivering in the field, but they remained like dead bodies on the ground for many minutes after the wails of the captured refugees had been silenced, along with the sound of motorcars driving off into the night.

Renée was the first to pull herself to her feet. Viv followed suit, stiff and cold to the marrow of her bones. As they set off once again across the field, Viv spotted something on the ground a few feet ahead. When she drew nearer, she bent down and seized the small object, no larger her hand.

"What is it?" Renée whispered, remaining ten feet to her right as they headed across the landscape.

"A little doll. It must have been dropped by…"

Viv couldn't finish her sentence.

The Jewish refugees had come so close to escaping…

What would happen to the little ones, she wondered? To their poor parents? To the nice young man who had shared his bread with them, or the elderly couple with luggage that had slowed them down and put the others at risk?

On such small things their fates had turned, Viv thought, tears clouding her eyes. Her throat tight, she set off again with Renée following close behind. Beyond the small stand of trees, a road appeared. Emerging on to it, Viv heard Renée let out a gasp.

"Look," she said, pointing. "What's that glow in the sky?"

"Geneva, I should hope," Viv answered.

"It doesn't look that far away."

"The distance can be deceiving at night," Viv warned. She inhaled a deep breath and squared her aching shoulders. "Let's go."

———◇———

Viv had been right. The lights in the distance had definitely been deceiving. It seemed hours before they finally spotted a road sign on a high wooden post.

"We're *not* in France anymore, and we're beyond no-man's-land!" she exclaimed. "These high signposts mean we're in Switzerland. The winter snows, remember?"

"I haven't been in this country since I was five when my mother married my American father," Renée replied. "But are you sure we're truly across the border? Those soldiers back there spoke German."

Viv felt laughter bubble up in her throat. "But didn't you hear their *accents*?"

"I was so petrified, I just heard their yelling."

Viv nodded with understanding. "But, in normal speech, their accents would be different because it just dawned on me: they were speaking *Switzer Deutsche!*"

"Swiss German!" Renée nodded, a grin suddenly lighting up her face. "Oh, my God, Viv! Is it possible we've actually *made* it?"

Viv's gaze swept the field they'd just crossed. "Yes. I do. I think we've made it! And with any luck, the rest of our group was arrested by *Swiss* guards, not German—although I suppose that the Swiss could send them back to France if they wanted to. Us, too, if we'd been caught."

Sadly though, Viv thought, there'd probably be no way ever to know of the fate of their fellow travelers. Renée suddenly threw her arms around Viv.

"Can you believe it? We *made* it!" she shrieked.

With Renée still clutching her shoulders, Viv looked beyond the nearby wooden signpost and felt a stab of panic at the sight of a bicycle coming directly toward them. In the next moment, a uniformed member of the military jumped off the seat.

"*Halte! Police de frontière!*" he cried.

At least the soldier on his bicycle was speaking *French*! Viv could feel a huge smile spreading across her face. His words and language confirmed they had stumbled into the French-speaking section of Switzerland. From the look on the border guard's face as he scrutinized her fake documents, Viv knew she was destined to be questioned at the headquarters for the border patrol.

But at least they'd be Swiss interrogators, not Nazis.

CHAPTER 18

Viv could hardly believe how quickly her life and Renée's had changed now that they were in a neutral country. After they were both thoroughly questioned, Swiss border officials contacted the American consulate where an attaché negotiated their release with amazing dispatch. Best of all, a young man named Erik Thoman from the Swiss Foreign Office arrived to confirm Renée's dual citizenship to the Swiss border officials.

As they prepared to leave the detention facility, a tall, unusually handsome young Deputy Swiss Border chief who'd originally interrogated them appeared at the door. With a smile that seemed to Viv almost congratulatory, he handed back the knapsack that was confiscated when she had been taken to the cross-examining room.

"*Bon voyage, mademoiselle,*" he said, adding in perfect English, "wherever it is you're off to."

Viv had smiled back, but Renée's Swiss escort was waiting to transport them to the inexpensive hotel that he'd booked.

Within a few days and thanks to Erik's recommendation, Renée had secured a level-entry clerical job with a branch of the Swiss government's foreign office in Geneva. In another great stroke of luck, the American attaché assigned to Viv had booked an appointment with the very man Adrienne had mentioned before Viv had left Paris.

"If Allen Dulles believes your story, you'll have a new American passport issued you," her rescuer assured her.

Dulles was "associated" with U.S. officials in Bern but worked out of what she'd been told was his "private headquarters."

Did it matter she'd heard he was a spook—a paid spy working for the American government? But then she thought, who *better* to pull the levers of power in the bureaucracy? Just like Erik Thoman had done for Renée, could someone like Allen Dulles be able to secure speedy documentation of her American *and* British dual citizenship so she could get to England to volunteer for the war effort?

Viv borrowed the fare for the train trip to Bern from the happily employed Renée. Upon arrival, she followed directions to an address in a narrow, cobblestoned street located in an upscale part of the city built on a horseshoe-shaped ridge and surrounded by the Aare River a hundred or so feet below.

Standing on the opposite side of the street from her destination, Viv had to laugh as she swiveled back to look toward the entrance of the villa at Number 23. Allen Dulles lived on a street named *Herrengasse*—translated: "Gentlemen's Lane."

"Well, I hope he *is* one," she mused, gazing at the elegant front facade squeezed in between its imposing neighbors—all with views of the distant, yet magnificent peaks of the Jungfrau range of the Bernese Alps, their summits still clad with snow.

How does a person behave with a spy? she wondered, her stomach tightening. Especially since she planned to assert she was who she *said* she was—but had absolutely nothing in her possession to prove it. Dulles could very well think that *she* was on an espionage mission, having turned up in Switzerland with forged documents.

Should she reveal her connection with the American Hospital and their clandestine activities there? To Dulles, Viv was merely a refugee from Nazi-occupied France. Would a spymaster like him give one hoot about her aspirations to do something—anything—to help the Allied war effort?

Crossing the street, she walked up a few steps, inhaled a deep breath, and lifted the brass knocker. Immediately, a young woman answered and promptly showed her inside, asking her to take a seat in a small anteroom. After a few minutes' wait, the young staffer returned and announced, "Mr. Dulles will see you now. Come with me, please."

Allen Dulles's domain was in reality a spacious apartment situated on the ground floor. Viv was ushered into what appeared to be his private study. Red velvet drapes framed a view overlooking an attractive back garden. To her right was a massive fireplace with a leather sofa facing it. Viv noticed a small butler's table under the window that was stocked with a forest of bottles containing every imaginable alcoholic beverage. The tall man waiting to greet her had the physique of a lifelong tennis player, probably in his forties, Viv guessed. This spring day, he wore a light gray tweed jacket and sported a pipe in his hand that she speculated he kept with him at all times as a sort of gentleman's prop. Dulles stood beside an impressive mahogany desk, peering at her critically from behind rimless glasses, his slick, thinning light brown hair parted slightly off-center on his left side.

"Ah... Miss Vivier-Clarke, is it? You certainly don't *look* Swiss—or French for that matter. With the phony documents found on you, you must be clever indeed, to have made it through the border check."

"Well, we made it under the barbwire," she acknowledged, "but not much farther into Switzerland after that."

"So I understand," Dulles said with what Viv judged was a slight sign of amusement at the corners of his mouth.

She remembered how Renée's new friend, Erik Thoman, at the Swiss foreign office in Geneva had offered Viv a word of warning.

"Dulles may present himself as a diplomat and assistant to Leland Harrison, head of the U.S. Mission in Switzerland, but make no mistake, he *is* a spy. He has his own operation in Bern, and his job is to gather intelligence about everything, even concerning people who are working and on the same side, including—you should know—the Brits."

Absorbing the sight of her host garbed in his impeccable tweed jacket, Viv recalled that Adrienne Vaud's friend, Gaston Dupuis, in Paris, had also volunteered that Dulles was a cagey fellow.

"Nobody is certain what the man's actual mission *is* in Switzerland."

Remembering Gaston's words, Viv had asked Renée and Erik on the day they'd seen her to the train to Bern, "So this Dulles guy is not to be trusted?"

Erik had offered only the barest shrug, saying, "If anyone can, Allen Dulles is probably the only American in Switzerland able to get you where you want to go."

Her host took a step beyond his desk, and as if reading her mind said, "I'm forgetting to formally introduce myself. I'm Allen Dulles, in charge of everyone claiming to be an American."

Annoyed by this show of blatant intimidation, Viv extended her hand.

"Well, I *am* an American. In fact, I have dual citizenship," she declared. "A holder of 'Allied passports,' you might say. I'm American, thanks to my father, who died flying in the Great War, and I'm British through my mother, who is now interned by the Nazis at a camp outside Paris."

Dulles glanced over at a folder on his desk.

"In Vittel, I understand."

Viv could only stare. Only someone with access to a high level of intelligence information would know precisely *where* her mother was incarcerated in France.

Dulles gestured and said, "Please take a seat on the sofa in front of the fire. I'll just sit here, if you don't mind," he said smoothly, sinking into a nearby leather club chair. "I have your phony Swiss identity card in my file, here. Now, tell me why I should believe you're a documented American and not just a Brit or someone from some other country masquerading as a U.S. citizen?"

Just a Brit? So much for the alliance between our two countries...

"I do, indeed, have dual citizenship," she retorted, knowing she must immediately tame the tartness of her tone if she wanted to succeed with this man. "However, at the moment, my U.S. passport is buried in the ground in a secret place in Paris and my British passport is locked in my family's safe at—"

"At a steel ball-bearing plant in North Carolina?" Dulles interrupted.

"No. At our family's apartment in New York," she corrected him, pleased to score a point.

"But your stepfather has done quite a bit of business with the Germans, yes?"

Oh, Lord! Dulles thinks he can put me off by insinuating that I'm a German collaborator or a double agent?

Well, she'd bet a dollar the file probably also noted that she'd studied German in Berlin, so he figured he could play this little cat-and-mouse game to rattle her by hinting she was up to no good with the enemy.

"Yes, Karl Bradford has done business with Hitler's thugs," she confessed calmly, adding, "and I think it stinks. In fact, until recently, I've been in Paris driving a Red Cross ambulance bringing back wounded French and British soldiers from the front." She met his gaze. "Look, Mr. Dulles. I was told to see you about finding a way to get to England to see if I make some contribution to the fight against the rotten Nazis. If you don't believe me—"

She pushed against the arms of the sofa, as if to rise.

"Sit down!" he ordered brusquely, and then more conciliatorily, "please. Miss... Bradford? Clarke? Vivier-Clarke? Which do you prefer, by the way?"

Viv inhaled a deep breath and summoned a forced smile.

"Vivier-Clarke is my hyphenated legal last name. Bradford is the name of my mother's second husband. Officially, I'm Constance Vivier-Clarke, but everyone calls me 'Viv.'" She graced him with another obligatory grin.

"Ah...'Viv' it is, then." He leaned back to reach a button under the corner rim of his desk and pushed it. "But I suppose being part British, you'd probably like some tea?"

Without waiting for an answer, he looked behind her as a door opened.

"Roger? Would you have Mrs. Van Meter fetch us a pot of tea and a cup-and-saucer, for our guest, please? I'll help myself to a whisky."

Viv turned her head and emitted an audible gasp at the sight of the figure standing in the threshold. Her hands flew to frame both sides of her face.

"Oh, my God!" she exclaimed. "Roger Gianakos! The last time I saw *you* was on a dock in Marseilles!"

CHAPTER 19

Viv barely suppressed a wave of laughter that threatened to wash over her as she took in the wispy presence of her former 'minder' from the American embassy in Athens. How could she forget the very man who'd been assigned to make sure she boarded the ship in Marseilles bound for America the week war had broken out? Roger's mouth dropped open at the sight of her as his face began to flush the exact hue of the room's scarlet velvet drapes.

To fill the uncomfortable silence she exclaimed again, "Roger *Gianakos*!" giving the pronunciation of his Greek surname a flourish. "How amazing to see you!"

She couldn't believe that the person she'd outwitted in order to hop a train to Paris in '39 was working for Allen Dulles, of all people, as part of the American Mission in Bern.

Gianakos' suit hung loosely on his skinny frame, his face burdened with black-rimmed glasses too large for the shape of his narrow, balding head. He took a step farther into the room and literally gaped at Viv.

"*You!*"

The accusation exploded from his thin lips. He pointed a trembling forefinger at her. "You gave me your word of honor!" He was nearly shouting now. "You almost ended my career in the State Department, damn you!"

"Goodness, Roger," Dulles admonished mildly, shifting his gaze from his underling to his most recent petitioner. "I take it you two know each other."

Viv tried to sound matter-of-fact. "There was an occasion when we were on the same ship traveling from Greece to the South of France."

She felt a sudden stab of worry. After all this time, Roger was obviously still furious at her. She wondered what would happen if Dulles learned the entire story of how she'd deceived the twit in order to remain in France.

Gianakos again pointed directly at Viv. "This woman's father—"

"*Step*father," Viv interjected, trying to sound helpful and also to remind Dulles that Karl was no blood relation.

Gianakos wagged an angry finger in her direction as he addressed his boss.

"The North Carolina industrialist, Karl Bradford, cabled this young woman a *huge* amount of money to our Athens embassy, along with a ticket to get her safely on a ship back to America the very day that Britain declared war on Germany. *I* had the unfortunate task of making sure she left for the United States." He turned to face Viv, his expression suffused with both mortification and fury. "You *lied* to me! You gave me the slip and I missed the ship's sailing. I caught hell for it from the Ambassador!"

Viv tried to appear penitent. "I am *so* sorry Roger. It's just that I wanted to—"

"That you would *stoop* to saying you needed to buy a supply of…of…"

She glanced over at Roger's superior, knowing it would not be a good idea to mention the ruse of needing to buy sanitary napkins in front of a man like Allen Dulles.

Maybe a play for sympathy was best?

"Really, Roger, I couldn't be sorrier for what I did to get myself back to Paris, but my poor mother—"

"Oh, God," Gianakos groaned, slamming the palm of his hand against his forehead, dislodging his glasses so they slid down his nose.

Dulles narrowed his gaze in her direction and sternly admonished both parties, "Now calm yourselves, both of you. Roger, please just fetch the tea, will you?"

Gianakos stood frozen on the Persian carpet. Viv could tell that he was aghast that she should ever appear in his life again, or even worse, that he should lose all control in front of a superior like Allen Dulles.

Attaché Gianakos finally summoned the will to spin on his heels and scurry off to fulfill Dulles's request to procure a cup of tea for the despised visitor. Viv's host walked over to his drinks table and poured himself a Scotch while Viv endeavored to regain her composure after this most unexpected encounter.

"Well, Mr. Dulles" she said as he turned to face her, his crystal tumbler filled to the brim, "you now know one *more* thing about me, and that is that your attaché Roger can certainly vouch for the fact I'm truly an American citizen."

Dulles regarded her thoughtfully. "And, I'd say, a young lady who apparently—and rather cleverly—gave him the slip."

———◇———

A few days following Viv's extraordinary encounter with Allen Dulles, to say nothing of seeing Roger Gianakos again, Viv was summoned back to Number 23 *Herrengasse* for another audience with the man who held her fate in his hands.

Her fingernails were bitten to the quick with nervousness as to what would happen next. Now that the shock had subsided of encountering Gianakos again and the reality of her precarious stateless situation reasserted itself, she realized the angry young staffer did, after all, work for the man who would determine her future.

Erik Thoman, Renée's Swiss friend at the foreign office in Geneva, had mentioned that Dulles had put it out he was working as some sort of special "emissary" for President Franklin Roosevelt. Perhaps the spymaster wouldn't see Viv's duplicitous treatment of his underling, Roger, as clever as it had at first seemed to him.

For the second time, she was ushered into Dulles's dark-paneled study and once again took a seat on the sofa facing the fireplace. Without preamble, Dulles asked her a question she had least expected.

"Miss Vivier-Clarke," he said, staring at her steadily as if observing her every twitch and swallow, "would you be willing to return to France as an undercover operative?"

Dumbfounded by his proposal, she never expected Dulles to

come back to her with anything other than his permission to have a replacement American passport issued to her. To her shock and utter amazement, the elusive intelligence officer was asking *her* to sneak back into the country she'd just fled and to serve as some sort of secret agent. On one hand, she was certain she could be useful back in France—as long as she stayed clear of Paris. And yes, she knew the country, its language and its present conditions under the heel of the Nazi invaders. But what *exactly* did this strange man have in mind?

Viv met Dulles's gaze. "Return to France?" she repeated, her mind whirling. She thought of the poor Jews who'd been caught at the border and allowed another moment of silence. "Yes," she agreed after another moment's pause. "I'd be willing to go back to France and help the Allies if I could."

"Very well," Dulles replied, appearing pleased with her response. "I want you to return to Geneva, first. I'll provide you with funds to refurbish your wardrobe."

He paused and surveyed her with a critical eye.

"It may not be particularly easy to disguise yourself, what with your striking looks and your height." He rubbed his chin with the thumb of his hand holding his pipe. "But I'm hoping your language and first-aid skills and your proven knowledge of how to make your way behind enemy lines outweigh any risk." He nodded, as if he'd successfully convinced himself his decision was sound to send her back into harm's way. He bent down and scribbled something on a piece of paper at his desk and handed it to her. "So, change the color of your hair, if you can find a way to do that—or tone it down somehow. Our people in Geneva at the address I've given you will advise you where to go next."

Stunned by this swift turn of events, Viv blurted, "But what do you want me to *do* in France, exactly?"

Dulles cracked an easy smile. "Oh. That. Yes. Well… I'll see if I can employ you as a courier or a guide in our French underground organization."

A secret operative! In a French Resistance circuit, like Toquette!

Then a thought struck her, sending a spike of terror into her chest. "But I shouldn't be sent back to Paris, Mr. Dulles. The SS was about to—"

"Yes, yes, I know all about that," Dulles intervened as if the information bored him. "They were going to arrest you for sure. But don't worry. You won't be sent there."

"So, where *will* I be sent?"

Dulles gave her a sharp look.

"First lesson...may I call you 'Viv?' Stop asking questions. You will find that people in your line of activity are always, and *only*, on a 'need-to-know' basis. Wait until you are *told*."

He rose from behind his desk and rang the hidden buzzer. Roger Gianakos appeared so quickly, Viv wondered if he'd been listening at the keyhole. Without offering a word, the young man showed her the way out. She felt his hostile eyes on her back while she made her way down the ancient cobbled *Herrengasse* and disappeared around the corner.

CHAPTER 20

Back in Geneva, Renée helped Viv find a modest hotel to stay in. Thanks to the financial stipend and an address Dulles had provided, a seamstress outfitted her with a small but attractive wardrobe with proper French labels, suitable attire for a bourgeois young woman living in wartime France. Renée also located a hairdresser who put a brown rinse on Viv's burgundy-colored tresses, although the recipient wondered how she would maintain the shade once she crossed back into France.

Then the waiting began.

Each day, Viv phoned the American Consulate in Geneva, and each day her call was met with "No news for you yet, I'm afraid, Miss Vivier-Clarke. Please be patient."

The longer she waited to hear from someone official concerning the next steps of her mission, the more she found herself pacing the floor of her tiny hotel room. She gazed into the mirror, hardly recognizing herself with her dull brown hair and her bourgeois wardrobe tailor-made for her tall, slender form.

She'd never been good at waiting, she realized. Never been one to just sit still. She'd always been on the move, diving into the next adventure, the next ski trip, the next rendezvous, restless and anxious not to stay with her mother and Karl for any extended length of time.

Staring at her reflection in the streaked and peeling hotel mirror, she wondered, suddenly, if her peripatetic style of life had been her way of outrunning her hatred of her stepfather and all he stood for in his business and personal dealings. When Karl had first married her mother Pamela, he had treated young Viv as a necessary nuisance, forbidding any mention of his wife's first husband or the sacrifice the flyer had made fighting in the Great War.

Once Viv became a teenager and challenged Karl about his business dealings in Germany, the very country that had killed Group Captain Charles Vivier-Clarke, her stepfather actively sought every means either to dismiss or punish her for her outspoken views. Banishing her to boarding school for five years had been the ultimate control he'd held until she'd reached eighteen.

For Viv, waiting for news from the American Consulate these last days had been a grim reminder of her growing up years when her fate had been solidly vested in someone else's unfriendly hands.

The following Monday, an unfamiliar voice on the phone speaking to her from the Consulate informed her, "I'm afraid the decision has been made that courier work is too risky for a girl like you. Someone else has been chosen. So sorry."

And whoever it was abruptly hung up.

"*Merde*!" Viv hissed at the phone receiver in her hand. "Shit, shit, *shit!*"

Viv was certain that it was Roger Gianakos who had managed to put the kibosh on her assignment through some sneaky, low-level bureaucratic maneuver. After calling Renée to meet her at their favorite café, Viv stormed to her table and sat down in a fury.

Detailing the latest development, Viv pointed to her head. "I'm nixed for the job *and* stuck with fake hair! I cannot believe that little piss-ant could do this to me!"

"He probably couldn't forgive you for his humiliation," Renée replied, taking a sip from her steaming cup of coffee. "I've seen things like this happen at the Swiss foreign office too. Some minor rubber-stamp guy with an axe to grind can put a wrench in the gears, and the bosses never even notice. A little fish gets drowned in a big pond."

Viv continued to seethe. "I'll go back into France on my own, then, and find a Resistance circuit to work for!"

"You're crazy!" Renée protested with alarm. "Face it, you're basically a woman without a country. You don't have documents that prove *any* identity—real or fake! You have no contacts outside of Paris. And, by the way, your French accent isn't that good. You'd be spotted by the first SS goon that stopped you."

"Thanks for the encouragement," Viv retorted.

Renée countered in a softer tone, "At least you have a claim to dual citizenship. Why don't you just try to find a job at the British consulate here in Geneva? It'd be a lot safer, given what's going on in France."

"But, Renée, the Nazis are nasty customers, and I was given a chance to *do* something! I can't believe Roger would be able to block what Dulles ordered. Especially since there's such a need for building up local resistance to the occupation!"

"I'm telling you, the lower bureaucrats practically run everything," Renée insisted glumly. "I'll bet Dulles has no idea about this, but he wouldn't go to bat for you, even if he did. Wouldn't want a 'scene' with his deputy over such a small thing."

"Small thing?" Viv echoed, a flash of memory hearing the screams of the women and children apprehended in no-mans-land when they'd crossed the Swiss border. "*Gianakos* is the 'small thing.' What a total creep."

"O...kay," Renée said slowly, as if she'd made a sudden decision to take pity on Viv. "If you're *certain* you want to return to France so you can make your way to England and do your bit for this blasted war, I'll speak to Erik Thoman at the foreign office. *Maybe* he would speak to our boss about you."

"He's *Swiss!*" Viv said, her voice laced with discouragement. "What's the Honorable Mr. Neutral going to be able to do for me?"

Renée put a steadying hand on Viv's arm.

"You might not believe this," she said lowering her voice, "but not everyone in the Swiss government is so neutral. So calm down, will you? Let me see what I can do."

Viv sat up abruptly, jiggling their table and splashing coffee over the cup's rim.

"Oh, *would* you, Renée? At least Erik's speaking to his boss about me offers a glimmer of hope. Meanwhile, is there any way we can find out what happened to all those people that crossed the border with us? I just can't get them out of my mind."

Viv pictured the little Jewish girl's small doll that she'd stuffed at the bottom of her knapsack. Often, she found herself waking up at night with the thought of that sweet child's fate and conjured all sorts of terrible scenarios.

Renée looked around the café as if she feared someone might be watching them.

"Look…let's deal with one thing at a time. I've got to go. I'll leave a message at your hotel if anything develops."

———◇———

A few more days went by, and again, Viv received no news, other than the chatter she overheard in the café she frequented that General Dwight D. Eisenhower had arrived in London on June 24, half-way through this difficult year of 1942. Viv was at her wits end by the time Renée suddenly got back in touch and told her to meet her at the café.

"If you still want to do this crazy thing, you can leave tomorrow," she said in hushed tones with a glance over her shoulder at the other patrons in the café. "It's been arranged through the Swiss Secret Service. Even though the Swiss are supposedly non-combatants, I guess certain factions of the government are more sympathetic with the French Resistance than with the Nazi SS."

"Well, that's something, at least," Viv murmured.

Then it dawned on her. Something was actually happening!

I'm being given an assignment! But, what? And by whom?

With a rush of gratitude, Viv reached across the table to give a quick squeeze to the hand of her former traveling companion.

"This is such good news, Renée! Thank you *so* much for somehow managing all this." Viv had another thought. "By the way,

I know I keep asking, but were you ever able to find out what happened to those people we crossed the border with?"

"The Swiss authorities sent them back to France," Renée replied with the barest shrug of her shoulders. "My boss said Switzerland has had its fill of refugees."

Viv sucked in a breath. "*We* could have easily ended up refugees ourselves, you know," she reminded Renée sharply, "or been sent into the arms of the SS."

Looking away, her friend replied, "In this world, Viv, you do what you can do. Otherwise, I promise you, you'll just go crazy."

It's the world that's gone crazy. Someone *has to stand up and—*

Viv inhaled another deep breath. Renée had been very decent to locate someone in the Swiss government who felt as Viv did that the Nazis must be stopped. She thought of her mother in the internment camp at Vittel and wondered what Pamela's view of the Nazis was *now*?

"Look, Renée, I'm sorry if I sounded critical," Viv murmured, lowering her voice as she was acutely conscious they were in a public place. "I really *am* appreciative for what you have done. What time do I leave?"

Renée also began to speak barely above a whisper.

"After dark tomorrow. A Swiss secret agent will fetch you in the alley behind this café at nine o'clock and will drop you off near the border of Saint-Julien."

Viv felt a bubble of excitement expand in her chest. She was headed back to France to work with the Resistance!

Renée paused. "I was told to let you know that you won't get any identity papers until you meet with a man called Clément Grenelle in a French village near Frangy."

"Without documents, how in the world will I get beyond the border?" Viv worried aloud. "And even if I do, how do I make my way to England to try to volunteer for the Allied war effort fighting to free France?"

Before Renée answered, she swept her eyes around the café to be sure no one was listening to their conversation.

"One step at a time, Viv. The Swiss agent will give you initial instructions, and then this Grenelle guy will tell you what to do next…but you must be really careful."

"Kind of my only choice, wouldn't you say?" Viv replied with a rueful smile.

"Well, here's as much as I was told to tell you," Renée said, her voice hushed. "You'll have to make your way on your own from the Swiss border to the tiny French village of Chaumont. Find the church there. You will hear the word 'rain' repeated three times, a signal that is your contact. He will provide you with a very important message that you're to memorize *exactly*. Grenelle in Chaumont will instruct you from there."

"This sounds like a bad movie plot. Why don't they just send a *wireless* message to England? What do they need *me* for?"

"Honestly?" Renée replied, flinging her hands in the air, clearly annoyed that Viv had been peppering her with so many questions. "I have absolutely no idea. Do you want to do this, or not?"

Chastened, Viv replied, "Yes, I do."

She suddenly remembered Dulles's last words to her. "Viv," he'd said, "people in your line of activity are always, and *only,* on a 'need-to-know' basis." His message? "Don't ask questions. Wait for answers as you go along."

Sage advice from America's overseas spymaster, Viv thought, clamping her lips shut.

If I want to stay alive, I'd better start following it.

CHAPTER 21

The next evening, Viv glanced at her watch for the twentieth time, noted the hour and the exact minute, and reached for the strap on her knapsack resting on the floor next to her feet. Dishes clattered in the background and the café hummed with its usual nightly conviviality of coffee and cocoa drinkers. A minute later, she rose from a table in the corner and quietly let herself out through the side door precisely as Renée had instructed.

The alley was shrouded in darkness, although the bustling Geneva night owls could be heard celebrating in nearby streets. She swiftly exhaled with relief at the sight of a nondescript black sedan that was parked nearby, a figure silhouetted behind the wheel.

When she approached from the rear, the person inside leaned over, and suddenly the passenger side door swung open. Viv slid in next to the driver. She was shocked to see he was the same Swiss intelligence official who had originally questioned her at the border headquarters following her arrest by the officer on his bicycle. She remembered thinking at the time that the interrogator assigned to her case was a remarkably handsome young officer who had exhibited surprising compassion when he made the decision to release Renée and her into the streets of Geneva.

Viv leaned forward a bit to have a better look in the dim light of the car's interior.

"*You?*" she marveled.

"Yes, it's me, at your 'secret' service," he said with a quirk of a smile. "I *thought* you'd be surprised."

"That I certainly am. Who are you, really?"

"I'm the person who questioned you for illegally crossing into Switzerland."

"I *know* that," she replied impatiently. "But what's your *name*? Your job?"

"Let's just say you can call me Kurt."

Viv could guess that wasn't his real name, but then Dulles's warning about not asking so many questions came to mind.

"Kurt it is, then, and I suppose you remember my name?"

"I saw a file, but I have no idea if 'Constance' is the name given you at birth." He studied her for a moment and added, "You don't look like a 'Constance.'"

Viv laughed. "Smart cookie. Call me Viv, and by the way, you don't look like a 'Kurt.' More like a 'Christopher' I should think."

Kurt's eyes widened in what Viv thought might be genuine surprise. He quickly smiled back as if to cover his startled reaction. Oddly—since it was June and much of the snow had melted on the lower reaches of the Swiss Alps—her lanky guide was nevertheless dressed in a black skiing outfit. She had to admit he cut quite the impressive figure sitting across from her on the driver's side.

"I understand you ski, yes?" he asked. "Even trained for the Winter Olympics?"

Someone must have obtained access to travel visas that testified to Viv's many ski holidays in Switzerland over the years, along with her aborted training with a ski coach before the war started.

Zermatt, St. Moritz, Verbier... I certainly was living the good life in those days...

The Swiss officer declared, "If you and I are stopped, our cover story is that I'm in search of the last of the spring skiing higher up on the mountain. We got friendly this afternoon in a local ski shop, and I offered to give you a lift up to the slopes. I just want to be sure we keep to the same story since we supposedly have just met."

"Sounds good," she agreed. "So how about you return my Swiss identity card?"

She'd been worrying all week that she was crossing the border without possessing even mildly official-looking documents.

"Sorry. I can't give the card back to you." He put his vehicle in gear and moved into a main thoroughfare. "Someone else is already using it. You'll get a French one where you're going."

"Without anything to show at the border, I doubt I'll get very far," Viv replied, weary of always having to play the role of constant petitioner ever since she'd left Paris.

"I have every confidence that you'll make it across," her escort asserted. "Look how you managed to enter Switzerland undetected with all those Jewish refugees you guided. If they'd followed your instructions and not clumped together with all that luggage and noisy chatter, they probably *would* have gotten through." He shot her a grin, adding, "And you and your friend would not have encountered Agent Anders coming on duty like you did."

"A random case of bad things happening to good people, right?"

Viv thought of the sweet little girl and the doll she'd left behind. Could *this* be the Swiss official that had sent that small soul back across the border into German custody?

The man who called himself 'Kurt' pulled a pack of cigarettes—French Gauloises—out of his pocket and indicated Viv was free to take one.

"Thanks, but I don't smoke. I had asthma as child. I still have a few allergies."

Kurt nodded and returned the pack to his pocket. Silence soon fell between them. She stared out the window as their sedan glided through the darkness. The officer shifted gears as he rounded a corner and headed west, out of Geneva.

A few more miles down the road he volunteered, "I've cancelled the patrols for half an hour on a particular part of the St. Julien section of the border. That should give you time to get across safely."

Viv regarded him with a skeptical, sideways glance. "You can do that?"

"It's the birthday, today, of a friend of mine in the guards. I told him and his partner to take a longer dinner break to celebrate. When I give you the signal, it'll only be a short distance to sneak up to the wires…a long, high wall of them that you can slide *under*. On the other side, you'll see a dirt road. Don't take it," he advised. "Cross over it and slip into the vineyards there. Pick a row between the vines and keep going along it. You'll eventually reach an open field. Cross it, and you're out of no-man's-land."

"That doesn't sound too bad," Viv murmured. "The vines will give me cover."

"Eventually you'll see a barn on your left where you can get some rest until daylight. But be careful. There are German and Italian patrols and the *milice* roaming about these days. You want to stay invisible until you reach Chaumont."

"How far from the barn to that village?" she asked, unsettled to hear that the violent, Vichy-supported militia, the *malice,* were also in the area.

"A good twenty kilometers. You'll come to Chaumont at about five kilometers before the signs say you're nearing the larger town of Frangy."

Viv groaned. "On foot all the way, right?"

"Right," he confirmed, keeping his eyes on the road. "Outside the barn, *more* vineyards continue and also fields of various crops. Pick another row of vines and stay in it. Once it ends, you'll see— again on your left—a hill with some castle ruins. The village of Chaumont is perched next to them." He reached under his seat with one hand. "Here are some Gauloises and some French food coupons. Your contact in Chaumont, Clément Grenelle, has a family to feed. Kindly give these gifts to him with Kurt's compliments. He will know you as *Mademoiselle* Violette Charbonnet and will secure your French identity documents in that name."

Viv smiled in the darkened car. "'Violette.' At least it's close to 'Viv' so I'm likely to remember it," she declared. "And how will I find this *Monsieur* Grenelle?"

"Hard to say." Grinning again, he said, "He's been told you're coming and has your description: a tall American with brown hair that used to be the color of burgundy wine and who—"

"Who doesn't look French," she interrupted, completing his sentence for him. Viv asked, "*Why* are you doing this for me?"

"One less refugee to deal with."

"C'mon!"

"That's a joke." He remained silent for several long moments. Then he said, keeping his eyes on the road, "Maybe I envy you."

"Envy *me*?" she echoed, surprised by his response.

Kurt's lips had formed into a straight line. "Maybe I don't like the Germans either. In my job, I hear and see with my own eyes what they're doing every day. I know I'm supposed to be 'a neutral Swiss,' but I confess a great sin: I want the Allies to win." He briefly looked over at her again. "It won't happen for a long time, I don't think. Your side will need all the help it can get—even from a tall American girl like you who speaks bizarre French but has shown she has…courage."

The full force of the smile he then bestowed upon her was devastating.

He couldn't possibly *be the Swiss official that sent that little girl and her mother back into the arms of the Germans…*

In fact, for Viv, the Swiss officer's off-kilter compliment and his quiet stance in favor of the Allies filled her with a poignant but powerful sense of gratitude—along with an unexpectedly bittersweet combination of *what if* and *if only…*

Viv recognized that like Marcel Delonge, this attractive young officer would have drawn her like a magnet under different circumstances. She was nearly thirty now, she thought. Practically an old maid by any standard. Would she ever marry? Have children of her own? A piercing foreboding made her wonder if all the good men like Marcel and this Swiss renegade would be in their graves before this terrible war finally ended.

And maybe she would be as well...

For a brief second, Viv pictured Colonel Marcel Delonge, the man with eyes the color of coffee. He, too, had had the same strange effect on her as this good-looking, fair-haired Swiss, his tall form trim in his black ski clothes. And, as different as Kurt was from Marcel, she knew in her bones they were of the same mind: they hated what the Germans were doing to their world and had become willing to risk their own safety to try to do something to stop them.

The car slowed.

"We're almost there," he announced quietly.

He cut the headlights and the engine. The sedan silently rolled to a halt, and as it did, Viv felt her heart speed up. Her driver turned to face her. It was time for her to leave the safety of Switzerland.

"I'll come with you to within a few meters of the razor wires," he said. Viv nodded, reaching for the door handle. He placed a hand on her sleeve and warned urgently, "Don't slam it when you leave the car."

Viv slid out of the front seat, stood up, carefully closed the car door, and settled her knapsack over her shoulder. In the distance, she saw a massive tangle of wires. The barrier was higher, it seemed, than the fence she had faced at the other border crossing.

Lowering her voice, she said, "I paid no attention to the name plate on your desk the day you interrogated Renée and me. Do you honestly go by the name Kurt?" she asked, whispering now as they drew even closer to the fence. "And if you don't, can't I know your real name, now?"

"No. It's better that you don't," he murmured.

If she got caught, she couldn't betray him, and that was good, she decided.

As they walked side by side toward the menacing fence, the thought occurred to Viv that it felt so comfortable to be with a man several inches taller than she. He gently guided her toward the shelter of some bushes and bid her crouch beside him.

His voice low, he said, "Don't move for the next little while, and we won't talk. The last patrol leaving a half hour early at my behest will come by any minute now. I'll give you a push when it's safe for you to go."

After a few minutes more of silence, she heard the sound of

heavy boots on the ground nearby and low voices speaking Swiss German. Her haunches soon started to ache from the strain of sitting on her heels. When she could hear the guards no more, she turned to gaze over her shoulder. Her companion bent forward and startled her with a kiss of benediction on the forehead.

He whispered, "I can't say it later so, good luck…and Godspeed."

For several more minutes, neither moved a muscle. Viv thought she'd never be able to stand up without a crippling leg cramp, but suddenly he whispered, "All right, go! *Go!*"

Viv made a run for the fence, pushing her knapsack under its bottom wire to hold it up a foot, a maneuver that made room for her to wiggle through. Once on the French side, she stood up with remarkable ease and liberated her small piece of luggage.

When she looked back through the wires, the man whose name wasn't Kurt had disappeared into the starless night.

CHAPTER 22

The twenty kilometer walk from crossing the border at St. Julien to the tiny village of Chaumont was exhausting, but in Viv's view, mercifully uneventful. She never had to dive into a ditch at the sound of a German or Italian patrol. And much to her amazement, she managed to find the barn where she'd been advised to grab a couple of hours sleep with nary a French gendarme or thuggish member of the *milice* in sight. Burrowed beneath a pile of hay in the loft above a deserted horse stable, she barely remembered closing her eyes. Unfortunately, when she awoke, tears were cascading down her cheeks and her entire chest was congested.

Merde… I hate having allergies! Dry hay is the worst!

Coughing and sneezing as she climbed down from the loft, she found a horse trough with a shallow puddle of water and splashed her face. Still sniffling, she ate some cheese and a bun she'd saved from the café the previous night. Just before dawn broke, she was on her way again through vineyards that seemed to stretch southwest for miles. As instructed, she kept walking along the same row of entwined budding vines until she reached a paved road with a stone marker that declared: "Frangy, 9 kilometers."

Thank God I'm in the Free Zone.

Here, at least, in the supposedly unoccupied part of France, the Germans had not yet ordered all the road signs changed to their own language. She wondered how long *that* would last?

As the morning sun began to peek above the horizon, she spotted a mass of stone buildings high on a hill. Ruins of a turreted fortress rose above her head. Directly below was the beginning of a steep trail that wound around to the top of the ridge. Wearily trudging up the nearly vertical rocky path, her heavy boots began to raise painful blisters on her heels and her eyes still itched from a night of sleeping on hay. In the warming sunshine, sweat gathered on her upper lip and ran down her sides under her wool coat.

At length, the trail ended at the edge of a cemetery next to a church built of the same gray-colored stones as the abandoned ruin. There, across scores of tilted, lichen-covered tombstones, a man of middle years was wielding an outsized shovel. Both his hair and scruffy beard were a salt-and-pepper color, and the dirt-streaked blue beret on his head looked as old as he was.

When she drew within a few feet of the open grave, he looked up and volunteered, "I don't think we'll have rain today."

Viv stared back at him blankly. Was *this* the man Grenelle?

Scowling, he continued, "Rain used to come here in early June, but no more since the war began."

Before she could acknowledge the password that Renée had told her about days earlier, he barked, "We've had a hot spring, so far. We need *rain*!" He slammed his shovel into the mound of soil beside the rectangular hole he'd dug. "Can't you count, *mademoiselle*?"

"Ah…y-yes…*rain*…three t-times," Viv stuttered.

By some miracle, she'd found Clément Grenelle as soon as she'd set foot in Chaumont! Maybe she'd make a good secret agent yet. She reached into her knapsack.

"Will two packets of Gauloises and some food coupons make up for how fuzzy my head is right now? I'm literally dead on my feet. I *walked* the twenty kilometers from the Swiss border, by the way."

The gravedigger shrugged as if what she'd endured was no great feat and snatched the peace offerings out of her hand.

"C'mon with you, then," he grumbled, his gaze measuring how tall she was. "Let's not have the village wondering if I have taken a mistress a foot higher than I am."

In your dreams, monsieur...

But Viv merely nodded politely, following in his wake and wondering if she would have any chance to soak her feet.

———◇———

Clément Grenelle, his wife, young son, and a pair of five-year-old female twins lived in a village house that also matched the same gray stone as the local church and the tumbled-down fortress.

The family's clothing was threadbare, its furniture battered, and a single iron pot hung from a metal arm that extended over a fireplace hearth in a corner in what passed for a kitchen. The children silently observed their visitor over the chipped rims of soup dishes placed before them by an equally taciturn *Madame* Grenelle.

As Viv took her place, she acknowledged the circle of stares with what she hoped was a friendly smile. She took a first sip of thin broth tasting of the barest hint of a potato and perhaps some greens from an anemic kitchen garden somewhere, given the surrounding rocky soil of this hill town.

Whatever the Grenelle family did to subsist in this barren village—other than *monsieur*'s grave digging—remained a mystery. At least, the food coupons she'd brought should have bought her some goodwill with the lady of the house, although Viv could plainly see that the woman would be very happy when her husband's latest "guest" was sent on her way. She found herself wondering if wives got a vote as to whether a family joined the Resistance.

One of the Grenelle twins sat to Viv's right. The little girl's elbows were on the table, and she was pressing her small left hand against her flushed cheek. With her other hand, she held her spoon, but wasn't scooping the scant evening meal into her mouth. The child looked as if she might be running a fever.

Viv inclined her head and asked, "Are you feeling all right?"

Before the girl could answer, *Madame* Grenelle declared without sympathy, "Nicolle has a tooth coming in and thinks if she complains enough, she'll be excused from her chores." To her daughter she said sharply, "Your sighing and moaning will do you no good, *mademoiselle*. Be grateful for what has been set before you and eat!"

"But *maman*," the little girl protested, "it hurts so much that I can hardly open my mouth. Now, my other side has begun to—"

"Quiet!" her mother commanded. "Your father has business to do with this lady once we finish supper, so I don't want to hear another *word*."

Despite her mother's command, the little girl quietly put down her spoon. Viv reached for the child's other hand resting in her lap and gave it a sympathetic squeeze to signal she understood how miserable a toothache could be. Nicolle met her gaze with tears filling her eyes.

She is *in pain, poor little thing.*

Viv volunteered, "*Madame*, I have aspirin with me. May I give her one?"

Clément's wife remained silent for a few moments, as if absorbing an offer she was surprised to receive from a complete stranger whose presence put them all at risk. She shrugged. "I'm not sure her tooth is as bothersome as she pretends. Let us see how she is at bedtime." Her stern expression softened. "But thank you, *mademoiselle*."

Viv quickly finished her soup and looked at Clément inquiringly. He wiped his lips with his sleeve and rose to his feet.

"Come," he said without preamble. "Bring your knapsack with you.'

Viv rose from the table and gently ran the back of the fingers of one hand against Nicolle's swollen cheek that radiated heat.

"Feel better, *ma petite*," she murmured.

"Let's go," Grenelle commanded. As they left by the stone house's solitary door, he said over his shoulder, "You will sleep in the back. We leave tomorrow morning on the first bus from Frangy."

Viv halted in the dusty side yard. "*You* are my *passeur*?" she said, startled.

"*D'accord*," he replied with a nod. "It's been agreed that I'm the one to lead you. I have other business in Carcassonne and told them

I could escort you first to Annecy to hear from the *maquis* there about the messages you are to deliver to London. From there, we will make our way to both our destinations."

"The '*maquis*?'" she asked, wondering what organization or splinter group she was to deal with.

"'*Maquis*' is slang for 'underbrush'," he explained with a look that signaled she must be a very green recruit to the Resistance not to know this already—which she was, of course, she thought grimly. "The High Command is starting to require that our young men be transported to Germany to work," he said. "Instead, they're going into hiding, often in the mountains or deep into the forests. 'Into the underbrush,' yes?"

Her host continued to lead her around the side of his house to a wood hut that reminded Viv of the one in which she and Marcel had sought shelter on their way to Dunkirk. She shuddered at the memory of the wreckage after the *Luftwaffe* had dropped its solitary bomb. Pushing such recollections aside, Viv speculated on what role this scruffy middle-aged man could possibly play in the shadowy world of the Resistance.

Other business in Carcassonne, he'd said.

She couldn't help but wonder why Kurt, the handsome Swiss border agent, as well as Erik, Renee's contact in the Swiss foreign ministry, forged connections with an ordinary grave digger in a forgotten village called Chaumont. Very strange bedfellows Viv thought, ducking her head to enter a small loft filled with hay that she so dreaded.

Oh, God... I'm sleeping here?

Immediately she suppressed a sneeze.

Welcome to the glamorous world of clandestine operations, she thought wryly.

A few scrawny chickens pecked at the dirt floor scattered with a sprinkling of plant cuttings, probably scraps not put in the soup they had just consumed. Grenelle leaned against a wooden post that held up a roof with patches revealing the last rays of daylight. He pulled out one of the packs of Gauloises she had given him and offered her a cigarette, which she declined. He lit up, inhaled deeply, and then blew out a stream of smoke that only added to Viv's struggle not to sneeze. He glanced down at her feet.

"I'm glad to see you're wearing boots. Once we get to Annecy, we will have a meal and then leave the town to do some alpine climbing."

"That's fine," she replied with studied nonchalance, pushing away the thought of more blisters on top of the ones she already had. "I've skied a lot in France, including cross-country. I'm sure I can manage a hike to…?"

Her question dangled in the air between them.

"You'll know when you get there," he replied tersely. "A group of *maquis* want you to take messages to London for them."

"So I've heard. I've been told I'm to deliver them to the Brits. If the Brits won't see me, though," she wondered aloud, "what about the Americans?"

Clément retorted almost scornfully, "Stick with the Brits, although we'll see if they end up supporting everything that upstart, de Gaulle, demands. All he does from the comfort of his London headquarters is declare on the wireless to those of us under the German boot, 'France lost the battle, but will win the war.'"

Was Clément a Communist? Viv had heard the Resistance movements that opposed the German takeover of France were far from unified. Many a Frenchman was opposed to the far-right power elite that had ruled France before the war started. And there was *another* French general, Girard, whom Viv had heard it said was organizing resisters and was a fierce rival of de Gaulle. Maybe Grenelle was in *Girard's* camp? Who the heck was she working for, she wondered?

"And this particular group of *maquisards*?" Viv ventured. "Who are they, exactly?"

"As I said, there are some boys in the Haute-Savoie we want to keep out of the forced labor camps. We've sent them into the mountains to a plateau above Lake Annecy. It's a good place to hide. It's rough getting up there, and usually there's a cloud cover."

"So, in other words, these are Resistance fighters who take to the hills…take to the 'underbrush,' as you put it earlier?"

Clément shrugged. "They're not fighters—yet—but we hope with training and weapons, they will be by the time the Allies invade. That's where *you* come in."

Viv opened her mouth to ask the first of a torrent of questions, but her host shook his head. He pointed to the hayloft.

"You'll learn more when we get to the Plateau des Glières. Now, get some rest. Here's a bucket to relieve yourself, and there's a horse blanket up there for you. I'll come fetch you before dawn." He raised a hand whose fingers were close to being singed with the glowing tip of his cigarette. "And thanks for these."

"Wait, a sec," Viv said, digging into her knapsack. She pulled out a small tin of aspirin, handing her host two tablets. "I think your daughter might have a fever. You could have her take one before sleep and another tomorrow morning. They might ease the pain of that tooth."

The look of gratitude transformed the man's expression.

"That's very kind. Thank you." He folded his fingers around the little white pills.

For all *Monsieur* Grenelle's gruffness, this *passeur* was a damn sight nicer than the ruffians who'd taken Renée and her to the Swiss border, Viv thought. Without bidding her goodnight, he ducked under the low doorframe and disappeared around the corner.

Viv climbed a shaky wooden ladder into the loft and placed the horse blanket flat on the straw. Not bothering to undress, she held her breath against the dust and rolled herself up like a sausage in the scratchy wool. With her knapsack for a pillow, she hoped these arrangements might help her keep her distance from the blasted hay.

As she closed her eyes, a voice echoed in her head.

And once you get to London and deliver the maquis' messages— if you ever do—then what's next, Mademoiselle Violette Charbonnet?

CHAPTER 23

The day after Viv and Clément Grenelle arrived at the safe house he'd arranged for them in a back street of the lakeside town of Annecy, they immediately prepared for their departure to the Plateau des Glières. At two that afternoon, a driver and his truck materialized to take them to a destination some 34 kilometers up a road flanked by nearly mile-high limestone promontories. The further they drove up a steep-sided valley toward the town of Thones, the colder it became inside the truck. Their driver stopped the vehicle at the foot of the plateau, where Viv and Clément climbed down to the road. Within seconds, the truck turned around and headed in the direction from which it had come. Viv cranked her neck to stare up at the encircling alpine cliffs rising higher than the plateau itself.

"Whoa," she murmured. It was going to be quite a hike.

By the time they'd tramped uphill less than a few kilometers, the blisters on Viv's heels were bleeding inside her boots. Gulping in the thin, alpine air, she realized how long it had been since she'd skied in top shape.

And today, we're only hiking...

It seemed eons ago that she and Grenelle had enjoyed an ample lunch that day, sitting in a dark corner at the Café Lyonnais. The establishment was on a street that ran parallel to one of several quaint canals running through in the town of Annecy nestled at the northern end of the spectacular lake of the same name. The restaurant's proprietor, Anton La Salle, whom Viv guessed to be a leading member of some underground group in the region, treated them as honored guests. After weeks of reduced rations, the roasted herbed chicken and potatoes and sautéed *courgettes*—lovely little baby zucchini squash—had been like dining at the Hôtel Ritz during Viv's headiest days in Paris. But as the thin air began belaboring her lungs these few hours later, she wished she'd accepted the second cup of "real" coffee La Salle had so generously offered.

"Wait!" she gasped, grabbing for Clément Grenelle's sleeve while reaching out with her other hand to lean against a bolder to steady herself. "Just let me catch my breath a moment." It upset her to realize that she was this seriously out of shape for such strenuous exercise at high altitudes.

"Aren't you supposed to be an expert skier?" Clément replied skeptically. His even breathing showed he was unfazed by his superior age and the steady pace he'd set for them to move steadily up the steep trail.

A bolt of irritation fueled her response.

"Actually, I *am* a good skier. I was training for the Olympics before the war started," she fibbed in her defense. "I'm just a bit out of condition. I'm okay. Let's go."

She took off ahead of him, wondering how much further the steep trail would take them. Even in late June at these heights, there were patches of snow on the ground and more on the crags arching overhead. Viv's fingers were numb, as were her toes. In fact, she could no longer even feel her painful blisters rubbed raw on her heels.

"How many men are hiding out up here?" she puffed over her shoulder as she continued to fight for breath.

"Only a few right now, but more will come," Clément said as he overtook her stride. "Some stay here during the day to drill and practice their shooting and then sneak back down to their farms and homesteads at night. The more the *Boche* try to deport our youth, the sooner there will be an army of young men from the Haute-Savoie eager to fight for France." His piercing, pale blue eyes held hers for a moment. "We are mountain people, Violette," he declared. "We don't like strangers coming in to tell us what to do, and we certainly aren't willing to be sent like *slaves* to work for the German war machine, which is designed to kill us."

Viv thought of all the times she'd rebelled against Karl or her mother telling her what she could and couldn't do. Here, however, the stakes were life itself.

"I understand," she nodded, tugging her wool cap more securely onto her head. To Viv's surprise, *Madame* Grenelle had urged her to take it with her for warmth just as they were leaving Chaumont to head for Annecy.

"The aspirin you gave to Nicolle helped her to sleep," Clément's wife had volunteered. "I think she really does have a bad jaw with a molar coming in." She had thrust the ailing twin's cap into Viv's hands. "Here, wear this. It's loosely knit, so it should fit. You can return it to Clément when you get to wherever you're bound."

Now, grateful for the warmth of Nicolle's cap in temperatures that seemed to grow colder with each step, Viv estimated that it would take at least another half hour of climbing before they'd reached the top of the rocky trail.

When they finally arrived at the summit, she was ready to drop in her tracks. Breathing heavily, she paused to take in the sight of the huge, flat expanse of the plateau ringed by mighty mountains above it. The landscape before her stretched like some giant meadow the size of a large lake—only instead of a grassy field one might expect in spring—the Plateau des Glières was still coated with a thin layer of snow. A quarter of a mile away was a wooden chalet of modest size, its roof covered in a dusting of powder.

Cross-country skis would be nice right about now, she thought.

She and Clément set off toward their destination where they were to rendezvous with the *résistants* taking refuge in this remote hideaway. They had barely reached the chalet's ice-glazed stairs when the door opened, revealing a burly young man in a heavy, black turtleneck sweater. He held two mugs that he extended to the visitors.

With a broad grin aimed at Viv, he said, "Welcome to the Plateau des Glières. I'm Julien." He handed her a mug filled with an inky brew that she guessed was made from ground acorns, not real coffee as at the Café Lyonnais, but its warmth felt sublime.

The three entered the chalet, a small, dark structure that looked a lot like the warming huts on the slopes of some of the ski resorts Viv had frequented when in school.

"Julien, this is Violette," said Clément, making his introductions brief, as Viv suspected was the habit when a new person was introduced to any resistance organization. "Our friend in Switzerland sent her."

Viv wondered silently which friend that was—Renee's colleague, Erik Thoman, at the Swiss foreign office, or the mysterious Kurt, obviously an intelligence officer, and not a common border functionary as Viv had originally assumed?

Their host bid her take a seat on a wooden chair facing what served the group as a kitchen table. Clément melted into the shadows beside them. He took his place among the young men seated on wooden benches against the wall listening attentively, their curiosity piqued that a solitary woman had joined their company.

Her *passeur* had only disclosed that the plateau was one of the locales poised to recruit young men threatened with deportation to the enemy's work camps. He and other secret leaders had arranged for this hideout, preparing it for even more men, should the Germans and Italians invade the Free Zone, as rampant rumors forecast.

"I hope you have a good memory, Violette," Julien said, his friendly demeanor swiftly turning deadly serious. "We have several messages for you to deliver to the war office in London, but none that we will permit you to write down. You must memorize each one, word-for-word. Many lives will depend on your doing this perfectly."

Viv nodded, with both excitement and growing apprehension. What if the mission the handsome Swiss officer had set for her challenged her in ways she wouldn't be able to meet—and people died?

Julien leaned forward, his hands clasped and resting on the table.

"As Clément has surely told you, we are forming a band of...how you call them? Guerilla fighters. *Saboteurs*."

Viv glanced over her shoulder at the youthful audience behind them. The volunteers were clad in all manner of work clothes, odd pieces of military attire scrounged, perhaps, from a father or grandfather who'd fought in the Great War more than two decades earlier.

She found herself thinking how young they all seemed, just boys, really, with peach fuzz barely growing on some of their eager faces.

This group had apparently gotten the word they might soon be scooped up at random by German soldiers that currently and indiscriminately snatched young men from street corners and cafés, loading them at gun point onto trains and into canvas-covered trucks.

"From there," Julien explained, his voice dark with anger, "our French brothers and sons are transported deep into Germany to serve as virtual slaves in the Nazi war machine's munitions, tank, and aircraft factories."

Julien slammed a fist on the table. Startled, Viv glanced at his audience, whose eyes were glued on the two of them.

"You must tell Mr. Churchill that we are ready to recruit platoons of anti-fascists who will strike at night, blow up train tracks where German supplies are sent into France from their homeland, and kill as many of the invaders as we possibly can!" Julien's eyes were now aglow with fury, and his voice sank to a rasp. "But they'll be slaughtered if we don't soon get Allied help."

He expects me *to gain an audience with Winston Churchill?*

Viv inhaled a deep breath and kept her eyes on Julien, focusing on each word he said, praying she could remember it all.

"We will need weapons dropped on the plateau by parachute," he elaborated harshly. "If they want to win this war, they must send us *tons* of guns and ammunition…medical supplies…and food to equip at least a thousand men. If you make it to London, tell this to the British High Command. *Tell* them! It's the only way to smooth the path for the Allied troops we pray will invade to free us from these barbarians!"

His eyes narrowed to slits. From his sudden, skeptical expression, Viv wondered if he had judged that she, a mere woman, wasn't up to the task he'd laid out for her.

As if to confirm her fears, Julien turned to address Clément who was smoking one of his precious Gauloises and leaning against the back wall.

"Why did they not send a *man* for a man's job?" he demanded of Viv's *passeur*.

Viv was both moved by Julien's fierceness of purpose and highly offended by his concluding remarks. She swiftly raised a hand, signaling that she wished him to pay close attention to what she was about to say.

"I was sent here, Julien, because there are people whom you do not know that believe a *woman* has a far better chance than a man to get back to Britain through enemy lines. The Nazis suspect every Frenchman under forty wandering the streets to be AWOL from the military after France so *quickly* surrendered to the Germans," she said, deliberately abrasive, "or they're a possible spy."

There! One insult deserves another!

Julien settled back in his chair, expressionless. Viv pointed a forefinger at him.

"You should be glad a woman—especially this one—is taking your messages to London," she asserted, speaking in a voice loud enough for the young men on the backbench to hear every word. "The Nazis so disrespect your French women that they cannot conceive of a female pedaling through the center of town on a bicycle whose wicker basket is full of hand grenades hidden under a caged chicken, or that she would *dare* attempt to pass through a check point with blatantly fake identity documents or a pillow under her dress, feigning pregnancy. We women couriers have done all those things, so a woman like *me* is far more likely to out-fox the foxes than any of *you*!"

Julien wore a shocked expression that told Viv she might have well crossed the line to have spoken to a leader of a *maquis* in such a disrespectful fashion in front of his recruits. She could hear the young men behind her shift their weight on their bench. Clément cast her a look of unease mixed with a hint of admiration.

For a long moment, Julien bit his bottom lip in thought as he stared at the surface of the wooden table that separated them. Then, he looked up and met her glance while she did her best to keep her own gaze steady. He gave a sharp nod, as if he agreed with himself about something. His friendly grin returned.

"*Vive le France!*" he burst forth, looking over her shoulder at his compatriots. He stood up from his chair, walked over to Clément and clapped him heartily on the back. "I agree, *mon ami*. You have brought us exactly the right person for the job."

But am I truly the right person right for this dangerous, demanding work, Viv wondered silently?

Could she pass as a citizen of France long enough to make it to the Spanish border and somehow find her way from there to Great

Britain? Would she be able to remember "each word" of Julien's demands and requests by the time she got there? Would anyone of import at the London War Office even be willing to *listen* while she attempted to convey the urgency of these brave people in this remote area of war-torn France?

And most treacherous of all, Viv wondered, how would she make it through every German checkpoint…evade every patrol…cross every border to safely escape France for a second time?

CHAPTER 24

Just as Viv feared, the trip south from Annecy and then west to Perpignan near the border with Spain where she was to flee across the Pyrenees had been fraught with peril. Every single moment she and Clément battled to stay one step ahead of the authorities. Each day she held her breath every time Vichy authorities and local gendarmes checked her fake French identity papers that Clément had somehow produced in the name of Violette Charbonnet. On several occasions they observed French officials being as ruthless as their German counterparts grabbing Jewish escapees off trains, from the streets, out of their homes, and from their places of business.

One older woman had been dragged from Viv's railcar just before their train left Cannes en route to Perpignan. Two arresting officers accused the unfortunate soul of having the wrong color ink stamped on her documents, a dead give-away that the papers were as phony as Viv's were. "Violette Charbonnet" felt the weight of guilt press down on her when neither she nor Clément intervened as the terrified Polish refugee was manhandled out of their compartment toward a fate too horrifying to contemplate. Witnessing this, Viv felt a strange, new compulsion to make it to London to in some small measure fight against forces that could be so cruel and inhumane.

On the third day of the journey, Viv roused herself from these depressing thoughts as she saw out the window that their train had finally entered the far end of the Carcassonne station. The car came to a halt with a shudder and screeching of brakes. Viv and Clément made a show of casually gathering their belongings, exiting the train, and then sauntering the length of the platform. At a shaded table outside a closed café, they took a seat to wait for their final train to Perpignan. The station was blessedly empty at this early hour, except for a worker pushing a broom at the other end of the rail yard. Viv cradled her head in her arms on the table and promptly fell asleep.

———◆———

The sound of a train whistle roused Viv from her stupor. She sat bolt upright, alone at the table with Clément nowhere in sight. A dull ache had begun to pulse in her jaw. Groggily, she rubbed the side of her cheek.

A toothache? Oh, God...how can I be getting a toothache now?

Both her right cheek and parts of her neck were swollen, the skin taunt and hard to the touch. She thought of Clément's poor little twin daughter, moaning in pain at the dinner table the first night she'd arrived at Chaumont. A toothache like that was the *last* thing she needed right then. It had been ages since she'd been to a dentist, and she found herself thinking about all the chocolate and sweets she'd consumed as a schoolgirl.

Just then, the train soon bound for Perpignan came to a halt four tracks away from where she sat. She jumped up from the table and grabbed her knapsack, gazing around with her heart in her throat, frantic to know where her *passeur* had gone, as she had no ticket to board. Two gendarmes were chatting with each other where earlier she'd seen the janitor sweeping the floor.

Her cheek was throbbing even more than when she first awoke as she turned and saw Clément coming around a corner. He was pointing in the direction of their train and walking slowly toward it so as not to attract attention from the local police who evidently were just coming on duty. Viv forced herself to adopt Clément's leisurely pace, relieved to see they would board a car on the side hidden from the gendarmes.

"Where *were* you?" she muttered under her breath.

"Can't a man take a piss?" he answered irritably. He handed her a baguette wrapped in newsprint. "Take this," he hissed. "Make a show of giving me a chunk of bread if anyone comes through the car checking our identity papers."

The carriage became increasingly crowded at each subsequent stop as more passengers bordered the train making its tortured way to the southwest corner of France. Much to Viv's alarm, her throbbing toothache was growing worse by the minute. By the time they pulled into their final destination, she was in a thoroughly miserable state.

"I must find a dentist," she mumbled. "I can hardly move my jaw."

Clément didn't answer but led the way out of the car arriving in Perpignan, one of the largest French cities on the Mediterranean some forty kilometers from the border with Spain. At the exit to the station, Viv dug for her documents as the line neared the checkpoint. When it was her turn, she could feel her heart speed up as it always seemed to do in these situations. With one hand, she handed her fake travel pass and ID to a local guard while pressing the other against her swollen cheek, wincing as she met his gaze.

"Toothache," she managed to whisper between her clenched jaw.

The grizzled guard whose own teeth were either black or missing barely glanced at her papers, offering an understanding nod. "My sympathies, *mademoiselle*. I have often suffered from the same myself." He looked at the next person in line, waving her through.

When Viv and Clément emerged into the bright, warm sunshine, she sagged against the nearest wall. By this time, the pain in her neck and jaw had become excruciating.

"I've never had a toothache this bad," she said apologetically, having to pause to catch her breath. "Where do you suppose I can at least find a pharmacy for some stronger pain medication?"

"You can't," Clément replied shortly. "It's dangerous to hang around a train station, especially this one. Let's go. Take one of your aspirins, why don't you? Perhaps the *patron* will have something stronger to give you."

"What '*patron*?'" she said, gritting her teeth against the throbbing in her jaw.

Clément merely shook his head as they began to make their way through Perpignan's city streets. The roads were flanked by buildings with red tiled roofs that looked more Spanish than French.

Finally her guide said over his shoulder, "You need to understand that the word of this particular *patron* is law among *résistants* in this region, so don't do or say anything stupid, all right? Once we meet up, he'll take over and be the one to point your way to the path across the Pyrenees toward Barcelona. But first, we have to find some bicycles."

As they threaded their course through a labyrinth of passageways, Clément explained that some twenty kilometers from the foothills, the Germans had created a "forbidden zone" similar to others that skirted the eastern border with Switzerland.

"The area here that stretches to the foot of the mountains has become a natural jumping-off place for anyone trying to escape into Spain." Viv merely nodded to show she was listening despite the pounding in her head. Clément halted his forward progress to emphasize a point. "And I'm warning you, Violette. The people here exist in a world of their own. Most in this region live on isolated farms or vineyards. They were smugglers even before the war. Now they go in for it in a really big way—smuggling human beings looking to gain freedom in Spain."

"So they know the best passes to take through the mountains?" Viv asked.

"Every pass, every path through the highest peaks," he confirmed.

And with that, he stomped off, not waiting to see if she were following. Despite the pain that now had invaded the other side of her jaw, Viv broke into a trot in an effort to catch up with him as they approached a small bistro.

Viv asked, "So the man we're meeting up with is a smuggler?"

"A far more important partisan than *that*," Clément replied with a rare show of amused irony. "He's French, but looks both Basque and Catalan, and as a leader in this area, I should warn you that he can be just as disagreeable as me. These people are more fiercely independent than even the *Haute-Savoyards*, and that's saying something." He pointed to an alley where two battered bicycles leaned against a stone wall. "Ah! For once, I don't have to chase these down," he mumbled. He strode toward the door of the café. "First we eat. Then we ride."

"And after that?"

Clément frowned. "You ask too many questions."

———◇———

After hours of cycling west down dusty roads, it seemed to Viv as if her *derrière* was permanently affixed to her bicycle seat. Not only was her jaw shot through with racking pain, but the padding on her bottom's sit bones had developed what she could only imagine were genuine "saddle sores," raw patches to match the ones on her heels caused by the climb to the Plateau des Glières a few days earlier. At least there was no snow on the ground in sunny Perpignan, but she was now certain she was running a fever.

Ahead of her, Clément pedaled energetically, leading the way down a road he appeared already to know. After a brief stop for water in a tiny nondescript village, they next began to climb a narrow road bordered by extensive vineyards. A citadel with crenellated walls loomed on their right against the cloudless sky. Sweat poured down Viv's back muffled in her winter coat she would need crossing the Pyrenees.

Finally, her *passeur* turned into a dirt track that led to a stone farmhouse, its roof clad in the ubiquitous red tiles of this region so near to Spain. Viv was beyond exhaustion, the pain in her head as well as in her jaw reverberating throughout her body. The dirt track, peppered with rocks, veered left toward a wooden, wall-less outbuilding where a big plow and other farm implements were housed under its roof. Zigzagging to avoid the stones challenging her front wheel, Viv felt the landscape fairly swimming in front of her. Clément's bicycle abruptly came to a stop. In turn, she screeched to a halt, nearly colliding her front wheel into his back one.

A strangely familiar voice prompted her to look up from her rusted handlebars.

"Ah…so Miss America has made it safely across the breadth of France."

Viv could only stare, speechless. Finally, she managed to murmur through her swollen jaw, "Oh…my… *God*!"

Marcel Delonge's tanned, scarred visage with its high-bridged nose bore an inscrutable expression. His dark eyes took in her sorry state. He was clad in dirty overalls, a crumpled navy beret tilted at an angle on his dark hair. In his hands he held a large, rather menacing-looking pair of pruning shears.

"Welcome to the vineyards of Chateau Delonge," he addressed them both with amused irony. "From the looks of *you*," he added, directing his comments to Viv, "you appear sorely in need of a glass of wine."

"Better yet, how 'bout an injection of morphine?" she mumbled, dismounting from her bicycle. She was stunned to realize that the man she'd driven to Dunkirk was now the French Resistance's *patron* in control of the escape route to Spain. She pointed to the lumps near her jaw line, too exhausted to mention that the skin on her heels stung like fury and her rear end felt like it was burning in hell. Struggling to stand upright next to her bicycle, the world began to fade before her eyes.

The last thing she heard was Marcel murmuring, *"Mon Dieu,"* as she collapsed onto the dirt beside his mud-caked boots.

CHAPTER 25

Viv had no idea how long she'd been asleep—or rather, semi-unconscious. Hearing voices murmuring nearby, she struggled to force her eyes open. Marcel was standing at the foot of her bed, along with another man snapping shut a doctor's bag.

"You were right, Marcel. I'm afraid it's mumps," declared the stranger. "The swelling on both sides of her neck...her high temperature. Every symptom she has points to it." Viv heard the man chuckle. "But as for those nasty sores on her *derrière,* I expect those were produced by the prolonged cycling it must have required for the *mademoiselle* to arrive at your door."

"Yes," Marcel replied, and Viv could hear amusement in his voice as well. "I put some ointment I had on them, as well as on the popped blisters on her heels. I imagine both...uh...areas will make a full recovery."

Viv felt her cheeks and neck growing even warmer than her fever warranted at the thought that Marcel Delonge, of all people, had rubbed both her heels and her bottom with salve when she'd been out of her head! She quickly clamped her eyes shut again so they wouldn't see she was awake.

Marcel asked, "How bad a case of mumps do you think she's got?"

"Pretty severe," the doctor replied. "There's no known medicine for it, so we'll have to see if there are further complications."

"Like what?" Marcel asked, and Viv took a tiny bit of comfort that he actually sounded concerned.

There was a moment of silence in her sickroom. Then the doctor said reluctantly, "Well, in really bad cases, I've seen everything from heart trouble to deafness to possible problems with fertility."

Viv closed her eyes even tighter, not wanting even to think about what the doctor had just said, but, even so, her thoughts spun in all directions.

Because of the stupid mumps I could have a heart attack or lose my hearing?

And then she felt like someone had punched her in the stomach at the possibility she might never be able to have a child. She suddenly remembered Clément's daughter, Nicolle, who'd had the exact same symptoms the night the little girl sat next to her during supper in Chaumont.

And I thought it was just a bad toothache...

"How long will she be contagious?" Marcel asked.

"For at least another few days. Tell everyone to keep their distance, including you."

"Oh, don't worry," assured Marcel with a laugh. "I had a case years ago."

The doctor replied, "Well, I haven't heard of anyone ever getting mumps a second time—but do be careful."

Marcel was exiting toward the door of Viv's bedroom.

"When my sister makes our visitor her meals, I'll have Marie leave them outside this door. The rest of us will definitely steer clear." Viv heard the two men's voices grow fainter as they moved a foot farther down the hallway. "When I saw the way she looked," Marcel told the doctor, "I realized right away what bad shape she must be in. I put her to bed and immediately washed my hands. Then I sent for you to come."

"Good decision, washing your hands," agreed the doctor, "otherwise we might have to deal with a serious outbreak around here at a time we can least afford it." Viv's eyes still clamped shut, she heard the doctor ask, "Who is she, by the way? She's so extraordinarily tall for a woman. She certainly doesn't look French."

"No? You don't think so?" Marcel replied blandly. "She's a friend of a cousin, here to help us with the harvest later on. Her accent is faintly Alsatian, I'd say. My cousin told me her family comes from that part of the country, and *you* know how often that benighted area has gone back and forth between us and the *Boche*."

The doctor's tone of suspicion subsided. "Ah, yes. Poor Alsace. A region of excellent white wines that the Germans have stolen, lock, stock, and barrel, yet again. Such bad luck to live there. At least in our land of superb reds, we only have a few Krauts to contend with in the Free Zone."

"For now," Marcel deadpanned, "but the rumors are…"

Viv couldn't hear the rest of Marcel's cover story for her because the two men had ambled farther down the hallway. Her last thoughts before falling into a drugged sleep were that Marcel had read her file somewhere, somehow. Otherwise, how would he have known that her father's people *had indeed* hailed from poor, "benighted" Alsace?

———◇———

By the next day, Clément had departed for Carcassonne. Viv's fever had abated, but she was still suffering from severe swelling in her cheeks and neck. Following another fitful night's sleep, she pulled herself to a sitting position and wondered when Marcel's sister, Marie, would put her breakfast on the tile floor outside her room?

Marcel suddenly appeared at the threshold, holding a small tray with coffee and a hunk of bread soaked in milk so she could force it between her sore jaws. In the season's sunny days, her host's face had gained a deeper shade of tan. With the thin scar slashing down his left cheek, his powerful but slender figure reminded Viv of a world-weary bullfighter who had lost a match a time or two in the ring.

Setting down her breakfast on a bedside table, he announced without preamble, "If you're to make it across into Spain, you must leave for the mountains tomorrow."

Oh, God... Viv groaned.

He retreated to the doorway and leaned a shoulder against the frame.

"The passes that I was able to obtain for you elapse in two days' time. If you should be stopped without them on the French side, you'd immediately land in jail. It's against the Armistice Agreement, but the Germans are now patrolling the border region here night and day between France and Spain. A pair came by yesterday, but when I said we had someone in bed with the mumps, they left us alone."

Viv stared up at him, wide-eyed. "That was close," she murmured.

To her surprise, Marcel actually cracked a smile.

"The Germans are very strange when it comes to contagious diseases. They're fanatics about cleanliness and health. Mumps, smallpox, measles...they go crazy. Even so, what their visit tells me is that it's not safe for you to stay here any longer. Anyone around here could betray us for money or a loaf of bread."

Viv gazed up at him from the bed, at a complete loss for what she should do or say next. Marcel turned to gaze out the window in the direction of the mountains whose summits were shrouded in a late spring snowstorm.

"The problem's been that I've had the devil of a time trying to find any *passeur* willing to guide you across. The coming storm could be brutal at the summit. Even the seasoned smugglers think it's too big a risk to go tomorrow."

"So, what should I do?" she demanded, sinking back against the bedroom wall. "You're not just going to toss me out to the wolves, are you?"

He let out an audible sigh, either from irritation or exasperation.

"No. I'm going to serve as your *passeur*."

"*You?*" Viv exclaimed. "According to Clément, you're the big cheese around here, even if the Free French movement is practically non-existent these days," she goaded him. Thanks to Clément, she knew as much as Marcel did about the internal squabbling that was wracking the various *résistants* and anti-Vichy groups among the French. "How can *you* be the one to take me across?"

"For unexpected reasons that have nothing to do with you, Miss America, it would seem that I, too, am headed for Spain."

She could tell she'd gored his ox referring to how unreliable so many French citizens were when it came to standing up to their German conquerors.

"Have you ever done the trip?" Just her luck to be guided by a first timer.

Marcel's eyes narrowed. "Consider yourself damn lucky that I have to make the journey myself. But if you choose not to go with me, you are correct. You'll have to leave my place when I do," he added, tight-lipped. "Any other options are non-existent. I tried to get one of the local fishermen to take you along the coast to Barcelona or Valencia, but they all refused."

Viv brightened hearing this. "That sounds like a good solution. I have great sea legs."

"It's not a good idea at all. My sources say the minute you put into any port along the coast, Franco's goons will be certain to lock you up in a remote jail where there isn't an American or British consulate for miles and miles. You're likely to *never* be released, and I don't need to tell you, life in a Spanish prison for a woman can be a very unpleasant."

"Well, can't I just stay here for a while and help with the vineyard until you can get me a new pass?"

Marcel gave an emphatic shake of his head.

"I can't risk my sister and niece's safety having you here any longer. You either come with me tomorrow, or you'll have to fend for yourself."

She was acutely aware that he was calling her bluff to prod her off her bed of pain so she wouldn't be a danger to his sister and niece. In the time she'd been lying in her sickbed, Viv had hardly exchanged a word with either of the women in Marcel's family, but the head of household was obviously protective of them—and she couldn't blame him. She had a sudden memory of the moment he had rushed into the shepherd's hut to drag her under the chassis of the ambulance when the German plane attacked them on the road to Dunkirk. Marcel Delonge might be a prickly son-of-a-gun, but his instincts were to safeguard people, not risk their lives. She found herself oddly disappointed to think his action to save her life was probably just routine with him.

Marcel cocked his head to one side. "You shouldn't be worried about crossing the Pyrenees. Weren't you training for the Olympics before the war started?"

Viv could only stare up at him from the bed. How would he even know that she'd had a short-lived dream to make a British or American ski team? Some file on her *must* have been passed from Kurt to Clément to Marcel. It was obvious that Marcel was determined she'd leave Perpignan and cross the mountains into Spain, come hell or high water.

"The war put an end to any plan about the Olympics," she replied, seeing no need to mention her skiing coach had fired her for her lousy work ethic and lack of discipline.

And then she had another thought: perhaps the "wolves" were closing in on *him* as well. She decided to test his threat to kick her out on her own.

"You're a *poseur,* as much as a *passeur,*" she accused, tilting her swollen chin in a gesture of defiance. "You wouldn't throw me or anyone who hates the Nazis as much as I do into the Krauts' clutches—or Franco's either—if you could help it."

Marcel didn't answer. He regarded her for a long moment. Finally, he asked, "Tell me the truth. Do you think you're well enough to make it across the mountains?"

Secretly, Viv wondered the same thing. Would crossing over a treacherous range like the Pyrenees with a bad case of the mumps actually finish her off? And what grave danger would she put *him* in if she became a burden? If she stayed in Perpignan, she would be putting his entire family—and herself—at risk.

She thought back to her narrow escape at the Swiss border when all the Jews had been caught within feet of Renée and her. She felt a burning sense of outrage that Hitler's goons thought nothing of hurting children like the little girl who dropped her precious doll as she'd fled in terror. In the next moment, Viv experienced a rush of determination unlike any she'd ever known.

I swear I'll make it over the mountains and on to London.

Viv knew, then, there was only one way out of their mutual dilemma.

"When do we leave?" she asked, pain shooting through her neck as she spoke. "And just so you know, I will crawl over the Pyrenees on my knees, if I have to. I've got to complete my mission to London and prove I can be a bona fide intelligence agent."

Marcel gazed at her with a skeptical expression. "Your accent...your height... your half-brown, half-red hair. You'd eventually get caught, you know."

"I'll work on my accent!" she insisted. "And I'll dye my hair all brown again—or maybe even wear a wig. I want to come back to France!"

She swung her legs over the edge of the bed and nearly fell sideways as the room swirled around her in a disconcerting circle. She forced herself to sit up straight, willing him to believe she had found something in her life to which she could totally commit.

"I *know* France, Marcel," she insisted. "I've learned the stupid little things a secret agent must know to avoid getting caught. The right ration cards, the proper color ink on identity documents, the latest jokes. All the little details that matter."

Marcel cocked an eyebrow above his scarred cheek in reaction to the vehemence of her words. He voiced no reaction regarding her vow to return to France as a secret agent.

"Well, if you truly decide to come with me tomorrow," he said over his shoulder as he left the room, "meet me in front of the farm building where I witnessed your collapse on the ground." Turning back to face her he asked," Surely you remember the spot?"

"Of course I remember," she snapped, offended that her impassioned words seemed to make little impression on him. "Don't worry. I'll be there."

"*D'accord.* My sister will wake you at four with coffee and some bread. Eat it, pack the extra food she will leave, and dress in every item of warm clothing you own."

"I wish I hadn't returned that wool hat to Clément," she muttered.

Marcel shot her a stern look. "And don't be late. It may be the end of June, but there's plenty of snow in the high country, and from the looks of the sky right now, we may be getting another dusting." He turned and disappeared from the doorway.

It'll be the Plateau des Glières all over again...or worse.

A few minutes later, Viv was startled when her host reappeared with a wine bottle and two glasses in hand, along with a bundle under his arm.

"I think you need some serious fortification before we set off tomorrow."

"Even before I eat my breakfast?"

She wondered if wine would make her inflamed glands worse. Marcel placed the glasses on her bedside table next to the coffee and bread, then seized the wine bottle and deftly pulled the cork. Pouring from a label that read *Cuvée Bisconte Chateau Delonge 1937,* he handed her the other glass.

"Before we drink, I have something else for you." From under one arm he withdrew two pairs of heavy woolen socks. He tossed them onto the coverlet at the foot of her bed. "They fit me, and since I've had a closeup view of your feet, I'm guessing they'll come close to fitting you, too. Wear the heavy pair on your way up the mountain, and the lighter one as we descend. The proper socks can prevent blisters, you know."

Viv grimaced again at the thought of Marcel rubbing ointment on her lacerated feet and bottom the first day she'd arrived in Perpignan.

"Well, here's to your improving health," he said, raising a glass in her direction. The Delonge vintage glowed the color of garnets in the morning sun that glinted through the window facing the Pyrenees. "If anyone can cross that snow-packed track up there with a raging case of the mumps, it will be *you,* Miss America."

He was watching her with obvious interest as she gingerly took a sip of the wine. Despite the pain in her jaw and her scratchy throat, her mouth reveled in the taste of Grenache redolent of dark berries, soft and ripe on her tongue.

"Well?" he asked, for once a supplicant of her good opinion.

"I can barely swallow," she replied, enjoying a perverse satisfaction that she was refusing to offer him a deserved compliment on his excellent vintage. Why did this man challenge every fiber in her body, and yet draw her to him like butter on toast, she thought crossly? She set aside her glass and fell back against her pillow, feeling as ill and miserable as ever. In a fit of pique, she pulled the bedcovers up to her swollen chin.

"I can't drink anymore," she mumbled.

"Until tomorrow, then," Marcel said.

He abruptly left her room, taking his wine bottle and the two glasses with him.

"Until tomorrow," she managed to whisper with no one nearby to hear—and no one to calm the onset of fear that had begun to gnaw at her gut.

CHAPTER 26

Viv's world inside the moving farm truck in the shadow of the Pyrenees was black and cold. A trusted vineyard worker had driven Marcel and her along a remote dirt road that led to a narrow bridge where they stopped. A light dusting of snowflakes coated the wooden boards they were now poised to cross. Viv would never admit it to Marcel, but she was more than grateful for the extra pair of socks donated by her new *passeur* that she'd put on over her own. Her boots were snug and, thus far, her feet were warm. But given the biting cold, it was anybody's guess how long that would last.

"Too bad about the weather, *patron*," the driver said, ignoring the presence of the other passenger. He offered a brief nod as Marcel reached for the door handle, a pair of binoculars in his other hand. "Goodbye and good luck, sir."

"Thank you, François," he replied, slipping the leather strap over his head and settling the field glasses against his chest. "And remember, you have no idea when I left or where I've gone, understand? As for her," Marcel added with a curt nod in Viv's direction, "if anyone asks, she was too sick to help at the vineyard and returned to Alsace. *Your* life and your family's—as well as ours and my sister and niece's—depend upon keeping this morning's activities a secret." He clapped a hand on the driver's shoulder. "It may be a while before the Delonge Vineyards see me again."

"I know nothing, *patron*," he replied solemnly. "*Au revoir*."

"Good luck with the fall harvest while I'm gone."

"We will do our best, *patron*."

Viv couldn't help wondering if this farm manager would remain loyal if ever questioned harshly by authorities while the vineyard's owner was away. Pushing aside such a gloomy thought, she exited the truck and stood on the frost-covered ground.

The farm vehicle made a turn and retreated down the road, its noisy engine giving way to the sound of the fast-moving river a few feet from the road. Marcel knelt on the bank to fill the gourd he carried with icy water and then slung its strap over one shoulder. He gestured to Viv that it was time to set out across the slick, rickety bridge where the trail disappeared around a bend.

At first the going was fairly easy. They climbed up a rocky track that Viv assumed had been carved by goats. She soon began to wonder, though, how quickly the blisters on her heels would reappear, given patches of her skin were still pink and tender.

Within another mile, she had her answer and had to slow her pace.

Even in these low foothills, the unseasonable overnight storm had left a thin coating of new snow in its wake. Marcel, far in the lead, moved uphill along pastureland toward a pine forest where the soft, spring powder grew deeper with each step. He waited for her at the next ridge, lifting the binoculars to his eyes to stare down the trail.

When she caught up with him, he said, "We're lucky that we only got a half-foot from that spring storm, so try to keep up. It will get much colder the higher we go," he warned. He sought her gaze. "Viv, I do realize how sick you've been, but we have to keep a good pace." He raised his field glasses again and made a small gesture. "I just spotted two soldiers at the bottom of the trail that might be Germans or Vichy. They were gazing up in our direction for a long time. If we can just get to the next ridge, I doubt they'll try to tackle the mountain, dressed as they are."

"Troops? Oh, God!" Viv exclaimed. "What if they take aim at us as we—"

Marcel interrupted and grabbed her by the hand, "Whoever they might be, we're nearly out of range. Let's go!" He turned and started pulling her up the path.

Feeling like she had a target on her back, Viv stumbled along behind him. She was already chilled to the bone and painfully aware that the swelling in her cheeks and under each ear had hardly diminished. Her hands and feet were numb now, but her face had begun to feel alarmingly warm. What if her high fever was coming back? What if those soldiers were following them? She repeatedly glanced behind her but could see nothing beyond a few feet of the rocky trail receding downhill as they kept climbing.

Marcel said over his shoulder, "We haven't heard shots yet, so let's hope that whoever those guys were decided we weren't worth the chase."

If they'd started their trek even ten minutes later, Viv thought, they could have been picked off by sharpshooters. But would those soldiers somehow get word to any confederates in Spain that two escapees were headed in their direction?

She and Marcel climbed for another hour, entering a biting, swirling mist that rendered the hillside nearly invisible, making it impossible to gauge what lay ahead.

More cliffs, she guessed glumly, a stitch in her side stabbing her ribcage. Marcel had finally let go of her hand and again picked up the pace. She soldiered on, her mind a blank except for watching first one boot, then the other, take step-after-step in terrain that grew steeper with each passing minute. She had no idea how many hours had elapsed, but afternoon shadows had begun to stretch across their path.

"There's a small chalet at the summit," Marcel informed her, looking back. "We can build a fire and you'll soon get warm."

The only way Viv found she could keep going was to grab for low-hanging branches of wind-blown trees and pull herself forward, hand-over-hand. That was, until there were no more trees to hold onto. She forced her mind to focus on the promised cabin and a fire to warm her hands and feet—but how far away *was* it?

Soon, they started up a trail flanked by sheer escarpments of rock on one side and a terrifying drop downhill on the other. With each step, every part of Viv's body that wasn't numb ached with the falling temperature.

I was completely insane to do this. I will die on this mountain. I can't...take...another step.

Viv collapsed against a large, slanted, snow-covered limestone rock, squinting through the mist as Marcel disappeared around a curve in the trail. Lulled by the utter quiet and a crushing fatigue, she closed her eyes as the mountains faded into oblivion.

———◇———

"Viv! Viv! Get up! Come on, now! You *must* get up!"

Marcel's commands were harsh, slicing into the cold silence that had cocooned her in its soporific embrace. She forced open her eyes. Marcel's expression was grim, the scar on his cheek white against his tanned skin.

She peered down at the path they'd trod that was swallowed up by mist.

"Oh, no!" she whispered, her shoulders shivering uncontrollably. "A-Are the Germans right behind us?"

"No," Marcel replied. "But you've *got* to keep going or you'll freeze to death."

All feeling had left her hands. Even so, he grabbed her arms and hauled her to her feet. Snatching her knapsack from her shoulder, he slung it over his own next to the strap attached to his water gourd. He held one of her hands in an iron grip, literally dragging her up the mountain behind him.

She would never understand how she struggled on, her feet having no feeling of where she was setting them down or picking them up. Her neck and jaw were as sore as ever, made worse by her teeth chattering in the biting cold as they climbed higher.

"Stop!" she screamed finally. "You have to let me catch my breath!"

Marcel obeyed her command, and sat beside her on another flat, snow-covered rock that faced the sheer precipice a few feet across from them. His arm around her shoulder, she inhaled deep, steadying breaths and began to feel a strange surge of energy.

"Just give me another second, will you?" she croaked, her voice sounding hoarse to her own ears. She took several more gulps of frigid air deep into her lungs. "I-I think I'm actually getting a second wind," she said, marveling at the slight but noticeable increase of energy. She met his gaze. "You don't have to drag me anymore, so let go of my hand."

"Good that you're breathing better," he said, "but I'll keep hold of one hand to make sure you don't fall off the cliff."

Fortunately, they were approaching the top of another steep incline where a dilapidated wooden shelter offered them a brief break from the wind.

After a few more minutes rest, Marcel insisted, "We have to move on." His voice was urgent and sounded as raspy as hers. "The cabin's on the next ridge where we can rest for the night, but we have to get there before dark." His gloved fingers pushed aside her woolen scarf and his searching gaze surveyed her neck.

Viv asked, "Still swollen, right?"

She remembered the doctor's words about serious complications from mumps and wondered, suddenly, if the next thing she knew, she'd go deaf.

"Still swollen," he confirmed with a nod, "but a little less so, I think." Then he braced his fingers under her chin, leaned forward, brushing his cold lips against the lumps protruding from each cheek. He leaned back. "Your skin feels warm. I'm afraid your fever may have come back."

Oh, God...what if I get horribly sick again and put Marcel's life at risk...

Before she could even finish the thought, Marcel urged, "Let's get you to the cabin. C'mon...it's not much farther."

Viv nodded, thinking how nice it felt to be kissed but suddenly worried that she might still be contagious.

"I heard you tell the doctor you had the mumps when you were a boy. Can a person get it twice?"

"You're worried that your *passeur* might collapse before we reach Spain?" he asked, his lips in a straight line, but his eyes filled with something akin either to amusement or possible pleasure that she might be concerned for his health. "Don't worry," he assured. "Most people believe this plague only strikes once." A gleam of triumph in his eye, he urged, "Come, you've nearly made it! We've only a few more kilometers to go."

———◇———

Despite the welcome offered by a small, dilapidated structure situated a good way off the trail they'd been following, Viv felt as miserable as ever. They had arrived at a narrow plateau that looked down on Spain in the far distance. Fortunately, a cluster of trees and shrubs hid the rugged wooden sanctuary from the view of anyone who didn't know where it was. Once inside, Viv's feet tingled painfully the more the numbness from the cold wore off. Shivering wracked her body even as her face felt hot.

Luckily, there were a few logs near the hearth left by previous travelers that had stayed overnight in the warming hut. One piece of wood in the stack was actually a scarred, wooden rifle butt.

"It probably belonged to someone in the Republican Army," Marcel speculated, selecting it from the pile and throwing it on the fire. "The defeated troops fighting Franco's dictatorship took this escape route in '39, fleeing into France."

"Oh, that's right," replied Viv wearily, accepting a drink of water from Marcel's gourd. "We're sneaking into the victor's country, aren't we?"

"Yes. The home of a strongman just like Hitler," Marcel reminded her. "Fortunately, the Brits at the consulate in Barcelona have been alerted to look for us in jail should we be arrested on our descent."

"How reassuring," Viv murmured, sinking to the floor in front of the fire and wrapping her woolen scarf around her torso like a shawl. "But how do you know that they expect us? The Brits, I mean?"

Marcel shrugged. "Friends in high places?"

"You've done this journey plenty of times before, haven't you?" she declared. "You knew this hidden hut was at the top of the trail."

"I've lived in Perpignan most of my life, before and after I was in the army. Everyone around here knows these trails."

"Except the *Boche*, I hope.

"They've only recently started sneaking from the Free Zone into the area around Perpignan. I doubt any have discovered this place—yet."

"But *you* knew about this place. You know about everything," she asserted.

"Let us hope I know enough to have gotten a message to the right person at the British Consulate," he said.

"I suppose I could also contact the American Consulate in Barcelona to come bail us out if we get arrested when we enter Spain."

Marcel shook his head in the negative. "If I were you, I wouldn't let them know you're hoping to work for British intelligence," he advised.

"Why ever not?" she protested. "Aren't Britain and America *allies* in this war?"

"Allen Dulles rejected you for an assignment in France, yes?" asked Marcel. Viv stared at him, startled he knew about this embarrassment. "And so," he continued as if he'd read a report, which Viv now assumed he had, "you were handed off by the sympathetic Swiss intelligence agent to a network of *résistants* fighters in France, one that's desperate for the Brits to help their clandestine activities, correct?"

"Yes but—"

Marcel interrupted. "So, trust me. Only deal with the Brits, and for now, forget about the Americans if you want to get back to France to try to help. At this stage, the English are much better organized than the—how you call them? The Yanks?"

Clément must have told Marcel everything about my last few months...

"So, what group are *you* with?" Viv demanded, wondering if the enigmatic Marcel Delonge would ever give her a straight answer.

He surprised her.

"When I left the Foreign Legion, I served in the regular army with de Gaulle. He's dependent on the Brits now, so I have to be in two camps: de Gaulle's and his benefactors in Britain."

"Why did you join the Legion?" she asked, her curiosity about the man piqued.

Marcel's eyes lowered to half-mast. "You ask too many questions, but why do you suppose most men join?" was his curt rejoinder.

"Because they're escaping something. What bad-boy thing did *you* do?"

"It was my young wife whom you might consider 'bad.' When I returned from fighting in the Great War, she'd run off with a neighbor of ours."

Viv grimaced, immediately penitent. "That's terrible! I'm so sorry."

"We divorced, which was a scandal, and I took off. A simple story."

"And you never married again?"

"You *are* a pushy, inquisitive American!" he exclaimed with a look of irritation. "No. I never married again and don't ever intend to!" He offered a mock leer. "But girlfriends are fine...now that I've recovered from my latest round of shrapnel."

"In your dreams, Colonel Hush-Hush!"

Marcel snorted a laugh and guided the conversation away from his personal life, returning to the subject of de Gaulle. "I doubt the Americans know or care that much about Charles de Gaulle—and if they do—I think they consider him a mere upstart."

"So does Clément," Viv said, waiting for his reaction.

"Clément is a good man, but he only supports the *Savoyards* fighters in the Alps. As you may have observed, he doesn't like any central authority telling him what to do." Marcel paused. "But if we want to drive out the Nazis from France, all sides are going to have to come together and coordinate their efforts."

"Hmmm...it all sounds complicated to me." Viv felt her calves beginning to cramp in reaction to the long, uphill trek they'd made. Fatigue was once again invading every bone in her body. From her place on the floor near the hearth, she leaned over and began to rub her legs vigorously with both hands. Keeping her gaze focused on her calves, she conceded, "I'll consider what you've said, though, about not contacting the Americans—at least until I play it out with the Brits."

"And you should know by now, in the spy game, there are invariably bureaucratic turf wars, even within the same intelligence services. That's another reason that, even with your dual citizenship, it's better if you declare for one group or the other."

"Well, since my own country wouldn't employ my clandestine skills, such as they are," she groused, "the Brits are sounding better by the minute."

When she quit rubbing her legs, she curled up on the floor as close to the hearth as she could without catching on fire. To her surprise, Marcel also lay down, settling himself next to her.

"Here," he said, stretching out and tucking her body within the contours of his own. "Pretend you're a spoon."

"Marcel!" she protested, thinking of their previous conversation about girlfriends.

"Don't get too excited," he said, his warm breath brushing against her ear. "It's what soldiers learn in survival training to keep from freezing to death during the night."

"Ummmm, body heat," Viv murmured.

The sensation of him cradling her backside was distracting in the extreme, made even more so when he pulled her ever closer, his warm breath ruffling the hair on the back of her head. She matched him inhale for exhale. Soon, her fatigue was more potent than even the heat of Marcel's body glued to hers. Reveling in a remarkable sense of safety, she began to relax as if encased in a wonderful, warm hammock. She recalled their strange embrace under the ambulance chassis when the German plane's tail gunner shot at them, and before she knew it, sheer exhaustion lulled her into a deep sleep.

———◇———

As dawn broke, a shaft of sunlight bathed Viv's eyes, forcing her to pry them open. Still squinting, she watched Marcel pour water from his gourd into a cup he'd heated over the fire with a spoonful of coffee grounds. He swirled it with a stick.

"Drink this, eat some bread, and then off we go," he said. "How do you feel?"

Viv cupped both her hands around the swollen mounds protruding from each cheek.

"Pretty rotten, I'm afraid."

"Well, at least it's downhill from this plateau. Time to get going."

"No sign of any Nazis climbing up here?" she asked, sensing they had returned to their *passeur/voyageuse* relationship.

Marcel snorted a laugh and pointed to the field glasses slung around his neck.

"No sign of them, *chérie. Allons-y.* Let's go," he repeated in English.

She began to gather her belongings and then stood stock-still. On the table was the colorful Hermès scarf in which she had wrapped the bread and cheese for Marcel before he'd dashed down the cliff at Dunkirk. This day, the silk square held the remnants of their morning meal. Marcel met her astonished gaze and gave a shrug. He swiftly seized the scarf and shook it out with studied nonchalance, stuffing it into his haversack.

"Yes, your lovely Hermès. With it, I miraculously made it safely back to England, remember? It's now my...how do you say in America? My lucky rabbit's foot."

Viv was speechless. She returned what she hoped was an equally nonchalant shrug. Then she bent over to pull on the other set of wool socks Marcel had advised her to wear on their descent. Her every muscle complained, along with the soles of her feet. Standing once again, she raised her arms, clasped her hands over her head, and leaned side-to-side to stretch out the worst of her body's kinks.

Once leaving the cabin behind, the two tramped across the rest of the plateau and were soon headed down a steep trail. With each step, the air grew warmer. In front of them was a horizon free of snow.

———◇———

Just as Marcel had predicted, Franco's sharp-eyed soldiers on patrol spotted them in the lower foothills and immediately incarcerated the "illegal refugees," herding the two of them into the same filthy cell in Figueres, a town outside Barcelona.

The smell inside their narrow confines nearly made Viv gag. Marcel gently chucked her under her swollen chin.

"Have faith, Miss America. I'm sure the cavalry is on the way."

"You've watched American cowboy movies, have you?"

"A few," he acknowledged.

"They played them in Perpignan?" she asked skeptically.

He laughed, and then lowered his voice so the guard wouldn't hear him say in English, "No. I saw them when I lived in Washington D.C. for a time."

"*What*? When was *that*?" she demanded.

Marcel put a finger to his lips. "You never heard me say that."

———◇———

Looking back a day later, Viv figured it was some kind of miracle, courtesy of Marcel's "friends in high places," that the British attaché in Barcelona arrived at their jail within hours to argue for their release. In Switzerland, she and Renée Reynolds had only been detained at the border for a day. A Spanish jail was an entirely different matter, and Viv was hugely relieved when the British functionary waved his magic wand—or more likely—a wad of *pesetas*—and a local judge ordered them set free.

That same day, she and Marcel were escorted to Madrid, and from there to the British base at Gibraltar a few miles across the water from the North African city of Morocco. The narrow waterway between the two points of land straddled the gateway between the Spanish Gulf of Cádiz—and beyond it, the Atlantic Ocean. In the opposite direction lay the Mediterranean Sea. Within seventy-two hours, Marcel had been whisked away on some military transport plane. Meanwhile, Viv had been left to cool her heels in the town of Gibraltar until passage to Britain by boat could be arranged.

Before his departure, Marcel imparted his final advice in the lobby of the modest hotel at which an unnamed British consular official had arranged for them to stay. Viv had seen little of Marcel, which left her feeling oddly miffed. They bid farewell in the lobby, where he handed her a scrap of hotel stationery with notes in his scrawl.

"If you're still serious about wanting to work for France's liberation, here's the name of someone to look up when you get to London."

It read:

Vera Atkins, assist. to Col. Maurice Buckmaster,
SOE – French Section, 64 Baker Street, London

There was a telephone number added below. Viv stared at the note.

"'Baker Street?' Of Sherlock Holmes fame?"

"The very place, although if you're considered for a job in intelligence, you'll probably first be sent for an interview to Orchard Court around the corner."

"What, exactly, does 'S.O.E.' stand for?" she asked.

Marcel threw back his head and laughed, the skin near the scar that began just below his eyes crinkling with unbridled amusement.

"You really *are* a baby spy, aren't you?" he said, enclosing her hand holding the note in his and giving it a squeeze. "The SOE is Britain's Special Operations Executive, an intelligence branch under MI6, but rather independent from it. For its part, MI6 considers Churchill's new SOE agents 'amateurs,' but I've heard F Section is pretty desperate to recruit French speakers, wherever they're from."

"Even *me*, although I'm ridiculously tall and my natural hair is too bright?" she challenged, wondering why she'd seen virtually nothing of him while in Gibraltar.

He gazed down at her. "I like how tall you are, and your hair is stunning, but both make you conspicuous. And yes, your French accent *is* atrocious, to say nothing of the fact that you ask too many questions and talk back to your superiors."

The former French Army colonel was teasing her, she knew, but he had continued to hold her hand. Viv suddenly felt bereft at the notion he would soon disappear in a plane flying to God-knew-where.

For a long moment, they looked into each other's eyes, neither of them pulling away.

Marcel said, "The women recruited to SOE's French Section are nicknamed 'Churchill's Angels' because it was *his* notion that women agents could operate in France with less suspicion than draft-age men. How amusing if you, the most un-angelic woman I have ever met, become one of them."

"What a compliment," she said, jutting her chin in the air.

"It is, actually."

Viv felt her breath catch, and for a moment she couldn't think what to say. Finally she murmured, "I just want to be sent back to France to try to do some good if I can."

And still Marcel kept hold of her hand.

He said quietly, "The SOE would be lucky to have you, but you'd be much better off in America, Viv. Things are going to get really bad in occupied countries before anything starts to get better—if it ever does. A lot of us will die."

Marcel...die? No! Not ever...

Viv tried to ignore the jolt of electricity that traveled from the hand he held directly into her solar plexus. Marcel leaned forward, brushing his lips European style against either side of her cheeks where the painful swelling had finally subsided.

Murmuring into her ear, he said, "The Brits are fully aware of your admirable deeds escorting Jews from France into Switzerland. They also are informed about how you got yourself back into France, unscathed, and climbed over the Pyrenees to Spain, sick as a dog. If you're determined to return to France, I say make the most of it, *chérie*."

Viv withdrew her hand and leaned away from him.

"And how do the Brits know all that about me?" she demanded, the memory of his farewell kiss now imprinted not only on her cheeks, but also buried in her brain.

Marcel was clearly trying to tame a self-satisfied smile.

"With the good word I put in for you with our escort to Gibraltar about your guts crossing the mountains with a bad case of the mumps, at the very least you might stand a chance getting a post somewhere in the London intelligence maze. It's a job that will keep your body and soul together for a while until you can re-contact your family."

"I have no family I wish to 're-contact,'" she replied sharply. "And I don't want to end up in London just typing up meeting notes for a bunch of desk-jockeys!" she protested. "I want to actually *do* something in France to fight the Nazis."

"Then, definitely, Vera Atkins at SOS is your best contact."

And with that, Marcel had turned to go.

Impulsively she'd asked, "Can't you at least tell me where you're flying to?"

Marcel swiveled his head. "No. Of course I can't."

He bent down to take hold of a new, smart-looking, Moroccan leather suitcase he'd somehow acquired during their stay in Gibraltar. Standing to his full height, he was at least half a head taller than she was.

"So, I guess this *is* goodbye," she said, avoiding his glance.

"Yes, it is…but you never know." She looked up at him in time to catch another glint of amusement in his dark eyes. "We've met twice, now," he said. "Once when I was wounded. The second time, when you were ill. Who knows if a third time's the charm?"

And with that, he'd headed down the hotel's entrance stairs and opened the rear passenger door of a waiting car that would take him to his plane at the airbase.

Viv walked beyond the hotel foyer and stood in the warmth of a sultry Gibraltar afternoon. She gazed down on the car and the steep, winding street that offered a view of the harbor below and the famous cliffs etched against a blue sky. Just before Marcel slipped into the rear passenger seat, he glanced up and saw that she had followed him out of the hotel. He broke into a rare grin as if he'd won a silent bet with himself.

Sensing that, she merely nodded her head in reply to his jaunty salute and showed him her back, marching stiffly into the hotel lobby.

He's gone...and in this war, I seriously doubt we'll ever meet a third time...

PART III
CHAPTER 27

London, Summer 1942

Viv stepped onto English soil with a sense of near disbelief that she'd managed to survive her rough Atlantic voyage on a tramp steamer dodging German U-boats en route. Once in London, her entire life turned upside down again—and all because Colonel Marcel Delonge had obviously "put in a good word for her."

In fact, he must have put in several good words with the powers-that-be in the "maze," as he had called it, of British intelligence services. Much to Viv's surprise and pleasure, her call to the office of Vera Atkins the day she arrived in London resulted in two appointments scheduled at the SOE's French Section that same afternoon.

Even more surprising, her first meeting with Maurice Buckmaster, the director of SOE's "F Section," had been an absolute breeze. Viv could only surmise that the man, as Marcel had indicated, was truly desperate for agents not only willing to risk their lives for low pay behind enemy lines, but also candidates that spoke less-than-perfect French.

Viv was shown into a small, unremarkable office in what appeared to be a former apartment bedroom. It was part of an ordinary block of residential flats in Orchard Court adjacent to Baker Street. Author Sir Arthur Conan Doyle had placed the residence of the fictional Sherlock Holmes at Number 22, with SOE's official headquarters at Number 64.

"New recruits never go to Number 64," Marcel had explained

when they were in Gibraltar, "but are first interviewed just around the corner."

"Too hush-hush for baby spies?" Viv had asked wryly, and Marcel had pulled a droll expression. "*C'est vrai*. Too true."

Colonel Buckmaster awaited Viv's arrival perched on the corner of his desk. As she expected, he was clad in a British Army uniform, and as soon as she crossed the threshold, he stood to his full, lanky height and extended his hand in greeting.

"Ah... Miss Vivier-Clarke. Delighted to meet you at last."

He resumed his place poised on the edge of his desk, his long legs sheathed in crisp khaki swinging back and forth as he eagerly asked her about her initial journey across the border from occupied France into Switzerland.

After she'd described her particularly harrowing escape, along with the unfortunate capture of the Jewish refugees in her group, Buckmaster nodded in sympathy and swiftly followed up with his next question.

"And then, I understand, you did the reverse? Is it true you managed to sneak back *into* France again without getting apprehended by the border guards on either side?"

Not wanting to put the Swiss agent "Kurt" in any professional jeopardy, she cautiously explained, "A very nice person whose identity I'd prefer not to reveal made all the arrangements. I merely followed his instructions and managed to get through the barbed wire unscathed just after the guards made their rounds." She paused for breath. "But, sir, there is something far more important about that trip that I need to tell you."

She leaned toward him and recited from memory all she had been asked to convey from Julien, the *maquisard* she'd conferred with in the chalet atop the Plateau des Glières near Lake Annecy.

"They say they'll soon have a thousand recruits to prepare the way for an Allied invasion coming from either the north or south," she declared, encouraged that the colonel's gaze had remained riveted on her the entire time she'd been speaking. "More young men have been arriving each day, but they need supplies. Food, weapons, ammunition...that sort of thing." She paused and then added, "They are willing to lay down their lives to free their country, Colonel. They desperately need Britain's help."

Buckmaster reached back and seized a file from his desk, fingering the corner.

"Well, thank you for all that. Most interesting."

"Would you like me to write it up in a report?" she asked, concerned by his tempered response that the colonel hadn't taken Julien's urgent requests to heart. In her mind's eye, she could see the line of civilian recruits sitting on wooden benches in the chalet, listening to their leader in awe. With a sinking feeling that she was failing the young fighters, she said, "Julien Paquet insisted I only memorize what he wanted me to tell you, so there would be no other record of his requests that might be stolen as I made my way here. He'd want you to have the details—"

"Sounds like a good man," Buckmaster interrupted approvingly, but he didn't take her up on her offer to make notes of Julien's petition. Instead, he pointed to the file in his hand and said, "I also understand that you crossed the Pyrenees with a rather painful case of the mumps. Quite remarkable, I must say. Tell me about it."

"At first, I thought it was a toothache," Viv confessed with some embarrassment, "but by the time I arrived near the French-Spanish border, a doctor confirmed I had a pretty bad case."

"But all that didn't stop you from getting yourself to Perpignan, though, did it?" he said with admiration. "And you *still* made it over the mountains. Good show, m'girl!"

Without any further questioning, he abruptly bid her to come with him out of his office and escorted her down a short hallway. Viv followed in his wake, a feeling of frustration and failure dogging her steps.

"I hope, sir," she said as they reached a door on the right, "that you'll seriously consider the requests I've conveyed about the Plateau des Glières *maquis*—"

But Buckmaster had already entered another nondescript room that also might have been a former bedroom.

"Vera Atkins," he said jocularly, "may I present our new American friend, Miss Constance Vivier-Clarke."

"Please call me Viv," Viv hastened to add, taking a seat where indicated.

The colonel addressed his deputy, "Ah... Viv and I had a most interesting chat. Now, I leave it to you, Vera, to handle the details."

Buckmaster backed out of the room, leaving Viv with a vexing level of uncertainty whether her messages from the desperate *maquis* would be given the slightest attention by the country likeliest to provide weapons and needed supplies.

Her new questioner smiled and said, "I'm so pleased your file says that, besides your native tongue, you speak French, Italian, and some German."

Before Viv could reply, Vera Atkins commenced conducting the interview alternating smoothly between the three declared foreign languages she spoke as well.

Startled by the woman's flawless French, Viv did her best to concentrate on the rapid-fire questions asked by Buckmaster's deputy. Even so, she couldn't help noticing that her inquisitor was a handsome woman, perhaps in her late thirties or early forties, with softly permed dark hair, distinctive arched eyebrows, and bright red lipstick. She was clad in a smartly tailored suit and silk blouse that appeared to match her curious combination of toughness and empathy.

For more than forty minutes, Atkins quizzed Viv closely about every phase of her adult life, switching languages without warning as she jumped from topic to topic. Her inquisitor probed Viv as to her attitude toward her schooling in Switzerland. Then, in Italian, she pressed her closely about time spent after Viv had concluded her education.

"I understand you traveled quite a bit throughout Europe. You got as far south as Greece, I understand. Doing what, may I ask?"

"Not much of anything useful, I confess," Viv replied, her mind spinning over choices of Italian vocabulary. "At that stage of my early twenties, I really didn't have any idea what I would do next. What I was even *fit* to do, frankly. I began to get a sense of direction when I volunteered for the ambulance corps at the American Hospital in Paris."

Atkins nodded and glanced down at the papers on her desk.

Looking up she smiled as if the interview might be over. She switched to English, asking, "Do tell me a bit about your passion for skiing. You had a skiing coach, did you? Hoping to try out for the Winter Olympics? I understand you didn't make a team."

Viv tried to disguise her amazement that Atkins would know anything about that.

"I was good, but not *that* good."

It was an honest answer—as far as it went.

Atkins smiled faintly and then asked, "What places did you ski in France? Chamonix? Albertville? Val d'Isère? I quite liked that place when I was a younger woman and had time for that sort of thing."

"Chamonix was my favorite," Viv answered promptly. Relaxing against the back of the chair, she added, "My father taught me to ski as a very young child in upstate New York…three or four-years-old, I remember. He was a wonderful coach, I guess you'd say. Kind. Encouraging, even when I took a tumble. I've always loved skiing… such a sense of freedom schussing down mountains, don't you think?" Atkins merely nodded. Viv continued, "And of course, when I was sent to school in Switzerland by my mother and stepfather, I skied at all the usual resorts. But in France, for sure I love Chamonix the best. I never made it to Val d'Isère, though," she disclosed. "It's pretty remote."

Abruptly switching topics and languages again, Miss Atkins began to query Viv in German on the specifics of her time in Berlin. Why had she gone there? What had she seen? Did she have views about her stepfather doing business there?

"I hated Berlin," Viv said, unable to keep her bitterness from showing. "Karl Bradford insisted I learn some German, so I went to language classes for six months, but I couldn't wait to leave. I thought he was wrong to have anything to do with the place. Those rallies," she shuddered. "I had no idea of how bad it was going to get back then, but I saw from those frantic, adoring mobs that Hitler was eventually going to be a threat to Europe. To the entire free world." She met Miss Atkins' gaze and said in English, "I am ashamed my mother married a man like my stepfather, who has aided and abetted Britain and France's enemy. I hope you understand that."

Atkins offered a slight nod and moved on to exploring the methods Viv had employed sneaking out of and then back into France, followed by the tale of her trek over the Pyrenees into Spain.

"I am a bit curious," Atkins asked pleasantly, "why you turned to the British Consulate, rather than the American, to make arrangements to come to Great Britain and show your interest in joining us here at the SOE?"

Viv stared at the papers on her questioner's desk.

"My willingness to return to France to aid in the Resistance was initially turned down by the Americans in Switzerland," she disclosed, wondering if she was completely blowing her chances with the SOE. "At first Allen Dulles in Bern said he was giving me an assignment as a courier. Then, the Geneva mission called and said they'd gotten someone else for the job. Fortunately, a different opportunity immediately presented itself, so I decided to see if I could offer my help to Britain—the other country where I hold citizenship," she finished, meeting Atkins' steady gaze.

"And why are you feeling compelled to offer your services to the Allies in the *first* place?"

Viv sensed this was the all-important question to intelligence officers like Atkins. *Why* was she, an American, willing to risk all to help rid France of its oppressors?

"My father was French-American and loved France, and I've always loved it, too," she began. "I've seen the cruelty of Nazism first-hand. The brutality toward the innocent," she said, her voice dropping so low Vera Atkins leaned closer to hear her. "It wasn't just the rallies in Berlin I witnessed. It was what they're doing to the children. To one family, in particular, that I tried to help across the border, but they were caught. A little Jewish girl was taken…" Viv pictured the doll she'd picked up off the ground and stored in her knapsack. "I just thought, 'I can't *bear* this. It has to be stopped.'"

Atkins remained silent for several moments. Then she said, "And you made your way across France and Spain through some very difficult circumstances, I understand."

Viv merely nodded. Then Atkins switched topics again.

"When you were at Lake Annecy, what was your opinion of the *maquis* you met with on the Plateau des Glières? How reliable a fighting force did you judge them to be?"

Viv attempted to hide her surprise. Buckmaster hadn't had time to tell anyone what she'd told *him* just now about Julien and his loyal men, so how the hell did this Atkins woman know anything about her rendezvous with the *résistants* in the Alps?

Then it hit her.

Marcel! Marcel has met with Buckmaster and Atkins! Clément must have told Marcel everything about my going to the Plateau des Glières—and Marcel told these two.

While Viv answered her question that the forces were young and needed training and weapons but were willing to risk their lives... her mind was a whirl.

If Marcel had met with the SOE brass recently, wasn't it possible that Colonel Hush-Hush was *still* in London? The lurch in Viv's stomach nearly knocked her off her chair.

Will this interview ever end?

Vera Atkins relaxed once again and smiled.

"Well, you certainly have lived up to your advanced publicity, but I am a bit worried about your French accent, Viv. Even though you and I speak a common language or two," she said, her lips turning up with amusement, "I'm afraid that I detect when you speak French the pronounced hint you're definitely from the eastern United States."

Merde! Hadn't Marcel said the same thing? she moaned inwardly.

Miss Atkins continued, "It could present a bit of a problem if we try to pass you off in occupied France as a native. And you are quite tall for a typical European."

Viv, fighting a sense the interview was suddenly veering in the wrong direction quickly volunteered, "Well, my father also was tall...his family was originally from Alsace. He—"

"Yes, I know, poor man. Died serving in the Great War, I understand. Bailed out over the Channel, did he? Malfunctioning parachute?"

Viv swallowed hard and remained silent. She'd never told Marcel about the way her father had died.

They know everything about me...

Staring across the desk at Vera Atkins, Viv had the distinct sense that Buckmaster's deputy was debating the pros and cons of her resumé. Obviously, Viv was someone who had lived in France under the Nazi boot and had coped very well. But what about her reputation with the skiing coach as a "washout?" But then Viv thought, perhaps with a war raging, they couldn't contact him?

Miss Atkins rose from her chair, indicating their interview was, finally, over.

"I think we have everything we need," she declared. "Thank you so much for contacting us. Let us know where you'll be staying in London, and we'll be in touch."

Viv left her second meeting of the day in a swirl of anxiety. After all this, would she get a call—as she did after her sessions with Allen Dulles—informing her that her abilities weren't up to snuff? On the other hand, weren't recruits who had at least a grasp of French so desperately needed that she would be accepted as an SOE trainee? If she were, would she be sent to what she'd heard referred to in whispers as "Spy School?"

The alternative—being stuck at a desk job typing reports in some bureaucrat's office at the War Ministry in bombed-out London—filled her with dread.

CHAPTER 28

"Call for you, miss," said Viv's new landlady following a knock at her door.

Two days had passed since her interviews at the SOE. In the interim, Viv thought she'd go mad with the lack of news one way or the other.

"Thank you, Mrs. Jennens," she said, her heart beginning to pound alarmingly. She followed the woman out of her rented room in a Notting Hill "Young Lady's Residence" and sped down the hall. As soon as she'd picked up the receiver, an unidentified male voice declared he was calling at Colonel Maurice Buckmaster's behest.

"We'd like to take your potential enlistment to the next step. Would it be possible for you to report to Wamborough House in two days' time?"

"Y-yes, of course!" she exclaimed, nearly exploding with joy and relief. Then she asked, "Where *is* that, by the way?"

"In the New Forest, outside London," he answered, his tone just shy of insulted that she, an ignorant Yank, didn't know as much. "I suppose it's best if I just take down your address and send a car to fetch you on Thursday around eleven o'clock."

"Wonderful!" Viv declared, and then lowered her voice. "Please tell Colonel Buckmaster I'm delighted to accept."

"Yes, miss," he replied, evenly. "Be advised, though, that at Wamborough, you'll go through a further psychological assessment before being accepted as a recruit."

"And if I pass muster, what's next?" she asked, disappointed to learn there was still another hurdle to clear. In fact, probably several she hadn't even thought of.

The voice answered in clipped tones, "You'll be advised from there, Miss Vivier-Clarke." He proceeded to dictate an address where she could be fitted for "an appropriate military uniform. Arrive there today before closing at five, please. The master-sergeant in charge will be expecting you," and the disembodied voice hung up.

Viv replaced the phone receiver and leaned one shoulder against the wall. She could only guess Buckmaster must have overridden any doubts Miss Atkins might have raised as to the quality of Viv's accent in the foreign languages she'd so haphazardly acquired in her youth. Surely they must have weighed the possible liabilities to herself and other secret agents that her deficiencies might present.

A wave of doubt swept over her. Was she utterly foolhardy to risk returning to occupied France again? What if her shortcomings got her fellow agents killed?

Her mother's voice rang in her head.

Constance, you can be so utterly useless at times. The headmistress at Le Manoir is constantly sending me notes about your sheer idleness when it comes to your studies. According to her, you do nothing but go skiing at the slightest provocation. Karl says...

For the first time in Viv's life, she deeply regretted how careless she'd been in the way she'd acquired the languages she'd learned and had given her other studies such short shrift. In doing so, she'd certainly succeeded in annoying Karl and Pamela but, in truth, she'd only hurt herself. From this moment on, she vowed she'd concentrate on improving her spoken French. Her German, too, if that proved a requirement.

Viv pushed away from the wall next to the phone and padded down the hallway to her room, scolding herself for allowing her parents' negative views to spoil the news that she had made it this far with the SOE recruiters.

Maybe I'll be going back to France!

The fact she actually knew what life was like under the Nazi invaders had obviously weighed heavily in her favor, along with whatever Marcel had said about her to Buckmaster or his higher ups.

Bless you, Colonel Hush-Hush...

And then, for as many days as it had been since she'd last seen Marcel Delonge in Gibraltar, she wondered where *was* the handsome, exasperating man with the battered beret and a scar on his cheek?

Viv leaned into the mirror and carefully applied lipstick that was a close cousin to the hue of her restored, burgundy-colored hair. What a luxury to be able to buy a *new* tube, she thought. It had taken scurrying in and out of half a dozen of London's sandbagged shops and various chemists to find the right shade—a very guilty pleasure given the horrific pounding the city had taken courtesy of Hitler's *Luftwaffe*.

London was a shocking shambles, and Viv could tell a possible German invasion of the island nation was on everyone's mind. She'd seen women on duty manning anti-aircraft guns in Hyde Park. Enormous gray balloons floated overhead whose purpose was to force German pilots to fly at higher altitudes during their sorties to rain down terror on the city. The Horse Guards at Buckingham Palace were no longer dressed in their resplendent scarlet coats and tall, black beaver hats, but now wore drab khaki uniforms. And everywhere there were red-painted arrows pointing "To The Shelter."

When she arrived at the haberdashery's address, the fitting of her uniform was performed with precision and efficiency.

"We'll just make these few adjustments," said her assigned tailor, gesturing with the skirt he held in his hand. "It won't take long...so take a seat here, please."

Less than a half-hour went by before the supply sergeant re-entered the fitting room.

"Here you are, miss," he announced, walking toward her with her custom-tailored olive-green wool uniform on its hanger. "Why not try this on one more time with your new brogues to make sure the skirt length's right?"

Viv smiled her thanks and slipped into the curtained area. The military's designated tailor had let down the hem to cover her knees a bit more. Once dressed, she donned the jaunty cap that she deemed far more attractive than the one she'd worn as an ambulance driver for the American Hospital. Returning to the open fitting room, the supply sergeant and the tailor gazed at her reflection in the three-way mirror.

"Fits you to a T, doesn't it just?" the tailor said, admiring his handiwork.

"And the belt is perfect, too," Viv said with a smile of thanks, pointing to the wide swathe of brown leather cinched tightly around her waist. She pointed to a badge on the shoulder of one sleeve.

"What's this stand for?"

"Why, miss, don't you know?" the tailor asked, and Viv could see he was highly amused by her question. "You are now a new recruit in the First Aid Nurses Yeomanry."

"Well, at least I'm not a total fraud," she replied with a laugh. "I took a first aid course when I drove ambulances in France."

The sergeant nodded his silent compliment and then said to the tailor, "You can't blame her for not knowing what unit she's in, Tom. Issuing these FANY uniforms is what they *do* with these SOE ladies. Not that I imagine they'll be doing much nursing from what I hear," he added with a wink. To Viv he said, "I don't think the War Office knew *what* division to put you lot in."

Meanwhile the tailor held out his hand. "Let me just bundle up your street clothes, love," he said cheerily, "and you'll be on your way."

———◇———

It was late afternoon by the time Viv emerged from the tailor shop carrying the brown paper parcel containing her street clothes tied with twine. She peered across the road, looking for a bus to take her back to Notting Hill. A few feet from her, near the curb, a figure pushed away from a light post and took a step toward her.

"Well, well. Don't you look *très chic*."

The man was in a uniform of similar hue to the one she was wearing. He had a collection of medals pinned on his chest and insignia decorating his shoulders, cuffs, and on the brim of his officer's hat that told her he was someone of a rather elevated rank.

And he probably thinks he can pick up any woman he pleases, she thought with a hint of annoyance.

Then she looked closely at the man's face under his brimmed brigadier's hat.

Eyes as dark as black coffee met hers. The man was more than half a head taller than she, and his sardonic smile was so familiar that her heart nearly stopped beating.

But there wasn't a *scar* slicing down his left cheek!

"Have you no greeting for me, Miss America?" he asked.

"Oh, my God," she expelled in a strangled whisper. "Marcel! What in the *world? How…?* What are you doing…? Your *face!*"

"You really should stop asking your infernal questions!" he said with a smile that no longer caused a slight puckering around his left eye. "Come with me," he commanded.

He seized her elbow and ushered her a few steps into a nearby teashop whose entrance, protected by a high wall of sandbags, required some serious navigation.

Leaning toward her ear, he murmured, "I'll tell you as much as I can that's not part of the Secrets Act. By the way, that's something you'll be signing, too, if you pass your psychological tests at Wamborough."

"How do *you* know that's where I'm going? I-I-I just can't believe this!" Viv sputtered as Marcel settled the two of them at a small, round table in a corner and signaled the waitress.

"Tea and scones for the lady. Coffee for me, if you will." Looking pleased with himself he chuckled, "When in Rome, do as you please. I prefer coffee."

Viv demanded more loudly than she intended, "What has been done to your *face?*"

"So you didn't recognize me at first, yes?" he asked, his gaze scanning hers intently for an answer.

"No, I did *not*—not at first. But don't forget, I bandaged that mug of yours a couple of times, so it's not really a fair test."

"*Qu'est-ce que c'est* 'mug' *s'il vous plait?*" he demanded in two languages.

Ignoring his request for a definition of the word 'mug,' she said, "I never thought you a vain sort of man but—"

Marcel interrupted her, switching solely into French. "Would you believe that I was *ordered* to have this done, paid for by General de Gaulle, who most likely got the funds from his British benefactors?"

"You were *ordered* to get a face-lift?" she asked, shocked.

Marcel leaned forward and winked. "Trust me, it was not to make me more beautiful than I already am."

"I guess you *are* vain after all," she interjected, trying not to smile.

Marcel shook his head with mock solemnity.

"The brass called it a 'face alteration.'" He settled back in his chair. "My scar was an identifying feature that certain factions in France already know and could communicate to others whom we'd rather not learn of my future presence in my country."

"Like my being spotted by the SS in Paris because of the color of my hair or my height," she replied.

"*Bon.* You understand now why this was done."

She paused, pointing to the insignia on his shoulders. "You were promoted to brigadier."

"Advancement is fast during wartime."

"So you *are* going back to France?"

He raised a dark eyebrow but remained silent.

"To Perpignan?"

"The Resistance network there was completely blown," he said, and she heard the bitterness as he said it.

Viv felt her breath catch. Had Marcel's partisans been betrayed because of her? Did someone tell the authorities about the strange, unusually tall woman arriving on a bicycle who then collapsed in his vineyard?

"And your sister and niece?" she asked anxiously. "Are they all right? And what about Clément Grenelle? Any word of him?"

"All fine, as far as we know. It happened right after you and I left. Fortunately, Grenelle was long gone. Most of the arrests were in a town some miles away from Perpignan—but it compromised the entire region's *résistants.*"

"Who was caught, then?" She thought of Marcel's various vineyard workers she'd met and his farm manager who'd driven them to the base of the mountain.

"People you don't know."

"And you won't tell me anything else." It was a statement, not a question.

"You know I can't," he replied.

She nodded with resignation, taking closer note of the several medals on his chest. One was the *Légion d'Honneur* and the other a *Croix de Guerre.*

She reached out to touch his sleeve. "Thank you, by the way, for opening doors for me at the SOE."

"They know they'd be lucky to have you." Then Marcel's expression grew grave. "I do wonder, *chérie*, if I've done you any favors."

"I know, I know," she said with a dismissive wave, "it's a dangerous world and it's getting worse. But really, Marcel! What else should we be doing as France is being crushed—and maybe England, too?"

Meanwhile, she couldn't stop herself from staring at the smoothness of Marcel's face and the fact that the skin on both cheeks now matched. The bump was gone from his nose, rendering his entire face as handsome as she'd remembered his right side was.

He'd noticed her staring. "So what do you think?' he asked. "Will my sister or niece allow me to return to the winery someday?"

Viv scanned his visage critically.

"Whoever knew you well before will probably recognize you…eventually. But to others, you're a new person."

"*Bon.* Let us hope that's so."

Viv continued to stare at him over her steaming cup of tea. "So all the time I was on the high seas dodging U-boats," she said, "you've been in a London hospital, recovering after a Harley Street plastic surgeon had his way with you."

Marcel nodded. "*Exactement.* And now I'm ready for whatever comes next."

Viv fell silent. Whatever came next for him was bound to be full of risks at every turn. She was shocked to realize how frightened for him that made her feel. De Gaulle had ordered the surgery, he'd said, which had to mean the exiled leader of France had big plans for the promoted Brigadier Hush-Hush…

Marcel was a soldier. A former *Legionnaire*! He'd been given high priority evacuation orders from Dunkirk. He'd already been sent back into France once where he'd been a leader of a resistance network in the area near his family home below the Pyrenees. He'd made no secret of believing that to win France's freedom, the various disorganized and highly fractious Resistance groups *had* to put their rivalries aside and find a common purpose to work in unison to defeat the invaders.

Viv felt her stomach clench. She would bet her new prized lipstick that Marcel Delonge might be just the man the de facto leader of the Free French had been seeking. Marcel was the perfect choice for de Gaulle to forge the disparate groups in country into a viable civilian fighting force, ready to assist the Allies when the invasion of France was ultimately launched.

If it ever will be, Viv thought to herself bleakly, taking a sip of her tea.

"Marcel," she said. To her horror, she suddenly found she was fighting tears that had begun to cloud her view of him across the table. "Please tell me that your next assignment *isn't* to try to convince all the underground fighters to put their enmities and ideologies aside—and work together?"

Marcel reared back in his chair and she knew, instantly, that she had hit upon the truth, or close to it. But what a nightmare, she thought, a feeling of alarm surprising her with its intensity. He'd be sent all over France with the SS after him at every turn.

Marcel stared down at his coffee cup. "What a clever girl you've turned out to be."

"But they've given you an impossible task!" she protested.

She'd seen for herself what a tangled mess the supposed Resistance had become.

There were the Communists. The youth camping out in the woods to avoid conscription to Germany. The *maquis* fighters hiding on mountaintops for the same reason. And then there were the fiercely independent and irascible brave souls like gravedigger Clément Grenelle refusing to be conquered by *any* outsiders. How would a de Gaulle deputy dodge the SS while attempting to get partisans throughout France to agree what should be done—and *how*—when it came time to rise up and reclaim France from Hitler's mammoth war machine?

Marcel sounded tense and almost angry now. "While I appreciate your insights as to any of my future assignments, you know that I can't discuss this subject, Viv."

But Viv couldn't help herself. "So you've agreed to take on the deadly task of consolidating these competing factions for France and *de Gaulle's* glory?" She had stated her question in a harsh whisper, although she expected that her outrage was probably coming through loud and clear. "Did General de Gaulle, from the safety of his London headquarters, concoct this dangerous—no, *suicidal*—plan you're to execute for him?"

For some reason, she realized she was as angry as she'd ever been. Had Marcel been designated a sacrificial lamb, just like her father?

She leaned closer. "Was *that* why you submitted to surgery to lessen the chance that old enemies would recognize you? Don't you realize that you've done this in the name of an obscure officer whom many, as you probably know—since you know everything—consider a common *upstart*? What makes you think *de Gaulle* knows what's best for France? It's easy for him to command such an operation, but *you're* the one marching into the lion's den!"

She fully expected him to storm out of the tearoom, but instead, he leaned toward her to grasp her free hand. He even smiled.

"My dear Viv, I am overwhelmed by both your deductive powers and your apparent concern for my safety. Believe it or not, I agree with everything you've said."

"Y-you do?" she stammered in shock.

"Even so, de Gaulle—and other top leaders, by the way—are right. France can only free herself if we unite the partisans. Someone has to try, and I'm the chosen one."

"*But*—" Viv could hear her protestation had become almost a wail.

Marcel squeezed her hand hard to rivet her attention.

"That's the decision. I've accepted it. So have several others. We all must." His smile was almost beatific, as if she'd satisfied something he never expected. "But I'm here now, *chérie*. Let us make the most of this, our third rendezvous. You must have surmised that I asked to be informed when you made it to London, and *voilà*! Here you are."

"Here I am," Viv murmured. "And yes, amazing that we meet for a third time."

"*Ah...oui*. And let's hope, indeed, our reunion today proves to be the charm, *chérie*." He reached across the table to graze the back of his fingers along the side of her face. "No more chipmunk cheeks, I see. You've made a complete recovery from the mumps?"

"Yes. Finally. And I still have my hearing and my heart continues to tick."

Her skin tingled from his touch, and she could only keep staring at his left cheek that was as smooth as her own. Marcel leaned closer across their small table.

"We have so little time before we must—as you Americans say—get this show on the road. I've made us a reservation at the one restaurant in London that serves decent French food. After that, my dear Viv, I hope you'll wish to accompany me to my—"

Just at that moment, the spiraling wail of a siren pierced the air.

"*Merde!*" they declared simultaneously.

The proprietor of the tearoom shouted, "Shelter's on the corner! Shelter's on the corner outside and around to your *right*!"

Viv took a last, hurried sip of her tea and Marcel, his coffee, and then they bolted for the door.

CHAPTER 29

An air-raid warden, clad in his vest and helmet, urged the crowds, "Step lively, now. Off you go! Follow the arrows down to the Tube! Jerry hasn't been over for a while. He may make a night of it. Hurry, there!"

Viv and Marcel joined the others streaming downstairs into the underground train station. From far off, they could hear dull thuds of bombs hitting somewhere in London, along with gasps of fear from a few of the shelter seekers nearby. Most everyone except the two of them carried pillows, blankets, and even mattresses in their arms.

"Look," Viv said, tugging Marcel's sleeve.

Walking down the steps in front of them was a man carrying a typewriter and a satchel of books tied with a canvas strap.

"As good a place as any to get some work done, I suppose," Marcel replied.

As they reached the foyer near the ticket booths, accordion music spilled out, played by a French sailor accompanied by an American soldier puffing into a harmonica.

"Sounds like a café in Paris," Viv said as Marcel pulled her beyond the crowds that had stopped to listen.

Nearby, a woman at a teacart was dispensing cups of the hot brew, while on a section of the platform where trains normally arrived, several card games were already in progress. Those carrying mattresses and other aids to promote sleep had slipped down to the tracks themselves and placed their household items between the rails, as there would be no trains passing by while the air raid was in progress. A few people even began to dance to the music echoing through the tunnels.

"May I?" asked Marcel, holding out his arms.

The parcel he'd been carrying containing Viv's street clothes was soon sandwiched between his hand and her back. The swelling crowds allowed them only a few steps before they had to halt and merely shuffle in place. Viv was intensely aware of Marcel's thighs rubbing against hers as his military medals pressed against her breast.

"*Chérie*, let's find somewhere to sit,' he whispered in her ear.

Before Viv could agree that's what she wanted, too, a skirling sound rent the air. Marching down the stairs was a kilted figure, sporran swinging, bagpipes wailing.

Marcel shouted, "*Notre Dame de Misère*... My God, what *is* that?"

"A lonely Highlander," Viv shouted back over the din.

"*Mon Dieu*, let's get away from that hideous noise!"

Even louder than the shrieking sounds of the Scottish classic, "The Gay Gordons," came an enormous thud, this one very close. The entire tunnel shook. The music stopped abruptly, followed by screams of those standing under the ceiling near the pay booth where a crack was forming in the plaster.

Marcel grabbed Viv's arm, guiding her through the milling throng and along the corridor. Together, they bolted up the exit stairs until they were standing outside behind a high wall of sandbags.

"We can't go out any farther," Viv gasped, trying to catch her breath and fearing an air-raid warden might be close by. "We'll be picked up immediately."

Marcel turned and took her in his arms. "My poor baby spy. What a reunion this has turned out to be. Not at all what I planned." He pointed to a low pile of leftover sandbags wide enough for them both to sit upon. "Let's crouch here for a while and at least get some air." He pulled her down beside him with his arms still around her shoulders for warmth. "Can you see the searchlights up there? They're beautiful."

Viv relaxed against one side of Marcel's chest, gazing at the sky in awe despite the niggling fear that an incendiary bomb might suddenly whirl down in their direction.

"I keep thinking of that direct hit on the shepherd's hut," she murmured.

Marcel looked down and framed her face with both his hands. He leaned forward, their lips inches apart.

"Well, think of *this*, instead," he whispered, and began kissing her, softly at first, then with an intensity that made her think his probing lips were the lethal weapons.

When she finally came up for breath, she murmured, "I don't want to think at all."

Marcel proceeded to spend the next half hour making a thorough exploration of her most outstanding contours under her new uniform while never taking his lips from her face and neck.

"We're shameless," Viv giggled against his ear, "acting like teenagers."

"We are not," contradicted Marcel with Gallic aplomb. "We are making limited love under exceedingly difficult circumstances. May I touch you here?"

Finally, the all clear sounded just as they were both starting to shiver in the night's cold air. They could hear the crowd begin to tramp to the top of the stairs. Marcel rose from their perch on the sandbags and pulled her to her feet.

"Come, I've been given an apartment not too far from here. A friend of mine who's in Washington currently lent it. We'll have a warm bath and a whiskey. It will do us good."

As far as Viv was concerned, it definitely would accomplish *that*—and probably a great deal more. What else could they do in the aftermath of such possible death and destruction? She wanted to laugh in the face of the terror reigning down on London tonight. Laugh and make love.

————◆————

By the time Viv awoke the next morning, the space next to her on the bed was empty, but the distinct aroma of burnt toast filled the bedroom. Padding out to the kitchen, she found that to make up for Marcel's unfamiliarity with an American toaster, he'd slathered on the bread's blackened surface the remnants from their host's jar of peanut butter.

Munching on a bite, Viv teased "Mmmm…not very French, but an interesting combination of flavors." She studied his face as they choked down their toast. "You've lost some of your suntan, and I have to say, I miss your scar just a bit."

"Let's hope the Germans will too. Buckmaster wouldn't allow me to get in touch with you until it had fully healed. He wanted a report if you recognized me right away."

"Well, I didn't—right away—so he'll be happy." She looked at him steadily across the kitchen table. "So, thanks to your new face, you're definitely going back," she said, unable to keep herself from wondering for the thousandth time in the last sixteen hours if they'd ever see each other again. A sudden, fierce joy came over her that she'd thrown caution to the winds and made love with Marcel the minute they'd entered the flat and shut the door.

Marcel put down his coffee cup and pointed to his left cheek.

"Now that I have this new 'look,'" he replied, "they want me to leave fairly soon. And you?" he asked, seeking her gaze. "Word is you did well in your initial interviews," and then he quickly added, "but I never told you that… agreed?"

Viv was relieved to know that her being honest in her sessions at Orchard House about her flaws as well as her successes had been the right decision, especially with Vera Atkins. Then she breathed a sigh.

"But I still have to be 'psychologically evaluated' at Wamborough," she reminded him. "If I pass muster, I imagine I'll first be sent somewhere for training. What *kind* of training, I haven't a clue—or where the hell they'll assign me in the end." She inhaled a deep breath, adding, "Just as long as it isn't Paris. I told them about nearly getting arrested when I was working at the American Hospital."

"No Paris assignments, then, I expect." he assured her. "I have every confidence that you'll pass all tests with flying colors, including learning how to dangle in space at the end of a parachute."

Viv put down the last corner of her charred toast and stared at him, feeling the blood draining from her face.

"Marcel, you can't mean that? They'll want me to *parachute* into France?"

A kaleidoscope of unbearable images of her father falling from the sky flashed through her mind, and she felt she might be physically sick.

"Of course you have to parachute," he said, matter-of-factly, taking a sip of coffee.

"Not *me*," she said, pushing back her chair.

"Oh, yes, you," he insisted with a stern shake of his head. "It's a nonnegotiable part of every agent's training."

CHAPTER 30

Viv jumped up from her seat next to the kitchen table. "Oh, please, *no*! There is absolutely no way I can jump out of an airplane!"

Marcel rose quickly and in one long stride took her in his arms.

"Buckmaster showed me your file to see if I could corroborate everything they knew about you," he said soothingly. "I saw the notation of how your father died. I'm so very sorry, Viv. But your father isn't *you*, and it's no longer 1918."

Feeling a sense she was choking, she burrowed her forehead into the shoulder that she'd once bandaged for Marcel on the road to Dunkirk.

"*N-No one* ever said *anything* about para…c-chuting!" she said, gulping down a tide of swift-rising panic.

"Darling, I'm sure they thought you'd realized that on your own. Every SOE recruit has to make a couple of practice jumps. How did you *expect* to return behind enemy lines?"

"By fishing boat," she protested, "or climbing over the Pyrenees again!"

"Perhaps they're sending you to a place that isn't near water," he said gently.

Viv suddenly remembered Vera Atkins asking her about how well she skied—and where? They'd both reminisced about shushing down the slopes at Chamonix.

"Oh, God!" Viv cried, "What if they're sending me to the Haute-Savoie? They know all about my going with Clément to the Alps around Lake Annecy and the Plateau des Glières."

Marcel's expression told her she'd likely guessed right, or something close to it. Winter was coming on in a few months, creating a need for clandestine couriers who could ski. If Marcel knew the Alps were her destination, he also knew that the only way to get there was to parachute in.

Viv covered her face with both hands. Crashing from the air into the side of a mountain would be even worse than falling into the English Channel! Marcel rocked her gently in his arms while they remained standing in the middle of the kitchen.

"*Mon amour*…you're the bravest woman I've ever known. You'll get through this. You'll see."

"I can't explain it, Marcel," she said softly, emotion nearly cutting off speech. She felt as if she were a five-year-old child about to burst into a fit of hysterical crying.

"No need to be scared," he crooned. "Parachuting is not as bad as you think."

Viv raised her head from his shoulder, blinking back the tears filling her eyes.

"For *you*, maybe, but all I can think about is my father falling three thousand feet into the water." She shook her head, staring at him. "His body was never found!"

Marcel pulled her close again and refused to let her struggle free from his arms. In a corner of Viv's mind, she was filled with amazement that this tough-minded, often sardonic, bare-knuckles fighter could be so kind and comforting.

"It had to be a horrible thing for a little daughter to learn," he said, scattering small kisses on her neck and cheek. "But Viv...that was years ago. Everything about jumping out of airplanes has improved enormously since then, including the meticulous packing of the chutes. *Your* parachute *will* open!" he insisted almost sternly while pulling her hands away from her face to make her look at him. "I've done it many times in training and several jumps for real. I was frightened, too, at first, but now I even *enjoy* it. Once the chute opens, there's this amazing, peaceful sensation—"

"Oh, *God!*" she moaned, wrenching herself out of Marcel's arms and turning her back. She instantly felt a gentle slap on her *derrière*.

"After what I saw you could do, even with a raging case of the mumps, I never thought a parachute jump could have *this* effect on you," he scolded. "You'll just have to buck up, Miss America, if you expect to become one of us."

Turning in place, Viv could only stare at him, mute.

"Believe me," he said, his voice harsh and uncompromising, "there are many aspects of being a secret agent that will test your courage." He refused to allow her to look away. "And jumping out of an airplane is one of them. You'll just have to deal with it and meet the challenge—or quit right now."

"I don't quit!" she shot back. "But—"

He cut her off. "Good. Now, go get dressed. You and I are both headed for the New Forest today."

Viv stared.

"You're also going to Wamborough?"

He laughed. "I've *been* psychoanalyzed. I'm merely delivering you there."

"Where are you going after that?" she demanded.

"Can't tell you."

His face assumed the same opaque expression she'd noticed whenever she asked him specifics about his work. Marcel's shoulders had stiffened, and he remained silent. Viv's own body ached from their lovemaking, and she despised the feeling that had just come over her of sudden abandonment. She turned and seized the dishes off the table, took them to the sink, and ferociously turned on the water full blast. Ignoring Marcel, she rinsed the plates and cups and placed them one by one on the drain board with a thump.

Marcel came to stand behind her. He reached over her shoulder and flipped off the water. Then he spun her around to face him, his gaze softening. His hands gripped her shoulders as if he were willing to communicate something important.

"After I leave you at Wamborough, I'll be sent for some specialized training."

"But you can't say *where*, right? That's always the answer."

"In war, it has to be."

"I get it, believe me," she replied with a peevishness she couldn't seem to control. "I've started to realize that we're just ants on the anthill doing whatever ants are supposed to do for God and country—until we meet our end."

"We are not ants," he said quietly. "We're trying to be patriots, you and I. But combatting what's happening in our world has to take precedence over our attraction for each other, Viv. Even over the love it should seem obvious that I feel for you."

Viv's eyes widened, and she wondered if she'd heard him correctly. Or was he just trying to manipulate her into not making any further fuss?

Were his words just a clever, sweet-sounding bribe?

Shades of Karl Bradford and her mother! Marcel had said "the love it should *seem* obvious" he felt for her. But did he really feel it? There was nothing obvious about Marcel except his perpetual elusiveness. Yes, he liked her. Possibly felt some sort of genuine affection for her. And, yes, she liked him. In fact, she feared she *had* fallen in love with him. And it certainly seemed obvious they'd both liked the way they'd been together in bed. Even so, she was sorry now she'd let her guard down. Everything linked to this mysterious man felt as scary as jumping out of an airplane.

Marcel reached for her hand. "Viv, the best chance for us to meet again is if you pull yourself together and learn to parachute behind enemy lines. *Look* at us. Here we are—in London. We've already defied the odds."

"Which narrows them even more, don't you imagine?" was her glum reply.

Marcel gave a frustrated shake of his head.

"*Mon Dieu*, have a little faith there'll be many more times together for us." He flashed her a rare grin. "You never know when we might find ourselves together in France at times. Don't forget those 'friends in high places.'"

Marcel pulled her to him again, cupped her chin in his hands. His kiss was slow and thorough as if he were trying to convince her they *would* see each other again. It came to Viv that after years of her parents' subtle abuse, she might have been too quick to suspect Marcel of being like them. But he was not like them in the least. His kissing her so tenderly was as generous as he was. She had been a witness to the ways in which he constantly looked out for the welfare of others. He'd been a superb and thoughtful lover. And she had to admit he was right about one thing: she *was* going to have to "buck up." Otherwise, what would she do with her life during this horrible war if she didn't make it as an SOE recruit?

Marcel took a step back, his hands moving to clasp both her shoulders once more. She forced herself to take a steadying breath and meet his assessing gaze.

"You're right. I'd...better go get dressed." She turned away from him, walking out of the kitchen. Sensing his eyes on her retreating back, she strode down the hallway to the room at the far end with its unmade bed. The truth was Marcel Delonge would soon disappear from her life. Whatever happened next was totally up to her, but one thing was certain. If she were ultimately accepted as an SOE secret agent, she would somehow find a way to avoid being flung through a moonlit sky from a low-flying British Halifax.

Viv stooped to collect several pieces of her new uniform that she'd discarded with abandon on the floor the previous night—and made a solemn promise to herself.

I will figure out some other route to return to France besides *dangling from a parachute that might not open...*

CHAPTER 31

Marcel pointed to the road sign just ahead of their car as they entered the Borough of Guildford. Minutes later, he pulled into a gravel driveway that led to a rather massive red brick Elizabethan manor house. Wamborough, a country estate that had been requisitioned the year before by the SOE, was surrounded by clipped grass and weathered wooden fences that marked it as the bespoke home of aristocrats it had always been. Beyond the estate's several looming gables with steep, slate roofs, Viv could see the rolling hills of Surrey's farmland stretching for miles.

"And what, exactly, do they do here," Viv asked, "besides inspecting my brain to assess if I'm fit to be one of their agents?"

Marcel laughed.

"That… plus teaching you unarmed combat and the art of silent killing." He reached over and squeezed her hand, adding, "but I expect they mostly want to see how clever you are at evading the enemy. It's a very handy skill, if you end up a courier. They need to weed out those not suited for undercover work and train those that are."

He pulled up in front of the manor's entrance and turned off the ignition.

"So this is goodbye," Viv said, steeling herself to make a dignified exit.

"*À bientôt*," he said with a smile.

"Until we meet again?" she parroted back to him.

"Even better. 'See you soon.' And by the way, I won't be far away."

Viv stared at him behind the wheel. "I thought you were—"

"Leaving for France?" he interrupted, "Soon, I imagine, but not as soon as I had thought. It turns out I have some...special training to do—just like you—along with a refresher course in parachuting." Before Viv could react, he leaned across and grasped her chin between his slender fingers, kissing her soundly, and leaning back. "*Bonne chance*, Miss America."

———◇———

Viv's initial weeks at Wamborough Manor turned out to be nothing she couldn't handle. As Marcel had advised, she answered every question posed by her superiors with absolute honesty and was deemed "psychologically stable." She also passed every physical fitness challenge put in front of her in the fields around the estate, showing as much skill as most of her male counterparts. Once the physical and mental assessments were completed, she was called before Major Roger de Wesselow, the Coldstream Guards officer that ran the training establishment at Wamborough. He stepped in front of his desk and held out his hand in congratulations.

"Well done, miss, on all accounts," he declared, handing her a copy of the Secrets Act he then asked her to sign. Retrieving the executed document and putting it on the desk, he said, "Not too many women could have succeeded with this course. And not a lot of men either, I'm here to tell you. Of course, you're tall, and that probably helped. It's my job to whittle out the ones not fit enough or ill-suited for undercover work, but so far, you've turned in an excellent performance." He seized a manila envelope from his desk and handed it to her. "These are your orders. You've been granted three days leave before starting your next phase of training."

"Am I allowed to ask what that is?" Viv inquired.

"I'm afraid not," replied the major, "but you'll know soon enough. Enjoy your weekend and be at London's Euston Station well before ten p.m. on Sunday."

"May I ask where I'm going?"

The major cast her an exasperated look. "One thing you will need to practice a bit more, miss, is not to ask questions. You will be informed of everything you need to know from here on out." His expression softened slightly. "One thing I can tell you regarding the next phase of your training: Bring woolen socks."

There was a light knock on the open door to the book-lined study that Viv supposed had been formerly the owner's private lair.

"Sir," said the major's adjutant, "a car and driver has arrived to fetch Miss Vivier-Clarke. Shall I tell him to wait?"

Startled, Viv swiveled her head and stared out the casement window to the major's right. Parked on the gravel turnaround was the same car that had brought her to Wamborough Manor, with the same driver at the wheel. It was Marcel.

———◇———

"So you're friends with the major?" Viv asked, slipping into the passenger seat.

"De Wesselow?" Marcel put the car in gear. "He was awarded the *Légion d'Honneur* in the same ceremony I was."

Viv shook her head, amazed. "That's how you know I finished the course here?"

"And that you were given high marks? Yes. The major was quite complimentary."

"You are too much," she laughed. "I must admit," she added happily, glancing at Marcel's profile, "it's lovely to have a chauffeur take me back to London."

The apartment belonging to Marcel's American friend was their ultimate destination, but not before Marcel proposed he take her to the French restaurant he'd promised the night they'd been caught in the air raid.

It was unfashionably early when they entered the tiny *Mon Plaisir* bistro on Monmouth Street in Covent Garden. The half a dozen white-cloth tables stood empty and a solitary waiter with a luxuriant handlebar mustache stood polishing glasses. Clad in black trousers and an ankle-length white apron around his waist, he looked up at the sound of the front door opening and smiled broadly.

"Ah-ha! Finally, the brigadier. And with *mademoiselle,* as you promised," he cried, setting down his dishcloth. He stepped out from behind a bar that Marcel had revealed to Viv on their way there had been imported from a brothel in Lyon. The host ushered his only guests to a table slightly secluded from the others. "We start with an *apéritif, oui*? Followed by *l'escargot,* and then—"

"I leave the menu entirely up to you, my friend," Marcel

intervened, "except that we will start with champagne. Veuve Clicquot, if you have it."

"Sadly, no *monsieur*. We heard that the damn *Boche* nearly pillaged the whole supply when they invaded Reims, but we do have a Pommery Brut, '32."

"*D'accord...*"

When their dinner of roasted leg of lamb in red wine, accompanied by perfectly cooked string beans and scalloped potatoes with melted cheddar cheese (in lieu of *Gruyère*) arrived, Viv figured the chef must have a direct line to the black market.

The evening sped by, as did the two nights and days of Viv's leave during which she was awash in a cascade of sensations of taste and touch that she realized would have to nourish her for months to come.

Sunday morning she and Marcel lay in the darkened bedroom where they'd first made love, sated and comfortable with each other, but painfully aware of the hours ticking by.

"Shall I make us some breakfast?" Viv asked, tracing her forefinger along the bridge of Marcel's nose, now minus its Gallic bump.

"Do you know how?" he demanded, and in a quick move, had her on her back with his entire frame hovering above her.

Looking up at him she retorted, "Not really, but I can definitely manage the toaster better than you can."

"We are quite a pair, aren't we? We love food but we're hopeless as chefs." He lowered himself a few inches, his chest brushing lightly against hers, his lips inches away from her mouth. "What I wouldn't do for a croissant and a cup of real coffee."

Viv reached her arms around his shoulders and pulled him toward her.

"What I wouldn't do for...*you*."

Marcel nuzzled her neck. "You'd even parachute out of a plane?"

Viv tensed and then forced herself to relax. She knew agents had been delivered to France in submarines, warships, rubber dinghies— and not only flung from the sky.

I will somehow find a different way...

She smiled up at him. "Who knows how they'll get me back into France? But first... come closer, *Monsieur* Frenchman..."

———◇———

Euston Station was eerily deserted except for the cluster of uniformed men and women milling beside a set of tracks on the far side of the cavernous space. The group stood next to the night train scheduled for a destination that remained unidentified, even to the recruits about to step aboard. Marcel had talked his way through the security check, given his rank and the decorations on his chest. Now, he and Viv stood apart, waiting for the sign from the conductor that it was time to depart.

"Will your 'friends in high places' still be able to keep tabs on me once I leave London?" she asked as casually as she could. "Will you have any idea where I am?"

"For a little while, *chérie.* Don't forget, Colonel Buckmaster isn't my true boss. He's my friend."

"Ah…yes…you report to General Upstart. Well, tell *him* to keep you safe."

"I'll try to do that for myself," Marcel responded, holding her gaze, "and you be sure to do the same."

"At explosives school? And what about 'How to survive an SS interrogation' class?' I guess *my* safety depends on how talented I turn out to be at acquiring some new skills."

As she mentioned her future curriculum, Viv suddenly felt as if she were being banished to an institution for sanctioned sinners. For the first time in her life, she wished she and Marcel could just be a couple of vintners in the sunny South of France, worried only about the upcoming harvest.

Marcel grasped both her hands.

"You'll do *well,* Viv. You've got what it takes to be a great agent. Remember that."

"I want *you* to be the greatest agent of all and stay alive, damn you!" She was truly fighting tears, now. "Me? I'll just probably be schussing down the Alps with a few encrypted messages in my pack," she said, her voice tightening, "having a grand 'ol time."

Before Marcel could respond, a voice rang out, "All right, chaps…and—ah—ladies. Time to get aboard."

Two other women and four men were waved toward the last car of the train. Marcel swiftly bent and brushed his lips on both of Viv's cheeks.

"Always *à bientôt, mon amour*…"

Viv nodded, barely able to speak, but she finally managed to say with false cheer, "Absolutely, *Monsieur* Hush-Hush. See you soon. We never say *au revoir,* right?"

"You've demoted me," he laughed. "Not 'yes, Brigadier, sir?'"

"No... I'm just imagining you someday back in your dirty overalls, wearing your beaten-up blue beret, and wielding those wicked pruning shears."

"Come along, now, cadet!" barked her escort officer, a buxom woman straining the seams of her FANY uniform. Then she noticed Marcel's rank. "Oh. Well, yes...it's time to say our goodbyes. Never fear, sir... I'll keep a sharp eye on her."

Viv followed her leader into the coach and stood by the window of the sleeping compartment she was sharing with the only other female recruit.

At exactly ten o'clock, the train made a lurch and then moved down the track away from Marcel's tall, lean figure.

À bientôt, mon amour...she cried out silently as he disappeared from view.

———◇———

Viv knew exactly what ground they had covered when the overnight train pulled into the station. Out the window, she spotted a towering up-thrust of rock with a castle perched on its plateau.

"Look! We're in Edinburgh!" she blurted. She'd loved this Scottish city she had visited as a child.

"Hush up, you dolt!" It was the escorting officer standing at the threshold to their compartment, glaring at Viv. "Come away from that window!" Her ample figure squeezed past the two female recruits and yanked down the shade until the castle disappeared. "We'll be leaving shortly, so it doesn't matter where we are right now. Meanwhile, keep silent about this stop, will you please?"

Duly chastised, Viv nodded her obedience.

In the next instant, their coach nudged sharply against a fresh locomotive and soon they were on their way once more. Viv could tell by the position of the morning sun that they were still headed north.

"It looks like where we're going is very hush-hush," whispered the young woman whose name Viv had learned was Marjorie Winchester.

"So it would seem," murmured Viv with the realization that she would never hear the words hush-hush without thinking of Marcel.

CHAPTER 32

The second female friend Viv acquired in the SOE besides Marjorie arrived two weeks after Viv had been at Arisaig House, a requisitioned hunting lodge hidden away in the remote Scottish Highlands.

Catherine Thornton, a striking blond with arresting green eyes, arrived late one evening at the gray stone mansion situated as part of a lonely estate outside Inverness to the west of Fort William. She, Viv and Marjorie were three of some sixty women in various stages of training the Brits had recruited for possible clandestine duty behind enemy lines. Catherine and Viv bonded immediately as fellow Americans, close to the same age and both equally and physically fit. They took mutual pride in keeping up with the majority of male recruits at a facility devoted to paramilitary and guerilla hand-to-hand combat training.

The day after Catherine's arrival, much to their surprise and disappointment, Marjorie suddenly vanished. Viv learned from the drill sergeant that she'd failed to physically defend herself in the course of the various "take down" exercises and had been duly dispatched to the "Cooler."

"God Almighty, what's that?" Catherine had asked when she and Viv arrived back at their barracks to find Marjorie's bunk stripped to its ticking and the mattress rolled up on the steel bed springs, awaiting another recruit to take her place.

"'The Cooler?'" Viv repeated with a slight shudder. "I was told it's another isolated hunting lodge where washouts are virtually under house arrest until the powers-that-be determine the knowledge they've gained no longer has relevance for fighting the war."

"But that could mean waiting out the entire conflict!" protested Catherine, adding "That is, if this blasted nightmare *ever* ends."

"You got that right, sister," Viv replied, glad that somewhere along the line an old boyfriend had taught her some jujitsu that had gained her commendation during the last few days of training. With Marjorie gone so suddenly, Viv was determined to teach Catherine some moves before their next class in hand-to-hand combat.

Unlike Viv, Catherine spoke flawless French. When Viv pressed her about it, she reluctantly admitted she'd graduated from the Sorbonne with honors when her father was attached to the American Embassy in Paris as a Marine security expert.

"Do you suppose we could speak *en francais* at night so you can correct my rotten pronunciation?" Viv pleaded.

"You mean, help you get rid of your adorable New York honk?" Catherine said with a laugh. "*Pas de problème, mademoiselle.*"

But how long would they both be at Arisaig? Viv wondered. Would there be enough time to correct her dangerous habit of speaking French interspersed with English whenever she couldn't remember a word?

On the evening following Catherine's first day of training, they both were bone tired from hours spent tracking each other up and down the moor a good distance beyond Arisaig House itself. As soon as dinner was concluded in the hunting lodge's grand dining room, the two women repaired to their barracks in a former stone outbuilding and began to prepare for bed.

"The men get the elegant chambers with four-poster beds, upstairs in the lodge," Viv disclosed wryly, "but at least, with a night guard on duty walking the perimeter, we don't have to worry about any unexpected visitors padding down the hallways in the wee hours." Catherine merely raised an eyebrow. Viv gestured toward the sparse furnishings and a few iron cots pushed against the stonewalls. "This place probably housed the beaters who flushed out the prey for local lairds during the shooting season."

Catherine sank onto her narrow bed, her eyes fastened on the embers glowing in the small stone fireplace built into a nearby corner.

"This certainly seems a long way from the D.C. British embassy," she murmured.

"D.C.?" Viv responded. "Not Paris? Whatever were you doing in D.C.?" Then she apologized. "I know. We're not to ask about our lives before the SOE."

"I was in D.C. because of my husband's job," Catherine stated flatly.

"You were married? *Are*, I mean."

Catherine nodded morosely. "Witness before you the long-estranged American wife of a British diplomat—and that's absolutely all I have to say on that subject."

Viv was taken aback to hear even this much. She couldn't help but have noticed when Catherine had arrived she wore no rings and there had been undeniable electricity when the stunning young woman greeted Viv's fellow recruit, a Frenchman in his early forties with a classic Gallic nose and a full head of salt-and-pepper hair. To Viv, Henri LeBlanc had been a good friend to her from the day she arrived. From their first training session together, he'd been cheerful and welcoming. Before long, he'd also become a trusted partner in lock-and-key class when they shared the task of making wax impressions to fashion keys in situations where there were none.

"Wait a minute here," Viv teased Catherine with mock indignation. "What gives between you and Henri Leblanc? It was pretty obvious that you two had met before."

"It couldn't have been *that* obvious?" Catherine said with a look of alarm. "That doesn't speak very well to our future as secret agents."

"Well, before you arrived here, Henri and I had become pals, of sorts." Catherine's gaze narrowed, and Viv knew she'd guessed right. They *did* know each other well before Arisaig. Viv held up two hands as if to ward off whatever Catherine planned to say. "Truly, we're *just* pals," she emphasized. "I like him. He had my back, and I had his in every class we took together. But that's all, I promise you." She longed to say how much she wished Marcel could magically drop into her life like Henri had into Catherine's. "C'mon my dear! What's the story about *you* and the dashing *M'sieur* Leblanc?"

Silence filled the room except for the soft hiss of coals on the hearth.

"Word of honor you won't tell anyone, okay?" Catherine answered.

Viv nodded an emphatic yes. "Henri and I have been lovers from the time we were both in Washington, D.C." She grew silent once more and glanced again at the hearth. "When I arrived here, I almost had a heart attack when I saw him amongst the crowd of recruits greeting me in the foyer. I had no idea he'd be in training here, too." She paused and then said, "He's leaving tomorrow, but of course he can't tell me where they're sending him."

Viv could only nod again, this time with complete sympathy. Every single day it had been drilled into them to "Trust No One." But sometimes it was necessary to trust *someone*, and Viv was beginning to see that the art of being an intelligence agent was in sorting out who that could and should be.

Catherine apparently trusted her, Viv thought with pleasure.

"Henri slipped this to me at dinner," Catherine murmured, revealing a small square of paper she had been holding crushed in her hand. She showed it to Viv. "Can you tell me what a 'bothy' *is* and where I can find one?"

Viv sat bolt upright on her cot.

"Well, if it's what I think it is, it's a deserted stone cottage up on the moor that we used in one of our field exercises before you arrived."

"Henri wants me to meet him there tonight, if I can."

"You *do* know, don't you," Viv said, handing back the note, "that you could get thrown out of the SOE if the brass discovers you broke curfew?"

"Of course I know," Catherine countered, fingering the slip of paper from Henri.

Viv's thoughts were filled with memories of the shepherd's cottage the night a German bomb almost ended her life if it hadn't been for Marcel dragging her under the ambulance.

She managed to smile at her new friend. "I can tell you how to get there."

"Oh, God, Viv. Would you?" Catherine asked eagerly. "If I get caught, I swear on my life never to reveal who told me about the bothy and where to find it."

"Hey," Viv replied, remembering all the frightening moments when she was certain an SS or Vichy officer would apprehend her with her fake documents. "Fooling the colonel here will be good practice if you ever get nabbed by the Nazis." She walked to the window that faced the moor and pulled back the blackout curtain a few inches. "Okay," she said, pointing. "See that big tree across the lawn? Behind it is a trail…"

———◇———

The next morning, Viv wasn't quite so happy that she'd assisted Catherine in going AWOL. She awoke with a start just before dawn, mildly panicking when she saw that Catherine wasn't back in her bunk. Their group was to assemble on the mansion's front lawn at six for calisthenics, followed by a swim in the loch before breakfast. Viv pulled on her clothes and a heavy jacket, peered outside the wooden door to see if the coast was clear, and bolted like a gazelle down the gravel path. Grateful no one was outside yet and that the nighttime patrol had probably gone in for a warming cup of coffee, she made for the windswept moor on a path starting from behind a huge pine tree.

The stone-and-thatched bothy stood on a lonely rise a quarter of a mile away. Viv was huffing and puffing by the time she pounded on the door.

"Catherine! Hey, Thornton! If you're in there, move your ass!"

She heard Henri declare, *"Merde!* Oh, God…it's after five! Catherine, wake up!"

Viv heard Catherine's protesting, "No-o-o…"

This exchange was followed by loud movements and more curses. Viv tapped her boot impatiently on a patch of turf sprouting near the weatherworn front door. Finally, she reached for the wrought iron handle and rattled it loudly.

"Look, I don't want to get court-martialed—or whatever they do to us SOEs for disobeying the rules—just because you two are so slow getting out of the sack!"

More sounds of movement, but no Catherine. Growing alarmed at the minutes ticking away, Viv slowly opened the door a crack and absorbed the sight of Henri and Catherine, fully dressed and standing in the center of the dirt floor, arms entwined.

Pushing the door open wider, Viv declared, "C'mon, Thornton. Chop, chop. We've got fifteen minutes to make it back before reveille."

Henri gave Catherine a gentle push towards the threshold. "Viv knows a way around the moor that's completely obscured by a forest until you reach the back of Arisaig House." He turned his attention to Viv. "I salute your uncanny ability to pick locks and the fact you've been a wonderful friend. *Au revoir, mon amie.*"

"Likewise, *mon ami,*" she smiled. "I'll miss you, too, Henri."

"Good luck when you get to parachute school," he added.

Viv swallowed hard. She'd confided in Henri how the mere thought of jumping out of a plane terrified her.

"I swear to you both," she said, "the SOE will just have to get me into France some other way!" To Catherine she urged, "C'mon, spy sister. We've gotta get going!"

———◇———

By mid-morning, Viv and Catherine had finished their daily calisthenics, and Henri Leblanc had been whisked away from Arisaig House—destination unknown. Viv could tell that Catherine was doing her best to hide how much she missed him, now that he had been most likely deployed on his first assignment in France.

For the rest of September 1942, the two women and their class of recruits buckled down to the serious business of learning to handle explosives safely in a variety of dicey situations. Viv and a male recruit were assigned to blow up one end of a bridge which—much to her relief—was successful.

Coming down from the moor, she caught up with Catherine, whose partner that day setting up explosives with her on a stretch of railroad track had been another young American their age named Sean, who turned out to be a cousin of General Dwight Eisenhower.

"Did you see our end of the bridge blow sky high?" Viv asked Catherine excitedly. "Thank God I passed. How did you two do?"

Sean Eisenhower beamed at Catherine. "With good teamwork, we passed too."

"Bravo us!" exclaimed Viv. "Here's to surviving the *next* place they send us."

———◇———

Within the week, and without even a day's warning, Viv received orders to report to wireless school at Bletchley Park in southern England. Much to her chagrin, she knew within two days that she was—as she had been with her Olympic ski instructor—a total washout, but certainly, this time, it was not because she didn't give it all she had.

"I'm just God-awful at remembering these damn dots and dashes," she exclaimed to the woman next to her who seemed infuriatingly skillful, tapping away the practice messages that made up the day's exercises.

The instructor came up behind Viv and barked, "No talking! No wonder you're so hopeless at this, miss!"

Later that day, Viv was called into the colonel's office who ran the school.

"I'm afraid, miss, wireless transmission is never going to be your forte."

Viv gazed across the desk at the man who held her fate in his hands and agreed.

"I'm so sorry, sir. I tried. I really did, but I just can't seem to get the hang of it."

"The problem is, I'm afraid, that we are in desperate need of pianists right now," he said, employing the slang the British Army used for recruits that could lug a leather suitcase around France, sending messages back and forth to the War Office from the keyboard hidden inside. "Therefore, I'm afraid—"

Pure terror gripped Viv. She was about to be let go from the SOE and likely be sent to the 'Cooler' for the duration of the war!

"But what about being a *courier*?" she interrupted, trying to suppress her panic. "I'm sure you've seen from my file that I performed that service when I was in France before."

The major tapped a forefinger on the manila folder in front of him.

"But it says in here you've voiced many times your aversion for being trained to parachute into Europe." He gazed at her with surprising kindness. "I understand your father had a very unfortunate accident when his parachute didn't open, but, even so, I'm afraid I must—"

"I'll *do* it!" she almost shouted. "Send me to parachute school! I swear I'll be all right. *Please*, sir. I want to be part of all this!"

The colonel stared at her across the desk that separated them. He shook his head, his expression doubtful.

"Each parachute trainee is a drain on our war treasury, my dear. If, in the end, you cannot manage to—"

"You have my *word* on my father's grave—which was *in* the English Channel, by the way—I'll jump, no matter what!" She was amazed to hear the words coming out of her mouth. She blinked away her tears. "It's what my father would expect of me."

CHAPTER 33

"Oh, my God, Viv!" cried Catherine Thornton. "I can't believe it. You're *here*!"

Viv's friend from Arisaig House leapt up from her cot the second she caught sight of Viv walking into the women's Quonset hut, the designated sleeping quarters at Ringway Field, a military air facility outside Manchester.

"I was a total idiot when it came to learning wireless," Viv confided, throwing her duffle bag and knapsack on the empty cot Catherine pointed to.

"But you always said you'd never jump—"

Viv interrupted, "Well, it was made very clear to me that doing a decent job in this course is the only chance I have of being sent into enemy territory, so here I am."

"But how many times did you tell me that you absolutely would refuse to throw yourself out of an airplane?" Catherine persisted. With a look of empathy she added, "Given what happened to your father, I can hardly blame you."

"You're correct. I said 'hell no' to every big wig I've met," Viv admitted, wishing she'd kept her mouth shut.

"But now?"

"The colonel at wireless school told me, basically, to pull my socks up and get on with it. If I can somehow get through the parachute course, I'll most likely end up a courier in France for some SOE circuit leader or something."

Catherine came over to Viv's cot and sat down beside her, giving her a hug.

"You'd be a *great* courier for a unit coordinating with local Resistance leaders, Viv. The SOE obviously doesn't want to lose you, so they're giving you a second chance." Catherine rose to stand, her hands on her hips. "Think of it this way. There are only a handful of American women in this corps," she reminded Viv, "so no matter how hard it gets, we've got to show the flag, right?"

Viv laughed. "Thanks for the pep talk, although I'm mostly doing this for France, not the U.S."

And for my father…

———◇———

Viv stood in line behind Catherine as they waited their turn to climb up a ladder to a platform from which they were expected to jump onto a pile of mattresses, followed by what the sergeant said was a "land roll."

Fortunately for Viv, Catherine was a week ahead of her in the training.

"So what's a 'land roll?'" Viv asked in a hoarse whisper.

"You tuck your head lower than your shoulders, put your forearms over your face, glue your legs and feet together and roll on the ground," she explained. "They have us practice this for hours…so you'll catch on," she encouraged. "We jump off higher and higher parapets as the day goes on. If you don't go out stiff from the airplane, though, you'll break your nose…or something even more important."

"Oh, God," Viv groaned. "I'll never live through this." The line of recruits was moving briskly toward the ladder of the lowest platform. "When do we get taken up in a real plane?"

"Not before you learn how to fold your parachute."

"We pack our own parachutes?" Viv gasped.

"No, but they want you to know how it's done."

And that's supposed to give me confidence the damn thing will open?

Catherine put one foot on the first rung to the platform towering over their heads. "When they take us up in the plane the first time, we lie on our stomachs looking through the hole in the fuselage where eventually we'll jump. But don't worry...they do that just to get us used to how it all feels."

All Viv could reply was, "It *feels* like I'm in the middle of a nightmare."

———◇———

During her week of practicing jumping off of increasingly higher platforms onto the pile of mattresses, Viv managed to substitute the thought of leaping out of a plane with the happy memory of facing a steep hill on which she was about to ski down. She learned to take a deep breath and just *go*—banishing all thoughts while keeping her legs and ankles locked together as if she were about to schuss down a mountainside.

Viv couldn't believe it was October 1, the day she knew there was no escaping her fate. The moment had arrived when she was to jump into the void from the thing she dreaded most: a low-flying Halifax.

She was even more unsettled that a lumbering twin-engine bomber, called the Whitley, had been substituted. Numbly, she followed Catherine into the hold of the plane and took a seat beside her on a hard wooden bench that ran along the interior fuselage. The plane had been modified to carry nine parachute trainees and a dispatcher in one go.

Viv gazed at all nine passengers in full jump gear filling the square-shaped tail. The engines revved to a roar, and soon they were airborne.

"My back's killing me...is yours?" Viv yelled over the deafening noise. They were circling the flat, bleak drop zone over Ringway airfield. "This equipment we've got must weigh a hundred pounds."

Catherine nodded, shouting back, "With our chutes, helmets, and overalls, I thought we looked like a bunch of hunch-backed crabs boarding the plane!"

Just then, the dispatcher barked, "Standby! Move forward! Move forward!" He waved on the seven trainees ahead of Viv, with Catherine holding up the rear. Each parachutist was connected to a static line that would ultimately release when the jumper left the plane. The dispatcher had one final caution: "Don't let go of your ripcord—*ever*!"

Viv's stomach was churning like a flushing toilet.

"I think I'm going to be sick!"

"Not now, you aren't!" Catherine shouted. "Go, hurry. Go, scoot! HURRY!"

Like a zombie, Viv lowered herself from the wooden bench and slid her bottom near the round opening in the fuselage, allowing her feet and calves to dangle in the open space. She felt a frightening rush of wind on her legs and held the rim of the open fuselage in a death grip.

She fought against the vision of what it had been like for her father to push off into the void as flames licked his cockpit, only to realize his parachute was failing.

Don't think of that! Don't! Remember all the training...

She grasped the rim of the open exit hole even tighter, the mantras of her parachute instructor beginning to fill her brain.

Keep your head up. Never look down through the hole. Go out stiff. Shove off hard when you hear...

"GO!" yelled the dispatcher.

Later, she would never know how she'd summoned the blind courage in that instant to push her entire body out of the plane and into the abyss of space. The noise of the Whitley's two engines was ear splitting. The wind yanked her sideways, buffeting her frame beneath the looming plane that swiftly passed over her head. For several endless seconds, she was caught in the plane's slipstream, hanging suspended in the air like a doomed prisoner dangling from a noose.

Oh, Daddy...will I die like you? Will I just plunge...

Somehow, a voice overrode her despairing thoughts with a command.

Count! Count to ten and then pull your parachute's ripcord, damn it!

Ten seconds later, she managed to yank the cord. She didn't have time to wonder if it would open, because in the next second she felt a painful jerk wrenching her shoulders as the chute pulled away from the packing strapped to her back. She felt its load zoom into the sky above, clearing the plane's fuselage by a safe distance.

She glanced up between the strings tied to the chute and marveled that the puffy canopy was placidly ballooning to its proper fullness above her. Her training blessedly taking full possession of her thoughts, she reached up to grab hold of her rigging lines, drawing them closer to her body to steady the chute. She looked straight ahead at the horizon for a minute or two and recalled Marcel saying that after a few jumps, he'd actually enjoyed floating to earth.

Then she made the mistake of looking down.

The imagined scene she'd long held of her father jumping out of his flaming plane came rushing back in just the same way the land of Ringway Airfield was speeding up to meet her. In the next second, she hurled the contents of her stomach straight down and wondered if she'd simply be a pathetic casualty, dead the second she hit the earth.

A voice on the ground was shouting up at her.

"Pull your rigging lines to the right. To the *right*! Good! Now bend your legs. Bend! Forearms over your face! That's right. Put your head down. Head DOWN! Hunch your shoulders! Now *roll*!"

Viv landed with a thump and was dragged along the field by her air-filled chute, stopped finally by a tall, dark-haired instructor. Catherine, too, had landed several hundred yards away, and those already free of their equipment ran to help both women untangle themselves, offering excited hugs of congratulation.

"Careful," Viv warned them with embarrassment, pointing to the front of her jumpsuit. "I was sick coming down."

"But you did it!" Catherine cried, running to her side.

Viv shuddered, "I did it, but I hope I *never* have to do this again!"

"You have to do *two* jumps to pass the course," Catherine reminded her gently.

The instructor who'd verbally called out to Viv to guide her landing grabbed her elbow and led her to one side.

"You might not have to do a second jump," he said in a conspiratorial whisper. His broad, "I'm-a-God-around-here" smile hinted that a payment for his good offices might well be demanded in return. He held out his hand by way of introduction.

"I'm Lucien Barteau, and I'll be the new Air Operations Officer, stationed somewhere outside Paris, charged with receiving you agents arriving in France."

"Goodness, how impressive," Viv replied. He appeared oblivious to her gentle sarcasm and seemed pleased by her response. "When do you take up your post?" she asked, intrigued in spite of herself.

"Very soon," he replied, "but of course I can't tell you when."

"Of course," she replied demurely.

Air Officer Barteau was a tall, well-built young man in an ordinary sort of way, with dark, wavy hair. He was dressed in a stiff canvas flight suit, topped off by a silk ascot at his throat. Viv would guess he was a young Frenchman in his early thirties, confident, bordering seriously on cocky. She felt his appraising glance taking in her figure, and it occurred to her that he expected her to do the same to him: assess him for his obvious good looks and impressive bearing.

He favored her with another smile. "I used to fly for Air Bleu, and because of that experience, I suppose, I have the good fortune to be the one deciding who parachutes into France and who returns in the Lysander instead."

"A Lysander?" Viv repeated, wondering if this rather full-of-himself Lothario could possibly serve as her rescuing angel.

"It's our new short-takeoff-and-landing airplane. It can put down in a farmer's field and take off in short order. No need to jump out of it with a parachute," he explained. He raised a dark eyebrow as if to say, "Wouldn't that be lucky for *you*?"

"Sign me up!" Viv said promptly, taking off her helmet and shaking out her shoulder-length dark red locks in a show she hoped would prompt Officer Barteau to put her name on that clipboard of his. *Anything* to avoid that ghastly moment when she looked down at the earth that appeared to be rushing up to snuff her.

Lucien Barteau smiled yet again, his teeth not as white as he might have wished. Viv was certain the man was signaling to her that he was speaking to her in his own, seductive secret code. He gestured to his clipboard.

"I can easily put your name on my list for the Lysander and tell your trainer there's no need for you to do a second jump," he said.

"Oh, Lucien," she practically cooed. "That would be so kind of you!"

Two can play this game of cheese-and-mouse…

He added confidently, "I'm usually the one who keeps track of where F Section is assigning departing agents and make their deployment arrangement accordingly."

"You're my hero," she said, and cast him a coquettish smile that would have made her mother, Pamela, envious.

She'd do whatever it took—almost—to hang up her parachute for good! Given her prowess at jujitsu, she figured she could handle a guy like Barteau if he got out of line.

Just then, a voice prompted her to turn around.

"Let me add my congratulations. It's good to see you're in one piece."

Marcel stood before her in his full brigadier's uniform, medals and all. He was eyeing Lucien Barteau as if he were the other lion in the ring.

CHAPTER 34

Marcel Delonge and Lucien Barteau stood facing each other eye-to-eye in the airfield. Nobody moved while a small fighter plane noisily tore down a distant runway and took off. Viv struggled to regain her composure and moved to introduce the men to each other.

"I'm quite aware of *Monsieur* Barteau," Marcel said, demoting him in his address. "Weren't you a former stunt pilot in an air circus for a while?"

"And then I flew for Air Bleu, sir," Lucien said stiffly.

It would have been obvious to anyone that the two men apparently were not the best of French compatriots. In an attempt to soothe the charged atmosphere, Viv offered, "Air Officer Barteau has said he'll try to get me deployed on the new Lysander, Marcel, so I wouldn't have to parachute into France."

"You did well today," Marcel noted mildly. "Parachuting, I mean."

"I threw up. In the air."

"It happens," he replied.

"I hated jumping. I dread ever having to do it again."

"Yes, you hated it and you were afraid, but you did it anyway," he said. "That's the definition of courage, you know."

Lucien offered a feeble salute to his superior and then turned to address Viv.

"Well, since *mademoiselle* doesn't enjoy parachuting, I'll do my best to get you on one of the Lysander flights. Goodbye to you both."

He whirled on his heels and headed into the center of the landing field to speak to the other instructor who'd been supervising the day's series of jumps. Marcel watched Lucien walking away. Then he turned to Viv.

"Just for the record," he said, "I asked the colonel for a favor. If you could make at least one jump successfully, he agreed he'd put you on the list for the new Lysander."

"But Lucien said—"

"Lucien, is it now?"

Viv looked up at Marcel, astonished to realize that he was even the least bit jealous of Barteau's attentions to her. She laughed.

"Marcel! I just met him less than ten minutes ago!"

"Glad to hear it. I don't like him. I don't trust him. Neither should you."

"Wha—?"

"But don't worry. You *will* be on a Lysander when you head for France." He continued to gaze at her with a somber expression. "Meanwhile, you and I have been granted a couple of days' leave. That is, if you'd like to spend them with me?"

Viv stared at him. "Of *course*! I'd love nothing more! Where are we going?"

"No questions allowed, as usual," he chided, nodding over his shoulder in the direction of Lucien's retreating back, "especially here."

Viv realized Marcel had an extreme dislike for Barteau that obviously predated her meeting a man bent on dazzling an insecure parachute trainee like she was.

Seizing his hands, she said earnestly, "Thanks for the warning about that Barteau fellow, Marcel. I promise you I'll take it seriously. It's just that I honestly don't think I could make myself jump again." She held up her hand to prevent him speaking. "Yes, I did it once because I had to so they wouldn't kick me out of the SOE. And by some miracle I survived. But if you *or* this full-of-himself guy can get me a seat on a Lysander, I thank you both for taking pity on me," she pleaded. Impulsively—and despite the exposure of where they were standing—she reached up and kissed him firmly on the lips, whispering, "You are the only man I want in my life. I can't believe you wangled both of us leave at the same time."

Marcel pulled her hard against his chest and growled, "Believe me, it took some doing. Now, let's get out of here."

———◇———

"Where in the world did you get your hands on this adorable machine?" Viv shouted over the wind streaming by their open-air sports car. The jaunty British racing green Morris 8 Series E convertible with its contrasting black fenders had garnered enthusiastic waves from bystanders all along their route down from London.

"It belongs to the same friend who is loaning us his cottage," Marcel shouted back. "Or rather, his stables."

Viv shot him a startled look from across the dark green leather passenger seat.

Marcel laughed. "Not to worry. Nigel said we'd find the converted livery barn quite comfortable." His lips suppressed a smile as he added, "No, we're not sharing it with any four-footed creatures. Our absent host swears it's quite cozy."

Viv laughed. "I hope he's a *good* friend who isn't prone to exaggeration."

"The best," Marcel replied, sober now. "He's the pilot flying you over to France."

Hearing this news, Viv's breath caught, and she tilted her head against the leather seatback and tried to relax. She hadn't really allowed herself to dwell on the fact that she soon would be headed across the English Channel in a plane that would have to dodge anti-aircraft flak on its approach to the shores of France. These precious two days might be the last time they would see each other.

She turned her head away from Marcel to gaze at the rolling patchwork of fields and forests speeding by. Overhead, the bright blue skies were pure pleasure after the gloom of Scotland, along with the long ride they'd taken on a stuffy train from Manchester to London. When they'd emerged from the train station, Marcel had miraculously produced the dashing little Morris convertible to take them the rest of their journey to the southeast.

For several hours, they'd been driving from London toward Sidlesham, a small village near Chichester Harbor and a scant six miles to Tangmere, a secret RAF airfield outside London that would be their ultimate destination in two days' time.

"The cottage is convenient to the base where we'll both be deployed—but on different days," he'd warned, "and *no*, don't ask me exactly when or to where."

Viv's heart speeded up at the reality they soon would be going their separate ways. She would be a newly minted SOE agent; he a major player in de Gaulle's plan to try to unify the unruly factions among France's *résistants*.

The borrowed little Morris hummed along the road and eventually turned down a narrow lane where she could just catch a glimpse of the coastline curving toward Portsmouth. Marcel made another turn into a dirt track marked Rookery Farm. He continued on until it led to a redbrick and flintstone cottage that once had housed a few farm animals. The sight of a modern door painted pale blue reassured Viv that it had, indeed, been converted for use by two-footed creatures.

Marcel parked to the side on a square patch of gravel and handed Viv her knapsack and duffle bag, then grabbed hold of his own. He pulled an elaborate iron key from his jacket and opened the door.

"After you, *mademoiselle*," he said with a gallant sweep of his hand.

Inside, Viv's gaze took in vaulted, beamed ceilings and a small fireplace fitted with a wrought iron coal burning inset. Whitewashed walls alternated with patches of brick peeking through the plaster here and there. A terracotta-tiled floor sported a few scatter rugs. Two well-worn leather chairs flanked the hearth, and to the left against one wall was a compact kitchen area, a small round table with seating for two, and a steep staircase leading upstairs to the area that must have once been the hayloft.

"Oh, Marcel…" Viv said with a happy sigh as she turned in place. "It's as adorable as the car! Aren't we lucky?"

He followed her up the stairs that led into one large room, also with whitewashed walls and rough beams overhead. Pushed against the far wall made of old brick, also painted white, was a large fourposter bed that might have been installed a hundred years before their arrival. Viv let her two pieces of luggage slide from her hands to the floor, thinking that they had been gifted with the perfect honeymoon cottage. She gently seized Marcel's duffle from him and deposited it beside her own. Then, without a word, she reached up and put her arms around his shoulders, pulling him close.

"Thanks to your friend, Pilot Nigel," she whispered, "we have two whole days…"

———◇———

Viv and Marcel scarcely left their four-poster except to eat and take walks the mile or so down to the edge of the English Channel. On the third morning, Marcel awoke, stretched, and nuzzled Viv awake.

"Hungry?" he whispered. "For food, I mean," he amended.

"What meal is this?" Viv mumbled, her eyes still closed.

In their time at the cottage, the pair had existed mostly on eggs and toast, along with many cups of tea flavored with real—not powdered—milk. The precious glass bottles had been generously left for them each morning on the front step by whoever ran Nigel's family farm in his absence.

"Our last breakfast," Marcel said. "I'll do the scramble if you'll make the damn toast. What I wouldn't give for a croissant!"

Viv opened her eyes wide, turned to face Marcel in their feather bed, and threw her arms around his naked form. She held him close, keenly aware that this was the last time they would wake up in bed together, and also conscious of the steady rhythm of his heart beating against her breast. Blocking thoughts beyond where they were that second, she concentrated on reveling in the closeness and safety she felt lying next to him.

At length, Marcel pulled away and stretched out his hand to the bedside table for the protection he dependably employed. Relishing the next exquisite moments, she found herself wondering what the child they would likely never create together might have looked like.

On their last stroll down to the high cliffs overlooking the water shared with France some 88 nautical miles in the distance, Viv and Marcel held hands and remained silent for several long minutes. Viv spoke first.

"I had almost begun to forget there's a war on."

"The setting definitely helps," Marcel agreed, turning from the spectacular view to face her. "And so do you. Help me forget about the battles to come, I mean."

He took her in his arms, then, and kissed her deeply with the sound of the English Channel lapping gently on the rocky beach below. Viv laced fingers of each hand into his dark hair and leaned in to kiss him back. A feeling came over her that they had both been trying to imprint memories of these last moments together from the second they had awakened. And now, with the air and sunlight embracing them, Viv recognized a desperate need to gather impressions that might sustain her in the days and months and perhaps even years ahead.

When finally they released one another, Marcel's voice was low and filled with an emotion Viv had never heard before.

"Our time here went by so quickly," he said. He seized both her hands. "You realize I can offer you no guarantees?" he said. "I can only promise to do my best to stay alive. And you must promise to do the same. *D'accord, chérie?*"

Viv nodded, her throat tight.

"And if by some miracle," he said, "this nightmare ever ends and we both—"

"Yes, yes, *yes!*" she whispered. She couldn't bear to say the words *if we survive this war* and fought against a sob that nearly choked her.

Marcel dug into his pocket and brought out an embroidered insignia, holding the patch representing his parachute squadron for her inspection.

Viv stared. "You had a pair of wings like that sewn on your flight suit at Manchester."

"They *were* on my flight suit," he replied, smiling faintly. "I pried them off. I will go out of my plane totally hush-hush, as you say, in a business suit worn under my flight gear. Once I land, I'll bury the gear and my chute in the field." He placed the small, silk-stitched parachute canopy in the palm of her hand flanked by an embroidered wing on each side and folded his fingers around hers. "Find a place to hide this inside the lining of your jacket or somewhere it's unlikely to be found if you ever get searched. I want it always to remind you of how brave I think you are."

Viv stared up at him, her eyes swimming with tears, not feeling brave in the slightest. Marcel leaned down and brushed his lips against her forehead.

"Just remember your training, and I promise you, you'll stay safe." When he pulled away, his dark eyes focused on to hers. "And do remember… I love you."

Startled by his declaration, she could only murmur, "Oh, Marcel, I lov—"

Before she could finish, though, he leaned forward and kissed her hard, then pulled back quickly, and said, "We have to leave for Tangmere, *now*."

Viv nodded. They were due at the base by late afternoon. She turned to look up the path they'd taken from their brick and stone cottage whose roof was just visible at the top of the rise. She reached for his hand again. Side-by-side, they walked back to Rookery Farm. They packed their belongings in silence, but Viv hid a smile when she saw Marcel tuck her Hermès scarf into his duffle bag. Their luggage stowed into the Morris 8's back seat, they got into their midget car and drove the few miles in bright autumn sun toward the uncharted days that stretched ahead.

CHAPTER 35

To Viv's surprise, their next destination was also a cottage. This one, on the Tangmere RAF base itself, was covered from foundation to roofline in a thick blanket of ivy. Once a chapel, the ancient brick building was now home to the "Moon Squadron."

"These are the SOE's pilots like my friend Nigel," Marcel explained as he swung the Morris into a designated parking place at the back of the cottage. Several other official-looking sedans were already in their slots. "Britain's 161st ferries the lion's share of SOE's secret agents to France," he continued, "either those who parachute from Hailfaxes, or lucky ones like you, who land by your preferred mode of transportation: the Lysander. Mostly the pilots at Tangmere operate during periods of a full moon, given they're generally not landing at regular airfields with normal lighting."

"Hence their name, The Moon Squadron...how fitting," she murmured.

Viv knew that the Lysander, a small, single engine aircraft, could carry only two to four passengers, depending on the amount of cargo that was also on board.

"What if bad weather blocks the moon?" Viv asked, tamping down her anxiety.

"Well, it *is* October and it's getting colder," Marcel reminded her, grabbing their duffle bags from the back seat of the Morris and flipping the baby-buggy canvas top to fasten it to the front windshield in case of rain. "One or both of us might have to wait if the weather gets iffy. Sometimes, they even have to scrub flights completely until the next month's full moon," he said, guiding her toward the cottage's front door.

"Now, wouldn't *that* be nice?" Viv joked, hoping it sounded as if she weren't quaking in her flight boots. "My birthday's October fifteenth."

"I'll be sure to think of you that day," Marcel replied, his hand on her elbow guiding her through the cottage's front door.

Inside the foyer, she caught a glimpse of a small group of uniformed men and one woman chatting amicably while sipping cocktails. She quickly recognized Maurice Buckmaster and Vera Atkins from her initial interviews at SOE headquarters. Viv wagered silently that the tall, youthful officer in a leather flight jacket had to be Marcel's friend Nigel, for he gave a friendly salute and waved them over.

"Oh, golly," Viv whispered, her hand on Marcel's sleeve, halting their forward progress. "Do you suppose that older officer is my new boss?"

"Major Merrick?" Marcel asked. "*Oui, chérie.* The one with the mustache."

Viv absorbed the sight of the man's graying temples and receding hairline, as well as the thin salt-and-pepper mustache on his upper lip. His narrow face and slightly round-shouldered posture looked to her as someone who might have been a single-practitioner solicitor in civilian life.

"Oh, *no*," Viv groaned. "I'm a full head taller than he is."

"He's known as a soldier's soldier," Marcel reassured her. "And old enough to be your uncle. I hear he's a good man."

"But he's a *man*," Viv emphasized, "and all my life, any guy who has to look up to me to carry on a conversation soon excuses himself from my company."

In recent days, Viv had found herself growing apprehensive about this first meeting with Major John Merrick, whose code name she'd been told was to be "Pierre." The only other thing that had been disclosed to her was that his mission was to create a new clandestine network in the Alps called, aptly enough, Mountaineer. Their further assignment was to coordinate missions among the various French underground groups and forge them into an effective guerilla fighting force, ready to assist when an Allied invasion was launched. A similar assignment to Marcel's, Viv mused. Would Marcel and Merrick be stepping on each other's toes in their efforts behind enemy lines?

Marcel's grip on her elbow tightened as if he sensed her desire to back out of the small, paneled room that served as the Moon Squadron's pub. The man with the mustache turned toward Viv as they drew closer. The Major's gaze swiftly surveyed her from her feet to her wine-colored mane. Marcel made introductions.

Before Viv could say more than, "Lovely to meet you," which was the last thing she felt, Merrick said, "I was pleased to hear you're reputed to be a crack skier. I've tried it myself a few times, so I expect we're going to get plenty of exercise." His gaze drifted upwards. "In your white camouflage ski suit, the Jerries undoubtedly will think you're tall enough to be a man, which won't be a bad thing, you wager, Maurice?"

Ignoring Viv, he turned to the director of SOE's French Section for an answer.

"That was our thought," Buckmaster replied as if Viv weren't even in the room.

Vera Atkins smoothly took charge.

"And speaking of clothing, Viv, I'm so glad you got here in plenty of time. I've not only brought you your white camouflage ski suit, but also the French wardrobe we measured you for in London. Let's go upstairs so I can show you everything, plus I have a few last-minute instructions to review."

Viv barely had a moment to bid Marcel and the others goodbye. Upstairs, the seventeenth century cottage featured a long hallway off of which Miss Atkins explained were small bedrooms reserved for pilots when their flights were delayed. "There's a free one down here at the end."

When they entered, an open leather suitcase lay on the bed with clothing laid out on the bedspread, neatly folded.

"I've already checked to be sure the labels are properly French." Miss Atkins pulled the lining out of one of the pockets. "We also make certain that there are no laundry tags, matchbooks, or any telltale signs that you have actually come to France from England. Even the buttons on your wool jacket are French," she added with a hint of pride.

She began to stow other items in the suitcase, showing Viv a packet of French cigarettes, a recent French newspaper, and a photograph she tucked in the silk pouch that was part of the lining in the suitcase's lid. As promised, a white camouflage ski suit was folded at the bottom.

Pointing to the photograph, Vera said, "This is your 'half-sister' named Yvonne Charbonnet who lives on a farm outside Annecy in the Haute-Savoie. You, on the other hand, were a skier training for alpine events in the Olympics until the war started. You have been trying to find employment at various resorts in eastern France, but so far, to no avail. Your money came from modeling you did for companies making ski equipment." Atkins looked at her intently. "Now, tell me the firms you've worked for."

Viv dutifully recited the names of since-bankrupted ski equipment manufacturers that her spy school instructors had provided as part of her new identity.

"Excellent," Vera complimented her. "The best policy for agents is to concoct a cover story as close to the world they know as possible." She regarded her silently for a moment. "And if you are ever found out to *not* be French? What then?"

Viv responded automatically.

"I'm to admit that I'm a rather dim-witted young American woman, caught in France hoping to try out for the Olympics when war broke out, and that I'm rather spoiled." She tried not to laugh at a perfect description of herself a year earlier, except for being a dimwit. Pausing for breath, she added, "I'm American from a wealthy industrialist family in North Carolina, trying to find my British mother whom the Germans interned at Vittel. My stepfather is the American industrialist Karl Bradford, a steel ball-bearing tycoon."

Viv found it totally galling that in this second narrative, she had to pretend she rather admired Karl and his achievements, but the spymasters who'd worked out her "back-up" cover story felt the SS could easily check Berlin to verify Karl's activities before the war. Her instructor had said, "It might just prevent them from torturing you too badly—or at the very least, prevent your execution."

"All right, then," Vera said with a satisfied nod. "Let's get you dressed and meet the others for dinner. I've left out the wool skirt that's actually split into culottes so you can easily ride a bicycle until the snow falls and you take to your skis as Major Merrick said." She pointed to a matching jacket and blouse. "You can leave your FANY uniform on the bed when you're dressed. It will be waiting for you when you return."

If I return... she thought, wrestling not only with rising fear of what might lay ahead, but also sensing she might never see Marcel again, the only man besides her father she knew, now, she truly loved.

Viv turned toward the bed, expecting to hear Miss Atkins leave the room.

"One or two more details," she said with a quiet air. Viv turned around in time to see Buckmaster's deputy reach into her jacket pocket. She pulled out a small, gold compact, handing it to Viv. "Colonel Buckmaster and I want to give you a token of our deepest appreciation for the journey you've agreed to undertake." She turned it over, pointing. "There's an engraving in French 'To darling Violette.' The story is that the compact was given to you by your mother when you reached twenty-one."

If only... Viv thought with an unexpected jolt of sadness.

"Here, let me open it for you," Vera instructed, and retrieved it from Viv's hand.

"It's lovely," Viv murmured, touched by their thoughtfulness. "Thank you so much."

Miss Atkins inserted a fingernail between the mirror and its golden shell. In the hollow was a capsule tightly wrapped in cellophane.

"Did anyone tell you what this is?" she asked Viv.

"The L pill," Viv replied, suppressing a shudder. "As in 'lethal.' To take when there's no way out."

Atkins nodded. "It works in thirty seconds when you squeeze it between your back teeth. Keep it near you at all times." She clicked the case shut. "Only take it if you think you can't keep silent about your operation for at least two days so others in your network have time to scatter." She nestled the compact in Viv's palm and turned to go. "And now, get dressed. Your flight suit and parachute gear will be at the hangar."

"*What*?" Viv reacted in horror. "But I thought—"

Miss Atkins, one hand on the bedroom doorknob, held up her other hand like a crossing guard. "Odds are excellent the Lysander will land in the field as scheduled, but you'll wear your standard parachute gear during the flight, just in case." She smiled brightly. "I'll see you downstairs."

Viv's hands trembled slightly as she donned her French wardrobe. She peeled back the lining of her sturdy French shoes and slid in the small, embroidered wings-and-parachute patch Marcel had given her as a good luck token. Slipping the shoe back onto her right foot, she stared at herself in a narrow mirror on the back of the door.

"I guess I'm as ready as I'll ever be," she said to her reflection, and headed down to dinner.

———◇———

Viv sat next to Marcel and the others on wooden benches that flanked long trestle tables in a room in the cottage adapted as the "Officers Mess." Their group was served a plentiful meal of boiled meat, along with potatoes and carrots Viv suspected had been grown in a kitchen garden out back. She could barely eat a bite.

"Not exactly French cuisine," Marcel whispered in her ear in his native language, "but try to eat something. It may be a while before we get anything nearly as decent."

"Oh! Has it turned out that you're flying out tonight, too?" she whispered back, attempting one more time to learn what was next for him.

"I'll be there to see you off," he murmured, taking a sip of ale which Viv knew he'd rather exchange for wine.

As usual, he offered an answer that was no answer.

After servings of English "pudding"—a caramel custard dessert concoction that might also be considered a genuine pudding in America—the party gathered in the foyer and donned their coats. They filed into two sedans that were waiting, engines running, outside. The moon had risen, clear and crisp in the October air, a sight that soothed Viv's rising anxiety that she might, in the end, have to parachute out of the Lysander about to carry her to France.

Once the cars entered the airfield and pulled up in front of a large

Quonset hut next to the runway, Vera Atkins bid the men farewell and instructed Viv to follow her.

"See you soon," Marcel whispered. "You're just going to put on your gear."

Assuming the role of a mother hen, Vera guided Viv toward a room with a tin door that opened into a women's changing room that looked more like a housekeeper's closet.

"Everything you're to wear over your regular clothing is hanging in here," she said. "Except for your knapsack, your luggage is being loaded aboard the Lysander right now, so you've nothing else to worry about."

Yeah, right… Viv already felt her stomach twisting into a knot as Akins closed the door behind her.

Viv struggled into her canvas flight suit and pulled it up and over her woolen skirt and matching jacket in whose right pocket was the "L" pill incased in the gold compact. Reaching down to her knees, she tugged the long zipper that went up on a diagonal to her shoulder, encasing her entire body. Then, she picked up her helmet and gloves and emerged into the chilly hangar, her eyes seeking Marcel's familiar figure still wearing his regular uniform. She spotted him speaking to Nigel who was outfitted in his flight gear. The pair stood next to another young man who also looked as if he were preparing to board an airplane for a flight into enemy territory.

"Ah, Viv," Marcel said, holding out his hand as she approached. "Meet your seatmate, Paul. He's Merrick's radio operator. He's going out with you on the second Lysander while the Major will be on the first, along with quite a bit of equipment."

Nigel laughed and clapped Paul on the back. "Actually, since this man is a pianist," he said, using the slang term for a wireless operator, "we call him 'Fingers.'"

"Paul Mallory in real life," Mallory laughed. "Fingers" looked to be in his early twenties, a fresh-faced, eager young American. "Pleased to meet y'all."

"You're from Georgia?" she asked.

"Close. New Orleans, Louisiana. *Laissez les bons temps rouler,* ya know." He flashed a friendly grin. "Marcel, here, tells me you went over the Pyrenees with a wicked case of the mumps. You sound like the kinda gal it'd be good to have on this adventure."

Viv summoned a smile, although her stomach was still turning over.

"If you passed wireless school," she said, "you have my undying admiration. The only thing that saved me after my disastrous attempt to master that skill was the powers-that-be apparently need someone who can speak French and ski." She thrust out her hand, mildly cheered by Paul's friendly demeanor. "I assume you made it through parachute class, too, but aren't we lucky to be landing on the ground in France?"

"I guess so," he said. "You should know that I've never had on a pair of skis in my life. And I'm kinda disappointed that we won't be jumping. I had fun during training."

Viv tried to suppress her look of horror. Marcel slung his arm around her shoulder and addressed Paul Mallory.

"Let's assume the plane will land, as planned, in a field near Loyettes, east of Lyon," Marcel said with a wry smile, "but if our Viv shows a moment's hesitation, Fingers, just push her out the jump hole."

For the second time that evening, it felt as if the men surrounding Viv had forgotten she was standing in their midst. Just then, Major Merrick joined their group. He, too, wore a flight suit over what Viv assumed were French-style civilian clothes provided him by F Section haberdashers.

"Well, chaps," he said, his gaze sweeping the circle surrounding him, "what time do you think we'll leave?" Buckmaster and Vera Atkins were walking toward them, along with the duty officer. Merrick pointed toward the hangar's gigantic door, open to the shadowed landing field beyond. "How's the weather forecast?" he asked Nigel.

Nigel shrugged, "When I checked earlier, they said it was reasonable, although there would be some clouds and rain to fly through over northern and central France.

Viv wondered if the weather turned bad, how hardy was a plane only thirty feet long that flew low and had been adapted to plop down in fields behind enemy lines? At that moment, another leather-jacketed man approached their group.

"Good evening, gentlemen," Group Captain Hugh Verity greeted them. Spotting Viv and Vera, he added, "and ladies. It's a go, although we have to keep an eye out for a mild, warm front lying right across our track. If the winds behave, we'll be fine and the risk of fog will be negligible." Viv shot a look at Marcel.

Nigel saw the exchange and said cheerfully to Viv, "Well, I imagine you're glad not to be jumping. It's going to be cold over there." Viv merely nodded. Nigel looked at her intently, "But if you have to jump, you would, right?"

Viv could tell everyone in the group that had ever seen her SOE file had come to attention waiting for her answer.

"Yes, of course," she managed to reply.

"Good girl," Nigel said, casting a glance at Marcel. "But I hope you won't have to. Air Officer Lucien Barteau will be on the ground to greet us."

This time, it was Marcel who stiffened at the name of Barteau. Viv remembered his warning: *I don't trust Lucien Barteau. Neither should you.*

Meanwhile, Hugh Verity was saying, "Apparently, the Air Officer has found a nice, level field, but there's a Nazi internment camp not too far from it, so don't hang around the plane once we're on the ground."

Marcel spoke up. "And why did Barteau select such a landing spot?"

Verity glanced at Buckmaster, allowing him to answer.

"Barteau wired that it was the best to be had to get you people as close to the Alps as possible." He shrugged. "Apparently beggars can't be choosers these days."

CHAPTER 36

Everyone filed into the Ops Room for a look at the big map of France on the wall. Once last-minute instructions were concluded, Colonel Buckmaster said jovially, as if he were flying out himself, "Well, then, time to get going, wouldn't you say, chaps?"

Meeting adjourned, everyone solemnly shook hands. The two pilots led the way over the dark tarmac toward their Lysanders parked wing-to-wing. Nigel vaulted up a metal ladder permanently affixed to the plane's back fuselage. Viv handed up her knapsack and turned to face Marcel. He leaned forward, lightly kissing her on both cheeks.

"À bientôt, chérie" was all the farewell that time and circumstances allowed.

Viv briefly closed her eyes, willing herself not to show the well of emotion she was feeling. After a second, she opened them, donned her crash helmet, and nodded her goodbyes. Scrambling up the metal ladder, she ducked just in time to avoid colliding with the rim of the open canopy.

Inside the Lysander, Viv crouched on a wooden bench fastened to the left side of the fuselage. Nigel emerged from the cockpit to attach parachute harnesses for Paul and her to static lines "just in case of an emergency jump," he said off-handedly. Then he showed them how their helmets plugged in to the intercom.

Viv and Fingers then wedged themselves toward the rear of the plane, surrounded by their luggage and wooden boxes of supplies— some marked as weapons and ammunition. There was even a pile of bicycle tires roped together which vividly brought back memories of wheeling past authorities in Annemasse at the Swiss border with a chicken squawking in her basket.

Nigel handed them each a blanket, announcing, "Our escort planes will shadow us until we reach the French coast. After that, we'll fly a bit beneath the ack-ack." With a wave, he squeezed through an opening into the cockpit and strapped himself in.

"Ack-ack?" Viv mouthed to Paul.

"Anti-aircraft flak trying to shoot us down."

"Wonderful," Viv murmured.

The engine roared to life and their plane began to roll toward the end of the runway, following the other Lysander. The noise of the two planes became intense as they waited their turn to take off. Viv heard Merrick's plane head down the field first.

With an accelerating rumble of their single engine, they, too, soon sped down the tarmac and were in the air. The moon over the English countryside shone brightly, clearly illuminating the patchwork of fields and rivers passing below. Viv was startled how quickly they left the coast of Great Britain near Bognor Regis and headed across the Channel. The intercom crackled with Nigel's calm, collected voice.

"We're going to climb to eight thousand feet, well above any light flak, but please, everybody, keep a sharp eye out for the odd German patrol plane, will you? We'll have to drop to about two thousand feet eventually, and that can get dicey. Cheerio."

Less than an hour later, the plane was approaching the coast of France when the light of the moon overhead suddenly disappeared. The Lysander's fifty-foot wingspan had plunged into a sea of thick, gray clouds, rendering the curved part of the clear canopy overhead completely opaque.

"Sorry for the fog," announced Nigel in Viv's earpiece. "Fortunately, we have a good ways still to go," he advised his passengers as Viv stared at the closed parachute trap in the belly of the plane, "so let's hope it clears, including the ground fog."

"The *ground* fog?" Viv repeated aloud, looking at Paul in alarm.

They were going to land in a farmer's field, for God's sake!

Viv was well aware that doing that in thick fog that extended all the way to the ground could be as fatal as her father's parachute failure.

Fingers peered at his watch and showed it to her. It was twelve-fifteen. They were about an hour away, plus or minus, from their destination. The two of them stared at each other and simultaneously began to inhale deep breaths. Blessedly, the boiling, dark clouds slowly began to dissipate as they headed steadily south and east toward the target area outside Lyon. At long last, the pilot's voice once again boomed over the intercom.

"Well, boys and girls, it would seem we've had a bit o' luck, weather-wise. Hugh Verity's plane looks as if it's about to land. We'll make a circle here while he lets off the major and the equipment, and then we'll have some fun of our own."

Fun?

Viv's nerves were as taut as the static line that was still connected to the parachute she prayed she wasn't going to need. She and Paul sat motionless on their hard, wooden bench as the plane banked sharply, and then banked again, lining up for their own descent to the field where the other plane had presumably landed and was about to take off.

"Here we go…stand by for a few bumps," Nigel warned.

All of the Lysander's thirty-foot length pointed sharply toward the earth as the two passengers clung to the edge of their bench to keep from sliding toward the cockpit. Viv braced for impact just as Nigel cursed loudly through the intercom, "Oh, bloody hell!" She felt the plane's nose pull up sharply to abort the landing. "*Bugger all*, we missed it! Verity didn't get airlift as soon as I thought, and I was going to overshoot!"

Their plane may have missed the makeshift runway, but the Lysander didn't execute an entirely clean get-away. Flashing by the glass canopy was a church belfry, and the very tip of the plane's wings clipped it, sending the shock of the impact reverberating up Viv's spine. In seconds, both she and Paul were thrown into the belly of the plane.

"Owww!" he yelled, as Viv's leather suitcase hit him in the back.

Viv's knapsack landed on her feet and shins, followed by the stack of bicycle tires.

"*Merde!*" was her automatic response, although, in the next moment, she realized it could have been far worse, given Nigel had, so far, kept the plane airborne. The wooden box of Sten guns slammed into the tail area as the Lysander pulled up and leveled off.

Paul was struggling to sit up as he pushed aside tins of ammo. Viv reached down to extract her feet and rub her lower legs. The barrier of her flight suit had probably kept her skin from receiving too much damage, although she imagined she'd be bruised and battered.

"You okay?" she asked Paul.

"Not great," he said, rubbing the small of his back, "but I'll live."

To their great relief, the plane kept flying as the two passengers grabbed the edge of the wooden bench and righted themselves to resume a seated position.

Nigel's impersonal voice penetrated both their helmets. "You two might have to jump after all, so do be prepared." Viv thought she'd be sick right then and there, but in the next second Nigel barked, "No, no! It's all right…it's all right. I see now that Verity's well off the ground and away. Standby for landing!"

The plane slammed onto the grassy field, its reinforced undercarriage miraculously intact. The second they'd rolled to a stop, she and Paul detached from their static lines, abandoning their parachutes on the bench. With her seatmate in the lead, Viv scrambled toward the metal ladder permanently affixed to the plane's side, its top rungs painted yellow for easy visibility.

A male voice on the ground yelled in French, "Hurry, hurry!"

She followed Fingers Malloy, missing the ladder's last rung and stumbling smack into a mud hole. Stunned by her fall, the wind knocked out of her, she lay there for a minute as moisture from the ground soaked her cheeks and chin. Slowly, she pushed herself to her knees and saw a tall figure striding toward her. Frantically, her gaze swept the field. Fingers was nowhere to be seen. However, extending a hand to her was the dark-haired figure of Lucien Barteau, a sarcastic smile on his face.

"*Ahhhh…mademoiselle… Violette, n'est-ce pas?*" In English he added, "My tall, lovely American who, I see, revels in savoring the soil of France. How did you like the Lysander I arranged for you?"

He helped her to her feet and turned to catch her suitcase, duffle, and knapsack that Nigel was poised to toss out of the plane. Continuing in French he ordered, "Take your luggage, make a run for that stand of trees over there and wait for me."

"Where's Pierre?" she demanded, using Merrick's code name. "And Fingers?"

Lucien pointed toward the trees and turned away without answering. A small band of ragged-looking men in farm overalls and moth-eaten jackets were swarming toward them to receive the battered cargo that Nigel pitched to them from atop the plane's ladder. Some six inches of the plane's left wing was crumpled, but the rest of it appeared in reasonable shape. Viv waved him her thanks and gathered up her belongings.

With Marcel's warning about the former aerobatic stunt pilot ringing in her ears, she made a dash across the field, weighed down by her leather suitcase and heavy duffle, along with her knapsack slung over her back. Once she reached cover, she collapsed, gasping for breath at the base of a wispy pine. She peered into the gloom and listened intently. Major Merrick was nowhere to be seen, and neither was Fingers Malloy. She thought of the Nazi internment camp she'd been advised was nearby. Had the sound of two planes landing alerted patrols that had spotted and apprehended her two companions?

Viv shivered at the thought that such bad luck could end their mission before it had even begun. The night air had more than an autumn bite to it. In fact, it felt downright frigid. Even so, she unzipped her flight suit, peeled it off her body, and rolled it up tightly like the sleeping bags of her youth. She wondered if one of her male companions would help dig the hole in which they were supposed to bury all evidence of their illicit arrival behind enemy lines. As she sat sorting out what to do next, the engine of Nigel's plane roared to life once more. Gathering speed, it raced down the field, heading back to England while she sat on the cold ground of France, alone in the dark.

———— ◆ ————

It was easily a half hour before Viv heard a voice speaking roughly and then felt a large hand on her shoulder.

"Come, we must go," Lucien said, looking down at her sitting on the frigid ground with a tree at her back. "I had to see that the men stored the guns and other supplies where the Krauts won't find them."

"Lucien, where are the two men in my Mountaineer network?"

Not answering her question, he offered one of his own. "Didn't they tell you my code name is Gilbert?"

"No, I don't think they thought we'd be anything other than ships passing in the night," she said pointedly.

He pulled her to her feet, keeping hold of her hands. "*Mais non, chérie*, never two ships passing."

"Where are Pierre and Fingers?" she insisted for the third time. "Aren't we supposed to be on our way east by now?"

"Change of plans. They've gone on to the safe house with one of my other men."

She cast him a skeptical look. Lucien/Gilbert had indicated they would rendezvous in these woods. She pointed to her flight suit rolled like a sausage.

"Shouldn't we be burying this gear?"

He took it from her and stuffed it in her duffle. "Someone could make good use of the fabric," he observed. "I'll get it from you later."

"But what if a German sees you have it," she protested. "They'd guess that—"

"Let's go," he interrupted. "You'll see Merrick and Paul at the safe house."

This guy pays absolutely no attention to security! she thought, hearing him use her companions' real names.

Lucien, a mere inch taller than Viv, cast her a tight smile.

"You seem to forget, *chérie,* that I'm in charge here. Let's go," he repeated, and there was not a hint of Gallic charm in his tone.

CHAPTER 37

Viv knew they had landed somewhere around the town of Loyettes in the Commune of Ain in the Rhone-Alps, east of the large city of Lyon. That meant they were southwest of Lake Annecy in the Haute-Savoie, which was the Mountaineer circuit's ultimate destination very near the Swiss border.

Not too far from my old skiing stomping grounds, she thought, grateful she had some grasp of the Resistance territory that was theirs to organize. The resorts at Chamonix, Mont Blanc, and Albertville all held memories of a carefree life she'd once known.

As Viv and the Air Operations Officer—whom she reminded herself to call Gilbert—began to walk through the trees, she spotted a river on her left, its flowing current sparkling in shafts of moonlight.

"The Rhone," she murmured. "It seems so incredible to be in France again."

Lucien merely nodded. They emerged from the woods onto a path that paralleled the bank with a large bridge visible ahead. Squat, two-story stone buildings, their painted shutters closed tight, were lined up on her right. Lucien veered into the street leading from the bridge and then immediately turned left down a narrower road with a church spire looming at the end of the lane.

"Good heavens, is that what the Lysander hit?" Viv whispered. "Why didn't we rouse the entire town?"

"No. Your pilot nicked another church steeple in the next village."

He turned into what looked like a stable yard, and Viv braced for another night sleeping in a hayloft, stifling her sneezes. To her relief, at the far end of the courtyard was a wooden door that led to the house adjacent. They entered a kitchen with a hallway that Viv assumed led to bedrooms where the others were already sleeping off the nerve-wracking trip. She set her belongings on the stone-paved floor and exhaled.

"We made it."

She looked over at Lucien, who smiled like a Cheshire Cat and replied, "And since you did so without the dreaded parachute, let us have a toast to your good luck at being assigned to me as your landing instructor in Manchester." He gestured toward a bottle of wine, half consumed, standing on a wooden table with two glasses positioned next to it. "A glass to celebrate."

"Thank you, no," Viv said. "I'm literally dead on my feet. Please, where do I sleep?"

Ignoring her, Lucien uncorked the bottle and poured red wine up to the brim in both glasses. Turning, he handed one to her.

She stood eye level and stared back at him, then carefully set her glass on the table.

"I guess you didn't hear me, Gilbert, but I don't care to have any wine at this hour. What I need right now is sleep."

He took a step closer and set his own wine glass on the table, his eyes riveted on hers. "Surely, there are more interesting things we could do than fall asleep."

As a reasonably attractive woman who'd dealt with her share of Casanovas, she could guess what he expected as recompense for claiming to secure her seat on the Lysander. She reached down for her suitcase and rose to her full height with her knapsack in her other hand.

"I do thank you, *Gilbert*," she said coolly, emphasizing his code name, "not only for me, personally, but for all you've done to arrange the landing for our group. Meanwhile, you'll have to excuse me. As I said, I'm exhausted and I—"

He grabbed one wrist, forcing her to let go of her knapsack and pressed it against his chest, abruptly pulling her close. Viv released the handle of her suitcase and rejoiced when he winced as it landed on his foot.

"Let me go!" she demanded hoarsely, aware there might be others just down the hall.

But Lucien grabbed her other wrist.

"I don't think so, *chérie*," he growled, pulling her toward the door they had entered. "I have such comfortable quarters next door, so you'd better show a little gratitude for all that I did to—*oompft! Merde!*"

Viv's mastery of jujitsu only encompassed a few moves, but her recent "silent killing" course in spy school prompted her to shove a hard elbow into Lucien's diaphragm. He gasped for air and released her wrists, his back slamming against the door. For once, Viv was glad how tall she was, which allowed her to place a swift, downward blow to the bridge of his nose with the side of her clenched right fist. Blood immediately gushed out of his nostrils, over his upper lip, and dribbled down his chin.

"Why, you bitch, I'll—"

"What's going on, here!" barked a voice from the hallway.

Viv whirled around just in time to see Major Merrick striding down the hallway in his undershorts, pistol drawn. The room fell silent while Lucien wiped his bleeding face with the back of his sleeve. Merrick's gaze swept from the Air Officer who had greeted their two Lysanders, to Viv, who stood with her fists clenched by her side, her suitcase, duffle bag, and knapsack strewn on the kitchen floor.

Viv spoke first.

"I imagine agent Gilbert, here, has a bit more to learn about the training provided to women SOE agents." She offered Lucien a saccharine smile. "I was demonstrating for him how we female recruits take the same self-defense course he received." She looked back at Barteau. "My last demonstration move seemed to have done damage. Sorry."

Merrick, his lips ajar in obvious shock, stared at the two of them frozen in place. Viv could almost read the major's thoughts. Lucien Barteau was very competent at the extremely important job of arranging landings and takeoffs of SOE's critical personnel. If Merrick believed he had to report Lucien's misbehavior, *she* didn't want to be the cause of Buckmaster or his superiors believing women agents "caused disruption in the ranks." She swiftly held up her hand before Merrick could rebuke her attacker.

"Please excuse us, Major Merrick," she began, in as pleasant a tone as she could muster, "if our arrival just now awakened you. No problem, right Gilbert?" Not waiting for his answer, she seized the handle of her suitcase and rising to her full height added, "I must say, I, for one, am completely knackered." She flashed a faint smile at their greeter whose head was tilted back to stop the bleeding. "Am I right in assuming there's a bedroom down the hall where I'm supposed to sleep?"

Lucien managed a slight nod, mumbling, "Last one...on the right."

"Well, then," she said with false cheer, "I bid you both a good night's rest."

She slung her knapsack over her shoulder and bent down again to retrieve her duffle. Acutely aware of two sets of masculine eyes staring at her back, she strode down the hall and entered the last door on her right. The room was dark, but the moonlight shining through the window revealed a cot with a blanket on top. Viv sank down on the mattress, her luggage slipping to the wooden floor. Her entire body was suddenly seized by trembling, and she covered her face with both hands, vaguely aware that the fist she'd used to deliver a blow to Lucien's nose now ached like the devil.

She forced herself to take slow, even breaths and felt her heart rate slow down. One thought revolved in her mind: Lucien Barteau, a.k.a. "Gilbert," might be an expert in the field of aviation and supposedly on the side of the Allies, but she felt she'd learned an important lesson this night about survival in wartime France.

Under certain circumstances, trust no one...

She understood in a totally new context exactly what that meant. Marcel had placed Lucien Barteau in that particular category, and she silently blessed him. Even so, it was a disconcerting notion that apparently there would be men on both the Allied *and* German sides she'd have to fight.

"Welcome to France," she whispered bleakly into the chill air of October.

Missing Marcel in ways she'd never expected, she'd never felt lonelier in her life.

———◇———

To Viv's relief, early the next morning one of Lucien's minions appeared at their door to guide Major Merrick, Fingers, and Viv into Lyon with no sign of the Air Operations Officer to be seen. For Viv's part, she hoped she'd never lay eyes on the man again and left her canvas flight suit on the bed for the creep to dispose of as he wished.

At the train station, each member of the trio boarded separate cars and collectively held their breath until they disembarked at Le Bourget du Lac, a less well-known destination than the nearby spa town of Aix-les-Bains. As autumn was giving way to winter at these altitudes, light snow had begun to fall in flurries.

"This is where *you* come in," Major Merrick announced to Viv as soon as they met up at a café down an alley away from the train station. "Can you locate three pairs of skis? We're headed for Lake Annecy, and later, I to Saint Jorioz. I'm told you know it."

Viv smiled happily. "Oh, yes. Saint Jorioz is a tiny town, a few miles down the lake from Annecy, but with a lovely prospect over the water."

"We're not going there to enjoy the view, Viv," Merrick replied brusquely. "I need to confer with a couple of agents there to establish the ground rules for our Mountaineer network. Peter Churchill has his own active operation in the region, and we don't want to step on his toes. Nevertheless, London has assigned Mountaineer to work with the *maquis* on the Plateau des Glières and several other underground organizations in regions east of there. We'll establish a safe house for you near Annecy, with a room there for me as well, although I'll be traveling most of the time between Resistance groups." He glanced at Paul. "We'll also need to find a spot somewhere around the Lake where Fingers' equipment can establish a decent radio signal to Britain."

"It'd better be pretty high up in the mountains," Paul replied, looking doubtful they'd have much luck broadcasting from a place ringed by the Alps.

"Faverges might work," Viv offered. "It's a few miles beyond the south end of Lake Annecy where the surrounding land flattens out."

Merrick nodded as if her suggestion had merit.

"But back to the skis. I think to avoid arrest and get around the Haute-Savoie in this weather, we may have to masquerade as three grown siblings on a bit of a winter holiday. We'll take trains or buses as far as we can and then take to our skis, if we have to."

"Have you two done much skiing yourselves?" Viv asked, keeping her tone neutral in the wake of Merrick's earlier comment about their mission not being a vacation.

The major fell silent a moment before he replied, "Oh…once or twice, on school holidays quite a few years ago it is, now." His expression hinted at the first smile he'd ever bestowed on Viv. "You may have to provide a lesson or two when we start out."

"For me, too, I'm afraid," Paul chimed in. "Remember, I'm a New Orleans boy."

Given that their radioman was a complete novice, and Major John Merrick, a.k.a. Pierre, had gray sideburns, Viv reckoned that for once, she'd be the expert in the group.

When the major rose to pay their bill, Viv asked Paul, "Who is Peter Churchill? Any relation?"

"Pretty distant, according to Merrick," he replied. "As you can imagine, though, the name always garners attention. Peter Churchill's code name is Raoul, by the way. He has a woman courier, too, I heard... Odette Samson, who goes by the code name Lise."

Outside the café, the snow had begun to fall in earnest. While the major and Paul finished their coffee in a back corner, Viv set off to find someone willing to sell her three pairs of skis. This, she imagined, would be no easy task, considering the shortages of just about everything in wartime France.

As she made her way down the main thoroughfare, she noticed a cluster of people filing into a church rectory with a poster proclaiming, "Church Bazaar Today!"

She joined the shoppers, who were perusing an odd assortment of discarded household goods whose sale would aid "our widows and orphans." To her delight, leaning against a wall near the entrance to the rectory were two pairs of battered but serviceable skis, poles, and metal-tipped boots to match that could be clamped into cable bindings.

"Any chance you know of one more pair of used boots, poles, and skies I can buy for myself?" she asked of the church volunteer, repeating Merrick's cover story that they were embarking on a short, impromptu holiday to take advantage of the early snows.

The diminutive, gray-haired woman overseeing piles of clothes, assorted pots and pans, and a collection of castoff sports equipment quickly glanced side-to-side and said under her breath, "My son was conscripted to work in Germany. We have no idea when he'll be back. I was going to break up his skis for firewood. I could sell them to you."

Viv leaned forward to speak quietly in her ear. "I would be so grateful if you would. Boots and poles, too?" She touched the woman's arm. "And may your son return safely."

The woman named a price and looked Viv up and down. "You're a tall one, aren't you, but I think everything will suit you fine. Shall I go home to get them?"

———◇———

Less than an hour later, Viv and her companions, each wearing heavy boots and carrying pairs of skis on their shoulders and ski poles in their hands, boarded a bus that took them to the train station in Aix-les-Bains. From there they entered a railcar, posing as a trio of holidaymakers hoping to find more snow in the higher Alps. Two hours later, they arrived in Annecy, the lovely medieval town situated at the top of the lake with the same name that Viv knew well from holiday trips during her boarding school days. The guards checking documents were local gendarmes, and thanks to the group's well-worn ski equipment, Viv, Merrick and Fingers were waved through with a cursory look at their phony identification.

"We're not far from the Café Lyonnais," Viv volunteered as the trio started down one of Annecy's quaint, snow-covered streets bisected by canals whose waters fed the lake. "I know the owner who looked after me when Clément Grenelle escorted me to the Plateau des Glières to meet with the *maquis* up there."

"Let's hope someone there can help find us a safe-house outside town," Merrick said, "so we can quickly get down to business. Now that the Allies have taken North Africa, the word is that the Germans may move any day now to occupy all of France beyond the Free Zone in anticipation of an invasion from the south." He grimaced. "With SS swarming around here, our mission to recruit and mollify the various factions of resistance in the Haute-Savoie will become twice as difficult—and far more treacherous for our personal safety." He shrugged, "But it can't be helped, so let us get on with it."

Viv pointed to the faded blue awning with its cracked yellow lettering declaring that they had reached the destination. Merrick looked over at Viv as if he had never expected her to find the restaurant with such ease.

"The Café Lyonnais is part of a small hotel," she explained. "The owner is a partisan. Perhaps he'd even let us stay in one of his rooms."

"It's the first place the authorities look," Merrick replied dismissively. "But we can certainly chance a meal in his café and see if he knows someplace else safer."

Viv gazed beyond the eatery at the bustling traffic and busy shops along their route. Life in Annecy, with its lovely canals and waterside eateries, was certainly less austere than the German-occupied Paris that she'd fled months earlier. To her amazement, standing at the restaurant's door as if he'd expected them, Anton La Salle, the *patron* of Café Lyonnais, recognized her immediately as she greeted him.

"*Bonjour, monsieur*! Do you remember me? I am—"

"Ah...*mademoiselle*! Of *course* I remember you!" he enthused with a glance at her head. "How good to see Clément Grenelle's burgundy-haired beauty once more."

Embarrassed by his effusive greeting, Viv held out her hand to shake his and introduced her companions. Anton pulled Viv into a bear hug, bussing both cheeks.

"Come, come... I'll get someone to store your skis and let me seat you and your brothers at a table in the back."

CHAPTER 38

It was long after the lunch hour, and Café Lyonnais was nearly empty. With a nod, Viv's boss encouraged her to follow their host into his kitchen to inquire if he could provide them with a safe house in the vicinity. As soon as they were alone, Viv glanced at a dishwasher working at the sink and asked Anton La Salle to step into the alley where she explained who they really were and the urgent needs they had.

"Finally!" Anton exclaimed. "The Allies are sending us some genuine help to fight the Krauts."

"Well, a least it's a beginning," Viv hastened to reply. "My *patron*, Pierre, is a key man in England," she explained. "Besides an out-of-the-way place to house the major and myself, we need to find a protected spot from which my other comrade can radio back to Britain about the state of things in this region...and about the requirements of the Resistance, here," she added as further enticement.

Anton let out a low whistle. "So... Clément was right to put such faith in you," he said. Viv found herself amazed to hear of such support from a man who seemed off and on to dismiss her. Anton smiled broadly. "He told me that you would somehow manage to take the messages from Julien Paquet and the Plateau des Glières *maquisards* to London—and you have!" He clapped her on the shoulder, clearly a supporter of the many local young men who'd literally taken to the mountains to avoid being sent to work in Germany. "My dear Violette, it is an honor to assist you and your major."

Anton's magnanimous expression suddenly grew grave.

"Is there a problem?" Viv asked quickly, worried she had raised La Salle's hopes too high, given Buckmaster's tepid response when she relayed to him Julien Paquet's impassioned plea for weapons and supplies from Britain.

"Just that my own eighteen-year-old son is now in hiding up on the plateau. Only by sheer luck, Jacques missed being caught in a recruitment grab for the factory work camps abroad. On the day a German conscription team swept through Annecy two weeks ago, my boy happened to be away helping on a friend's farm."

"So even in the Free Zone, the *Boche* are now forcing young Frenchmen to work in Germany? It's totally against the Armistice agreement!" she complained.

Anton snorted. "What isn't?" He leaned forward and lowered his voice. "Rumors are everywhere that the Germans are about to take over *all* of France with the Italians."

"We've heard that too, but why do you think there'll be no more Free Zone so soon?"

"We've had word there have been convoys of troops on the roads not far from here." He suddenly looked solemn. "God, how I hate the bastards!"

The alley's frigid temperature had begun to give Viv the shivers. She reflected on the way ordinary French citizens were beginning to recognize, now, that there were no compromises to be made with the occupiers, including with French Vichy collaborators.

Anton chided her, "Come. I can see you're feeling the cold. I expect you haven't had as good a meal as I gave you since the *last* time you were here, am I right?"

"*Absolument!*" Viv agreed, delighted at the thought of one of Anton's *potages*.

"You will eat," Anton declared firmly, "and then we will see what we can do to help you and your companions."

———◇———

By the end of their first day in Annecy, Fingers was installed in a tiny, out-of-the-way hideout above the village of Faverges at the south end of the lake. The wireless operator reported that he was able to get a remarkably clear signal.

"I've been amazed," Paul Malloy said a few days later. "The locals told me that no one has seen even one of Fritz's white vans around there." He was referring to the German military vehicles that roamed all over France with frequency-locating equipment on the roof, searching for forbidden Allied wireless transmission stations.

For Viv's own quarters, Anton miraculously found a minuscule, abandoned chalet tucked away off the main road between Annecy and the village of Thones. She and Major Merrick donned their skis and plodded out to the classic alpine cottage nestled near the base of the rocky up thrust that formed the Plateau des Glières itself. Merrick took a few tumbles along the way, proving to Viv he'd never skied often enough to master the balance the sport required.

Viv extended her ski pole, offering, "Here, grab hold. I'll help you up."

"No need, no need," Merrick huffed, but after a few more spills, he took her up on her offers without comment.

When they finally reached the chalet at dusk, Viv insisted the one bedroom at the back would be reserved for Major Merrick when he was in the region. A loft above the living room featured a quite respectable cotton mattress, along with ample woolen blankets provided by Anton's wife, Olivia.

"How lovely not to be sleeping on straw," Viv had said a few days later when offering Olivia her heartfelt thanks.

"You will be protecting our son, Jacques," Olivia replied earnestly, "by helping the *maquisards* on the Plateau des Glières get the supplies they need. Giving you a cotton mattress and a few blankets is the least I can do."

Viv's bedroom overlooked the open living room-kitchen area and a small, stone-fronted fireplace. Out the back door there was a ground-level entrance to a storage cellar burrowed beneath the house that Merrick thought would provide a good space in which to prepare explosive charges for "certain operations when the time comes."

"Now that the basics of our living arrangements have been settled, thanks to Violette and Anton," Major Merrick said during their final meal together at Café Lyonnais, "I'm off to see Peter Churchill—ah, Raoul—down the lake at St. Jorioz. Fingers," he addressed his wireless operator, "I will get a message to you to meet me near Faverges as I circle around on my routes." He shifted his gaze back to Viv as the three were going over Merrick's last instructions. His eyes drifted to her hair. "I do worry about how English your coloring is, and that your height makes you appear like the American you are. Either way, I fear you just don't look French enough."

Viv reared back in her chair. What was he actually saying, she wondered? That he would send her back to Britain as too big a risk to their mission? Reading her thoughts, Merrick shook his head.

"Don't misunderstand me. Your knowledge of this area has obviously been superb. I'm just afraid very few French women are nearly six feet tall like you, and people here might suspect you're not a native. That could jeopardize your safety…and ours too."

"I could do something to my hair," she replied in a rush. "I dyed it before and perhaps Olivia could help me with this." She fell silent, eager to think of something to convince Merrick she was more of an asset to their mission than a liability. The thought of endangering the others gave her pause, but surely he wouldn't banish her to England after all she'd gone through to get here.

Merrick raised a glass of tolerably decent red wine that Anton had provided them as soon as they'd arrived at the café.

"We wouldn't be nearly as ready to launch our recruitment project if you hadn't had such good contacts here in the Alps, so kudos to you," he said by way of a toast. "Along with my sincere thanks, I also must voice my concern for the good of the mission and urge you to take great caution in everything you do. Your most important *assignment*, if you will, is to do your best to try not to draw attention to yourself."

Viv sucked in her breath and blurted, "I'm working every day on my French pronunciation, and I'll definitely dye my hair." Suddenly she wished she could add, "But what do you want from me, Merrick? Make myself shorter?"

Viv's tacit admission that Miss Atkins and others detected a hint of New York when she spoke French was cut short by Anton's appearance carrying a savory lamb stew. The offering had been cooked in red wine, along with vegetables and herbs from Olivia's garden. The meal was served, family style, in a cast iron pot that he placed in the middle of the table, along with three bowls and a sliced baguette.

"A Café Lyonnais specialty made just for you, *patron*," Anton said with a flourish of the ladle he then placed in the pot. "May this fuel you for your coming journey." He offered a rather lopsided salute. "Until we meet again."

All three of his guests nodded their thanks from their table secreted in a dark corner of their host's establishment. After Anton had disappeared into the kitchen, Major Merrick spoke in hushed tones. "Violette, your next mission is to connect with your friend Julien Paquet and survey the men's current state of readiness on the plateau. Training, available arms, their medical supplies…that sort of thing. I need an accurate assessment."

"Yes, sir," Viv said with a nod, recalling her brief encounter on the plateau earlier that year. She wondered if Julien would remember her favorably after she'd so pointedly defended her qualifications as his envoy to Britain.

Merrick continued to address Viv, "Also, before I leave, I will be giving you more particulars on the messages I want you to deliver." The major paused and leaned forward, lowering his voice. "I will ask your old friend, Clément Grenelle, to meet you back in Annecy in two weeks' time, after your return from the plateau."

Viv nodded, holding back a smile. It would be good to see the familiar face of the *passeur* who had escorted her to Marcel's vineyard, even if it was cranky Clément's.

Viv asked Merrick, "Is it all right if he stays in your room at the chalet when you're not here? If not, I can make a cot for him in the basement."

"Fine either way," Merrick replied. "I want you to teach him how to cook up some timed explosives the way you learned during your training in Scotland. By the time you return from the Plateau des Glières, the supplies you need...plastique, pencil charges, detonators, and so forth...will have been delivered to you. In turn, you will supervise him in teaching a small, trusted group of locals to build the devices needed at a future date."

Viv tried to keep her expression impassive, while worrying whether or not she remembered each important detail about how to fashion a charge that could blow up a train track without killing herself or her comrades.

Merrick continued, "Be sure to emphasize to the men that we won't be launching any attacks yet, but that at some point, this collection of saboteurs will be able to cripple certain local industrial sites in preparation for an Allied invasion."

"Let's hope that's soon," commented Paul.

Viv kept her silent doubts to herself. 1942 was drawing to a close, and from everything she'd learned in her time in the SOE, the day the British and American forces would land in France seemed very far off into the future.

Viv stared into her glass of wine and wondered if the same held true regarding her ever again seeing Marcel.

———◇———

Merrick and Fingers Malloy had barely left Lake Annecy when the rumored predictions about the fate of the Free Zone came true. On November 11, in direct response to the recent Allied forces landing in North Africa, the German occupiers of northern France rolled their tanks and soldiers all the way south to the Riviera. Within days, they had taken control of all civil and military operations from the English Channel to the Mediterranean Sea, and from the Atlantic coastal regions to the borders of the European countries to the east.

Viv was only slightly relieved when she saw that in Annecy and in villages and towns around the lake, Germany's ally, Italy, was the primary occupying force assigned to monitor check points and maintain the Nazi stranglehold over the civilian population.

"This is true for all of the Haute-Savoie," Anton explained over a cup of coffee after Viv stopped by Café Lyonnais to confirm the rumors. "In fact, the Italians have been assigned all regions along the left bank of the Rhône River." Anton shrugged his broad shoulders. "At least I like cooking their style of food a lot more than German overdone breaded veal and smelly sauerkraut!" He pointed to a new menu he'd just had printed. "See? I'm offering my own version of Bolognese, made with local rabbit and the tomatoes Olivia put up from her garden last summer." He winked. "When they eat in my café, I pick up all sorts of intelligence I can then relay to the *résistants* here in Annecy."

"The ones that Clément will teach to wire explosives?" she confirmed quietly, although no one was nearby.

"*Mais oui*," he said with a nod. "Your *patron* has already arranged for explosive supplies to be parachuted down south of Faverges. Fingers will supervise."

Viv gave an answering nod, mentally reviewing her lessons on how to stuff a dead rat with *plastique* and a detonator and place it in the right spot on a railroad track.

Next on her list was to ask Olivia if she knew any hair stylist in Annecy that could turn her distinctive dark red hair to mousey brown.

———◇———

The following mid-November day, Viv set off alone on the steep trail she and Clément had taken that wound around to the summit of Plateau des Glières. That initial journey seemed like another lifetime ago, considering how much had changed for her since then. On this trip, Viv donned the socks that Marcel had given her to cross the Pyrenees, along with her warmest trousers and a woolen beret clamped down over her tucked up newly brown mane. In her knapsack, she carried a flask of cognac, a small jug of water, and some food to sustain her for the nearly five-thousand-foot climb to the top.

No skis this trip, she thought with regret, as her journey led her in no other direction than the quickest route straight uphill.

Earlier autumn snowfalls had mostly melted, and the landscape now had taken on a bleak, frosty, barren aspect. The sharp wind biting Viv's cheeks was a reminder that another storm could roll down the valley at any hour. She reached a bend in the uphill trail when she heard rhythmic voices calling out a marching pace.

Oh, God...is it the Italians already?

Her other worry was the local *milice,* the Vichy-supported militia that were now part of Nazi enforcement squads in the Haute-Savoie. These units were made up of mostly young French hoodlums dressed in black uniforms and berets embossed with a Greek insignia on the brim. Their main mission for the Vichy collaborators had been to ferret out Jews, Resistance members, Freemasons, and gypsies. Whatever the identity of the troops coming toward Viv, they would demand to know what a tall woman dressed like a member of the *maquis* was be doing on a lonely trail leading to the summit on such a blustery day.

Stopping to listen to the approaching voices, she glanced to her right, spotting a huge boulder directly off the path and ten feet below it.

What in the world were these men doing at so elevated an altitude? she wondered. Had they made some sort of scouting mission to spy on the *maquisards* on the plateau? Or were they even preparing a surprise attack?

Swiftly she slid feet first down the incline on her stomach. At the bottom rim of the boulder, she barely managed to insert the fingers of one gloved hand into a rocky fissure to stop herself from sliding into a ravine dotted with scrub and pine trees. She could hear the sound of water gurgling in a small, unseen stream twenty meters below the slope.

She caught a few words of Italian floating on the frigid air. Fortunately, her grasp of the language was proficient enough to hear one man complain to his companions that the army should have provided them warmer jackets appropriate for the alpine climate. Another shouted that after less than an hour on the trail, his feet were *blocchi di ghiaccio*—blocks of ice. To Viv, hearing this assured her that the group had never made it to the summit, for it took a couple of hours to ascend, and only if one knew the way.

She craned her neck and was relieved that she could no longer glimpse the path above her. The moments ticked by with agonizing slowness as the procession of what was apparently a small squad of newly arrived Italian occupiers filed past her protective barrier. Viv waited another five minutes in silence. The ground was slick with frost that was swiftly turning to ice, and her fingers had gone numb.

Hand-over-hand, she inched her way on her stomach back up to the path until she reached the trail once more and stood to her full height. Digging into her knapsack, she pulled out the flask of cognac and took a swig.

That's all I need...getting caught by the enemy on my first mission for Pierre!

It didn't bear thinking about.

———◇———

Dusk was descending by the time Viv had climbed up to the edge of the Plateau des Glières. She had eaten all the food she'd packed and was almost out of water. To her relief, the chalet where she and Clément had met with Julien Paquet months earlier soon came into view, a dark outline of a peaked roof against the gray sky with the higher Alps soaring above. At least, for now, the Italians hadn't discovered one of the few trails that could safely lead a hiker—or a group of *résistants*—to the summit.

Viv trudged the quarter mile in growing darkness across the open, flat field, finally reaching the bottom of the wooden steps to the *maquisards'* headquarters. As on her last visit, the wooden front door suddenly flew open. She realized immediately that the figure standing in the threshold and clad in a French Army issue black woolen turtleneck was not Julien. She peered through the gloom at a man with broad shoulders who was leaner and taller and sported a battered dark blue beret. Viv froze, one boot on the stairs.

After another moment's hesitation to be sure she wasn't hallucinating, she exclaimed, "I-I can't *believe* it! How did *you* get here?"

CHAPTER 39

Marcel Delonge's expression alerted Viv she should not reveal to the *maquisards* arrayed behind him that they were personally well acquainted. The less each clandestine network knew about the other, the less information that the SS could torture out of them about their fellow *résistants*.

"Good to see you, Violette—isn't it?" Marcel said as Viv slowly mounted the chalet's front stairs, doing her best to erase her look of astonishment. "When we spotted your approach across the field, I told Julien, here, how we briefly shared a jail cell in Spain before I was flown back to England."

He smiled casually and formally shook her hand. For her part, Viv could barely look at Marcel for fear Julien and the others in the room would guess how fast her heart was racing at the sight of the man she knew, now, she loved but feared she'd never see again.

Meanwhile, Julien greeted her as a long, lost comrade. With Marcel by her side, she was urged to warm herself next to the roaring fireplace and help herself to sausages on a plate that had been placed in her lap. Shortly afterward, Viv, Marcel, and Julien moved to a wooden table in the center of the room where Viv delivered Major Merrick's inquiries as to the Glières *maquis'* precise state of training and equipment.

Viv smiled to soften her words.

"My *patron* from Britain wants to learn about your group's state of readiness to take on specific sabotage missions he has in mind for you when the time comes."

Julien leaned back in his chair. Viv saw that he was choosing his words carefully.

"Please tell your *patron* we would be most happy to comply with his requests *if* he is able to supply the necessary air-drops of goods and equipment to sustain us. You can tell him that our numbers keep increasing—nearly four hundred now—as the Krauts attempt to ship more of our young men to work in Germany, and so they've come up here. As a result, our need for *more* weapons, ammunition, medical supplies, food, and shelter is dire. Those living down in the valleys below the plateau can only provide us so much. We have yet to receive any of the *materiel* from England that I asked you for last spring."

Viv understood his anxiety.

"I did, indeed, convey your previous messages to London. Sending me and my superior, Pierre, to the Haute-Savoie region is a first step, we hope, in obtaining what you've requested," she assured him. "I will tell my *patron* of your growing numbers and urgent needs. We now have a member of our team with a wireless to transmit intelligence and specific field requests. Hopefully, you will see a result in due course."

"I should hope that is very *soon*," Julien said with taciturn understatement.

Marcel asked questions as well. He probed Julien about the expected arrival of cadres of defeated Spanish Republicans fleeing Franco's regime who were willing to join the French fight against Germany.

"Yes, we do expect them," Julien acknowledged. "They say they are committed to our cause and will certainly swell ranks up here." He glanced at Viv. "Accommodating them will strain our resources beyond the breaking point, however, which is another reason we hope the Allies will hear our pleas and respond *very* soon."

While Marcel continued to quiz the head of the Glières *maquisards*, it dawned on Viv that his mission, like Merrick's, was to assess how well various in-country anti-Nazi groups could be molded into a single, cohesive national fighting force. Viv guessed, however, that de Gaulle wanted them all to report to *him*. In the next moment, her theory was proved correct.

"Once an invasion is launched," Marcel explained to his rapt audience in the chalet's main room, "General de Gaulle wants the various Resistance fighters who are already in France to link up with the arriving regular French Army soldiers returning to liberate the country in France's name. It is a matter of national pride that we—not Britain, not America—are seen as the driving force restoring the honor of the French Army."

With a little help from their friends, Viv thought, attempting to keep a wry expression from giving away her sentiments.

"*Vive La France!*" voices rang out to the chalet's rafters.

"We are ready!" cried a voice from the back of the room.

"Count on us! And our Spanish brothers!" shouted another.

There was a general uproar with the men slapping each other on the shoulder. As the hubbub died down, Julien declared the conference concluded. Turning to him, Viv quietly related her near encounter with the Italian soldiers she'd spotted on a lower trail.

Julien replied, his brow furrowing, "So these lackeys have arrived in the Haute-Savoie and are beginning to get the lay of the land. Hopefully, they don't have enough men to storm the plateau, but we obviously must post more sentries. They didn't see you?" he asked Viv with a worried frown.

"No," was her emphatic reply. "I hid down a ravine before they appeared on the trail. From my vantage point, though, I could see they were quite ill equipped, complaining loudly that they should have been issued warmer coats. They looked to be regular Italian Army soldiers, not mountain brigades. There were only about two dozen of them."

Julien nodded his thanks. "The Italian invaders are no angels, but they're a damn sight better than having the SS or even regular German troops dominating the entire region, as they have the rest of France."

"To say nothing of the *milice,*" Viv murmured, her revulsion of the black-shirted thugs who operated as the Vichy's de facto SS shared by everyone in the chalet.

Marcel joined in. "At least for now you'll just have to deal with Italian occupiers. Unfortunately, London is predicting that if the German High Command thinks an invasion of France is imminent—north or south—they'll push their Italian allies aside and will occupy every inch of this country themselves, including the alpine regions."

"Which is *why* we need more weapons and supplies!" Julien said, belligerently.

Viv imagined the poor man was reaching the end of his rope. Meanwhile, Marcel rose from the table.

"My plan is to depart at first light," he announced to his host. He turned to Viv and said casually, "And what about you, *mademoiselle?*"

Viv offered a nonchalant shrug, playing the role he'd prompted.

"I am expected down in the valley as well, so perhaps we can descend the trail together and keep an eye out for the Italian troops?"

Marcel paused as if he needed to think over her proposal and then gave a brief nod of agreement. By this time, he had donned his *Canadienne* and appeared ready to depart.

"Our hospitable friend Julien, here, has kindly provided another small chalet at the far end of the plateau with a room full of cots for visitors. Since it appears we are both leaving at an early hour tomorrow, perhaps I can show you where it is?"

Relieved she wouldn't be sleeping the night in a frigid hayloft, she tried to restrain the joy she felt at seeing Marcel once again, and the thought of where this totally unexpected rendezvous might lead.

"Those arrangements are fine," she said, fighting a giddy happiness that threatened to give away their ruse.

Her first mission for Major Merrick accomplished, Viv offered her thanks to Julien for his hospitality and promised to relay the revised details of his requests to the leader of SOE's Mountaineer network. Marcel shook Julien's hand, bidding him and his men goodnight. One of them opened the door as Marcel turned with a sweep of his arm.

"After you, *mademoiselle…*"

———◇———

The tiny chalet reserved for secret visitors to the Plateau des Glières was located on the northeast side of the meadow behind several large boulders that hid it from view. Someone on Julien's instructions had evidently laid a fire and lit it so the single room was warm and cozy when Marcel and Viv stepped inside. Several metal cots were pushed against the walls with a hodge-podge of blankets and quilts covering them. Near the hearth, a plate of cheese and a baguette sat in the middle of a table flanked by two chairs. Waiting, too, were a bottle of wine and a tin of coffee that Viv suspected was likely made from ground acorns.

"The *maquis* is generous with their limited provisions," Viv said, as she turned to survey the space that would shelter them for a single night.

She was acutely conscious that Marcel had shrugged off his *Canadienne* and stood behind her. Before she could turn around, his arms enfolded her and he kissed the base of her neck, resting his cheek against her hair.

"Pity, they made you dye your hair, but you still look wonderful," he murmured against her ear. "If I hadn't run into your major in Vercours, I wouldn't have known you were being sent to Glières. Pierre and I are playing a bit of tag, both surveying the state of readiness of these Resistance fighters. He for the Brits and I for the General."

Viv turned in his arms, her face inches from his.

"I honestly wondered if I'd ever see you again."

"You must have more faith in serendipity, as well as in my ingenuity," he said, scattering kisses on her eyelids, her cheeks, and at the base of her neck.

Viv laughed on a breath. "I certainly have faith in your amazing talent for ferreting out information. You seem to know a lot of important people at the center of this giant war machine in which I am the tiniest cog."

Marcel slowly unbuttoned her coat, eased it off her shoulders and down her arms, allowing it to fall on the wooden floor.

"I am a mere cog as well, *chérie,*" he said, his voice low, his eyes focused on hers. "But luck was with us once again, and here we are."

Viv leaned forward on her tiptoes and brushed her lips against his.

"Yes, here we are," she repeated, a part of her already dreading the moment they would part in the morning.

He cupped her chin in his hand, his brow creased. "*Pourquoi si triste, mon amour?*"

"I'm sad because…well…because seeing you like this makes me realize how much I've tried to ignore that I've missed you. A lot. And I'm sad because I fear for your safety every time we part."

She lowered her eyes. "Tomorrow we each go our separate ways, which gets harder and harder for me. Who knows if—"

Marcel put his forefinger to her lips to silence her. "It will drive us both mad to think about tomorrow and the tomorrow after that. The only way to keep our sanity, Viv, is to be *here*, now, in this chalet on the Plateau des Glières, in *this* moment."

"But—"

That was the last word Viv uttered on a night when snow began to fall in earnest on a high plateau in the Alps of France. Marcel sought her lips as the outside world fell silent of the sounds of war. Her final thought, before she was conscious only of the pleasure she was feeling, was that Marcel had always been the dispenser of sound advice.

I am here…in this moment…and it's all we have.

PART IV
CHAPTER 40

November 1943

Viv often had reason to remember Marcel's whispered words their last night together that November—that the present moment was all she could count on.

The final months of 1942 and the entire following year alternated between moments of sheer terror that her clandestine activities might be uncovered by the enemy, and its exact opposite—pride each time a mission succeeded. As Merrick's courier on skis in the alpine regions he supervised, she reveled in the fact that she, the major, and Fingers Malloy were outfoxing their adversaries. Their secret Mountaineer network of resisters grew ever stronger over the months they toiled to organize it.

Each day *was* all they had, she thought, and she tried to follow Marcel's advice to not dwell on the uncertainties that lay ahead. During the months since she'd seen de Gaulle's deputy, war had been raging intensely on all sides. Twice she'd come close to being arrested by local authorities at checkpoints and peppered with questions even though her identity documents were in perfect order.

"It's definitely my damn height!" Viv confided to Anton's wife, Olivia, one day when she helped her peel potatoes in the kitchen of Café Lyonnais. "Whenever I find myself having to look down on one of the damn Italian officers or the *milice*, they start quizzing me, especially when they hear my accent." She suppressed a shudder. "Sometimes, I think they're going to handcuff me right on the spot!"

In recent months, Viv and Olivia let it be known that the tall woman from Alsace with the muddy-brown hair was the impoverished widow of a La Salle cousin who had died in the battle that France had lost when the war first broke out. With this new cover story, Viv regularly did kitchen chores next to Olivia to convince any local who might be tempted to betray a neighbor and even other family members for money or a few bottles of wine. In return, Viv was given at least one decent meal a day.

Meanwhile, Major Merrick had left Anton and Viv in charge of the area around the northeast side of Lake Annecy while he moved westward to the district of Ain, headquartering himself in various safe houses and traveling in and out of Lyon. Near Vercours, another group of *maquis* had begun to gather—more young men dodging deportation to German factories and, instead, training in remote regions with few weapons in anticipation of the day the rumored Allied invasion would begin.

Now that another November had rolled around, Viv found herself waxing her skis in the basement of her safe house a few miles outside the town of Annecy in preparation for her next assignment for Mountaineer. There had been several moments since Viv had last seen Marcel when she'd begun to wonder if it were only a matter of time—along with bad luck in some form—before she was finally arrested for the fraud she was.

But it was the activities of Clément Grenelle and his deadly supply of *plastique*, pencil fuses, and detonators that proved to be the source of the most frightening few days of all. Her grizzled companion who had guided her to Perpignan before she crossed the Pyrenees with Marcel was his usual taciturn self when he arrived from his village with additional supplies to augment their little bomb-making factory in Viv's cellar.

"Do you actually know how to handle this stuff?" he demanded.

"I know what they taught me at SOE spy school," she replied, attempting to maintain a non-defensive tone. She had learned that it did no good to try to convince Clément that she knew what she was doing other than simply demonstrating it. "And you?" she countered. "Do you now consider yourself skilled at stuffing explosives into dead rats and putting them where they'll do the most damage?"

"After what you've showed me, I won't touch the bang-bangs anymore," he said blandly. "My brother-in-law blew off both his hands earlier this year."

So much for putting Clément in charge of teaching additional locals the art of bomb making! With a sinking sensation that she was basically now in charge of all explosives manufacturing in the region, she led the way to her cellar to store his latest delivery of deadly bounty.

"Where in the world did all this come from?" she demanded after she'd given him a swig of the cognac that Merrick had sent her via Clément.

"Another air-drop near Chaumont and one near Fingers outside Faverges," he said with a shrug. "Your major must have a great deal of pull with the dispatchers in London."

"He certainly must," she agreed, assessing the packages of *plastique*, pencil detonators, and other items necessary to build the devices. "Who is going to supply the dead rats this time?" she worried out loud. "I draw the line at trapping them."

Clément chuckled in a rare show of merriment. "Anton again, of course. Surely you must have noticed them running around his restaurant. I left a box of 'em outside on the sled I hauled from Annecy today."

"They're dead, right?"

This time Clément threw his head back and laughed out loud.

"I believe so," he teased. "I suggest you bury the box in the snow until you are ready to show your latest recruits what to do with the creatures."

Clément, who insisted he had more important duties than to teach former farmers the intricacies of bomb-making, spent the night sleeping in his chair facing the fire and was gone by the time she awoke the next morning. Later in the day, three young men from the plateau materialized at the back door of Viv's chalet: Jacques—who was Anton and Olivia's teenaged son—along with two of his young friends, Yves and Gaspard.

Dreading the next few hours, Viv sucked in her breath and led them back outside and down to the cellar where she prayed she could once again demonstrate the basic techniques of assembling an explosive device without blowing anyone up.

"First you must each clean out the innards of...uh...these rodents, here," she directed, pointing to the box of Anton's collection while feeling her own stomach churning in distress. "Once you have finished that chore, you dispose of the entrails outside by *burying* them in the ground. Then, call me and I'll come down to instruct you on your next steps: stuffing your explosive gadgets inside the rats."

"Why the rats? Why can't we just plant the plastique where we want to blow something up?" demanded Gaspard, the senior member of the trio.

"Because they're likely to be spotted by the Germans or some other authority before they explode," she replied tersely. She was heartily tired of having her authority questioned whenever she was solely in charge of a project like today's. Echoing the words of her instructor in Scotland she added, "Putting the charges inside the rats will disguise the device until the timers set them off. As guerilla fighters, our goal is to outfox the enemy, not to overpower them."

"Or rat them out," Jacques said with a sly grin.

Yves, who appeared to Viv to possess the most savvy when it came to following her instructions, eagerly began to order his fellow recruits to commence various tasks. Jacques obediently bent down to open the box of thawed rats and the trio set to their tasks. Meanwhile upstairs, Viv reviewed her written list of the sequence of steps needed to create a device suitable for blowing a bridge or electrical transformer to smithereens. After two hours of careful instruction, minus the detonators, Viv called their training session to a close and threw her notes into the fire.

"Excellent work, boys," she complimented them. "We'll have a refresher course when the time comes to make a stockpile of these."

"And what will we *do* with them?" demanded Gaspard with a belligerence that told Viv he definitely didn't appreciate being ordered about by a woman. "Who decides what we blow up around here?"

"First lesson," Viv declared, remembering her interview with Allen Dulles in what felt like another era. "*Stop* asking questions! When you choose to be a *résistant,* you accept that each one of us, including me, is on a need-to-know basis *only*." She summoned her most charming smile as she bid them farewell. "When the time comes, you'll relish what we're going to blow up to drive the German bastards out of France."

———◇———

Soon after Viv's latest bomb-making tutorial, Anton La Salle introduced her to a partisan by the name of Tom Morel. A career soldier in the defeated French Army, Lieutenant Morel soon afterward appeared on her doorstep on a clear, crisp evening bearing a precious loaf of freshly baked bread and a bottle of wine.

"I have been ordered by de Gaulle to start the process of using my experience in France's former mountain infantry brigade to transform the maquisards on the plateau into a military-style organization."

Startled to hear this, Viv asked, "By chance, have you encountered another of the General's men here in France, Victor Fernique?" She used Marcel's code name to maintain protocol.

Morel, a handsome young man with dark good looks, appeared equally startled.

"And you know this Victor Fernique *how*?" he asked, his expression sharpening. Viv realized that she was treading on dangerous ground inquiring about another agent with someone she'd just met.

"I trained in Britain at the same time as Fernique. He was sent into France for de Gaulle, as was I for the Brits." She offered a slight shrug. "I just wondered, since you're both former French Army, if you'd ever encountered him. It's always nice to hear one's colleague is…well…still alive," she said and was relieved to see Lieutenant Morel relax a bit. She offered a conspiratorial smile, adding, "Victor Fernique guided me over a few bumps on my way to becoming an SOE agent."

Tom appeared now to regard her in a friendlier manner.

"I saw him less than a month ago, so I can report he's well…. or was. He's sharp and knows his business, although he doesn't always agree with his commanders." He paused. "In fact, he doesn't think that we should organize such a large group as Julien's at all—but stay in smaller cadres and confine ourselves to sabotage."

"And what do you think?" Viv asked.

"I'm merely charged with following orders, and I let our General do the thinking," Tom replied. "I believe it will be useful and efficient to be in one place to train many men at once how to shoot and safely take cover when attacked." He paused again, casting her a penetrating look. "That is, if London ever sends us some weapons and ammunition. In fact, that's why I've stopped by to ask if you can tell me when we might expect this sort of help from the British."

"I wish I could tell you. Soon, if my major has anything to say about it."

Morel frowned. "Tell your major that meanwhile, we are drilling with tree branches."

Viv merely nodded and poured Tom a second glass of wine, later telling him he was always welcome to use the chalet as a safe house going to and from the plateau.

Recalling her conversation with the personable Tom Morel, Viv shivered in the dank, cold air of the chalet's cellar. Her task this day was to smooth the bottom of her skis with a homemade concoction of pine tar that kept the water from penetrating the wood and helped the slats glide over the snow. She tried not to think of the dangers involved in making her way to her next assignment. In contrast to Tom Morel's acceptance of his mission to instill a military standard of readiness in Julien's young recruits, she couldn't help but consider Marcel's final words as they'd descended to the foot of the plateau almost exactly one year earlier.

"I worry that with Anton and Julien's encouraging so many men to mass in such a large group on the Plateau des Glières, they'll wind up attracting a force of crack German troops capable of wiping them out in one, big land and air operation."

Alarmed by this, Viv had replied, "But Julien told me he expects their ranks to grow to at least a thousand! Wouldn't that give the German's pause before launching an assault using those steep pathways up to the plateau?"

Marcel wasn't persuaded.

"I think knowing those numbers would give the Germans the *incentive* to launch an all-out assault and make quick work of wiping out a large group of *résistants*." He'd sounded quite worried. "Julien's volunteer fighters are most effective when they work in small cadres, performing carefully planned acts of hit-and-run sabotage operations. Their job is to prepare the way for trained Allied soldiers when they land in France. Farm boys and the sons of café owners are no match for a Panzer division or a German battalion."

"But what if the Allies drop the arms and supplies to the *maquisards* that they've been begging for?" Viv countered. "Couldn't that make a difference?"

Viv had been startled by Marcel's grim expression. "They'd still be wiped out in a matter of days if the Germans decide to move on them. Julien's men should be trained as guerillas, not soldiers. The *Wehrmacht* is an overwhelming force to be reckoned with, to say nothing of the *Luftwaffe*'s bombers. We both know these things, right?"

Viv recalled that terrifying day when Marcel had saved her life during the attack that blew the shepherd's shed to dust.

"But *this* area is occupied by the Italians," she'd protested as they'd tramped through a foot of new-fallen snow on the same secret trail she'd traveled to reach the summit. "From what little I saw of Germany's ally, they're woefully unprepared to deal with a thousand Resistance fighters on the plateau."

"The Italians won't control this region for much longer, I fear," he'd answered. "As the noose tightens around the Axis troops in North Africa and the Allies attempt a landing in Sicily, Hitler won't trust the Italians to hold this part of France in check."

Marcel's predictions that day had proven all too accurate. Italy had turned against her ally and declared war on Germany in October of the current year, 1943. In response to the British forces taking Tripoli—and soon after the Americans landed in Sicily—the number of German soldiers in the region around Annecy had increased tenfold. Now, German forces had kicked out the Italians and had taken complete control of all regions from the left bank of the Rhone River to the border with Switzerland. Thanks to messages on Fingers' wireless, Viv knew the war was going badly for the Führer on numerous fronts and tensions had risen everywhere—especially in the Alps.

Mulling over all the events of the past year, Viv stood her skis on their ends in the drafty cellar and checked for any sections her pine tar sealant might have missed. Her journey dodging German checkpoints was a perfect example of the increasing danger to all SOE agents working in the region. Yet, everyone recognized the urgent need to connect with more *résistants* whom Major Merrick had enlisted to "hold the fort" until the hoped-for invasion. But hold it in small groups, or in large numbers on a plateau? That was the question.

On this blustery November day, Viv was bound for the ski resort of Val d'Isère where she was to enlist the help of an unusual man whom Major Merrick hoped would become the primary Resistance leader only a few kilometers from the Italian border.

But would such a Frenchman be persuaded to join Mountaineer by the female secret agent sent to convince him?

CHAPTER 41

"Dr. Jean-Paul Morand trained at the American Hospital," Major Merrick had informed Viv during a visit to Annecy. "For this reason, I thought you'd be a good bet to try to enlist him in the cause. He's originally from Alsace."

Viv had reared back with surprise. The doctor was from the same province as her father's family? Merrick hadn't even met the man, but from all reports, he considered him a good prospect to extend the Mountaineer circuit south and east. She prayed she wouldn't disappoint her leader if she failed in such a challenging mission.

Merrick continued briefing Viv.

"My sources tell me that Dr. Morand recently teamed up with a group of champion skiers, friends of his who also hailed from Alsace. These former Olympic athletes ended up migrating to the area around Val d'Isère after their parents fled the German invaders during the Great War. Morand's skier friends founded the new resort a few years before *this* war started. He was brought in as the doctor for skiers who injured themselves on the slopes or otherwise needed medical attention." The leader of Mountaineer had grimaced. "It was bad timing as far as their business venture was concerned, poor chaps. Few people are taking a ski holiday these days, so the place is going bankrupt."

"So you're guessing that Morand is no great fan of the latest German occupiers and might be willing to join us resisting them?" Viv asked.

"Exactly," Merrick replied. "He's been known to shelter a downed pilot or two during the past year. My guess is perhaps he'd do more if he had some support from us. Our intelligence tells us Dr. Morand is in an ideal position to help mount some serious resistance in that strategic region so close to Italy. When our mountain brigades fight their way up the boot of France's neighbor, we want local people like Morand and his ilk to greet them and show them the best ways to advance through the snowy passes into France from the Italian Alps." Merrick had paused and pointed a forefinger at her. "You're the expert skier among us, and you're an alumna of the American Hospital ambulance corps where Morand took his training. And since your Vivier family hails from Alsace like his, you're the logical person to make contact."

Viv wanted to be clear about Merrick's instructions.

"So you want me to see if the good doctor can organize young men there to form a resistance group in that region and to serve, himself, as an important way-point in an escape route from Val d'Isère to Switzerland?"

Merrick nodded. "Yes, that, and to find out if there are locals willing to be trained in arms and sabotage."

"In a ski resort?" Viv asked skeptically.

"In a ski resort that's located near a pass that we hope the American Tenth Mountain Division will use to invade from Italy," he reminded her.

Recalling the origins of today's journey, Viv glanced around her chalet to make sure she hadn't forgotten anything. She clapped her skis and poles together, threw her knapsack over her shoulder, and headed into the bitter weather outside.

With her sporting equipment heaved onto her other shoulder, she was assaulted by doubts her mission had any chance of success. She thought of Dr. Jackson and all the dedicated medical professionals she'd grown to know during her time driving an ambulance for the American Hospital in Paris. Dr. J would never plot sabotage, only dedicate himself to saving others from harm. Would a doctor like Morand, also devoted to healing people, be willing to recruit others to kill and maim their fellow human beings?

"Be extra vigilant as you make your way to Val d'Isère," Merrick had warned. "Fingers got a wireless message informing us that a German detachment has recently made their headquarters directly across the street from Morand's infirmary—which is housed on the ground floor of his private chalet. Various cadres come in and out of the village on the lookout for our forces expected, at some point, to storm through local mountain passes."

Oh great... Viv thought when she'd been informed of this scenario. *Lucky me.*

———◇———

Posing as a young woman on her way to visit a sick aunt in the mountains, Viv managed to travel without incident by bus and train from Annecy to less than four miles from her ultimate destination. She'd gone through Albertville, changing for the station at Bourg-Saint-Maurice. From there, with her skis still balanced on her right shoulder, she boarded a coal-burning "gazogene"-powered bus that stopped at Tignes du Lac, near the road to the ski resort of Val d'Isère.

She waited until the bus disappeared from view and then set out cross-country on her skis. She was relieved to see that clear skies and the little wind that blew across the snow wouldn't impede her journey to the village that sat at an altitude of 1850 meters. This she quickly converted to a breath-taking 6000 feet at the base. The Alps that ringed the resort itself soared to a formidable height of more than 11,000 feet, making it one of the highest ski resorts in Europe. Originally part of the feudal territory of the House of Savoy, at different times in its history the land had been part of France, Italy, and Switzerland.

In summer months, the landscape became a verdant, hidden valley, isolated from the outside world. In winter, the same territory sported some fourteen feet of snowpack, only accessible to the outside world by the Col de Liseran Road built six years earlier, in 1937. Not long afterward, a cable car had been added to a simple rope tow and T-bar lifts. This engineering marvel hoisted only the most serious of skiers, four to a car, to the heights of the spectacular

Bellegarde, whose sheer face provided the thrills sought by athletes like Dr. Morand's Olympic champions and investors.

That was, until the war ended everything. From what Merrick knew, Val d'Isère was now a virtual ghost town except for its despised occupiers.

Viv pushed her skis rhythmically through the snow beneath a pine forest that separated an even tinier village, Le Crêt, from Val d'Isère itself. The larger village had four hotels. Merrick ordered her to stay away from all of them.

"It may be isolated up there, as you know, but it's still a risky place to be these days. Besides a few SS, there are regular German soldiers, recently relocated from the Russian front, that pass through. They're known to lodge at the Hôtel des Glacier and probably at other hostelries in the village," he warned. "The place is totally Catholic and truly a conservative, right-wing society, so beware of collaborators there, as well. Many rather like the authoritarian approach of Pétain and his Nazi collaborators, and some may not particularly object to fascists being there."

The closer her skis drew to the edge of town, the more Viv began to doubt the odds of succeeding in such an unlikely outpost.

"And what about Dr. Morand?" she'd asked her boss during their final briefing. "Do we know his outlook on the invaders?"

Merrick replied with a steady glance, "From everything I've heard, Dr. Jean-Paul Morand is a complete anomaly. My sources say he despises the Nazis." He paused. "Even so, you need to be on the alert every minute. The small detachment of SS soldiers stationed there are assigned to monitor suspicious strangers in a village of less than two hundred residents."

Oh, wonderful... Viv thought glumly.

"I suggest you go directly to Dr. Morand's door and then figure out your next move."

———◇———

Viv had taken the most direct route from Tignes du Lac, but now she wondered if she should be seen in such open country. Perhaps she should have climbed to a ridge and surveyed the lay of the land from above before appearing as an obvious newcomer in a town with no "sick aunt" she could name, arriving via the only road into the village.

The high altitude's cold, thin air seared her lungs, causing her shortness of breath. Suddenly awash with doubts, she felt as if she were the least person likely to achieve this mission. Rounding a bend, she finally caught sight of the steeple of a seventeenth century parish church piercing the azure sky. Merrick had told her its square tower would be the landmark confirming that she had come to the right place. Her chest ached from the effort to breathe, and she rested a moment on her ski poles. Her gaze took in the solitary main street, which sported classic chalet architecture, featuring structures large and small, with the mountains on both sides disappearing into a cap of clouds.

As instructed, she looked for a substantial building with a peaked roof and a whitewashed, one-story façade. It would be topped by a wooden upper story with shutters flanking a series of windows that looked out on the spectacular alpine vista. She glanced over her shoulder and realized the German presence Merrick had warned her about had obviously taken over the local *gendarmerie*. Several SS officers, clad in their distinctive gray-green uniforms with silver epaulets on the shoulders and alarming scull insignia on their caps, stood in a cluster smoking and chatting with a knot of regular German soldiers. Her heart pounding at the sight, Viv powered her skis toward the chalet's front door, sensing their collective eyes boring into her back. She unsnapped her cable bindings, stamping her boots in the snow. Bending down to pick up the slats, she leaned them against the building and mounted the wooden porch with a sign that read:

DR. JEAN-PAUL MORAND - SURGERY
PLEASE RING.

Just as she reached out and pulled the cord on the small brass bell, a voice behind her commanded, "Halt! Papers, please!"

Viv turned around and saw the surprised look on the face of a blond, rail-thin SS officer who obviously had thought she was tall enough to be a man.

"I have not seen you in the village before," he said in German-accented French. "Let me see your documents, woman!"

Merde! I haven't even gotten past Dr. Morand's front door!

Viv fumbled for her knapsack to pull out her documents, her mind racing to figure out what to do next.

"Are you sick?" the SS officer demanded.

Seizing with ironic gratitude on this cue, she manufactured a loud cough, deliberately not covering her mouth.

"Yes, very sick!" she croaked. "I've come to see Dr. Morand."

She coughed loudly again, and the officer swiftly took a step back, neglecting to inspect her documents. Viv remembered Marcel telling her that Germans tended to be extremely chary of contagious diseases. Just then, the door opened.

"*Oui?*" inquired an elderly woman at the threshold. "*Bonjour, mademoiselle.*"

Viv turned back to face the SS minion who had accosted her and produced a hacking cough that would have frightened a battalion of germophobes. The officer raised both hands to shield his face and spun on his jackboots.

"*Mein Gott, fraulein,*" he said over his shoulder, "you should be in hospital!" and stomped across the street through the snow to return to his headquarters.

Behind the elderly woman who had greeted Viv, a man in a white doctor's coat appeared. At the other end of the corridor, a young woman clad in an apron also entered the hallway. Pretty in a Tyrolean, pink-cheeked sort of way, she looked to be near the man's age, although she wore a pinched expression and didn't appear particularly pleased there was a visitor at their door.

"Mother?" said the man to the older woman who stood at the entrance in front of Viv. "Isn't my next appointment not until four o'clock?"

Once the SS officer was out of earshot, Viv inquired in a normal tone of voice, "May I come in?"

Dr. Morand's mother stepped back, allowing Viv to cross the threshold, and then *Madame* Morand quickly closed the front door.

"Are you ill?" asked the young physician, coming closer.

"I was faking the cough," she admitted to the three standing in the hallway.

Dr. Morand looked at her with a pair of startlingly blue eyes that made a quick assessment of her clad in ski clothes. "Have you taken a tumble and hurt yourself?"

"No, I'm perfectly healthy. But I have some important

information from certain people who very much admire what you are doing here."

Jean-Paul Morand cast her a startled look and then motioned for her to follow him into his surgery where Viv assumed he treated his patients. The young woman in the apron swiftly disappeared through the door to a residence directly off the hallway.

As Viv walked behind Morand, she noted he had the physique of a skier: broad shoulders, trim waistline, long legs, and an easy stride. She calculated that he was only a few years older than she, and several inches taller. Given her own father's imposing appearance in photos when he was a young pilot, she imagined that Morand's sandy blond hair and high cheekbones were typical of men in his home territory of Alsace, a district that lay some 280 miles due north of Val d'Isère.

Over his shoulder Morand called, "Mother, if you would be so kind to explain to anyone else who arrives that I'll be with them as soon as I finish with this patient."

Viv realized, if a patient of Morand's were due soon, she'd have only a few minutes to state Major Merrick's case.

He closed the door to the brightly lit examining room. Before she could speak, he declared, "Promise me that you're not a plant from our neighbors across the street, trying to entice me into plotting against the Reich by sending over a tall, lovely young woman on skis who appears just the type that might convince me."

Oddly pleased by his compliment, she replied quickly, "Oh, I assure you, I'm no German siren, come to compromise you with my wicked ways. I'm with British intelligence, and before that, I drove an ambulance at the American Hospital in Paris where I understand you took your training with Sumner Jackson."

"And did you know his wife?" he asked, and Viv knew this was a test to be able to name her.

"Toquette? Yes, I got to know her quite well. An extraordinary woman."

Apparently satisfied for the moment that Viv was who she said she was, he gestured to a massive furry lump on the floor. "You have no objection, I hope?" One of the largest Swiss Mountain Dogs Viv had ever seen was curled up beside the doctor's desk, snoring gently. "We use Alphonse, here, for search-and-rescue when someone runs into trouble on the mountain. Don't worry, though...he may huge, but he has a lovely temperament." Dr. Morand leaned down to scratch one of the dog's ears. Alphonse opened an eye as the doctor spoke directly to him. "Don't want to scare any of the people you're trying to dig out of the snow, now, do we?"

Viv suddenly thought of the puppy her father had given her as a child. She longed to engage with the mammoth tan, black, and white animal, but knew her time was short.

"Actually, I adore dogs," she declared, smiling down at Alphonse. "He looks like a lovely big boy...aren't you, sweetheart?" she said, scratching him under his chin.

Dr. Morand gestured to a chair facing his desk. "Then you won't be afraid to sit here. No need, I imagine, to ask you to disrobe and lie down on my examining table," he added, and Viv could hear the humor in his voice. "Now, what's all this about?"

CHAPTER 42

Viv removed her ski jacket and cap, shaking her hair free, and quickly explained everything that SOE's leader of the Mountaineer secret network had asked her to convey. She concluded her long-winded pitch by repeating Major Merrick's wish that Dr. Morand could help assemble a select team of young men in his region willing to fight on the side of the Allies whenever an invasion might be launched.

Jean-Paul Morand gazed at Viv thoughtfully, clearly mulling everything she'd proposed. "I am correct in assuming you are an excellent skier, yes?"

"I'm not bad," Viv replied, "but now that I think about my arrival just now, that would have been very clever of the SS to use me as a decoy. As you saw, though, I scared away the goon asking for my papers when I coughed in his face."

"Really? I must have rounded the corner to the foyer just after that happened." He laughed. "Well then, you *are* clever."

"Your mother can confirm my ugly cough," she said with a laugh, "Luckily for me, the one who tailed me to your door was not the sharpest knife in the drawer."

Morand laughed again and then stated flatly, "By that 'sharpest knife' remark it would seem you're not native French, are you?"

Morand's casual observation caught Viv by surprise, and she didn't know what to say next. SOE training warned recruits not to employ colloquialisms or any language that might reveal their true identity—and here she'd used lingo that was a dead giveaway.

"We meet all sorts of people in a ski resort," the doctor said with a shrug, "skiers from all over the world. Somehow you just don't fit the mold of a French girl free to roam the resorts of Europe during a war." He cocked his head and asked, "You must tell me...how did a young American, and a woman, to boot, end up as an agent of the British intelligence services?"

Her mind spun in various directions until she decided the truth, in this case, was her safest option.

"My French accent is that bad, huh?" she began. "Well, I was born in New York, but raised mostly in Europe...first by my father, who was Alsatian-American, by the way." She was encouraged when Morand's gaze brightened at this news. "He died in the Great War flying for the Allies," she continued quickly, "and then my mother's second husband—also an American of a very different stripe—showed me how evil Hitler's Germany truly is."

Morand gave her a questioning look. "And he showed you this...how?" he asked.

"As a kid, I went with my parents to Germany in the Thirties when my stepfather was selling steel ball-bearings to the Nazi regime. I saw the rallies and the book burnings." She paused a moment. "So... when I was waylaid in Europe as the war started, I wanted to do something useful to combat the forces that were conquering the country I love more than my own, really. A friend opened a door for me at the SOE...so here I sit."

Jean-Paul Morand's attitude of intense listening prompted her to seek another area of common ground with this curious man to shore up their mutual connections.

"During the time I drove ambulances for the American Hospital, I picked up wounded after the disaster along the Maginot Line and worked closely with Dr. J." She hesitated and then asked a question herself. "What was it like taking your training there?"

"Dr. Jackson was the best mentor I could have asked for," he said, his eyes alight. "I considered him an inspiration. I still do. I learned English from the Jacksons, and they even provided me a back bedroom during my impoverished student days."

"At Number 11 Avenue Foch?" Viv marveled.

Morand smiled. "The very place. It's because of his being an American, I recognized the phrase 'not the sharpest knife in the drawer.'"

Viv began to relax and smiled back. "Dr. J and Toquette are a big part of my inspiration for the work I do, too."

Viv was tempted to tell this handsome young man about the Jacksons' most recent clandestine activities. Catching herself, she obeyed the strict "need-to know" SOE rule and said nothing about the couples' own efforts to help downed flyers escape the Nazis. Instead, she stuck to the purpose of her journey to Val d'Isère.

"My boss, the British Army major I've mentioned who is known here as 'Pierre,' has heard about your helping downed flyers escape to Switzerland. He thought, perhaps, you'd be willing to do more along that line. Are you?" she asked, holding his gaze. "The major also wants to know if you could recruit some locals to form a regional *maquis*?"

The young Dr. Morand glanced down at some papers on his desk. After a pause, he looked up and gave a faintly negative shake of his head.

"I think in America, don't all doctors take an oath to 'first, do no harm'? There's a version of that in France, as well. At least, that has always been *my* guiding principle. I hate the Nazis as much as anyone and have my share of reasons to feel that way," he said, as if willing her to understand why he would not agree to recruit men whom the Mountaineer resistance network would train to become killers. "I have come to believe that I can make my best contribution by remaining a healer."

"I do understand," she murmured.

And she did. The carnage she had witnessed as an ambulance

driver had convinced her that the only people benefitting from war were politicians and businessmen like her stepfather Karl Bradford, along with the arms merchants and their henchmen. Still, when innocent people were getting killed, shouldn't one...?

Morand interrupted her meandering thoughts.

"But you can tell your major that there is already a small cadre of men in Val d'Isère who have formed a Resistance group and say they are ready to fight for France."

"Really? That's wonderful!" Viv exclaimed, awash with relief that she could report this news to Merrick. "Would you be willing to ask them if they'd agree to meet with the leader of Mountaineer and perhaps coordinate some...uh...activities?"

Dr. Morand replied with a wry expression, "From what I've seen of their *activities*, they need all the coordination, expert advice, and support they can get."

"The major is an extremely respected soldier who runs his operation with very tight security. He also seems to have the ear of the London War Office, which means he's able to secure arms and ammunition for those whom he deems reliable compatriots."

Dr. Morand nodded. "I suppose you can say I'm considered a member of their group, but merely use the skills I have to tend to their medical needs and to spirit Allied military and others needing help out of harm's way if they cross my path here in the mountains." He offered a small lift of his shoulders. "If I can hide someone and speed them on to safety, my family and I are willing to do that."

Viv thought of the Jewish mother and her two children who were apprehended when she crossed the Swiss border. Now that the Nazis had taken over all of France, Jews that had initially fled to the South of France from Eastern Europe were being deported to German labor camps in droves. An idea began to take shape in Viv's head.

"Truly, I totally understand the non-combative role you prefer," she said, leaning forward in her chair. "In some ways, that would be my own choice, given all the suffering we see. But would you be willing for this chalet to serve as a Mountaineer safe house and be part of a designated escape route to Switzerland for Jewish refugees fleeing from Nice and Cannes, as well as downed flyers? I'm based near Lake Annecy and would find *passeurs* to take them from the town of Annecy across the Swiss border."

Jean-Paul Morand sat back in his chair and cast Viv a long, measured look. Finally, he said, "As you may have noticed, a few SS officers, along with random detachments of Germans soldiers guarding the local passes to Italy, have been circulating in and out of our village in recent months. My chalet is right under their nose. Given that, I'm not sure that expanding my services beyond what little I've already done is particularly wise."

"But you're a doctor," Viv countered. "Don't you see?" she rushed to assure him. "Your being a physician is the perfect cover! All I had to do today was display a hacking cough and that SS creep couldn't go back across the street fast enough. I promise you, we'll advise those we send to you to pretend they're on death's door."

"That's actually an excellent idea," he replied with a chuckle. "But just so I understand," he said, "you're proposing that my chalet in Val d'Isère become a halfway stop for those fleeing from the south of the country, up to our village, and from there, to *you* in Annecy, where you'll find agents to get them to Switzerland?"

Viv nodded. "Exactly. We have a small manufacturer working with us in Annecy who's a loyal partisan. He travels back and forth from Annecy to Geneva selling his wares in Switzerland." She omitted identifying the bicycle factory whose owner once rode several years as a competitor in the Tour de France. Valentin Hervé regularly smuggled refugees across the border in boxes that normally contained his shiny, up-market two-wheelers for enthusiasts in Switzerland with money to pay for them. "This contact has been a literal lifeline for us to transport escapees."

Dr. Morand folded his hands on his desk, his crisp white doctor's coat a startling contrast to his mesmerizingly blue eyes the color of the sky on a clear Val d'Isère day.

"So you're suggesting that we form a French version of the 'Underground Railroad' like the one for slaves during your American Civil War?"

"Something like that," Viv replied. "You certainly know your American history."

"Dr. Jackson was the one who told me about it. People in his home state of Maine apparently participated."

"Ah…that sounds like something he'd know about."

A silence ensued, and Viv realized she was holding her breath, awaiting his answer about allowing his chalet to become a refugee safe house for Mountaineer.

The ghost of a smile tracing his lips, he said, "Actually, now that you've convinced me you aren't a Nazi double agent, what you're proposing sounds right in my lane. As a matter of fact, I have a young woman hidden in my attic right now." He looked at Viv expectantly. "You might be able to tell me what I should do with her next."

Viv blinked. "You're hiding a refugee upstairs right *now*?" she marveled, picturing the German soldiers smoking cigarettes not twenty meters away.

"Yes, she's the niece of one of the founders of the ski school here. Her late mother was Jewish, and the daughter is in great danger of being deported now that those few SS arrived in Val d'Isère. As you can imagine, I would very much appreciate having more support in these efforts. I'm willing to do my best to provide a way station, when I can, but it would be a relief to have a better system for getting these poor, endangered souls through an established funnel into Switzerland. The Lake Annecy region seems quite perfect for that since it's so close to the border."

"And what about orphaned children?" Viv asked impulsively, thinking of the little girl whose doll still rested at the bottom of her knapsack. Merrick had told her that the Nazis were now routinely separating children from their parents, often leaving the little ones to cope on their own. "Could you handle them, too," Viv asked urgently, "should we happen to find children in need of rescue?"

"In reasonable numbers, I suppose. Yes." He offered a faint smile. "It helps to have one's mother and sister living under the same roof."

"Oh, that wasn't your wife I saw standing behind you in the foyer?" she blurted.

The doctor cocked an eyebrow. "No, that was Dominique, my older sister whose husband was killed fighting in the debacle at the Maginot Line."

Viv was ashamed to acknowledge how oddly pleased she was to learn that the doctor wasn't married. She wondered if the poor woman's husband had been one of the dead bodies she and Adrienne had seen lying by the side of the road when they drove casualties back to the hospital in Paris. She suddenly thought of Marcel and his shrapnel wounds, recalling their harrowing trip to Dunkirk. A stab of disloyalty at finding Jean-Paul Morand such an attractive, empathetic man burrowed in her gut, as she stopped to consider the way her life had been upended by the war. She was a young woman almost thirty years old now. The world's conflicts had put every one of her normal relationships on hold. She wondered if any of the struggles everyone had to contend with these days would ever be resolved.

Calling a halt to her strange swirl of disconcerting musings, she pressed, "Then I can tell my major that you're willing to be a safe house for Mountaineer, Dr. Morand? He'll come here, himself, for you to take his measure if you wish."

After a long pause, he nodded affirmatively. "Yes, I'll help your Mountaineer group in the ways I described." And as if the decision actually pleased him immensely, he smiled broadly, saying, "And do call me Jean-Paul." He lightly pounded one fist on his desktop. "*Mon Dieu!* What manners! I haven't even asked your name."

"Violette," she replied, extending her hand with a wink "Violette Charbonnet…but you can call me Viv."

Clasping her hand in a firm grip, he said, "My mother will insist you must stay for dinner, Viv. You can spend the night in our very comfortable attic getting to know our other guest. If any of our uniformed neighbors wonder why you haven't emerged from my chalet, I'll say we suspect you might have something very contagious and must be quarantined until we determine what it is."

"Tell them I have the mumps," she suggested with a laugh. "I had a horrible case, so I can definitely describe the symptoms."

"Nasty business, that one," Jean-Paul commiserated. "I hope you weren't left with any of the bad side effects."

"Not that I know of," Viv replied, thinking suddenly of the doctor in Perpignan mentioning sterility could be one of them.

"Glad to hear you recovered. Many don't who suffered serious cases." He smiled again a touch ruefully. "Let us hope we don't have any unwanted SS pounding on our door tonight. And if the weather cooperates tomorrow, you and I and our guest in the attic will set out on a day of skiing. I look forward to introducing you to our mountain."

Viv cast him a startled look. "I would love to, Jean-Paul, but no ski holiday for me, I'm afraid. I must go directly back to Annecy tomorrow and—"

"You misunderstand," he interrupted, grinning now, an expression that was almost boyish. "While our neighbors across the street eat their hearty breakfasts, I will get an operator to fire up our new cable car to take us to the summit. From there, I will show you a seldom-traveled trail that will take you all the way to Tignes du Lac, avoiding the problem of departing Val d'Isère by the road where there can be checkpoints when one least expects them. It will be a good test of your proposal, will it not, to escort *Mademoiselle* Marian Moraski Bardet to the next stop on your 'underground railroad.'"

Viv saw she was still on trial, so she nodded and smiled.

"The success of which will make it *our* underground railroad, don't you agree?"

"Touché!" he said with a laugh.

Viv was filled with a sense of satisfaction that Major Merrick was bound to be impressed by her success enlisting Dr. Morand to allow his chalet to serve as both a safe house for escapees and a base in the Mountaineer circuit. If the local *résistants* also turned out to have potential, Merrick would be doubly pleased by her efforts today.

Jean-Paul said, "Once you know your way on this particular trail I'm going to show you, you can also ski it whenever you make any return trips to Val d'Isère. Coming from the train station, it's a bit of a climb at points, but well worth it for security's sake."

At that remark, they exchanged looks in joint acknowledgement they would be seeing each other again, working as colleagues and maybe even become friends. Viv longed for the day she would see Marcel again, but there was something comforting to meet someone like Jean-Paul Morand who chose to fight for France in a fashion dictated by his conscience and Hippocratic oath. It would take both kinds of men to win this war. Men who fought, along with men who saved the lives of those that the war put in harm's way.

Filled with these thoughts, Viv bent down and stroked the mammoth head of the Swiss beast slumbering at her feet.

"Such a good boy, being quiet all this time," she murmured,

reflecting upon how much had been accomplished in this one meeting.

Alphonse opened his liquid brown eyes in response to her touch and rose from his prone position on the floor to put his out-sized chin on her knee.

"He's registered your scent and has clearly taken a liking to you," observed Jean-Paul. "If you ever got stuck in an avalanche, he could find you now."

"Find me *alive*, I would hope," Viv joked. She gently pushed Alphonse's huge head to one side so she could rise from her chair.

Jean-Paul also stood up from behind his desk.

"Let's hope Alf never has that task," he replied soberly.

Viv guessed that the doctor and his dog had dealt with many such emergencies on nearby slopes. Jean-Paul gestured toward the infirmary's closed door.

"Come, let my mother make you something warm to drink and we'll properly introduce you to my sister, Dominique, and also to our 'guest' Marian. For security's sake, Marian must remain upstairs for her evening meal, but the rest of us will dine together tonight in the kitchen where it's warm."

CHAPTER 43

When Viv awoke the next morning, she could see through the small window near the peak of the roof in Dr. Morand's attic that the weather had changed. By the time she, the physician, and the teenaged Marian reached the base of the cable car that transported the smattering of local skiers to the summit, visibility was next to zero and the operator had closed down the lift for safety's sake.

"Probably for the best," muttered Jean-Paul. The snowfall was so thick that they were looking at each other as if through a curtain of gauze. "A howling wind can make for a very frightening trip on the gondola. I'll get the rope-tow operator to pull us to the ridge half-way up." He cast a sympathetic glance in Marian's direction. "At least our feet will be on the ground as we move up the mountain."

Viv merely nodded, hoisted her skis higher on her shoulder, and trudged through the snow, finding that her stride fit Jean-Paul's perfectly. Marian lagged behind, her skis an unwieldy burden on her inexperienced shoulders.

Viv paused to allow the young girl to catch up.

"Have you had a chance to ski much at Val d'Isère?" she asked casually. She glanced at the towering slope on her right that had all but disappeared into thick, boiling gray clouds descending down the icy side of the mountain.

"Not very much," Marian replied meekly. "My uncle sent for me in the summer, and then, when the SS arrived here in early September, I've been in hiding ever since."

"But you've skied?" Viv pressed.

"My uncle owns the ski school, so I've tried it a few times."

"How did you do?" Viv asked, forcing a smile.

"I grew up in Cannes," Marian replied in a small voice. "I've only visited here twice."

"Ah…" Viv said. She saw that the figure of Jean-Paul had nearly disappeared behind a curtain of swirling snow. "Well, never mind…you'll ride the tow between Dr. Morand and me. Quick!" she urged the girl toward the platform where the rope apparatus revolved on a metal disk near the platform where they would each take off. Nodding at their arrival, Jean-Paul gestured for Marian to sidle up next to him with her skis parallel to his. He nodded to Viv to grab the rope first, with Marian directed to go right afterwards and Jean-Paul behind her. The forward momentum of the advancing rope launched the three of them on their tandem journey up the mountain.

Just as the apparatus lurched forward, Viv called out over her shoulder to Marian, who looked terrified as she clutched the rope in a death grip. "Don't worry! Once we get to the top, it'll be downhill most of the way to Tignes du Lac."

"How far will that be?" the girl shouted as the rope began the steep ascent.

Jean-Paul's deep voice answered, "Oh, only four miles or so."

Marian's stricken look told Viv everything she feared to know.

Jean-Paul kept the flat of one hand extended, ready to catch Marian if her skis veered off the rut carved by Viv's two skis plowing on ahead of them. Soon, Viv saw over her shoulder that the two of them behind her had nearly disappeared behind an opaque curtain of snow, thick and cold. Any further glimpses of Jean-Paul and Marian were blocked out by a silent world of white enveloping her in its frigid cocoon. Viv held on tightly as she was pulled, foot-by-foot, up the side of the tallest mountain she'd ever skied.

At the mid-way point the tow ended and Jean-Paul pointed toward a trail marker. Viv decided the best thing to do going downhill was to put Marian behind her with her arms around Viv's own waist.

"Put your skis between my legs and keep them parallel to mine," she directed the teen. "We'll go down the trail with you holding your arms around my waist, so you don't really have to ski on your own at all, Marian. Keep your knees slightly bent and flexible so your legs can take the bumps. Meanwhile, hold on tight to me and we'll be fine."

She turned to Jean-Paul who was gazing at the two of them with a doubtful expression. "She won't need her poles, so stick them in my knapsack, will you?"

Jean-Paul inserted them through one side of the flap and out the other. "Well, off you go," he said to the two of them. "*Bonne chance et bientôt*—especially to you, Viv," he added, mixing French with his very good command of English.

"Yes," she replied with a slight grimace that betrayed her nervousness. "*Bonne chance,* for sure. Please picture us safely on the bus leaving from Tignes du Luc."

Jean-Paul took a step forward and brushed his lips against both sides of Marian's cheeks. "You will return to us one day, *ma petite*, so be brave."

Then, more slowly, he offered the same farewell to Viv. His lips felt cold against her skin, yet they radiated warmth that lingered long after she'd pushed her skis downhill.

———◇———

The four miles along the obscure, snow-covered trail were slow and treacherous. Viv was well aware of Marian's sense of panic; the teen was clutching Viv's waist like a steel vise. Their four skis constantly sank into drifts with the track practically disappearing. Once or twice, Marian's weight shifted far off center and the two of them plunged into the freezing powder. Viv's legs were trembling with fatigue when she caught sight of the bus stop's snow-covered roof at Tignes du Lac.

Thanks to their pose as mother-and-daughter vacationers toting two pairs of skis and poles, they were waved through the remaining bus and railway checkpoints, arriving at the town of Annecy, exhausted but hugely relieved. At Café Lyonnais, Anton and Olivia spirited Marian up to a maid's room in their small *auberge* next door.

The following day, Viv escorted the young teen to the Hervè Bicycle Works. In a loading dock at the back of the factory, she directed Marian to slide, face down, into a large, rectangular box with a few discreet air holes punched at the end nearest her head. The box was closed, and the young girl was then loaded into a truck with additional boxes containing Hervè's new bikes stacked on top. Viv watched as the vehicle bound for various bicycle shops in Geneva pulled away and disappeared down the street. She could only beseech heaven that the Swiss Red Cross would guide Marian to a new home somewhere in the world where the Nazis couldn't hurt her.

Anton chuckled when Viv returned from the bicycle factory and demanded a cup of genuine coffee from Olivia's kitchen as her reward for a fraught few days. It seemed like a miracle to Viv that Marian should soon be safely in Switzerland.

"Clément Grenelle told me about that young Swiss intelligence agent he deals with," Anton remarked. "A very good sort, he says. Apparently, he's the reason Hervè's trucks loaded with bicycle boxes pass across the border with ease."

Startled, Viv asked, "By any chance, is the agent's name Kurt?"

"I really shouldn't confirm Kurt is one of us, but you obviously know him, so yes."

Viv was flabbergasted. The good-looking young man who had escorted her to the border to rendezvous with Grenelle had been part of the Annecy network all along? In contrast to her stepfather Karl, Viv added Kurt and Jean-Paul Morand to the list of men like her father, *Monsieur* Hervé, and Marcel Delonge. Each had proved steadfast and true to their ideals at great risk to their own lives. She offered a silent prayer that they all remained safe in their efforts to free France.

Anton poured her more coffee, commenting, "That fellow at the border risks a lot for France, and he's Swiss, can you believe?"

"Whatever he is, he's a very good man," she murmured, remembering how grateful she and Renée had been when Kurt released them after they'd illegally entered his country. "And now he can add Marian's name to the list of people he's saved."

———◇———

The early winter months of 1943 were among the coldest on record, making Viv's work traveling back with refugees more treacherous and nerve rattling than ever.

In mid-November, Merrick asked her to organize an explosives team she soon dubbed the "Boom-Boom Boys"—the same cadre that she'd trained earlier in the cellar. On Merrick's orders, Jacques La Salle and his longtime school friends, Yves and Gaspard, had blown up two pylons on the Ugine-Annecy railroad line, putting all the factories engaged in the German war effort in the Annecy area out of commission for a week. Three days later, the same team, also under Viv's direction, blew up the pylon on the 45,000-volt high-tension line between Cluses and LeFayet, cutting the power for the industrial sector for another four days. Each day the German factories were idle was a day that slowed their ability to fight.

In the bitterly cold cellar of Viv's isolated chalet, the "Boys" met on November 23 to prepare some more charges slated to destroy two transformers that would cripple the Schmidt-Roos ball-bearing factory in Annecy. Viv took particular pleasure in this operation, especially anxious that their efforts succeeded as she contemplated the thousands of ball bearings her estranged stepfather had sold to the Third Reich as crucial components for the German war machine.

Young Jacques La Salle seemed amused as he stuffed matching portions of malleable *plastique* into a row of seven large rat carcasses that his father, Anton, had provided.

"If we do this right," he crowed, "we can do several million francs' worth of damage and put the factory out of commission for a couple of months!"

"Well, don't count your rat carcasses before the explosives inside them detonate," Viv cautioned. She pointed to the third rat in a row of rodents lined up on the cellar's wooden workbench. "You haven't connected that pencil fuse properly. Pay better attention, Boom-Boom Boy, or you'll blow *yourself* up!"

Eventually, every single explosive went off exactly as timed, setting off reverberations that shook the windows and caused the snow to slide off roofs throughout Annecy. Predictably, the local Gestapo was enraged. They plastered posters on streetlight poles and walls everywhere around the town, promising dire threats of retaliation against anyone "aiding, assisting, or hiding these terrorists." The Café Lyonnais itself had one such placard attached to the front of the building.

On the fourth of December, the Boom-Boom Boys pulled off yet another attack, and an entire factory ground to a halt, expected to remain crippled into the New Year.

"We added a dead marmot carcass to our rat collection to hide the explosives," Gaspard declared proudly. "It doubled the boom-boom!"

"What's a marmot?" demanded Viv, annoyed the team hadn't checked with her first.

"An oversized squirrel," he said with a superior air. "They're common creatures in the Alps—bigger than a rat and we can fit more explosives in their body cavity. No one would think a thing if they saw a dead marmot near a transformer."

"We used double the amount of *plastique*," chimed in Jacques, "and got a *very* big boom-boom."

"Yes I heard it," replied Viv. "Bravo."

Two days later, Viv walked into Olivia La Salle's kitchen at her usual time to help her prepare for the lunch service. As she was hanging up her jacket, Anton came through the door from the café's dining area, looking grim.

"Because of the recent explosions, the Germans are sending another hundred men to bivouac in Annecy," he revealed in a low voice. "And this morning, they shot ten workers in reprisal, picked at random from the ball-bearing factory."

"Oh, God, no," Viv gasped. "Where are Jacques and the others right now? Did they leave town as I ordered?"

Viv had told the trio literally to head for the hills, up to the Plateau des Glières.

"Yes," Anton confirmed, with a look toward his wife. "But the damn Krauts threatened to shoot ten times that number if another act of sabotage occurs here again." He paused. "They still might execute more people, anyway."

"*Mon Dieu*," breathed Olivia, her face white with fear. "Our Jacques...and his friends—"

Viv laid her hand on Olivia's sleeve.

"It's Christmastime. I told the boys to lay low and stay out of sight, and apparently they have. I have no new orders, so all's quiet for now. That should be the end of it."

But would it, she wondered? She had carefully planned the sabotage to take place in the middle of the night so there would be no human casualties, only damage to property and a blow to the German war machine. But every action the French underground took now inevitably triggered a bigger *reaction* from the Germans. As the Resistance had grown in the Haute-Savoie, so had the German atrocities against civilians. Viv's throat tightened with emotion. Many of Annecy's townspeople had become her friends and comrades.

Ten innocent factory workers were lined up and shot because of what we did...

Anton cast uneasy glances both at his wife and Viv before retreating to the dining room to greet incoming patrons. The two women silently went back to work.

———◇———

Viv spent the next two weeks traveling from Annecy to Val d'Isère and back ferrying refugees posing as skiing enthusiasts. From there, per usual, they were taken to Hervé's bicycle factory where they climbed into boxes that normally carried shiny new two-wheelers and were loaded into trucks headed for Switzerland. Viv thought often of the receiving *passeur*, Kurt, on the other side of the French-Swiss border and mentally thanked him for every trip successfully completed.

The few moments of enjoyment she had during these stressful times were the days in Val d'Isère when she sat in front of the stone fireplace in Dr. Morand's downstairs living quarters at his chalet. *Madame* Morand welcomed her like a member of the family, and Jean-Paul's sister Dominique insisted Viv share her bedroom, rather than the drafty attic.

Ever since the doctor had shown Viv the challenging—but seldom traveled—back route to Val d'Isère, she skied down to the village from the ridge trail with a sense of happy anticipation. Her routine now was to enter and exit the infirmary from a side street, using the back door to avoid being seen by the SS contingent based across the street from the chalet's front entrance. Arriving escapees were ordered to take the same precautions.

In mid-December, as 1943 drew to its frigid close, Clément appeared at Café Lyonnais with instructions from Major Merrick that Viv was to take a break from her trips to and from Val d'Isère and go to the Plateau des Glières with a message for Julien.

"Lieutenant Tom Morel and a second key aide to General de Gaulle are to meet with Julien," Clément informed her. "The *patron* wants you there, too."

"Have the Allies agreed to start providing more airdrops with the supplies the *maquis* need up there?" she asked.

"Unclear," Clément replied. "There's an internal debate in London about the danger of so many *résistants* congregating there, attracting the Krauts' attention. Merrick wants you to inform him exactly what's been decided at that meeting between the leaders."

Her heart beat faster as she asked, "Do you know who de Gaulle's other representative will be?"

Clément looked at her oddly. "You mean our old friend, Marcel? He and Morel—along with another de Gaulle aide named Jean Moulin—all report to the General."

"Is it Marcel you're talking about?" she demanded. "Marcel *and* Tom Morel will both be there to meet with Julien?

As always, the irascible Clément failed to disclose everything he knew. "You'll see when you get there, won't you, Violette? Be extra careful, though. These days, the Krauts are lurking behind every snow drift."

CHAPTER 44

The next day, Viv set off in the familiar direction of the plateau where she battled her way in deep snow up the steep trail toward the summit. All was silent as she tramped through the scrawny pine forest at the beginning of the climb. Soon, she left the stand of trees behind and plowed upward for several hours until she reached the last mile through an unmarked crevice that rendered the area a perfect hiding place.

She considered herself safe, as long as no German planes flew over her secret route or spied the *maquisards* training on the broad plateau in plain sight. But the cold had become so piercing, she could barely move her gloved fingers or feel her frozen toes despite the trusty pairs of socks that Marcel had given her. At length, reaching the summit, she paused, her breath ragged, the gasps of alpine air stabbing at the lining of her throat like little icicles.

From the edge of the expansive meadow, blanketed in an icy crust, a line of perhaps fifty men with long guns raised shoulder-height were shooting at targets a hundred paces away. Startled by the sudden sound of gunfire echoing across the field, Viv felt suddenly apprehensive that the increasing number of German troops replacing the Italians in the alpine region would inevitably hear these same sounds amplified by the steep-sided canyons and echoing across Lake Annecy's waters. How long would it be before the Germans pinpointed the location of these clandestine activities now taking place a few thousand feet above the valley, a region that had slumbered in relative quiet—until now.

Viv squinted against the snow's reflection. She could smell the smoke drifting from the chimney of the larger chalet she had already visited twice. A finger of even thinner smoke rose from behind the outcropping that hid the visitor's quarters from view, the shelter where she and Marcel had stayed all too briefly many months earlier.

A figure at the end of the line of student marksmen turned as Viv waved with both hands to signal she had no weapons and was a friend, not foe. Julien Paquet trotted toward her as she strode from the opposite direction.

"Welcome!" he called out. "Tom Morel told us to expect you." Reaching her side, he let loose with a question. "Serving as the eyes and ears for your major, again, eh? I assume he's still judging whether he thinks us worthy of British arms and ammunition?"

Viv smiled and pointed to her knapsack. "Well, at least he judges you worthy of a fine bottle of Scottish malt whisky which I've carried all the way up the mountain to give you." She held out her gloved hand. "Good to see you, Julien. I hope everyone is well."

———◇———

The moment Julien and Viv entered the chalet's large front room, Viv's breath caught as Marcel and Tom Morel rose from chairs positioned around the kitchen table. She attempted to control her delight that her hunch Marcel might be at this important regional meeting had turned out to be true. She composed a pleasant smile that she distributed equally to everyone in the room. In truth, she actually felt light-headed at the sight of Marcel only feet away, alive and well. His face looked thinner, though, and pinched with fatigue. He nodded perfunctorily as if merely acknowledging Julien's and her presence.

Everyone took their seats while several *maquisards* busied themselves at household tasks in anticipation of the next meal. Others were departing outside to take their turn at practicing their marksmanship.

"We only have a limited number of Sten guns," Julien said pointedly to Viv, "so we alternate squads during shooting sessions, as you can see."

For the next half hour, Viv merely observed without offering an opinion as the three men argued over the wisdom—or folly, as voiced by Marcel—of gathering hundreds of fledgling fighters in a single area with few clear routes in or out. Once again, Marcel pointed out that there was a surge of German troops arriving in the Haute-Savoie, prepared to put down any threatened insurrection.

Julien countered, "But given our assumption that the Krauts barely know of this plateau other than its markings on their maps—let alone have the stamina to scale it—and currently have very few troops in the region, I don't see the worry." He gestured with both hands in frustration, adding, "And if they do discover us, we'll be ready."

Marcel looked over at Tom, his fellow professional soldier.

Former army Lieutenant Tom Moral, whom Viv immediately sensed was the mediator in the group, spoke up. "We're soon going to have some eight hundred men up here, who'd surely be able to hold the summit." He met Marcel's steady glance. "General de Gaulle wants the Free French to stand ready to liberate this entire region."

Julien cut in, "And to do it ahead of the Americans or Brits when we establish the new government. This way, it will be a *French* win without any outside interference."

Marcel shook his head. "Wait. As you say yourself, you haven't enough weapons and supplies as it is. What happens when a couple of hundred more men begin to mass up here? How do you feed them? Equip and train them to hold their own against perhaps three thousand crack German soldiers from their mountain brigades?"

"And whose fault *is* our lack of weapons?" Julien groused with a glance at Viv.

"Even *with* weapons," Marcel countered, "do you think this inexperienced bunch can possibly fight off a seasoned division of German fighters *or* the German Air Force, if it's unleashed against this location?" Marcel pounded a fist on the table. "You're sitting ducks up here, Julien!" He shook his head again. "In my opinion, you should be asking the Allies for small arms weapons and ammunition, along with explosive materials, in order to fight down in the valley, guerrilla style. Hit-and-run operations are what we're suited for at this stage to soften up the Germans and prevent them from bringing in more supplies. Leave it for the Allies—which will *include* French troops—to handle the open field warfare. Believe me, there'll be enough credit, blood, and glory to spread around."

Tom said quietly, "I've had no direct communication recently with London. Does de Gaulle agree with your assessment?" he asked Marcel.

Viv knew that de Gaulle, himself, had recruited Tom, just as he had Marcel, but communications between the leader and his deputies were poor. The General and his seconds-in-command went long stretches without any personal contact, making judgment calls in the field that much more difficult.

Marcel shrugged. "I have no idea if de Gaulle would agree that attempting regular warfare in these circumstances was folly, but if he could see the situation for himself, I think he might concur it is. As you know, a number of SOE and our own Free French secret networks were recently blown. The wireless operator I often borrowed was arrested last week. The entire region is fraught with possible disaster for us."

Viv thought instantly of Fingers Malloy, who was the lifeline to Major Merrick and the Mountaineer network's contact with Britain. Perhaps Marcel knew more than he was disclosing. He threw a glance in Viv's direction.

"I think I should warn you all," he said, his expression grave. "A key person in charge of expediting the transport of SOE agents to and from France is now suspected by some of us of being a double agent. In recent months, we've lost scores of new recruits almost as soon as their parachutes opened."

Viv felt an involuntary shudder, speculating that Marcel might well be referring to Lucien Barteau, a.k.a. "Gilbert," the Air Operations Officer whose nose she broke when he got aggressive with her the day she landed back in France. Lucien would make the perfect double agent, she mused. The former circus stunt pilot's good looks, ambition, and bravado might well render him the kind of character who'd do whatever necessary to advance his own interests. She cringed at the memory of how Lucien could have eventually overpowered her if Major Merrick hadn't walked into the room shortly after they all landed in France in October of 1942. Lucien Barteau had had plenty of time since that date to get up to mischief—informing the Germans in exchange for money whenever the SOE sent in additional secret agents to take the places of those arrested by the SS.

Viv decided to speak up.

"I can tell you from personal experience that the noose is tightening everywhere around the lake. The last time I saw our radio operator," she continued, recalling a recent conversation with Fingers Malloy, "he said he rarely slept in the same safe house two nights in a row these days. Now that the war in North Africa has gone so badly for the Germans, their attempts to eliminate Allied secret agents is at a fever pitch." She paused. "It seems very likely there will be a major, new influx of German soldiers, *including* air support, into the Haute-Savoie. Sooner, rather than later."

"And *we* will have the men by then to kick them back to their Fatherland!" declared Julien, whose flushed face signaled he didn't appreciate Viv supporting Marcel's views about the threat posed by German air and ground forces against his swelling ranks.

Tom's gaze swept the three sitting around the table with him.

"I say we continue to request arms and supplies from London, while training the men willing to join in our Resistance efforts. That way, we'll be ready, whether we partisans continue up here on the plateau, or we disperse into smaller units down in the valley to engage in sabotage efforts when the time is right."

Marcel remained silent, as did Viv. Julien inhaled deeply, and Viv could tell he was reining in his temper in reaction to Tom's mollifying proposals. Silence settled over the room except for the hiss of the coal crackling on the stone hearth.

"So, that's it, then," Marcel said, rising to his feet. "I must be off." He glanced out the window. "If I leave now, I can be down from here before dark."

Viv pushed her chair back from the table. "That goes for me as well." She turned to Julien. "I'll convey your requests for more Sten guns and the other supplies to the major and let him know about the increasing number of men in your *maquis*," then adding, "and I'll send up someone to let you know if any more additional German troops arrive in Annecy or the surrounding area. Fritz fully recognizes that the town is a key to funneling escapees into Switzerland. Trust me, our Mountaineer network will be the first to learn of any new measures the SS is taking to stop our operations."

Viv reached for her heavy jacket as Marcel donned his *Canadienne*. The four of them exchanged perfunctory nods—a moment that left Viv with a lingering feeling that their meeting had not truly resolved anything.

"I'll guide you down the least-known trail, shall I?" she offered Marcel. "It lets out on the Annecy-Thones road, and you can make your way from there."

"*D'accord*," he answered gruffly, as if his mind was solely focused on the next mission. With a brief nod to Julien and Tom he said, "*À bientôt*," and then strode past them and through the chalet's front door, with Viv trailing behind, wondering if this wartime quartet would, in fact, ever meet again.

CHAPTER 45

Viv felt Marcel's lips pressing gently on the back of her left shoulder. His body was cradled against hers, warm and comforting until she felt him move toward the edge of her narrow bed in the loft overlooking the small front room of her chalet.

"I must leave, now, *chérie*."

"Noooo…not yet," mumbled Viv.

He leaned down and brushed his lips against her back once more.

"I must. Get up, now," he urged. "I'll make us what passes for coffee."

Viv watched him rise, naked and leaner than she'd ever seen him. She imagined he'd noticed the same about her. Food had become scarcer than ever, and she figured she'd lost at least fifteen pounds despite her on-going cover story that she was a kitchen helper at a restaurant. Scars on Marcel's shoulders from the shrapnel he'd received in the early battles of the war stood out in stark, white slashes against his skin that remained tanned, even in a dark winter as cold as this one.

Viv reached for her clothing, dressed, and stumbled down the loft's ladder to arrive at the table as Marcel presented her with a mug of the hot brew—a drink they both wished was made from real coffee beans instead of ground acorns. He'd toasted two stale pieces of bread on the grate over the hearth that was now burning brightly. His canvas haversack, stuffed with clothing and other gear, was on a chair along with his jacket draped over the back.

If only we could be like this for a little while longer... she yearned silently.

Marcel had disclosed he was off to St. Jorioz on the west side of Lake Annecy to rendezvous with Viv's boss, Major Merrick, who'd been with the *maquis* in Vercours.

"He will be picked up soon to have meetings in London," Marcel disclosed.

"When you talk to him, tell him about the recent German reprisals in Annecy. And can you pass along the same intelligence that I told Julien about my fear we're due for an influx of more German troops in town?" she asked. Marcel nodded in agreement. "And what about Julien's pleas for a big airdrop of arms and supplies?" she added.

"If I have any means to do it, I'll convey exactly what he's asking for," Marcel said scowling. "I'll also give my view of the folly of a rag-tag assembly of patriotic but undertrained young men going to battle against Fritz's crack ground troops and the *Luftwaffe* positioned to annihilate them."

"You think that'll actually happen?" she asked, anxious at the thought of 17-year-old Jacques La Salle and the other young men hiding out on the plateau. "The Germans will even call in their Air Force in the end?"

"If I were commanding on their side, that's what I'd do, but who the hell knows?" Marcel reached across the table and seized Viv's hand. Meeting her gaze, he said, "It has been so good to be with you these last hours, *chérie*."

Viv nodded, her throat tight with emotion; she felt incapable of uttering a word.

Marcel's expression grew grave. "I need to tell you that you must be more vigilant than ever about your own safety, Viv. A major SOE network outside Paris was smashed a few weeks ago, with dozens of agents arrested. Things are going to get dark, indeed, in the New Year." He paused again. "Do you remember that scum we both met during parachute training—"

Startled, Viv interrupted. "You mean Lucien Barteau who became an Air Operations Officer? The one you warned me about and spoke of yesterday?"

Viv had never told Marcel about Barteau's aggressive behavior upon landing in France, fearing Marcel would literally kill him if he saw him again.

"Yes...code name Gilbert." Marcel paused as if deciding whether to confide in her. "I'm convinced more than ever that he's a double agent. Arrests invariably occur directly after operations he supervises."

"He headed the ground crew for my flight in on the Lysander," she confided. "After we landed, he got my *patron* and me to the safe house, but then..." Viv hesitated, and then made snap decision. "He tried to...uh...get fresh."

Marcel's dark eyes flashed. "*How* fresh? And where was Merrick?" he demanded.

"Asleep." Viv tried to sound offhand. "Turns out my hand-to-hand training came in handy. I'm fairly sure I broke his nose. Next day, Merrick and I were on our way, and I've never seen him since. I agree with you. He's dangerous and capable of anything."

Marcel's lips etched into a thin line. "If the chance presents itself, I'd like to shoot the bastard myself, but so far, those of us in the field can't seem to get Buckmaster and the others in London to pay attention to our warnings."

"Well, maybe it'll be moot. Won't the Allies be invading soon?" she pressed.

She felt a wave of longing that this endless war would soon come to some—any—conclusion. She could only pray the invasion would be launched before sheer fatigue exhausted agents like Marcel, Major Merrick, Fingers—and herself.

Or someone like Lucien Barteau betrays us...

"The Allies had better invade soon," Marcel agreed, his strain and exhaustion showing. "Apart from the Germans breathing down our necks, I can't take much more of the political posturing of the factions on *our* side, to say nothing of the endless regional infighting and clashing egos." He smiled wearily. "I just want to be back at Chateau Delonge picking my grapes and making decent wine." He leaned across the table and seized her hand. "I hope you realize how much I hope we might one day be there together, Viv." He barely brushed his lips against hers, a silent signal that told her he felt the same battle fatigue that had been plaguing her. "This may be farewell for a very long time, *chérie*..."

"I know," Viv whispered, fighting to subdue her tears.

"There's no guarantee either of us will make it through, but *if* we both survive..."

His tentative promise of a future together hung like the faintest of rainbows between them. Viv stared at the fire grate as he rose from the table, donned his coat from the back of a chair, and slung his army-issued canvas haversack over one shoulder.

Viv walked him to the door, and when she opened it, a blast of frigid air heralding a coming snowstorm swirled around them. They stood side-by-side on the wood-railed porch, both gazing down at the view of Lake Annecy and the white mountains ringing the water. War raging in the midst of such exquisite beauty was an abomination, Viv thought.

Neither spoke. Viv knew if she attempted a word, she'd start to cry, and that would make their parting even harder.

The moment passed, and Viv stared at Marcel's back as he trudged down the steps and set off, his booted footsteps etching his departure in the snow. At the end of the lane, he turned and waved. Viv waved back and then quickly reentered her chalet. Shivering from the cold, she walked toward the glowing hearth seeking its warmth. Viv sipped the dregs of the coffee from Marcel's cup, her lips grazing where his had been, and stared once more into the fire falling to embers. She turned her head slightly and gasped. Her eyes riveted on the chair where Marcel had placed his canvas pack and jacket when he'd arrived from their trek down from the plateau.

There, beneath the chair on the chalet's wooden floor, lay the Hermès scarf that Viv had given Marcel at Dunkirk to wrap food for his journey across the Channel, a piece of silk he had told her he had kept near him for good luck. In his haste to be on his way this day, it had slipped out of his pack and slid onto the floor, unnoticed by either of them.

Viv sank to her knees, scooped it up, and ran to the door, desperate to return it to him as his lucky charm. The snow had begun to fall in earnest. All trace of Marcel's footsteps had been erased, and the view of the lake was completely obscured.

Viv clutched the slippery silk in one hand, its folds frigid against her skin. Walking back into the chalet, she sank onto the floor in front of the dying fire and buried her face in its lingering scent of her Chanel No. 5 perfume. And then she began to cry, releasing deep, wracking sobs for the first time since her father had died.

CHAPTER 46

Soon after Viv's most recent trip to the plateau and Marcel's departure, Major Merrick arrived and claimed the back room at Viv's chalet.

"You've done well," he complimented her as they sat at her kitchen table that morning. "The information you gathered from Julien Paquet has been forwarded to London. Meanwhile, I've sent one of my agents to connect with the group whom your Dr. Morand recommended. An SOE contact in Nice will now be guiding certain key people north to Val d'Isère. You'll bring them to Annecy to be guided across the Swiss border, as usual. There may be times when the winter weather will make the operation impossible, but make as many trips as you think feasible." He stared at her a long moment. "Just be bloody careful whenever you enter Annecy. Word is that the SS is determined to find the cell leader that blew the transformers at the ball-bearing plant."

"Yes, sir," Viv murmured, her thoughts still riveted on her fears for Marcel.

Merrick took a sip from the cup of ersatz coffee Viv had managed to produce. He paused, and then set it aside.

"German mountain brigades are arriving now, so I want you to start wearing that white camouflage ski suit issued you as part of your gear. You're less likely to be spotted when you're traversing those mountain passes on your own." He pointed to a wooden box sitting on the floor. "I've got some small arms you are to take to the new group in Val d'Isère on your next trip. I'm hoping such token contributions will keep them in line until I can get the powers-that-be to air drop them supplies, including some for the *maquisards* on the Plateau des Glières." He tapped his forehead. "I'll have some messages you're to deliver about our future plans for the Val d'Isère group that we hope will come to fruition in the spring."

Viv tried not to display her nervousness at the idea of carrying hand grenades and small arms in her knapsack on public trains and buses when she set out for Val d'Isère with her skis on her shoulders. At any point the SS, the horrid *milice,* German regulars or Vichy authorities could stop her and demand to inspect whatever she was carrying.

"I'll do my best to get the arms into the right hands, sir."

But with each more dangerous assignment, she wondered if her best would be good enough.

"And Violette," Major Merrick added, his gaze steady, "getting that last group of children from Morand's safe house to Switzerland posing as the Head Mistress of an Aryans-only orphanage was first rate work."

Viv felt her face flushing. Merrick rarely offered compliments, but before she could thank him, he raised his hand to signal he had something important to add.

"I'm sorry to tell you, though, that the last handoff to the Swiss agent by the bicycle factory driver didn't go well."

"*Monsieur* Hervé's man was *arrested?*" she asked, suddenly feeling the lousy coffee she'd made churning in her stomach.

"No, he safely made it back to Annecy."

"Oh, thank God!"

Merrick appeared to gird himself for more.

"Things went awry on the Swiss side. The Swiss agent that once helped you—"

"Kurt?" Viv responded. "Oh, God, no! What happened?"

"A German patrol in the no-man's-land opened fire before he could get the youngsters into the safe zone."

Viv felt her heart constrict with horror.

"They shot the *children*?"

"Yes."

"And Kurt?"

"He was wounded by the gunfire and dragged back across the border into France."

Viv's heart began to race. "Do we know what happened to him?"

"The word that came back was that he was interrogated, tortured, then taken into a local square in Annemasse where a firing squad of ten men killed him."

"Oh, no… Kurt… *No*…" Viv said barely above a whisper. "And the children…"

"Beyond tragic," Merrick agreed. "And it means everyone in the Annecy chain of agents may be compromised, perhaps including you."

"No matter what the SS did to Kurt," Viv insisted, "he wouldn't tell—"

"He wouldn't want to, but there's not one among us who might not crack when the Gestapo starts putting lighted cigarettes out on your shoulder or pulls out your fingernails one-by-one."

Viv fought her tears and shook her head with vehemence.

"Not Kurt!"

"Did he know you were part of the circuit bringing refugees through Annecy to the bicycle factory?"

Viv was silent, her thoughts whirling through a list of all the people who knew even a slice of her involvement.

"I don't think he knew I had become a link in that particular chain. The La Salles knew… Clément Grenelle, of course. And *Monsieur* Hervé, although the drivers he assigned to various bicycle deliveries were never told who I was."

"The SS would have pressed Kurt for every name he'd ever worked with, and you're undoubtedly on that list." Merrick looked at her with an expression that bordered on compassion. "Odds are likely—if he cracked—he might have given them names he figured were far away from the Haute-Savoie by now."

"Names like mine," she murmured. "I'd told him when he helped me last year that I wanted to get back to England to see if I could contribute to the war effort. If Mountaineer security protocols were followed, he wouldn't have been informed I was back in France and working in the network with Grenelle and Hervé."

Merrick sighed. "That's what I thought. And that might mean he'd have figured your name was safe to disclose to his torturers in order to buy time for the others whom he *knew* were in Mountaineer to get away from Annecy. But if one of the other Mountaineers were caught because of Kurt and were later presented with your name..."

Viv felt her body go cold, as if she'd just climbed to the summit of the plateau. That Kurt might have inadvertently tipped off the local Gestapo of her presence in Annecy was a horrifying irony beyond anything she could have imagined.

Thank God he'll never know...

"The fact is," the major continued, "the SS executed Kurt, which might have meant he stubbornly refused to divulge *any* of what he knew, and therefore, you weren't named." Merrick shook his head. "But the problem is, Viv, we have no way of knowing that for certain. I tell you this to make clear why I want you to remain in Val d'Isère for a while after your next trip there until things cool down in Annecy. If nothing else happens, you can return to your job as *passeur* from the ski resort, but always on high alert, especially when you're near your chalet... you understand? Meanwhile, try to line up an alternate who can take the airmen and other escapees from the resort into Annecy."

Viv nodded distractedly, but her thoughts were spinning.

Clement...the La Salles... Jacques, Yves, Gaspard... Monsieur Hervé...even Major Merrick, himself, might be at risk...

Who knew how far the chain linking them to Kurt might have extended? Marcel had said that nearly every connection to the Prosper circuit in and around Paris had been blown. He'd declared darkly that he was convinced Lucien Barteau was somehow involved in the betrayal. As Viv took both coffee cups to the sink, she tried to absorb the implications of what could be happening to Mountaineer. And try as she might, she couldn't banish from her mind's eye the image of the handsome, decent man she knew as "Kurt"—being thrown against a wall, his body riddled with the bullets from ten guns.

"Well, I must be off," Merrick said, rising from the kitchen table. "Don't stay here long," he advised, "Two more days at the most.

And don't forget to take the grenades," he reminded her. "Give six to the *maquis* in Val d'Isère."

"What should I do with the rest?" she asked, still reeling from the news about Kurt.

"Wrap them in something and hide them beneath the floorboards under the kitchen sink. I have definite plans for all that later." He rose from the table and lifted his heavy jacket from a hook near the chalet's front door. "And, oh," he said, turning back to her, "I'm sorry if your place feels like a hot-sheet hotel, but Fingers will arrive tonight, so give him my room. Things got dicey in Faverges lately, too, so he needs to leave his area for a while, just as you need to stay away from Annecy for a bit. Just don't tell the La Salles or anyone in our circuit Fingers is here, all right? He'll base at this place and move around for security while you're with Dr. Morand."

"Fine," Viv responded, feeling hollow inside over Kurt's fate and the danger Marcel might be in at this very moment.

Life could turn on a dime she thought...*or should I say, on a centime?*

"Viv?" Merrick said in a way that told Viv he'd seen her mind wandering. "Be *sure* you wear that white camouflage ski suit. I've received word there's a new German mountain brigade coming that's been specifically assigned to this region. Be on the lookout for them. They're all sharpshooters, and the white suit will give you a better chance of not being seen on the slopes."

CHAPTER 47

Fingers Malloy arrived soon after Merrick had left.

"Merry Christmas a bit late!" he said, trailing snow into the front room of Viv's chalet. December 25th had come and gone with Viv spending it alone wrapped in several blankets thanks to the scarcity of coal.

Fingers had a canvas knapsack like Viv's slung over one shoulder and was toting his heavy leather suitcase. Hidden inside was the most modern version of a radio transmitter the SOE gave to its "pianists" for messaging back and forth with London.

"You sure it's Christmas?" joked Viv.

"Two days ago," he replied, speaking to her in English as he set his belongings on the floor. "Soon it'll be the New Year, you crazy Yank! 1944, Viv! We've been at this game two long years now." Hands on hips, he asked, "So, what've you been up to?" Before she could answer, he asked "Got anything hot to drink?"

"Lousy coffee, made lousier by yours truly," she said. "Or cognac, left by the major, I guess as a Christmas present," she added with a shrug. "No card, of course."

"I'll take the cognac, and let me sit down by this nice fire." He removed his leather gloves and rubbed his hands together vigorously to restore the feeling in his fingers. "God, I'm sure not in New Orleans anymore."

Viv poured two shots of the amber liquid, and the pair pulled up kitchen chairs facing the low embers on the grate. Viv then related Merrick's news that an agent she'd worked with had just been executed.

"Mountaineer might be compromised," she added, all humor drained from their conversation. "Merrick has ordered me to lay low in Val d'Isère for the same reasons you have come to Annecy. People know me here, but they don't know you."

Fingers took a long drink of his cognac. "The major can be a stiff, but he knows his stuff," he said. "The noose sure seems to be tightening these days."

Viv asked, "Have you heard about a suspected double agent causing this havoc?"

"Yup," he answered, staring into the fire. "I think that's why I started seeing those white locator vans cruising near Faverges more and more during the last few weeks. Somebody's got to be tipping off the SS about SOE operatives in our region."

Recalling the details of Marcel's suspicions about Lucien Barteau, Viv asked Fingers, "Do you remember that French guy who was in charge of meeting our Lysanders when we landed near Loyettes? What'd you think of him?"

Fingers gazed at her with surprise. "That tall, dark good-looking Frog? Yeah, I remember him. He seemed a pretty efficient operator. At least he got *us* off that field without being arrested."

Viv nodded and took a sip of cognac that burned its way down her throat.

"That, he did. But I've heard lots of other Joes like us apparently weren't so lucky. Over the last few months, a bunch was picked up within hours or days of arrival."

Fingers looked up from his drink, surprised.

Viv continued, "That operations guy knows where we three were headed, and knows about another agent that is pretty high up with de Gaulle. The major warned us to be extra vigilant as we move around here."

Fingers returned his gaze to the fire. "What was his code name? Gilbert?"

Viv nodded. Fingers remained silent for a long moment as if he were turning something over in his mind.

"Well, I'll grant you that he'd certainly be in a prime position to sell knowledge of our comings and goings if he felt like making a buck...or a couple million francs."

"My thoughts, exactly," Viv replied. "As a Frenchman working in SOE, Gilbert is in the perfect position to play both sides. Let's hope the powers-that-be in London have him on their radar." She stood up and stretched. "I'm bushed. You'll sleep in the boss's room at the back. I'm leaving first thing in the morning. As I said, the major wants me to keep out of sight around Lake Annecy for a while. The place is yours as long as you like."

Fingers looked up from the burning embers and nodded soberly.

"Thanks. I'll be coming and going as my gut instincts direct." They exchanged glances, neither speaking as several seconds ticked by. "I don't know about you, Viv," he said, shaking his head, "but I'm mighty sick of this war."

"Me, too, Fingers. Me, too."

Viv had turned toward the ladder that led to her sleeping loft when he declared, "You knew an agent who worked for the de Gaulle crowd, right?"

Viv whirled away from the loft's ladder to face her guest.

"Yes. What about it?"

"I think he may be the one I'm told was arrested in Lyon a week ago."

"What happened?" Viv demanded, trying to keep her voice from sounding shrill.

"The story I've gleaned in some messages back and forth is that soon as de Gaulle's guy got to Lyon, a witness reported that he was picked up by Klaus Barbie's goons. You know, 'The Butcher of Lyon.'"

Viv knew very well about the head of the Gestapo there whose sadism and cruelty were legendary by now.

Fingers went on, "Word is this agent, who was de Gaulle's number one or two deputy, was interrogated and most likely taken to Paris to be roughed up by the SS goons on Avenue Foch." Fingers paused and added quietly, "It seems this guy, whoever he was, is considered a very big fish. Nobody's heard anything about him since."

Fingers' expression of concern told Viv he recalled seeing Marcel bid her farewell the night she and Fingers flew to France. She felt her throat constrict so tightly, she couldn't speak and could only wave one hand in farewell at her guest as she turned and mounted the ladder to her sleeping loft.

Oh, God... Marcel!

During spy school there had been mock interrogations staged in the middle of the night. The SOE trainers described the techniques of torture the SS were famous for, especially when the Nazis thought they'd caught someone who was head of a clandestine cell, the sole aim of which was to sabotage the German war effort.

You mustn't think about Marcel! Only think about tomorrow's trip to Val d'Isère.

She forced herself to focus on the things she had to do in the next twenty-four hours to *not* get caught. It was her only chance to survive, or ever hope to see Marcel again. But her mind was reeling. How was it possible to concentrate on stealthily transporting six hand grenades and a couple of pistols all that distance without getting stopped? And if she *did* think about what might be happening to Marcel this very moment, she knew she'd go insane. Not bothering to get undressed, she wrapped herself in her blanket and sank down on the mattress.

A vision of Lucien Barteau rose in her mind's eye. What if he had been the one to betray Marcel? The two had definitely shown animosity towards each other the day she'd made her one and only parachute jump in Manchester. Was it possible Lucien knew the recent movements of de Gaulle's close deputy, making him ripe for a betrayal?

Don't! Don't think about that! Just think about the trip to Val d'Isère!

Viv lay in bed, forcing herself to plan each train and bus stop on her upcoming journey. She closed her eyes, only to imagine the SS pig in Val d'Isère who'd harshly demanded to see her papers the first time she'd come to Jean-Paul Morand's front door. She had to be ready with a plausible cover story if she ran into him again. She couldn't—*wouldn't*—allow herself to think that Marcel might be the Free French agent who'd just been arrested or accept the idea that his forgetting her Hermès scarf at the chalet was an ill omen if it were true that he'd been caught by Klaus Barbie's thugs.

Later... I'll think about Marcel later...

Exhaustion from her mental gymnastics finally delivered a few hours of fitful sleep.

———◇———

The next morning, Fingers Malloy stood near Viv at the kitchen table watching her pack a clutch of hand grenades into various pouches inside her canvas knapsack.

"You know not to touch the pins unless you're ready to blow something up, right?"

"Yes, thank you," Viv replied, arching an eyebrow. "Although I expect you realize that I attended the same small arms class in Scotland that you did?"

"Well...yes, but..." he replied uncertainly. "You'll be *skiing*. You just want to be sure the pins in those things are securely in place in case you take a fall."

Trust me, I don't need anyone reminding me, Viv swore silently to herself.

Even so, just to double check, she felt each pin on the devices that looked like miniature pineapples, confirming that none wobbled. The skies over the little chalet were overcast again, and the temperature that morning, three days before New Year's, had already dropped another ten degrees. She'd be skiing over snow-covered ice in many areas as she came down the slopes above Val d'Isère. Each turn, each mogul, each trail through a stand of trees could spell disaster, given the explosives in her pack. The trip would be especially hazardous as the sun went down. Shadows on the mountains made reading the steep inclines even more treacherous.

"Well, I'm off," she announced with forced cheer, pulling on her gloves. She glanced around the chalet's main room. "The place is all yours."

"Thanks," Fingers replied. "And good luck today."

His tone was grim. Both knew only too well that luck would be very much what she and her knapsack needed to arrive safely at her next alpine destination.

CHAPTER 48

December 29, 1943

The contents weighing on Viv's back were growing increasingly heavy by the time she'd made it to Tignes du Lac past several checkpoints with her skis slung over her shoulder. Not thinking about the hand grenades she was carrying was like not wondering if Marcel were the person Fingers had heard had been arrested. And ignoring the danger that carrying the concealed devices presented was like ignoring the likelihood Marcel had been taken to the notorious building in Lyon where SS *Haupsturmfüher* Klaus Barbie was known to personally torture his captives. His gruesome techniques almost guaranteed success at prying away his victim's secrets—unless they died first from his most barbaric method: dunking his prisoners, head first, in ammonia.

The skies were hanging heavy and low as Viv set off toward Val d'Isère. A cold wind whipped at her cheeks, and once again, she gave thanks for Marcel's socks.

Marcel!

She told herself for the umpteenth time she mustn't think about him now and trudged out of the train station like any other alpine resident. When she got off the local bus, she waited for it to pass and then mounted her skis, traversing the route for as far as she could before she had to carry them on her shoulder as she hiked up to the high-ridge trail. Once there, she pulled her white camouflage ski suit out of her knapsack and eased it over her brighter clothing that could easily be spotted if German patrols were scouring the area.

The shadows on the snow were lengthening by the time she clamped her skis back onto her boots and prepared to schuss down the last miles to a warm fire and a friendly welcome from the Morand family.

She hadn't gone far when, echoing from the trail below, Viv heard guttural voices bouncing off the sheer walls that lined the lower trail. Viv's German was good enough to translate a ribald exchange about the temperature being "colder than a witch's tit."

In the next second, she caught her first glimpse of two soldiers dressed in the same white camouflage ski gear she was, their skis hoisted on their shoulders as they trudged uphill on the same trail she had been skiing down. Their armband insignias told her they were members of an elite German mountain brigade.

She dug her skis' edges into the side of the trail and in the next instant, planted her poles into the snow. The grenades in her knapsack felt heavier on her back—and more dangerous—than ever before. Her mind raced over the few possibilities available to defend herself. One part of her brain wondered if this would be the day, after so many close calls, that her luck finally ran out.

———◇———

"Mein Gott!

Two young skiers clad in their unit's distinctive white ski apparel halted, mid-trail. Both soldiers were quick to note the white-clad figure looking down the track at them was not a comrade.

One soldier aimed his rifle and shouted in garbled French, "Halt, or I'll shoot!"

But they soon realized that they were not to win the contest with the tall stranger threatening them with a hand grenade poised to be pitched directly at them.

"No, *you* halt," shouted a voice in German that, to their astonishment, turned out to be a woman's. "I'll throw this before you can shoot, and we'll all be blown to bits!"

In the next moment, they were strangely relieved to be given orders that they were only too happy to follow in the way that they had learned to do without question as raw, young recruits who happened to know how to ski.

The next furious command was: "Cast your weapons into the ravine, *now*!"

They complied, as they did when ordered to march ignominiously past their female aggressor and up the trail toward their bivouac, not daring to look back. Their best hope was that there wouldn't be an explosion that would blow them beyond any hope of one day returning to Bavaria.

Their teeth chattering, not from the cold but from sheer terror, all the unlucky duo heard as they cross-hatched their thick boots up the steep incline to safety was the sound of another pair of skis whooshing down the mountain in the opposite direction. One finally summoned the courage to look around. There was nothing to see but falling snow.

———◇———

Viv fought against a persistent and annoying sense that someone or something was trying to rouse her from the cocoon of numbing warmth that now enveloped her. Her body was buried deep in snow that felt soft and welcoming.

For a second, she had a vision of two Germans in white camouflage gear, one of the menacing pair pointing a gun at her chest. She attempted to wave her hands to ward off an assault, but she couldn't seem to move her arms. Her next fuzzy thoughts were a memory of having escaped her aggressors but then having taken a curve in the trail too fast. Centrifugal force had done the rest. She'd lost control and...

She was vaguely aware of the trunk of a tree beside her. She couldn't feel her feet, even when she attempted to move them.

A stab of pain that felt like an ice pick lodged in her shin shot up her leg.

"Oh! Owww!" she moaned.

Then she heard barking.

Slowly she opened her eyes to see a large dog running circles around her prone figure and making a series of alarming, high-pitched yowls. The next thing she remembered was the sensation of a warm, rough tongue lapping against her cheek. The loud, persistent barks pierced her eardrums. As minutes went by, the yelps grew more frantic, echoing across the snowy ridge. Then she heard the crunch of boots drawing near.

"Good boy," declared a deep voice. "Good find!"

Someone was kneeling by her side and the barking stopped. She felt two woolen mittens frame her face. She tried to remain absolutely still. Was it the Germans, come back to finish her off?

And then a voice.

"*Mon Dieu*! Don't move, Violette."

Violette? Who's Violette?

Then, she remembered. *She* was Violette. She was a secret agent in France. SOE. French Section. She had been schussing down the trail with a knapsack full of hand grenades as if the devil were at her back when she'd hit the last turn before the final descent into Val d'Isère. A long stretch of ice had been hidden beneath the snow and—

"Wake up!" the voice shouted. "Wake up, Viv! You must wake up!"

The voice was deep and sounded familiar.

"Here. Drink this."

The cold rim of a flask was being forced between her lips.

"Try to take a few sips."

Brandy.

Viv felt its searing heat slide down her throat. She tried to voice her thanks, but the pull of sleep and the weight of something—a heavy jacket, perhaps?—settled against her upper body. A shard of panic pierced her consciousness. She should mention the danger of the grenades in her knapsack. It was a miracle none had gone off, but the pins had remained secure, thank God. And it was cold. Hand grenades didn't always detonate in sub-zero temperatures her instructor had told her. That was so long ago…

Viv attempted to assemble a warning about the weapons, but her thoughts were jumbled, and she couldn't seem to organize them into a sensible sentence.

"Alphonse?" the voice commanded the furry beast sitting beside Viv. "*Stay!*"

Warm breath blew against her ear. Was it dog or man? she wondered through a fog blanketing her brain.

"Alf will stand guard, Viv. I'll fetch a toboggan to get you off the mountain."

She felt a kiss linger on her forehead, followed by a thumb pressed against the side of her neck, then the pressure of two hands gently feeling along her pants' leg.

After several seconds, the voice reassured her, "You're in a bit of shock, but you're going to be all right. By the looks of how you landed, you may have broken your tibia, so don't move your right leg or try to get up. I'll be back as soon as I can."

Viv heard the sliding sound of skis on the snow, and then silence descended except for the heavy breathing of a large dog snuggling close to her backside to keep her warm.

———◇———

Viv barely remembered being transferred in the blackness of night down the mountain. Jean-Paul and Dominique wrapped her in blankets on Morand's toboggan and together brother and sister got her off the steep slope.

Likewise, she had no memory of the doctor setting her leg and then wrapping it in wet plaster from her foot to her upper thigh. Once it had dried, Viv wondered how the two siblings managed to transport her and her rigid cast up two flights of stairs to the attic hideaway where she'd previously slept in a cot beside Jean-Paul's transitory refugees.

When Viv finally awoke, she realized she had been transferred to Dominique's bedroom on the second floor. She also noticed that Alf had formed a very large, furry lump on the floor beside her bed. She heard heavy footsteps on the stairs and then the door opened. She breathed a sigh of relief to see it was Jean-Paul, himself.

"You're very lucky," he had informed her when the pain drugs he'd administered to her wore off in the hours after her rescue. "As I thought, it's a simple break of the smaller of the two bones in your lower right leg. You should be all right and able to walk and even ski again in about four to six weeks. We've put you in Dominique's room so you won't have so many stairs to navigate."

Approaching her bedside this morning, he cocked one blond eyebrow and offered a stern warning.

"I was informed by our friends in our local *maquis* that the SS has been all over the villages of Le Fornet and Le Crêt, looking for a tall woman who threatened two soldiers in their mountain brigade with hand grenades, yesterday." Viv lowered her eyes to her clasped hands in acknowledgement. Jean-Paul reached out and raised her chin with his fingers. "Forget about any heroics trying to leave here, understand? You will put us all in danger unless you stay in bed posing as a normal patient.

"Hiding in plain sight," Viv said with a rueful laugh, "although I doubt you'll ever consider me 'normal.'"

Jean-Paul's concerned expression grew tender, which startled Viv and sent an odd tremor down her spine.

"I consider you extraordinary, yes," he said. "But never 'normal.' Given that you are engaged in the same activities as are we in this house, neither of us could ever be counted among the sane," he replied with a glint of humor in his vividly blue eyes. "However, in the absence of your real *patron,* you must follow my orders and promise to do exactly as I say, agreed?"

Viv nodded obediently. "By the way," she said, "you and Dominique are the lucky ones. As you were lifting me onto the sled, I tried to tell you there were those six grenades in my pack, but I couldn't make my brain work to get the words out."

Jean-Paul threw his head back with the first genuine laugh she'd heard from him in months. A shock of his blond mane the color of amber honey fell across his forehead. The corners of his eyes and mouth crinkled as he described his sister discovering the cache of weapons stowed in Viv's knapsack.

"My sister nearly fainted when she sorted out your belongings and saw them," he admitted, "but luckily, the pins were secure and they hadn't exploded when you took your fall—or even when Dominique removed them from the bag."

"Thank God for that," Viv replied with a grimace. "Actually, I didn't land that hard when I hit that patch of ice on the curve, but rather, just started a long, slow, tortuous slide sideways... uncontrollably, as it turned out."

"And then the tree trunk stopped you from sliding into the ravine. Luckily, your leg hit it first, instead of your knapsack."

She shook her head. "The grenades still could have gone off when you loaded me *and* my knapsack onto the toboggan to take me off the mountain."

"Now, you wouldn't do that to a trio of good Samaritans like Alf, Dominique, and me, would you, now?" he said lightly.

Viv cocked her head. "Is that your version of French medical humor?"

The doctor merely shrugged as if admitting it was.

Viv asked, "Did you give the grenades to the *maquis* and tell them they were supplied by the *patron*?

"Your boss got full credit."

He bent down, pressed the back of his hand against her forehead and then took her wrist to feel her pulse. He gestured toward his dog.

"Both Alphonse and I agree that you are one of our more unique rescues." Silence fell between them while he consulted his watch counting the beats beneath his thumb and then nodded with satisfaction. "Your pulse is normal and you've no fever." The lines furrowing his forehead relaxed. "You'll live, and for that, everyone in this household is very grateful, including your new best friend," he added, shifting his gaze to the Swiss Mountain Dog that hadn't left Viv's side since the accident.

"It was a miracle anyone found me in the dead of night. I must have lain there for hours. How did you even happen to be anywhere near where I'd fallen in the woods?"

"A patient of mine is due to give birth in a month," he replied. "I went to Le Crêt to check on her. False labor. I always take Alf with me on house calls, and he caught your scent as I skied back to town. He's also the one we send out when there's an avalanche. He can pinpoint a human in the snow if he gets within two hundred yards. Especially someone he's encountered before as he did you from that first day you arrived at the chalet to enlist my help in Mountaineer." Jean-Paul bent down and rubbed behind one of Alf's ears. "Considering all your trips in and out of Val d'Isère, he considers you family." Jean-Paul gave his dog a big, approving pat. "As we came along the trail, his head went up suddenly, and the next thing I knew, he bounded uphill toward that stand of trees."

"All I wanted to do in the snow was stay asleep," she murmured. "Alf, here, just kept licking my face until you came back with the sled." She paused and then added, "I'm one lucky secret agent that *you* found me and not one of those German mountain brigade boys I'd run into earlier yesterday."

Viv had already told the story of her alarming encounter with the two nervous young troopers dressed, as she had been, in white camouflage. It had been pure bad luck they had been trekking up the same narrow mountain trail on which she'd been descending.

Jean-Paul took a seat on the side of her bed. The familiarity of the move startled Viv.

"My *maquis* contact told me there's a platoon of them camped pretty high up in a pass that leads to Italy," he said. "It was a wonder that you ended that little contretemps without you getting killed."

Viv gave him a worried look.

"Their leaders might send someone to search Val d'Isère, you know," she warned.

"We'll cope," he replied. He reached for her hand. His felt warm and reassuring, yet at the same time, his touch disquieted her. It wasn't Marcel's, but she was surprised to feel a strange magnetism between them.

Striving for a light tone, she said, "I suppose, by now, after all the missions we've done together, you're an expert in concocting reasons to explain the strangers temporarily residing in your chalet."

"It's true. I've had to become quite the storyteller."

Jean-Paul then fell silent, and Viv felt his gaze search her face. She averted her eyes to stare at their joined hands, mesmerized by the sight of his thumb grazing her skin, the tiny motion sending frissons of electricity up her arm.

He spoke first.

"You *do* realize you were very brave, don't you? I don't know if I—or anyone I know—would have been that quick thinking to hold up a hand grenade and threaten to blow yourself up—along with your adversaries—if they dared try to shoot you."

Viv gave a shaky laugh, withdrawing her hands from his.

"I have no idea why I thought of doing that. I guess it was because I couldn't get hold of my service revolver fast enough."

Jean-Paul refused to break their gaze. "Whatever your inspiration was, Viv, I'm very glad you only ended up this recent adventure with a broken leg."

"Well," she replied, "my major wanted me to clear out of Annecy because our network has apparently been compromised...so, yesterday I did just that, and look what happened. I guess you're stuck with me for a while," she joked, trying to break the odd spell that had been woven between them.

"I guess I am," he said, once again seizing her hand and giving it a gentle squeeze before releasing it. "When I first saw you lying in the snow, I feared the worst." His smile rueful, he added, "Now, it seems, having you here recovering under our roof as we start a new year might serve as a good omen at long last. Especially for me."

Viv found her body's warm response to Jean-Paul's tender touch truly unsettling. This tall, lovely man who seemed utterly unconscious of his golden good looks and instinctive penchant for good works was as courageous as anyone she'd ever met. Perhaps as courageous as Marcel, she mused—and then immediately felt disloyal for comparing the two.

Viv had observed from the beginning that Jean-Paul was willing to treat virtually anyone who arrived at his clinic. Inordinately kind and selfless, his brave actions had convinced Viv that he believed fervently in what she'd always considered to be the 'true' freedom-loving France, and not the Nazi-sympathizing minority that collaborated with the German occupiers.

She'd seen in the weeks she'd known him that Jean-Paul shared many of her own ideals, but unlike her, he rarely bothered to mask his personal feelings. He didn't disguise the fact that he liked her and that this emotion was growing to be more than that.

Viv brought herself up short. For sanity's sake, if nothing else, she and Jean-Paul had to remain just colleagues. Close friends and comrades were getting arrested, tortured, and killed. It could happen to any one of them, on any day of the week, *including* Jean-Paul. It had almost happened to *her*. And worst of all, it may already have happened to one of de Gaulle's most important emissaries.

Oh, Marcel! I just escaped the worst, but have you?

CHAPTER 49

January 1944

Viv would never forget the first week of the New Year. Following her exhausting attempts to navigate up and down a flight of stairs with her heavy cast, she had been dozing fitfully on Dominique's bed on the second floor. The skin on her right leg, encased in its plaster cast, had begun to itch something fierce. She became fully awake when she heard loud, insistent pounding on the front door of Dr. Morand's chalet.

Harsh, grating voices drifted up to the landing outside her door demanding to "Search the premises."

"Fine. Come in," she heard Jean-Paul's mild reply, as if this were a perfectly routine occurrence. "I have one patient recovering from a broken leg upstairs, so please, if you will, try not to disturb her."

"We are *looking* for a woman, a skier, who accosted German soldiers on the mountain three days ago, threatening to kill them," the voice declared angrily. "We will take this woman of yours to headquarters immediately for questioning."

Viv could feel her heart rate accelerating beneath her borrowed nightgown as loud boots tramped up the stairs. She gave silent thanks that there were no other fleeing refugees in the attic above. She stared at the outline of her broken leg propped up on a pile of pillows beneath the duvet. Alphonse, curled up on the floor at the foot of her bed, raised his head and gave a low growl.

As the intruders approached, Jean-Paul said with a laugh, "Well, I'm afraid you'll be disappointed in your search here. My current patient broke her leg *five* days ago, he lied with easy casualness, "so she can't be the one you're looking for. She's an American who came from Switzerland on holiday. She schussed down a slope far too advanced for her athletic skills. If you move her from here, you will injure her further," he insisted, adding pleasantly, "however, please feel free to ask her whatever questions you deem appropriate."

"I will ask whatever questions I *please*, Herr Doctor, and move her if I wish."

Hearing them approach closer, Viv kept her eyes on the bedroom's threshold, inhaling deeply to steady her nerves. She thought about the six hand grenades, grateful they were already safely hidden by the local *maquis*. The knapsack, itself, containing her telltale white camouflage suit, was now stored in a locked safe behind a moose head mounted on the wall in Jean-Paul's sitting room. She could only hope that the bedcovers concealed her height to some degree.

Viv swiftly shut her eyes, pretending to be asleep.

"So sorry to disturb you," Jean-Paul said in English, "but these gentlemen have a few questions to ask you." He turned to the officer, switching to Switzer-Deutsch, "She barely speaks French and no German, I'm afraid."

"I speak English," the officer snapped.

"I don't know your name," Jean-Paul inquired politely.

"Seitzer. Colonel Helmut Seitzer. The new Commandant here."

Jean-Paul made introductions while the colonel looked down at Viv who was doing her best to appear incensed at such an unwanted intrusion into her sick room. A uniformed companion standing behind Seitzer barely appeared twenty years old. Viv was relieved that neither man was the SS officer who had accosted her the first day she'd arrived at Morand's since she'd spoken decent French with him. Meanwhile, the jittery sidekick clutched the butt of his holstered gun as if readying to fire off a round.

The lead officer demanded, "Why are you in Val d'Isère on holiday in the middle of a war?"

While he was speaking, Viv noticed that the soldier's uniform appeared a size too big for him and its silver buttons hung loosely against his jacket's fabric, the result, no doubt, of the scarcity of rations in remote regions like this latest assignment. Skepticism was etched in his hollowed-cheek face, flushed a rosy hue due to his climb up the stairs. Earlier, when Viv had warned Jean-Paul that authorities might come looking for a woman who had threatened German soldiers, the two developed a cover story. Viv could only pray that this discontented soul would believe her when she told it.

In an exaggerated North Carolina drawl, she answered her inquisitor, "Why, sir, ah obviously came here to ski. W'all in America hear such *nice* things about this resort, and I've been dyin' to visit, ya know?" She intentionally made her reply sound as if the decision by a spoiled, wealthy civilian to come to Val d'Isère with a major European conflict raging was the most logical thing in the world. "It's the Christmas and New Year's holidays at my university in Switzerland, so I hopped on a train and here I am," she concluded brightly.

"And no one traveled with you?" he demanded, his incredulity obvious. "No one stopped you when they saw your American passport at the border?"

Viv's heart had resumed its wild tattoo in her chest, but she managed casually to look down and point to her cast. "I had my skis on my shoulders as I passed through the border control and they waved me right through. Never asked me for a thing!" she exclaimed. "My European school friends all had family to visit over the holidays, so I decided to cheer up my li'l lonesome by comin' here," she replied, making her remarks almost sound like an appeal for sympathy. "Ah had no idea, though, how *icy* it could be beneath all that snow, ya know?" She cast a kittenish look at Jean-Paul. "People here have been *so* hospitable, and the doctor says my leg isn't broken too bad. He says I'll be walkin' again soon, didn't you, doc?" With a rueful look, she turned her attention back to the SS officer. "Ah don't think I'll try zippin' down these slopes again, though." She gave a little self-conscious laugh. "I'm late gettin' back to classes as it is. My daddy's pretty mad at me."

"How did you get here?" Seitzer demanded, his tone harsh.

"I *told* you," she said, with the rudeness of a spoiled brat. "Ah came by train."

"I mean *here*, after your ski accident," the officer pressed, rising anger lacing his words as if he despised dealing with imbeciles. "To this clinic?"

Viv pointed to the large dog at her bedside. "This big fella found me buried in the snow and fetched the doctor. How lucky was *that*?"

Alphonse sat up, regarding the intruder with an air of distrust, another low-key growl vibrating in his furry throat. The officer and his deputy both took a step back, a hint of apprehension replacing their belligerence.

Jean-Paul intervened, leaning down to offer Alf a reassuring pat on the head.

"I was on a late afternoon house call and skiing back from Le Crêt." He paused and then added, "Feel free to check with the Laurent family to confirm all this. Their baby is due any day now," he added with a smile. He leaned down and patted the dog's head again. "Alf, here, who's been trained to find people in avalanches, was with me and started barking. He led me to Miss Clarke where she'd fallen in a stand of trees."

Viv and Jean-Paul had previously agreed that her cover story was best based mostly on truth in case anyone managed to check the facts or see if an American passport was registered to her with the U.S. Embassy in Paris.

"You couldn't have brought her down alone," the officer asserted. "Who else was involved?"

Jean-Paul replied calmly, "The dog stayed by her side while I skied back to the chalet to summon help. My sister, whom you just met downstairs, and I brought Miss Clarke back in a toboggan. She was suffering from hyperthermia as well as a broken leg."

Viv held up her hands, both wrapped in gauze to prove his point how close she'd come to serious frostbite.

"And your father you spoke of?" demanded the officer of Viv. "Where is *he?*"

"He's an American industrialist...back in North Carolina where his factory is." Viv offered a slight toss of her head against her pillow. "His company sold you guys lots of steel ball-bearin's before the war started." She shrugged. "Sorry he can't do that, now, but he figured it was okay for me to stay at my university in Switzerland after he went back to the States 'cause they're *neutral*, ya know." She shrugged again, repeating, "So here ah am, stuck with a broken leg." She offered a sarcastic smile. "Not exactly a great threat to the Fatherland."

Seitzer cocked an annoyed eyebrow. To Morand, the officer challenged, "I've seen a lot of traffic in and out of your front door. We watch such things, you know."

"That's not too surprising with my patients coming and going," Jean-Paul replied mildly. "I'm the only physician in the ski resort here, and also in the villages of Le Fornet and Le Crêt. People get sick, have accidents, give birth, and die. I've even treated some of your fellows," he added. "At this point, aren't we all just trying to survive this war?"

The officer didn't reply. His thin, rounded shoulders appeared to sink with exhaustion in reaction to the doctor's last statement. For a fleeting second, Viv wondered if Colonel Seitzer wasn't a chartered accountant or sold Volkswagens in civilian life? Given how thin he looked, Viv speculated that perhaps he'd been transferred to this current assignment from the deadly Russian front where Germans were being killed by the tens of thousands. Someone from the mountain troops Viv had encountered may have pressured officers like Seitzer to search for their assailant.

The colonel's eyes shuttered briefly, and Viv wondered if the man wasn't as sick of the war as she was. She held her breath, amazed he hadn't asked to see her documents to prove she was a foolish American college student. Apparently, the cast on her leg, her *faux* southern drawl, and the energy it took to cart one of Morand's injured patients down flights of stairs and across the street to his headquarters had convinced him her story was likely genuine enough. Without another word, he spun on his booted heels and stomped back down the stairs, his uniformed minion following in his wake.

Viv heard him mutter in German to his underling, "I seriously doubt whoever outfoxed those fools on the trail was a *woman*, and certainly not *this* stupid cow. The assailant is obviously long gone. Write that in your report and send it up the mountain."

Viv exhaled slowly. From the doorway of Dominique's bedroom, Jean-Paul winked and then trailed the unwelcome visitors down the stairs where he bid them adieu.

———◇———

Viv remained shaken by her close call with Colonel Seitzer, more than relieved to stay in Dominique's comfortable bed. By the second week of January 1944, however, guilt took over. Viv insisted on moving back up to the attic where she was joined by six-year-old twins. The children—a boy and a girl—were from wealthy Jewish parents that had somehow financed their escape with a *passeur* from Nice to Val d'Isère in the hope of getting them to Switzerland, and eventually to relatives in the United States. The boy, named Shavi, known as "Shay," and the girl, Sharon, had been whisked through the back entrance to the chalet and up the stairs to the attic. Dark curly hair and matching chocolate brown eyes were dead giveaways that they were Jewish. Viv had reached back to her childhood to invent word games they could play together to make the hours go by. Meanwhile, Jean-Paul searched for an emergency guide to take them from the ski resort where SS officers were a mere fifty paces from their front door.

"You are something else," she said to Jean-Paul when he brought up their dinners himself one evening. "You run this operation right under the Germans' noses."

Morand set down the tray and held up his hands in mock surrender. "I was here first," he declared matter-of-factly. "How was I to know a German outpost would take over the headquarters of our formerly friendly *gendarmerie*?"

A few days later, the children were taking naps one afternoon when Jean-Paul came to check Viv's temperature and her pulse as he did twice a day.

"I hope you don't mind sharing quarters with such little ones," he said, *sotte voce*, "but I really couldn't say no."

Viv shook her head vehemently. "Of course not," she whispered. "They're so sweet...and so frightened. They miss their parents terribly." She smiled sadly as she looked over at their sleeping forms. "I've racked my brain to remember bedtime stories my British nanny used to tell me. So far, the children seem relatively amused by them."

"Your mother didn't read to you at bedtime?" he inquired gently.

"*My* mother?" Viv scoffed, keeping her voice low. "After my father was killed and she was on the prowl for Husband Number Two, she parked me in London with her parents' servants." Viv paused to reflect. "Luckily for me, Mrs. MacLaird was a very nice Scottish woman who regaled me with tales of Highlander warriors' derring-do. I loved it—and her."

Jean-Paul chuckled and nodded in the direction of the sleeping children.

"Despite your own discomfort these last days, you've been quite wonderful with them," he complimented her. He paused, and then added casually, "Working with refugees might be something for you to consider...after the war."

Jean-Paul disclosed that he hoped someday to turn part of the resort into a winter ski school and summer camp for adults and children displaced by the war. "I've bought some land between our village and Le Fornet where we can build a series of small chalets and create a playing field for summertime games. We'll have hikes and arts-and-crafts and all sorts of activities scaled for children of all ages."

"What a wonderful plan," Viv enthused, "and I can see it's something that would be so perfect for you and so wonderful for these poor children," she added, glancing at her sleeping charges, "that is, if this war ever ends."

"All wars ultimately end," he said. He gently clasped her chin in his hand, murmuring, "And it's the kind of plan I can see you being part of...that is, if you wish."

Viv regarded his handsome face, tanned golden from skiing on his medical rounds under the winter sun. As their eyes met, she sensed an ardent tenderness that sent a *frisson* through her.

He definitely feels something for me...and I for him, but any plans for 'after' are mere fantasies. And besides...

Her thoughts leapt to her deadly fear that Marcel might at this very minute be suffering agony at the hands of the SS in Lyon if he was, in fact, the arrested agent of de Gaulle's that Fingers had told her about. And then there was poor Kurt. Like him, Marcel could even be dead by now. How could she think of anything else, she chastised herself?

All the warnings she'd been given in training to remain uninvolved emotionally with other agents came soaring into her consciousness. She certainly had ignored that rule with Marcel. Even more reason that she and Jean-Paul must remain only friends, she lectured herself. Even so, she couldn't deny how well they had worked together over these last months. It was almost uncanny how closely aligned their values were, along with their reasons for becoming clandestine operatives behind enemy lines. And from the moment she'd awakened with a cast on her leg, his concern for her seemed far more than merely professional. She'd been touched not only by Jean-Paul's warmth, but also by the kindness of both his sister Dominique and *Madame* Morand. Viv was shocked to admit that she'd felt cared for in a way she'd never experienced before.

Despite all this, who knew better than she did that sharing anything more than a compatible working relationship in the middle of a raging conflict could only lead to heartbreak—or jeopardy for all concerned?

"It's *you* who are wonderful with people, Jean-Paul," she urged quietly. "Both with your patients and the people you're trying to save. As for me? I can be a real bitch," she said with a harsh laugh, thinking of how she enjoyed torturing that Roger character who was her 'minder' escorting her from the Athens embassy to Marseille at the beginning of the war. "Trust me, I deserve no special kudos. I'm just following orders—including yours—to be kind to these kids." She faked a yawn and murmured, "And now, before they wake up, I think I'll grab a nap."

She closed her eyes and waited for Jean-Paul to leave the room. There was a long silence, and she could feel his gaze on her prone figure snuggled beneath an extra woolen blanket he had somehow managed to find for her.

Then, she heard him leave the attic, quietly shutting the door. She wanted to feel she'd done the noble thing, but her performance just then left her feeling like a louse.

CHAPTER 50

Viv finally received word via one of the couriers in the local *maquis* that Major Merrick had determined things were calm enough in Annecy for her to meet him at her chalet below the Plateau des Glières. Earlier, Jean-Paul had persuaded the young wife of another of the *maquis* to serve as *passeur* for the twins, along with a downed British pilot who had suddenly appeared at the clinic's door. Viv schooled the young woman in how best to make it through all the checkpoints, and miraculously, word came back from the *passeur* they'd pressed into service that all three had made it across to safety. Viv could only wonder what brave soul had replaced Kurt on the receiving end at the Swiss border.

"I take it that your *patron* doesn't know that you broke your leg?" Jean-Paul commented as he deftly removed her cast without bruising the skin on her shin.

Viv had hopped from the attic on her good leg all the way down two flights of stairs into Jean-Paul's surgery. Holding tight to the bannister and wet with perspiration, she reached his infirmary on the ground floor without assistance.

"I decided to wait to tell him when I saw him next," Viv answered, staring with trepidation at how thin her right extremity looked compared to her healthy one.

Jean-Paul scolded, "I'm not happy about taking this cast off a week before it's due. Except for sleeping at night, you must promise to wear your ski boot on this foot indoors and out for another two weeks."

"I promise. But I've got to get back to Annecy."

Since day one, Viv had been afraid Merrick would find an excuse to send her back to Britain for fear that her height, hair, and lousy French accent would prove everyone's undoing. If he knew she'd broken her leg, it'd be the end of her days as his deputy.

Jean-Paul noticed her worried look and apparently assumed it was due to her concern over the pipe-stem appearance of her recovering right limb. He laid his warm palm on her ankle and gave it a gentle squeeze.

"Actually, your calf looks pretty good. The fact that you're such a strong skier has served you well. Legs always lose muscle, tone, and strength after being immobilized in a hard shell for a few weeks," he reassured her. "For an hour each day until you leave, I want you to walk up and down in front of the chalet to build up your strength."

"In front of the Germans?" she asked, incredulous.

"Exactly. And if that goes well, next you'll get on your skis and do the same: slide on them on level ground in front of the clinic. We want Colonel Seitzer to see how that silly American who skied a hill too difficult for her skills is rehabilitating her leg so she can go back to Switzerland, sparing him the trouble of sending you to an internment camp."

Viv felt a swift intake of breath, but she knew that Jean-Paul's advice was sound. She had to keep up the masquerade by exercising in plain sight until she, the "stupid cow," was fit enough to make her way out of Val d'Isère—hopefully *soon*.

———◇———

The next few days were among the most nerve-wracking Viv had experienced since arriving behind German enemy lines. Each day, in full view of a few SS officers and regular German Army soldiers lounging in front of their headquarters enjoying a smoke, Jean-Paul would steady her as she struggled to maintain her balance and build strength in her marginally atrophied right leg. First in her boots and then on skis, he helped her slide along the snow fifty feet, make a turn, and then slide back again to the chalet's front door. Viv's hair, long since missing its vegetable dye, had returned to its deep, red color. But even with her tresses tucked into a woolen cap, Dr.

Morand's patient was beginning to attract more of the soldiers' attention that either she or Jean-Paul desired.

After five days of Viv moving her skis methodically across the flat area in front of the chalet, Jean-Paul whispered, "You're being ogled by too many of these men, I'm afraid." Within view of the "interested" onlookers, he reached up with both hands and pulled her woolen hat farther down to her eyebrows, tucking a few wayward strands of her hair under its ribbed rim. Meeting her gaze, he said quietly, "There…that's better. Now march! I expect another patient to arrive any minute."

Viv tensed when, as Jean-Paul had turned to leave, an unfriendly but familiar face crossed the street. The SS officer stood with his hands on his hips, his fingers adjacent to the pistol strapped to his waist.

"So you injured yourself, I see," said the German who had accosted her the first day she'd knocked on the door of the Morand chalet. "You don't live here, do you, or I would have seen your name on one of our lists."

Before Viv could reply in French, Jean-Paul offered a pleasant, professional smile.

"She broke her leg in a ski accident coming down Bellevarde and has been under my care as her physician for quite some time."

"When I saw her last, she had a hacking cough." His eyes narrowed and he addressed Viv directly. "It would seem, with all these visits to Herr Doctor's clinic, you would appear quite an unhealthy young woman."

Jean-Paul put a hand on Viv's shoulder, signaling her to remain silent.

"You've done well today, *mademoiselle*, but I think that's enough exercise. I want you to go back up to the infirmary and rest." To the SS officer he said, "Colonel Seitzer has already interviewed her and found all in order. So, if you'll excuse us…"

The officer seemed mildly alarmed at the mention of Seitzer's name. Viv breathed a sigh of relief realizing that this officious SS minion had obviously not been privy to his superior's visit to her sick room.

Viv merely inclined her head in his direction and allowed Jean-Paul to steer her into the safety of the chalet. Once inside the vestibule, Viv leaned her back against the wall and exhaled.

"I never saw that guy again after my first day and thought he must've been sent somewhere else," she said. "He definitely thinks something's fishy. We can only pray he and Seitzer don't compare notes on me." She shook her head, adding, "The longer I'm here, the more I put you and your family at risk." Her gaze met Jean-Paul's. "Between Seitzer, who thinks I'm a flighty American, and this guy, who thinks I'm some sort of weird Frenchwoman, I don't dare show my face around here again." She met his gaze. "Honestly, Jean-Paul, I've got to leave here."

She could tell he reluctantly agreed with her.

"I'll see about hiring a sleigh to take you all the way to the train. Your admirers across the street will see that you're well enough—and innocent enough—to depart in broad daylight."

Viv suddenly felt a weariness of mind and spirit. Under her thick woolen sweater and heavy coat, sweat from her recent exertions slid down her back and trickled between her breasts. She sagged against the wall, and to her horror, tears welled in her eyes, blurring Jean-Paul's face. Without speaking, he pulled her into his arms, wrapping them around her shoulders and pressed her head against his chest with one hand. She could hear the steady beat of his heart, and it comforted her.

"Ah... Viv," he said softly. "You're utterly exhausted, aren't you? You've been under such terrible strain for so long, now."

He swayed her body and his in a gentle, rocking movement. She felt him remove her woolen cap and nuzzle the damp skin at the base of her neck. As with Marcel, Jean-Paul's greater height and enfolding embrace enveloped her in a warm cocoon. She longed to simply sink against his body's heat and fall asleep, if only for an hour. It took every ounce of will she had to lift her head and summon a smile.

"I'm all right," she lied. "I'm just drained from all this exercise you're making me do." She raised both hands and laid them on his shoulders, gently forcing their bodies apart. "But I think your plan for my departure is a good one," she said, taking a further step away from the steady warmth of his gaze. "Do let's summon a sleigh." She slid her hands down his arms and clasped his hands. "You are one, amazing man, to say nothing of being a skilled doctor who put this pathetic Humpty-Dumpty back together again."

Jean-Paul cast her a quizzical glance, and Viv realized he had no idea who "Humpty-Dumpty" might be.

"You've fixed my broken leg," she explained, "and raised my spirits when I thought that was impossible—and for these kindnesses I will be forever grateful," she said, meaning every word. "And seeing firsthand the compassion and care you've shown complete strangers and those little ones in such desperate need of safety and shelter, you have shown me what true, selfless, non-violent resistance *is*." She leaned forward and feather-kissed each of his cheeks. "*You're* the brave one, my friend." Squeezing his hands, she murmured, "Please stay safe, if you can."

"Viv, I—" he began, but she put the forefinger of one hand against his lips.

"Let this be our farewell," she whispered. "Anything else is just too hard."

"Is it too hard to hear I've fallen in love with you?" Jean-Paul asked, refusing to let go of her other hand.

Viv felt the tears she'd been fighting spill down her cheeks. Without replying, she bowed her head and pressed her wet skin on the side of her face against the back of his hand. Then she turned and reached for the wooden bannister. Slowly, she pulled herself, step-by-step, up the stairs to spend her last night sleeping under Dr. Morand's roof.

With a sensation of melancholy lodging deep in her heart, Viv wondered if every man she cared about would always fall into the category of "Might Have Been?"

CHAPTER 51

From the top of the house, Viv heard the jingling harnesses of a horse pulling a sleigh along the snowy street below. Jean-Paul stood at the attic threshold holding her knapsack containing her few possessions—minus the six hand grenades—but including her white camouflage ski suit she'd worn on arrival.

"What if someone searches you?" Jean-Paul asked, his brow creased with worry. "Won't the white suit—"?

"No one will stop me, thanks to the crutches you've given me," she replied. "And if they search my belongings, I'll just say it was a gift from my German boyfriend."

Jean-Paul cast her a troubled look and helped sling the sack's strap over one shoulder.

"Come, then. No doubt there's an entire line of officers downstairs waiting to bid you adieu. Dominique will be the one to guide you out, as is customary."

Viv smiled her thanks. "Of course," she said with a laugh. "Herr Doctor would be too busy with patients to bid farewell to a pain-in-the-ass spoiled American who had so overstayed her welcome."

Jean-Paul halted, mid-stair, and turned to face her. He gently seized her chin with his free hand, leaned forward, and kissed her soundly on her lips.

"I was not letting such a fine actress leave here without doing that," he murmured, and then kissed her again, at first the pressure light and tender, then growing fervent, signaling without words that he didn't want her to forget he'd told her that he loved her.

Before she could say anything in response, he grasped her elbow and urged her to take hold of the bannister. Together, they gingerly descended the three flights of stairs.

As they neared the bottom step, she said with a shaky laugh, "What fine work you've done, dear doctor. Look how I can walk after barely four weeks in your care."

"But take it easy when you truly get back on your skis," he warned. "It will take a bit longer to build up those leg muscles. In a few weeks, though, you'll be good as new."

At the lower landing, Jean-Paul's mother Claire stood clad in her apron clasping a small box that Viv imagined contained whatever food could be spared for her journey by train back to Annecy. Dominique, too, was waiting, holding a thick woolen shawl she wrapped around Viv's shoulders. Alphonse sat beside her, methodically wagging his tail.

Viv's gaze drifted from one member of the Morand household to another.

"I can't thank all of you enough for—" She felt her throat constrict and forced herself to inhale a deep breath. "...for all the kindnesses you've shown me." Bending forward, she framed the dog's muzzle between her hands. "You, too, Alf, my rescuing angel."

The Morands had risked their own lives to provide her not only healthcare, but warm shelter and food when everyone in the village had so little to share.

Jean-Paul's mother held out the box to her and silently kissed her on both cheeks. Viv felt her heart lurch at the thought of leaving the security and safety of their home and wondered if her "getaway in plain sight" had a chance in hell of succeeding.

"*Adieu*," Jean-Paul murmured, also brushing each of her cheeks with the formality of a kiss. "We will miss you, as will our future 'travelers' who, sadly, won't have you as their *passeur*."

"Please know," she said, choking as she tried to speak, "I will miss you so..."

Dominique handed her a pair of hand-hewn wooden crutches made by the dozens by a local carpenter for Dr. Morand's patients, and then opened the front door.

"I've put your skis and poles in the sleigh. I hope you can find someone to help you carry them when you get to Annecy."

As Jean-Paul had predicted, there was a cluster of Germans lounging in front of their headquarters across the street. Off to one side, Viv spotted the presence of the bullying officer who had first accosted her at the Morand clinic's front door.

"*Go*," Jean-Paul urged under his breath, "and be sure to turn and wave."

For Viv, the twenty feet she had to traverse in the snow on crutches felt endless. She knew that Dominique was as tense as she was, both of them wondering if one of the onlookers would challenge them at any moment. When they reached the waiting sleigh, Dominique signaled the driver to hop down from his perch and pull back the pile of blankets, allowing Viv to take her seat. Jean-Paul's sister handed Viv's knapsack to her and then carefully wrapped the passenger in a kind of woolen cocoon.

"Are you sure you'll be warm enough?" Dominique pressed, making a show of handing the crutches to the driver to stow for the journey.

"The easiest trip I've ever made to the station," Viv answered under her breath.

Dominique nodded, whispering, "I've told the driver to find someone to help you board the train with your skis. Goodbye and Godspeed."

From the warmth of her tone, Viv guessed that Jean-Paul had confided in his sister about his strong feelings for his departing patient. As the principal character in this play for the German soldiers' benefit, Viv could only nod her thanks. She waved her goodbyes to the empty front doorway, knowing that a kind and loving doctor was watching through one of the chalet's windows.

Will any good and decent men survive this war? she thought for the hundredth time.

Viv stared, unseeing, at the driver's back, thinking of the horrible end that poor Kurt had faced. Would anyone in Annecy be able to confirm or refute if it had been Marcel who was the de Gaulle deputy arrested by the SS in Lyon? Squeezing her eyes shut, she tried to banish another terrible thought: if something ever happened to Jean-Paul or his family, how could she bear it? And would she ever know?

Viv's stomach began to churn with anxiety as she sank back against the seat and pulled the blankets more tightly around her shoulders. The driver picked up the reins, slapped the horse's rear, and the sleigh glided forward in the snow as if it were part of some lovely Christmas card.

Forcing herself casually to turn her head, her breath caught at the sight of gaunt, uniformed Colonel Seitzer emerging from the police station that the German troops had commandeered from the local gendarmerie. She inclined her head, acknowledging him as well as the array of officers watching her departure. As her final gesture of disguised contempt, she offered a gay wave of farewell to the murderous bunch.

Jean-Paul was right…this was a brilliant getaway plan!

An SOE secret agent had just made her escape from Val d'Isère in plain sight of a handful of Hitler's soldiers and secret police.

———◇———

"The crutches were the key!" Viv insisted.

Viv had spent most of the first evening of her return to Annecy regaling for Major Merrick and Fingers the amazing saga of transporting hand grenades to the tiny ski resort, outwitting two members of the German mountain brigade, breaking her leg, and eventually making her departure from Val d'Isère in front of Germans ensconced directly across the street from one of Merrick's top Mountaineer operatives.

"When one of the few taxis left at the Annecy train station saw me with my skis and my crutches, he offered to drive me home. I had him leave me off on the main road and hobbled here."

"And then sent *me* out in the cold to carry your baggage into the chalet," Fingers said with mock indignation.

The trio sat in front of the small hearth burning a pile of precious coal, fully aware that supplies in Viv's cellar were dwindling by the day. Just as the doctor ordered, she'd kept her ski boot on during her waking hours to support the leg she had broken.

"Where are the crutches now?" Fingers demanded with a grin.

"In the cellar, and you're welcome to them," Viv declared.

"I might use that trick trying to sneak back to the south end of Lake Annecy, now that you deem it safe enough," Fingers joked to Merrick.

"'Safe enough' is about all any of us can describe things right now," Merrick replied tersely. With a quick glance in Viv's direction he added, "I think both of you need to know it's been confirmed that de Gaulle's agent, rumored to have been picked up last month, was, indeed, arrested by Klaus Barbie's operatives in Lyon."

Before Viv could stop herself, she broke in. "Was it the de Gaulle agent you and Fingers met with me the night we flew out of England?"

Merrick hesitated and then nodded.

Viv felt as if someone had punched her in the gut. The fear had always been with her, she realized now, but knowing it *was* Marcel who had been jailed—or worse—was a likely outcome she'd refused to accept. She clasped her hands tightly in her lap to keep them from trembling.

Merrick continued, "Marcel Delonge—or I should say Victor Fernique—has been a key man serving the General, so there's been quite an effort to find out what happened to him since he was apprehended. He's either dead...or being interrogated further at Avenue Foch...or they've sent him east to a prison camp in Germany. We still haven't learned which." With another look at Viv he concluded, "The odds are, though, he's dead. We're told Hitler, himself, ordered him tracked down, arrested, and executed."

Viv released her hands and dug her nails into her knees to keep from screaming aloud. At length she was able to ask, "Do they think he was betrayed?"

Merrick gave her a peculiar look. "Do you have a suspect?"

"Yes, but absolutely no proof."

"Who?" Merrick demanded.

"I can only tell you Marcel once said to me he suspected treachery within the SOE." She inhaled a breath. "He didn't trust the agent whose code name is Gilbert."

Merrick's eyes narrowed. "The Air Operations Officer who met our Lysander near Loyettes, right? The one whose nose you bloodied when he...uh...tried some—what shall I call it? Funny business with you that same night."

"Yes. Him."

Fingers' gaze drifted from Merrick to Viv like a man watching a heated tennis match.

"Wowee," he said, his New Orleans accent pronounced as the three of them had been conversing in their native tongue. "Everyone I know says that agent Gilbert is a hell of a good air operations coordinator."

"Oh, he's that, all right," Merrick agreed, staring into the low-burning embers of their fire, "but his position provides the perfect cover for playing both sides."

"That was Marcel's view," Viv said, "but would London pay any of us a bit of attention, especially since the work he does is so essential to the SOE? Hardly!"

"A lot of our agents have been nabbed in the last six months," Merrick mused. He looked up and said to Viv, "You...uh...were quite good friends with Delonge, correct?"

Viv struggled to keep her tone neutral.

"I drove him in an ambulance from the American Hospital in Paris to Dunkirk, and then we encountered each other at various points during SOE spy school." She rose from her chair and added with her back to the men, "I hope to God he's somehow survived. De Gaulle was damn lucky to have a deputy like him in the field."

"That's what everyone says, poor bugger," was Merrick's response as he paused to light his third cigarette of the evening. "He and de Gaulle's other deputy, Jean Moulin, are now *both* missing in action."

PART V
CHAPTER 52

January 22, 1944

Viv knew that if she kept imagining all the horrible things the SS could have done—or were still doing—to Marcel, she'd go insane. The day after her return to her chalet outside Annecy, Merrick had sent Fingers back up to the Plateau des Glières. His assignment was to coordinate communications for a huge airdrop of weapons and supplies that the Allies had finally agreed to bestow on the *maquis* in that region, now that their numbers were approaching a thousand men.

"So the Allies aren't worried that the *résistants* up there will be sitting ducks if Fritz decides to use the big guns to take them out?" she demanded.

Merrick shook his head. "It's certainly not what I recommended, but London now thinks it'll show the world that there are thousands of Frenchmen ready to rise up when the invasion comes."

"Well, there are plenty who *are* ready to rise up, but is this the wisest use of these forces...putting them on a plateau where the *Luftwaffe* can pick them off?"

Merrick offered no further opinions on the subject. Instead, he advised her, "I'll be leaving, too, in an hour." The major pointed to Viv's leg. "Are you fit enough to execute our longstanding plan to blow up those locomotives in the Annecy rail yard?"

"Yes sir. Absolutely," assured Viv, praying she'd have the physical strength.

"Excellent. Do it no later than January twenty-fourth, understand?"

"Happy to be the demolition crew," Viv said, making light of a task that she knew would be a bear to pull off, to say nothing of possible German reprisals afterward.

"You? Demolition? Good heavens, no!" Merrick snapped. "You'll supervise, but this is a job for the lads you've recruited around Annecy. Fingers will get word to Julien up on the plateau to send them down here by Sunday."

"Jacques, Yves, and Gaspard, yes?" Viv nodded, naming the Boom-Boom Boys, as she'd come to call them to their faces. "You want them here by Sunday, January twenty-third, right? Only one day before we do the job?"

"That has to be the timetable," Merrick replied, his lips firmly set.

Viv's apprehension rose at the realization that Merrick's latest orders to blow up four locomotives literally in her own backyard was scheduled for a mere two days hence.

"Yes, you'll have one day to prepare," he repeated. "Things are heating up all over. Those locomotives bring in German troops," he said, as if she needed reminding. "Regardless of whether or not the Krauts use their air power, every day that the supply trains run makes an attack on the *maquis* on the plateau even more likely. The train depot demolition job must be done as soon as possible, and you're the only one I can rely on to see that it is." He gestured toward a back window. "I suggest you start immediately digging up and thawing those rat carcasses. Then start preparing the *plastique* explosives, the primers, the timer pencils and such. It's good you can begin assembling the various components now, yes?"

"Absolutely, sir. The Boom-Boom Boys can stuff the rats when they arrive."

Merrick offered her a deadpan smile. "I don't blame you leaving that job for last."

He then stomped his way to the back of the chalet where Viv assumed he would pack his canvas rucksack and soon depart. Meanwhile, she went over in her mind the many ways in which her latest assignment could go wrong.

And if the Boom-Boom Boys didn't show up, she wondered… what was Plan B?

Still reeling from the news confirming Marcel's arrest, she set off to find the shovel needed to dig up the rat carcasses behind the chalet, muttering, "I guess Plan B is me."

———◇———

Jacques, Gaspard, and Yves arrived at Viv's chalet on Sunday, the twenty-third of January exactly as she'd hoped. Then they told her the reason for their promptness.

"Earlier this week, there was a bloody skirmish with French Vichy forces on the routes up to the plateau. The bastards," Jacques began heatedly. "The Vichy viciously attacked their *own* country-men! We three barely got down off the mountain alive."

The trio unburdened themselves of their heavy coats and caps they'd worn against the bitter cold, aware there was a threat of yet another winter storm expected within hours.

"Basically, the Germans have declared a state of siege throughout the Haute-Savoie," Gaspard declared. "Anyone found carrying arms or assisting our local *maquis* is subject to immediate execution."

Viv realized that the more the local resisters threatened the Nazis' grip on political power, along with grim reports coming from the Russian front, and the more credible the rumors of an Allied invasion—the greater the German brutality against the civilian population in their area. Now, with this latest news of a siege unfolding against the thousand resisters holed up on the plateau, there was no avoiding the obvious. What she was about to launch with these three young men could mean certain death for all four of them if the mission didn't go perfectly. And even if it did succeed, heavy reprisals against the townspeople would surely follow.

Yves chimed in, "More and more men are gathering on the plateau, including a hundred French communist *résistants* and about fifty Spanish lumberjacks who migrated to France after losing the fight against Franco in their homeland."

"Maybe all this means the big show is about to begin," Jacques declared excitedly. "Did you hear, Viv, that Lieutenant Tom Morel has taken command on Glières? He even brought officers from the Twenty-Seventh Chasseurs alpine battalion!"

Viv silently wondered how those mostly untried recruits could hold out against thousands of German troops, bolstered by the notorious *milice*, even if the partisans were led by a talented professional soldier like Tom Morel and his deputies.

With a sigh, she announced, "Okay, boys, enough chit-chat. Let's get started. Down in the cellar you'll find the explosives already assembled and—"

Jacques interrupted almost festively. "And our job is to stuff them into the rats, right?" He looked at his comrades, both of whom were groaning with disgust. "Hey...let's name each rodent after a different enemy battalion!"

"There'll be new snow before morning," she intervened, "unless the wind blows it away. Remember, the cold can affect the timer pencils, so do *every* step with great care."

Viv wished she could use a detonating cord, instead of the pencil detonators, but the cord wouldn't give the saboteurs time to get away from the bombsite.

Another worry was if there *were* new flurries tomorrow, her team would leave tracks in the station yard. Doing a sabotage job in falling snow struck Viv as the height of folly, yet she knew in Merrick's view: the longer the mission was delayed, the less use the entire operation would be.

The Boom-Boom Boys would carry the Sten guns and the bag with the explosives stuffed in the rats' bellies. Ignoring Merrick's order for her merely to oversee the planning, Viv knew their best chance for success was for her to be the one to place the charges where they'd do the most good...or rather, the worst harm to the enemy.

"Stuffing the rats is enough to ask of anyone," she muttered, heading for the underground lair to watch over the boys' shoulders as she knew her superior officer expected.

———◇———

Just as Viv had predicted, the next day it snowed until past eleven a.m. After the sun came out, everything was crisp and fresh looking, with the surface of Lake Annecy itself looking like a cloudy mirror.

The sabotage team didn't leave Viv's chalet until after dark, slipping into town separately, and then rendezvousing in a storeroom off the kitchen at the Café Lyonnais until just before nine. Jacques' mother had looked upset to see her son appear with no warning, along with the others at the restaurant's back door.

"The *milice* were here a few days ago, looking for you," she said to Jacques, leading them to their makeshift waiting room. "As usual, we said you were up the valley, helping on a farm, but I know they didn't believe me."

Jacques merely grunted as the group filed past the threshold where the potatoes and other food stores were kept. Viv and Mrs. La Salle exchanged glances as Jacques' mother shut the door and urged Viv to stay with her, handing her a small bowl of soup.

"Olivia, don't tell anyone, even Anton, the boys have been here. We'll be gone soon."

Just then, the door to the café opened and Anton himself entered the kitchen. In the instant before the door swooshed closed, Viv caught a glimpse of a tall, good-looking man with dark, wavy hair lounging at the bar.

It can't be...please, God, no! Lucien Barteau? Why in the—

Without preamble she demanded, "When did that tall guy at the bar come in?"

"About a half hour ago. Why?"

"I know him, and it's not good that he's here. Keep a close eye on him and let me know if he leaves. And by the way," she added, "you've never seen a tall woman with dark red hair, okay?"

Silently regretting that it had been impossible to obtain the mousey brown dye to disguise her hair, she took in Anton's puzzled expression as he said, "And you don't even say *bonsoir, mademoiselle?*"

"*Bonsoir.* But don't forget, you didn't see me, right?"

Anton shrugged, grabbed a pitcher of water from the sideboard, and retraced his steps. Viv nodded briefly at Olivia and disappeared into the storeroom to wait with her explosives crew until the appointed hour to launch the mission.

Why would Lucien Barteau be in Annecy, of all places, unless someone had been tortured to reveal where the rest of the Mountaineer network might be found....

———◇———

Olivia reported that Lucien Barteau continued to lounge in the café. At the appointed hour of nine, Viv and the Boom-Boom Boys exited from the rear of the building and set off down the secluded back streets of Annecy. Viv reviewed each move of their mission while also processing her shock at seeing Lucien/Gilbert in a place he had no business being. By the time their foursome had turned into an alley and emerged on the outskirts of the snow-covered station yard, she'd forced herself to confine her thoughts to the step-by-step plan to blow up four locomotives.

Viv gazed back at the distinct trail left in the snow by their footsteps. She supposed the marks could have been made by rail workers—and the notion calmed her nerves a bit. Ahead of her she could just make out the glow of lights through the dirty windows of the station house. Beyond it, she could see the darker shape of the terminus shed where the unscheduled iron beasts were parked for the night.

Inside the station itself, waiting for the last train of the evening, innocent French citizens would be shoulder-to-shoulder with local German authorities and their French counterparts, the *milice*. Viv could only hope that Merrick's prior intelligence was correct—that the locomotives would be unguarded because the Germans judged that *résistants* like her group would never dare attempt a sabotage mission during the blanket evening curfew that went into effect each night at eleven.

"We have exactly twelve minutes to lay the explosives, light them, and get the hell out of here," she whispered.

She was glad she'd made the decision to position the explosive devices herself. If Lucien Barteau was nosing around, she couldn't afford a single slip up with their placement, and she simply didn't trust the young men to do it properly. She'd also secretly built in a margin of error that allowed for more time to make their escape. The cold temperature meant the time pencils might not ignite for seventeen minutes to half an hour after they were set to go off. It would give them extra time to get out of Annecy before the fireworks began.

Jacques and Yves quickly removed the disassembled Sten guns from the rucksack and clicked their parts together. The pair knew they had four minutes to reach their appointed stations as lookouts.

"You're to whistle to indicate caution or danger," she instructed them. "Gaspard, you come with me." She pointed to the bag of explosives he was carrying. "Stay close."

"I'm setting the explosives on the trains, though, right?"

"No. I am. You're the lookout in the shed."

"*You?*"

"Yes," she snapped. "On the last job, I heard you made Yves handle the rats while you just ordered him about. You didn't follow the plan."

"Did he tell you that?"

"Quiet. Let's go."

She had no time to argue or dress him down. Gaspard was only a kid with a lot of false bravado who didn't want to admit he hadn't been the one to plant the fuses the last time. As much as she hated handling the rats, she'd worn her warmest gloves and steeled herself to take on this crucial task. She just hoped she remembered the correct way to position the carcasses so their wired contents would explode as intended.

Grumbling an expletive, Gaspard set off along a set of tracks that would lead to the terminus. Viv followed a few paces behind him while Jacques and Yves took up their appointed lookout spots. She felt nakedly exposed as they walked slowly some twenty yards on the wooden crossties that led them directly to the locomotive shed. Once inside, Viv waited for her eyes to grow accustomed to the dark. Soon, the looming shape of the iron behemoths swam into view. It took only a few minutes to sandwich the first charge-filled rat between the steel wheel and its connecting rod at the front of the first locomotive she reached. She easily managed to wedge the second rodent into a similar prime spot on the locomotive standing in front of it on the same track.

Walking toward the third engine on a parallel track, she stumbled against a steel girder she hadn't noticed, and the noise sounded thunderous in her ears. A sudden flare of light shot up just beyond the snub nose of the iron monster. A man in trainman's garb was standing twenty feet beyond, silhouetted in a doorway to a backroom in the shed.

"Who goes there?" he demanded.

Viv froze, and her mind went utterly blank.

Chapter 53

The trainman's command that the noisemakers identify themselves was followed by complete silence. Viv called out the first mad thing that entered her head.

"I-I lost my dog," she shouted. "I think he ran in here. Have you seen him? And I just stumbled over something in the dark; I'm afraid I've hurt myself."

Viv sank to a crouch as if nursing an injury.

Without an order from her, Gaspard raced toward the trainmen and leveled his Sten gun directly at him. He thrust the barrel against the man's chest and growled, "Don't move or I'll—"

"*Mon Dieu*! D-Don't shoot me," the man stuttered. "I'll do whatever you say. I-I don't want any part of this!"

Viv rose to her nearly 5 feet 11 inches, furious Gaspard had taken action without orders from her. "Take him outside," she commanded. "Keep him there 'til I finish here."

Gaspard roughly marched his captive toward the door to the big shed where they'd all entered. Losing no time, Viv quickly set the other rat bombs in positions on the third and fourth locomotives where she figured they would do the most damage. With a final prayer that the timing pencils would go off as scheduled, she sped toward the entrance to join the others.

She was relieved to see Jacques and Yves were waiting for her. Gaspard was standing with them, along with the trainman, the barrel of the Sten gun now pressed against his back. The portly rail worker had a nice, middle-aged face, wrinkled and blackened from years of living with the effects of coal dust. His hair under his beret was pepper-and-salt.

"What were you doing at this hour in the storage shed?" Viv asked.

"Sorting out cigarettes I bring in from Switzerland twice a week."

"And you sell them," Viv confirmed. "On the black market, yes?"

After a moment's hesitation he nodded in the affirmative. Gaspard spoke up with the characteristic belligerence.

"Well, if you don't rat on us, we won't rat on you. Agreed?"

"*D'accord*," their captive replied, his manner mild now that he'd had time to take in the youthfulness of the team brandishing their weapons. "May I go home now?"

Viv nodded. "And you're to *go* home," she urged him. "Don't hang about nearby, selling your wares, you understand? You could get hurt."

"*D'accord*," he repeated.

She didn't dare let Gaspard be the one to make sure the man did as he'd promised.

"Jacques," she addressed the La Salle's son, "dismantle your gun, put it in the bag here, and escort this gentleman to his residence, please."

Viv was betting the conductor wasn't the sort to betray them since everyone in Annecy was only too aware of the severe penalties for those caught by the SS dabbling in the black market. She certainly wasn't going to kill the man since the major had ordered they were to do the job with no loss of civilian lives.

As the trainman and Jacques disappeared into the night, Viv gave instructions to the remaining duo. "Now, dismantle *your* guns and stow them in Jacques' rucksack."

Viv looked at her watch. The entire operation had taken fifteen minutes. Their tasks complete, Victor and Gaspard looked to her for further orders.

"Go directly home," she commanded, adding sternly, "Do *not* stop at any cafés and do not brag to anyone about our mission tonight, you understand?"

Some of the *résistants* of her acquaintance had proved incapable of keeping their mouths shut, and it wouldn't surprise her to discover that Gaspard or Yves might be among them. She handed Gaspard the rucksack with the weapons.

"Take these with you tomorrow," she continued. "Leave Annecy at first light and head straight for the plateau. Remember," she emphasized, "no one even knows you've returned here. To protect your families from reprisals, you *don't* want to attract any notice whatsoever. The sooner you're out of here, the safer it'll be for all the Mountaineers."

"I'm going back tonight," Gaspard declared. Viv could tell he was still put off by the dressing down he'd received from her earlier. He deserved even *more,* but she refrained.

"Then, I'll leave with Gaspard," Yves chimed in. "Jacques knows he's expected for more training, so I imagine we'll see him up there."

"Excellent. And yes, don't wait for him here in Annecy. Leave *now*." She forced a smile of congratulations, although she knew the job wasn't nearly finished until the explosions detonated and the locomotives were well and truly disabled. "Good work, both of you," she told the two young men charitably. They responded with broad, self-satisfied grins. "And tell Jacques the same. Now, get out of here."

As the novice crew melted into the shadows, Viv's next task was to remove herself from Annecy before Lucien Barteau had any idea how close he'd come to turning her in to the local SS and collecting a few more francs of his traitorous bounty.

Major Merrick was right. She mustn't show her face in this lovely town ever again.

———◇———

Viv's right leg had started to ache from the night's exertion as she walked alone through deserted side streets, at last reaching the road that flanked the lake. The storm had passed and the skies were studded with stars. Twenty-six minutes had now elapsed since she had laid the charges—and she began to worry. Any number of things could have gone wrong. Maybe the trainman *did* immediately contact his superiors and the bombs had been dismantled. Some other railroad official might have made a late-night inspection of the locomotive terminus and discovered suspicious bundles on the wheels. Even earlier, the Boom-Boom Boys might have jostled the explosives when inserting them into the rat carcasses. What was

344 | CIJI WARE

more likely, Viv, herself, might not have placed them correctly, or the pencil chargers were faulty, or...

Ten more minutes crawled by with an avalanche of doubts plaguing her. All Viv could hear were her boots crunching into the new-fallen snow and the slap-slap of lake water against the quay where a fleet of boats had once been moored during peacetime.

I hope it's only the cold that's taking the pencil fuses longer to ignite...

In the distance, the frigid air carried the sound of a gaggle of Germans drunkenly singing their way to their barracks north of town. Viv began to walk faster, yearning to reach her chalet down its tiny lane and burrow beneath her one blanket. If the pencil fuses really did fail, it didn't bear thinking what Major Merrick would say.

Viv began to feel a familiar numbness in her toes, a sensation that brought back the memory of the same bitter cold when she and Marcel crossed the Pyrenees that icy November. She attempted to pull her thoughts away from that dangerous subject of Marcel's arrest and the even more disconcerting, totally unexpected appearance of Lucien Barteau—worries that could make her lose her concentration.

She focused on the notion of using some of her precious coal to make a fire and sitting downstairs. She'd heat the last drops of cognac Merrick had left her and—

Good, God, would the damned fuses never ignite?

Maybe she'd forgotten to crimp them properly? Maybe—

Before her catastrophic musings could spin even more out of control, a sound rent the frigid air.

KA-BOOM!

The reverberations were sharp and very loud, riding on the sub-zero breeze wafting from town. By this time, Viv was a mere ten feet from the gate to her own property. The night was now so clear, she could see down to the lake, its shoreline sharply etched in black against the silver water. Grinning triumphantly, she opened the gate and trudged across the yard toward the wooden steps to her chalet's front porch.

BOOM!

The second charge went off, and almost immediately, the third exploded, followed by the fourth.

"Yes, *yes* YESSS!" Viv hissed, shaking her fists at the starry sky as she tried to tamp down her joy and relief. The explosives had finally detonated.

She pictured the heavy connecting rod shearing off the large front wheel of the first locomotive while the force of the other detonations crumpled the forged metal and crippled the other three engines as well. She only prayed that no innocent French traveler, waiting in the station house for the last train of the night, had been maimed by the flying debris. How wonderful it would be, though, if the treacherous Lucien had been taking a late train somewhere.

Exhausted by her whirling thoughts and her long walk home, Viv stumbled through the door of her borrowed chalet, its interior nearly as cold as the temperature outside. A strange trembling swept over her, along with foreboding that her fleeting moment of triumph might soon be supplanted by fears over the terrible vengeance she faced if discovered by her adversaries. She cursed herself for allowing the trainman selling black market cigarettes to go on his merry way. What if he decided to make a few extra francs by telling the authorities what he remembered about three young men and a woman with strands of red hair peeping from her woolen cap? Or, even more likely, what if one of the Boom-Boom Boys was careless and got caught before they could sneak back to the *maquis* on the Plateau des Glières? They'd be tortured, jeopardizing everyone who had helped establish Mountaineer.

Major Merrick had ordered the mission, but he certainly wouldn't be around to deal with its inevitable aftermath. Viv wondered what her next move should be.

She glanced across the room at the cold hearth, deciding against shedding her *Canadienne,* as she usually did, to hang it on the peg beside the front door. She knew, too, she hadn't the energy to fetch a scuttle of coal and light a fire. Instead, she gingerly mounted the ladder to the loft, her recovering right leg twinging at each step as she struggled up the wooden rungs.

Still fully clothed, she wrapped herself in her solitary blanket, closed her eyes, and prayed for sleep. When she finally sank into oblivion, she dreamed of Lucien, clad in trainman overalls, appearing in front of the locomotives with a phalanx of SS arrayed behind him.

CHAPTER 54

Viv spent the rest of February alone in the chalet, wondering where agent Lucien Barteau, a.k.a. agent Gilbert, might be lurking. Meanwhile, she waited for Merrick or one of his deputies to arrive and tell her what she was to do next.

But no one came.

Her food stores were dwindling by the day, and her coal supply was down to the last bucket. At the slightest sound of anyone approaching the chalet, she'd huddle in the freezing underground cellar, pistol in hand, hiding from the enemies who might come looking for her. With her knapsack packed and positioned near the door, she dreaded the thought of what reprisals must have come in the wake of sabotaging the locomotives.

The first week in March, the unmistakable sound of the gate outside her house opening and closing alerted her to someone approaching. When she peered through a small window just above the ground level in the cellar, she breathed a sigh of relief. Running out from the building, she dashed around the corner of the chalet.

"Clément! Oh, am I glad to see you!" she cried to the *passeur* that had guided her across the South of France to Perpignan and Marcel's vineyard. "I haven't left this place in *weeks*. Come in! Come in!"

"Well, no one *I* know wants to see you," he replied, his voice gruff as he stomped past her through the front door. He pointed at the hearth. "No fire? I'm a block of ice!"

Viv raced to the grate and lit the small pile of coal with a rag soaked in kerosene.

"It's been bad in Annecy these last weeks, right?" she said over her shoulder, using a pair of cracked, nearly ineffective bellows to try to get the flames to catch. She figured one of Merrick's deputies wouldn't have come to see her unless things were dire.

Clément sank into the chair usually reserved for the major and clapped his gloved hands together in an effort to restore feeling to them.

Without looking at her directly, he revealed, "Eight villagers—two for each locomotive destroyed—were shot in front of the town hall. Their bodies were tossed into the canal that flows past the jail. Plastered on nearly every wall and street pole are posters calling for the arrest of a 'Gang of Four Terrorists, led by a tall woman with red hair.'"

Viv sucked in a breath as if someone had punched her in the gut. "Jesus, Mary, and Joseph! How did they get our descriptions?"

"Young Jacques La Salle, it seems, sat at the bar of the Café Lyonnais after your operation and loudly recounted the great feats your team accomplished that night."

"Oh, God, *no*! He and the others have been told over and over never to say a word!" She cursed herself for allowing Jacques to escort the trainman home without first sternly repeating the standard admonition she'd given to Gaspard and Yves to never brag about any Resistance activities. "I told the other two to keep their mouths shut and leave immediately for the plateau," she said. "Jacques had one more job to do that night and left on his own. You would have thought by now the young pup would know *never* to do something so stupid."

"Well, all three got away from Annecy, no problem," Clément revealed with a scowl, "but the trainman was tracked down by whoever in the café overheard Jacques blabbing. The SS gave the poor soul a good work over, and he described who'd accosted him."

Viv could only speculate that Lucien might still have been hanging around the café's bar hoping to hear loose talk about Mountaineer and witnessed Jacques's bragging.

"What about the senior La Salles?" Viv asked, her throat tight.

"Whoever it was that went to the SS didn't apparently know that Jacques was the La Salle's son. So far, they're fine. But even if your accomplices have managed to get away, it's you, Viv, who are in the SS crosshairs. And the La Salles, too, if anyone connects you as their supposed kitchen worker. You've run out your string, here, m'girl. I've come to give you a direct order from our *patron*."

Startled, Viv looked at Clément quizzically.

"You've seen him? Major Merrick... I mean, Pierre? He hasn't been here in weeks."

"He went back to London for consultations and just returned."

"And?" she demanded.

"He says to take the small weapons you still have stowed here, deliver them to the plateau, along with the message that the Germans are about to make their move."

"They're bringing in more troops to the Haute-Savoie?"

"Two or three *thousand*."

"Oh, Jesus..."

"I'll fill you in on exactly what you're to say to the maquis."

Viv nodded. "Okay, I'll get ready right away."

"Tell them there'll be planes, too," Clément added. "Our thousand men are—"

"Going to be annihilated," Viv finished the sentence for him. "Merrick knows this, and Marcel feared their situation on the plateau from the very first."

"Marcel was right about that, and he was right about that lout, Gilbert."

"Fat lot of good it did him," Viv said bitterly. "Nobody would listen. I *saw* the traitor through the kitchen door at the Café Lyonnais that same night, Clément! I'm betting Gilbert is the one who's betrayed all of us around here, including Marcel!" She gazed at her French comrade-in-arms. "Is there any more news about—?"

"Our vintner?" Clément shook his head. "No word, but it's assumed he was arrested, and God knows what else. The damned invasion better come soon, or there will be none of us left!" He turned to force Viv to meet his gaze. "The major has informed London he's ordering you out of France for your own safety. Once you come down from the plateau, you are to head east to Switzerland. You'll have to find a way on your own to Chaumont, and from there, I'll do my best to get you safely across the border."

Viv thought it very ironic that she should be ordered to end her SOE tour of duty in the village of Chaumont where she began with Clément as her *passeur.*

Then, a thought struck her.

"Why can't I go from Annecy across the border in a bicycle box?"

"Too dangerous," Clément replied as if she were being dense. "If anyone sees you or arrests you, the Nazis would force you to give up everyone involved."

"*Never!*" Viv replied, firmly.

Clément looked her almost pityingly. "None of us knows if we could hold out, even for a day, given what the SS does to their captives."

"I have the L pill, you know," she retorted, offended that after all they'd been through together, he might think she'd betray any of the Mountaineers.

"Yes but...*no one* knows if the pill will be within reach at the moment it's needed, or if you'll have the courage to bite down on the capsule if it's in your hand."

Viv pictured the L pill she now kept at-the-ready in a side compartment of her knapsack and knew in her bones that what Clément was saying was true. One could never really be certain until the moment came. Would she be able to end her life in an instant to avoid betraying her compatriots? Did she actually have the strength not to tell SS torturers the information they demanded if a lighted cigarette was put out in her eye?

Viv admitted quietly, "You're right. For everyone's safety, including my own, I'd better leave Annecy today."

"And you must *also* leave the country," Clément reiterated. "I'll expect you in Chaumont in two- or three-days' time. Agreed?"

In response, Viv merely shrugged. She would, indeed, deliver the last of the small arms to the brave but perhaps foolish *maquis* gathering high on the Plateau des Glières. She'd long ago come to believe that Marcel's predictions were prescient. If the war were going badly for the German military in the Alps and elsewhere, as it apparently was, the Nazis wouldn't hesitate to launch an all-out assault to wipe out a thousand ragtag *résistants* gathered in the mountains, threatening their power and troop morale.

As for her leaving France as Merrick had ordered? Viv wasn't so sure *that* was a command she would—or could—follow.

———◇———

Viv discovered to her surprise the following day that Clément had risen long before dawn and left the chalet. She took his disappearance as a sign of the urgency of their current situation. She gathered the small cache of arms in her care and added them to her knapsack. With it weighing down one shoulder of her white camouflage ski suit and her pair of skis pressing down heavily on the other, she set out on the long hike up to the plateau that towered in the distance. If a German attack meant she had to make a quick exit from the campsite, she'd just ski down as far as she could and hope she was able to cross-country her way back to the chalet to safety.

For several hours on the upward journey, the gray skies lightened but no sun peeped out from behind the low-hanging clouds. Viv slipped and slid up the snow-covered trails, her ears primed for any suspicious sounds. Her neck began to ache, both from the heavy weights on each shoulder and because she kept looking in all directions, maintaining a sharp eye for any unexpected German soldiers that might be conducting reconnaissance along the few access routes to the plateau itself.

It was mid-afternoon by the time she arrived at the summit and immediately surmised that something terrible had happened. Rows of the *maquis* were standing in uneven lines around a makeshift flagpole, the illegal tricolor hanging limply over their heads. A hand-hewn wooden coffin rested on the ground near the pole with another French flag draped on its cover. It was clear to her that the group that had now attracted nearly a thousand Resistance fighters to its ranks was already burying one of their own.

Viv gingerly put a hand on the shoulder of one of the men she recognized from her first visit to this group of *résistants*. He stood at the rear of the massed group, and beyond him, she could glimpse the main chalet across the plateau's snow-strewn meadow. Everyone, including Julien Paquet standing at the front of the crowd, had gathered around the flagpole and the coffin to hear a priest intone the funeral mass.

"What has happened?" she whispered.

Recognizing her, the man she'd approached revealed in a choked voice, his eyes filled with tears, "One of our best leaders, Tom Morel, was killed yesterday."

CHAPTER 55

"Oh, *no!*" Viv murmured. "Not Tom Morel?"

Viv was deeply disturbed by the news that Lieutenant Morel had died. She'd seen for herself what a revered leader he was, a career soldier in the French mountain infantry brigade who had bravely thrown his fate with the *Résistance*. It was truly the worst thing that could happen at this moment for the group to lose the young lieutenant that had been put in overall charge of the Glières *maquis*.

Her informant continued, "There was a skirmish that our boys won yesterday at the village of Entremont below the plateau…but the Vichy police welched on a truce agreement, grabbed Tom, and shot him."

Viv gave his arm a gentle squeeze. "I am so, so sorry. He was greatly respected."

"What will happen to us now?" the man asked, his eyes full of fear.

"You will continue with your country's allies to fight for a free France," Viv sought to reassure him. "You will honor Tom best by doing that."

Despite her bracing words, she could only wonder silently if Lieutenant Morel's betrayal was merely another unlucky event in a string of problems facing the brave men who had assembled here.

"Well, at least we had a huge parachute drop of arms and supplies early this morning," the man informed them. "We think the Allies must be close to starting the invasion we've heard about all this time. Otherwise, why would they have finally given us what we've begged for?"

With his words ringing in her ears, Viv asked him to tell Julien of her arrival and request that she meet privately at the chalet after the service and burial concluded.

Within the hour, Julien and several others entered the chalet that had long served as the *maquis'* makeshift headquarters. Viv spoke first as she heaved a backpack full of service revolvers onto the rough-hewn kitchen table around which they sat.

"I wish I had more to give you," she said, "but this is everything my *patron* had left to send up to you before he went to London for consultations."

"Every bullet counts," replied Julien wearily, "as we've sadly learned just in the last twenty-four hours."

The lines etched on his face had deepened since Viv's last visit to the plateau. She imagined that she, too, looked and felt as mentally and emotionally exhausted as he did.

"And have you anything else to give us?" he asked half-heartedly.

"Only bad news, I'm afraid," Viv answered, her mind going over the list of things Clément directed her to tell Julien per the major's orders. "As I mentioned, Mountaineer's *patron* flew to London. Our mutual friend Clément reports our leader just returned by Lysander a few days ago to Ain in the region where that province butts up against the Haute-Savoie. He said to warn you that the Germans are very soon expected to bring in three battalions of *Wehrmacht* troops and two German police battalions, along with machine guns and a hundred and fifty howitzers."

Julien emitted a low whistle. "So we are to face some four thousand soldiers equipped with heavy weapons?"

"That was the intelligence I was asked to deliver to you," Viv disclosed with reluctance. "My *patron* and others in the Allied Command in Britain recommend that you should consider withdrawing from the plateau," she added delicately, reminding herself that when it came to the French, the SOE's role in these sorts of matters was only advisory. "It might be best to sneak back down in small groups and hide out at farms throughout the region until the call comes to rise up when the Allies begin to arrive."

Julien looked troubled, but the man sitting next to him abruptly stood up from the table and vehemently shook his head.

Introducing himself to Viv as Tom Morel's replacement in the chain of command on the plateau, Captain Maurice Anjot declared, "We cannot withdraw! They have killed Tom! We have his and our own honor to defend. We must *strengthen* our defenses."

Julien, whom Viv knew only too well was not a professional soldier like Anjot, declared with less than total confidence, "Surely, they will not be able to breach the heights here?"

"But the air assault forces will shoot you down, one by one, from their low-flying planes," Viv said quietly.

"The *Luftwaffe* is also being sent *here*...to join the fight against us on the plateau?" Julien asked.

Viv could plainly see the alarm invading the faces of both Julien and Captain Anjot.

"That's also what I was instructed to tell you. Certain transmissions apparently have been intercepted by the SOE, and it is now believed that calling in the German Air Force is a major feature of the enemy's future assault plan."

Silence filled the chalet except for the sound of the hissing fire.

Julien finally spoke. "When can we expect this...uh...supposed major offensive?"

Viv raised her eyebrow slightly at his use of the word 'supposed.'

"Expect it soon, I'm afraid. Perhaps within ten days or so... maybe even sooner. You should be prepared to see German mountain troops begin to explore how far up to the plateau they can get on foot. Your skirmish, as you called it, at Entremont, was probably just a test to see how ready you are and what weapons you have." She paused, and then said in a low voice intended only for their host and Anjot, "I must repeat: my *patron* urges you to disperse and wait for a signal that will come soon to rise up at the opportune moment to free France."

"And what do the rest of those in London say?" demanded Julien.

"And what says de Gaulle himself?" Captain Anjot asked quietly.

Marcel had told Viv that the top brass were far from unified on the subject. The most Machiavellian among them opined that if the Nazis saw proof positive that French civilians on the plateau were ready to fight the *Boche* in numbers, it would "at least hurt German morale even if the partisans were annihilated."

For her part, disgusted by this view, Viv murmured, "I can only report what I've just told you."

"Bah!" spat Julien. "It's nearly spring. 1944! We've been hearing an invasion is imminent for four *years*! Our alpine men have trained. They are ready to fight *now*!"

Viv shifted her gaze to Captain Anjot, a career soldier in the former French Republic and an experienced mountain infantryman. A man, who she fervently hoped, was not especially in favor of suicide missions.

"We are ready to defend the plateau and our honor," the captain stated, his voice flat with fatigue. He had assumed the manner of a man fatalistically ready to accept an honorable death like Tom Morel, his comrade-in-arms. As she observed him sitting with his arms crossed beside the kitchen table, his mouth downturned, he seemed to be weighing the odds whether any of his men could possibly survive an air and ground offensive on a steep escarpment that the *maquis* had considered impregnable.

Viv rose from her chair with a heavy heart.

"*Bien sûr,*" she said by way of signaling she had no more intelligence matters to disclose. "I am just the messenger. These are your men to command."

To Julien she said, "With your permission, I'll rest tonight in the visitor's chalet and head down the mountains at first light." To them both she added, "My sincere condolences about the loss of Lieutenant Morel. From my own meetings with him, I've known him to be a true patriot."

"The best," insisted Anjot sorrowfully.

Like so many, Viv thought, the face of Kurt and the coffin of Tom Morel flashing before her eyes. And what of men like Jean-Paul?

The best sort of soldiers in this cause...

And before she allowed her drifting thoughts to stray in Marcel's direction, she nodded to her hosts and walked out the front door into the frigid night.

———◇———

Before first light the next day, Viv donned her white camouflage suit over her clothing and headed out the chalet's door. She set out on

her skis across the broad plateau, her knapsack considerably lighter
without the weapons she'd delivered to Julien. Sliding along the
crust of snow that stretched to the edge of the summit, her right leg
felt less reliable than her uninjured left one, but she soon found her
rhythm and pushed her skis evenly along the meadow's flat surface
at a reasonably good clip.

She paused at the brink of the plateau, pondering which trail
down the sheer slopes would be the least likely to have been
discovered by any advance troops from the German mountain
brigades. She didn't have any hand grenades in her pack today, she
thought with a rueful grimace. Her service revolver was strapped to
one ankle, a factor that could make life complicated if faced with an
adversary while juggling her ski poles.

For an hour, she made good progress skiing downhill at an even
pace. Viv figured she was close to halfway down the trail in the
direction of the town of Thones when she spotted a cluster of men in
white ski suits like her own to the rear and a hundred yards above
her, slogging along a parallel ridge that would eventually join the
path she was on. She skidded to a halt, dug her poles into the snow,
and kicked her way out of her cable bindings as quickly as her
shaking fingers could release them.

Stowing her gear in snow off the track, she swiftly hollowed out
a bowl in the deep powder behind a rock. Like a hibernating polar
bear, she curled up inside it in a fetal position, wrapping her arms
around her knapsack and covering her head. With one gloved hand,
she scooped out airspace for her buried face to breathe and waited
for the platoon of some fifty soldiers to pass by.

For what seemed like hours, she could hear the low chatter and
the sound of men's skis schussing along the trail only a few meters
from her lair. Soon, her muscles began to cramp, ice seared her face,
and she began to shiver uncontrollably. Yet, she remained a round,
white lump surrounded by snow, invisible unless someone with
sharp eyes spotted her through high-powered binoculars.

Viv waited in the silence of the mountains where only the wind
swirling through the ravine made any sound. When, at last, she felt it
was safe to stand, at first she could hardly unbend her legs. She was
just about to fasten her second ski on her recovering right foot when
a bullet zinged past her left shoulder. She whipped her head around

in time to see a solitary soldier who apparently served as a rear guard for the group that had recently traversed the territory.

Viv ducked back behind the rock, flipped off the ski on her left foot, and scrambled to pull her service revolver from its holster tied to her calf. She could hear sounds of her assailant on skis coming toward her down the trail. She waited until she sensed the aggressor was close by and then leaned out from the rock and took aim. The sound of her pistol's shots reverberated off the sheer walls that stretched up to the plateau. She'd aimed at nearly point-blank range at an enemy dressed in white just as she was. His face obscured by the same type of ski goggles she wore, her anonymous attacker dropped his rifle as blood spurted from his chest, soaking his ski suit in a star-like pattern.

In the next moment, the soldier began a slow slide down the slope below the trail. Viv stared in shock as his body, along with his skis, carved a misshapen path dribbling blood in the snow until the marksman disappeared into the gloom of the ravine below.

Viv's mind spun with the ramifications of what she'd done. She had killed another human being. Her training from target practice in the fields of some aristocrat's country house in England had kicked in and she, Constance Vivier-Clarke, had just taken the life of a man who had tried to take hers.

If it had been Lucien Barteau, she would have done it happily, but she had just executed a poor soul doing his job, just as she was.

Adrenalin pumping, she wondered whether the group of soldiers that had skied by had heard the two sets of shots ring out. She fumbled into her bindings, stood to her full height on her skis while grabbing her ski poles, and pushed off down the trail. Her eyes swept back and forth across the landscape looking for other soldiers while she cautiously descended on the route until she could branch off in a direction she calculated the Germans wouldn't chance to take, as it ended up far off the main road to Thones. Once at the bottom, she circled back toward Annecy. Despite Major Merrick's warning that she shouldn't show her face anywhere near town or the villages around the lake, it was her only escape route in the cover of darkness.

Shaken and exhausted by her near fatal run-in with German mountain troops, she paused behind a tree to shed her white camouflage suit. She stuffed it into her knapsack and skied toward her chalet in the ordinary clothing she'd worn beneath. It was almost midnight by the time she reached the far end of the valley floor. Approaching collapse, she began the final cross-country slog through several fields toward her own, tumbled-down abode tucked at the end of a country lane. As she plodded along, cutting a line into the snow, a loneliness invaded her chest that she knew had nothing to do with the frigid temperature sweeping down from the Plateau des Glières.

A man—with a ravine for his grave—was dead by *her* hand. Somehow, she must find her way to Clément Grenelle in Chaumont. Only he could get her across the Swiss border beyond the grasp of the Nazis and the SOE agent named Gilbert who wanted her dead.

——◇——

By the time Viv finally reached her gate, every muscle in her body ached from the long trek. She gazed up at the roof of the chalet. As she'd expected, no smoke was rising from the chimney, which meant both Fingers and the major were long gone.

She had never felt so alone.

An icy wind off the lake brushed against her back as she went around to the rear of the small, wooden building. Breathing heavily from the last mile of exertion, she shed her skis and leaned them against the wall, also parking her boots on the top stair next to the back door. Her feet clad in socks wearing thin at the heels, she shaded her eyes and, by habit, peered through the window with its view through the kitchen into the main room.

After staring at the interior for a few seconds, she heard herself gasp. A figure—or was it a body?—swathed in the blanket from Merrick's bed was slumped in a chair in the middle of the room. The head of whomever it was was wrapped in a woolen scarf that Viv recognized as hers, usually draped on a hook near the door. One leg was propped up on a spindly wooden footstool. The hearth was black and lifeless. Viv could predict that it was as freezing inside the room as on the back porch.

Who the hell is *that…?*

Before opening the back door a crack, she reached down, pulled up the pants leg of her ski trousers and withdrew her pistol from its holster for the second time that day. Slowly, she entered the back of the house and crept silently toward the intruder. Cringing at the sound of a floorboard creaking, Viv was caught by surprise when the figure lying nearly prone in the chair reared up and held up one hand, his palm toward her.

"Don't shoot, Miss America!" he called out. "And thank God, it's *you!*"

CHAPTER 56

Viv ran toward Marcel, deposited her gun on the kitchen table, and sank onto her knees beside him. She was both laughing and crying, her joy at seeing him alive colliding with how obviously injured he was.

"Oh, my God, Marcel! I can't believe it! I can't *believe* it's you!"

"It's me, all right," he rasped, his lips crusted with dried blood. "And I'd probably be frozen to death in another few hours if you hadn't arrived." He stared up at her, the pain reflected in his eyes shifting to something softer, tender even. "So before you light the fire and wrap me up in something warmer, kiss me, please—but gently, mind you. Everything hurts." He reached out and ran the back of his fingers on the side of her cheek, adding, "I'd do the same for you if I could."

Viv leaned forward and brushed her lips lightly against his chapped and bruised ones and then nuzzled a spot beneath his nearest ear. She could smell the grime on his skin and inhaled happily. *Marcel was alive!*

"Ah...*chérie*..." he murmured, "you're the best medicine of all. I'd say to put me in your bed, but it might mean the end of me if I tried to mount those stairs to your loft."

"There's Major Merrick's back bedroom," Viv replied, "but it's an igloo back there. I'll grab blankets off my bed and get the fire going. We'll soon get you warm."

The mere effort of their exchange had exhausted Marcel, and his head fell back against the chair. As Viv scrambled up the ladder, she said over her shoulder, "They told us you were arrested in Lyon! That Klaus Barbie personally hunted you down and was sending you to Paris or Berlin for interrogation!" Pulling the covers off her mattress, she swiftly backed down the ladder and ran to one side of his chair. Carefully draping one blanket around his shoulders and over his lap, she knelt beside him once again, seized the hand nearest her on the chair's arm, and pressed her cheek on top of it. "I felt so guilty to think it, but when I heard the SS had grabbed you, I was almost sure that you might already be dead. Merrick thought so, too."

"I almost was," he said, his voice hoarse, "but here I am—and by the way, Barbie very much enjoyed torturing the hand you're now holding so sweetly."

"*Jesus*, Marcel!" she cried, jerking her face away and staring down at his misshapen palm and five black holes extending from his fingertips to the cuticle. Her eyes widened. "They pulled out your *fingernails*?" she said, enraged at the thought of the pain he'd endured.

Marcel gave a dismissive nod in the direction of his hand.

"My much bigger problem has been that I was shot in the leg during my escape."

"You're *shot*?" For the first time she took in the sight of the bloody bandages wrapped around his thigh. "How in the world did you get away and make it *here*?"

"Two other fellows and I grabbed our chance at the rail yards in Lyon. The SS was herding a bunch of us prisoners into a cattle car, headed north for Drancy Prison outside Paris. Somebody in another train car made a run for it just as an empty train on another track was rumbling slowly toward the main station to pick up passengers. The three of us rolled under the cattle car and ran toward the slow-moving train that turned out to be heading east."

"What a total miracle they only hit your leg and not your head," Viv murmured, rising to her feet to throw the last of her coal onto the cold hearth. Once she got it lit, she sank on her haunches beside his chair while she listened, spellbound.

"The other two weren't so lucky," he said, looking down at his mangled hand. "Both were riddled with bullets and couldn't climb onboard. Our pursuers thought they'd shot all the escapees." He cocked his head. "I left a calling card on that train, though," he said. "My leg bled all over the official German mail bags where I buried myself. As for my wounds, I'll need a bit of first aid from you, I'm afraid."

"More than a bit, from the look of you," Viv said, heading into the kitchen to fetch her few medical supplies from under the sink. "Don't tell me you got off the train in Annecy?" she said, grabbing the kit's handle. "The place is overrun with a division of new German troops."

"No, I got off earlier, but that's another story."

"And I want to hear it," she said, returning to his side. "But first, I need to tell you whom I saw in town a few days ago. Lucien Barteau."

"*What?*" Marcel demanded. "What the hell was that bastard doing in Annecy?"

"I think he's trying to help the SS round up what's left of Mountaineer."

"He didn't see *you*, I hope!"

"No. I've been hiding out here since we blew up four locomotives in the Annecy rail yard, that is, except for taking messages from Merrick up to the plateau."

Marcel paused, a wry expression briefly replacing his pinched, pained look.

"I only just learned that you've become an explosives *saboteur* and that the SS are tracking you the same way they're looking for me. Fortunately, I managed to slip off the train when it slowed on a curve before getting to Annecy at the ungodly hour of four in the morning. Then I crawled to a café near the lake."

"It was open at that hour?" Viv asked in amazement.

"No, but they know me there. I pounded on the door, and someone came down from their private quarters and let me in."

"How in the world did you make it here to the chalet? You've only been once before."

Marcel reached for her hand.

"How could I ever forget coming here, *chérie*?" he said with the familiar wry smile she loved so well. "A friend from the café where I occasionally met with your major brought me to your front gate in a hay cart."

"Ah…so *that's* where you two used to rendezvous," Viv mused.

Viv surmised that as one of de Gaulle's deputies, Marcel must have met with Major Merrick quite often to coordinate the various activities of their separate Resistance networks. Mulling this over, she tossed a bit of kerosene on the coals to get them to burn brighter and throw additional heat in Marcel's direction.

"What's even more amazing about my meeting you here," she said, "is that I wasn't even supposed to use this place as a safe house anymore."

"I know that," Marcel replied.

Viv whirled to face him.

"What do you mean, you 'know?'"

"Fingers was here when I arrived. He told me that your *patron* had ordered you to leave France after all the pyrotechnics and said that the German reprisals in Annecy have been severe. As soon as I got here, he decided he'd better leave, too. I was as surprised as you when you walked through that door." Marcel caught her by the wrist. "Fingers also said that there are posters with your description all over the Haute-Savoie."

Viv tried to avoid his gaze. "The reprisals were horrible," she murmured. "Innocent townspeople were taken out and shot in public view."

Marcel's voice was gentle. "You've done your bit, Viv. Too many people in the Haute-Savoie know—or have guessed—that you're an Allied agent. Annecy's a small town." He glanced at her hair. "People love to gossip about good-looking redheads. You are not a forgettable woman, you know? There'll always be one bastard who will betray his comrades for money. And if that sod, Barteau, is part of the hunt, it's even more dangerous. For your own safety and everyone else's, you need to leave the area and get yourself to Switzerland as soon as you can."

"I know," she agreed somberly, reaching for a kettle to heat water over the fire. "But what about you? Don't you imagine your number is up as well? You're pretty well known to the SS even around here, especially since you escaped Barbie's clutches. I'd imagine that every storm trooper in France is on the lookout for the undercover de Gaulle agent with five missing fingernails who walks with a limp due to a bullet in his thigh."

Marcel leaned his head against the chair back and closed his eyes.

"And you're such a specimen of health?" he countered. He turned his head, opened his eyes, and sought her attention. "Fingers told me that you broke your leg escaping a near catastrophe after threatening a bunch of Krauts by waving a hand grenade."

"My luck held that day, thanks to some very kind people in Val d'Isère."

Viv had a flash of memory of Jean-Paul framing her face in his hands, telling her she would be all right after she'd crashed into a tree.

"But what are the odds that luck will continue…for either of us?" Marcel asked, his voice thin from weariness.

Viv decided then and there against telling Marcel how close a brush with death she'd had merely hours earlier, or that she'd killed a man whose shot missed her by inches.

Marcel cast her a stern look. "But at least you can make a decent break for it, now. Fingers said you were to get yourself to Chaumont where our friend Clément will help you cross the Swiss border at St. Julien."

"Listen, you," she said quietly as she poured into a mug the last splash of cognac that remained in the bottle the major had left. "I am not leaving here without you, so let's concentrate on getting you in better shape while we figure where and how we go from here." She handed him the steaming mug saying, "Drink this, and let me have a look at that leg wound."

"You should save the cognac to disinfect it," Marcel suggested as Viv began unwrapping the bloody bandages round his thigh.

She tried to disguise her reaction when she saw that Marcel's thigh was swollen and had streaks of red surrounding the wound where the bullet had entered.

"It's infected," Viv announced flatly.

"Think what it would look like if I hadn't managed to dig out the slug during my trip in the hay wagon."

"Oh, wonderful," Viv murmured. "What did you use, a stick?"

"A spoon. From my mess kit."

"*Marcel!*"

"We should be sure to wash it before using it again," he advised, straight-faced.

Viv continued to clean the wound as best as she was able with the freshest cloth she could find. For the second time, she scaled the ladder to her loft and grabbed the Hermès scarf Marcel had left with her by mistake the previous time he'd been to the chalet.

"Look what I found," she said, waving it as she backed down the wooden steps. "The perfect bandage. You can even still smell a whiff of Chanel Number Five."

Marcel stared at it and reached out to finger its softness. "Have you heard that Coco Chanel has been living with a Nazi officer at the Ritz in Paris all this time?"

Viv stared at the scarf in shock. "*No*! How *could* she?

Marcel shrugged. "I swear that my getting picked up by Barbie's goons was directly due to leaving it here."

"Goodness, you *are* superstitious," she chided, teasing him, "but maybe it was Coco's perfume?" She treated and dried the area around the wound, then placed a square of clean white cloth over it. "There!" she said, wrapping the silk around the bandage and his thigh and tying it firmly, "you and your lucky scarf are reunited…and Coco Chanel be damned!"

She re-tucked the blanket around Marcel's shoulders, then gently washed his face and the cuts that sliced into his hairline and around his eyes and lips.

"Ow!" he winced when she removed the makeshift cloth bandage he'd wrapped around his head.

"This is Barbie's brand of bruising, right?" she asked, attempting to clean the area without hurting him more than she already had with her elementary first aid.

"Ah…this is nothing," he joked, opening his eyes wide to meet her gaze. "You should have seen me a week ago."

She sank to her knees beside his chair once more.

"I'm very glad I didn't." Glancing over her shoulder in the direction of the kitchen area she said, "As you've probably discovered, we don't have much food here, and even less coal, but we'll make do until you're well enough to leave." She raised her chin. "And when we do, you're coming with me to Chaumont. It's time for both of us to say *adieu* to France. At least for a while." Before he could interrupt, she tried to mollify the stream of objections she was certain he would raise. "Who knows? Maybe the brass will send us back before the invasion. For now, we'd both better skedaddle outta here."

"I have no idea what 'skedaddle' means," he replied.

"You never heard that when you visited Washington, D.C.? It means that now that you've come back to me, I'm not skedaddling *anywhere* without you."

With his good hand, Marcel reached for her palm and brought it up to his lips.

"The thought of seeing you again is what kept me alive," he declared, his gaze riveted to hers, "but where we each go next is a matter still to be discussed."

CHAPTER 57

During the next few days, Marcel's battered body showed some small signs of healing while the patient and his caregiver waged a war of wills over their future moves.

"You cannot just wander off in this condition!" Viv insisted.

"I'm not wandering off," Marcel shot back. "I'm going to Paris. I shouldn't tell you this, but the invasion is finally going to happen, and I have to be there."

"When? Where?" she demanded.

He pursed his lips, remonstrating her, "You know I'm not going give you details."

"But you're insisting you must go to Paris, so it's obviously going to happen in northern France somewhere."

Marcel shrugged and remained silent, absorbing Viv's scowl.

"If either of us go to Paris, we'll both likely end up dead before any invasion can take place," she declared. "We have a much better chance to be of use if we stick together and head for Geneva. I've even thought of a cover story because of your injuries."

Marcel looked doubtful, but before he could speak Viv rushed on.

"We can say you're a man wounded in an attack by *résistants* at the ball-bearing factory in Annecy where you worked for the German war effort. I'm your sister, taking you to a specialist in Switzerland."

"I like the medical specialist part," he said, straightening his lips to avoid smiling.

She pointed to the crutches she'd fetched from the cellar. "Look, we even have stage props for our performance at the Swiss border."

Marcel's jaw tightened. "I'm not leaving France," he insisted, "but *you* must. Fingers told me that Clément is expecting you momentarily."

"So let's both go to Chaumont!" Viv retorted with exasperation. "What good will you do anyone if you're arrested again, especially in your weakened condition? Paris is a nest of vipers, especially since our friend Barteau has worked his mischief with so many SOE networks like Prosper in Paris—and now, Mountaineer."

"You think that, too…" he murmured.

"Absolutely. Lucien has known from day one that you work for de Gaulle, and I imagine that that's worth a pretty penny in the world of double agents," she declared with loathing for the man who would have probably sexually assaulted her had she not known how to break an assailant's nose. "If he gets wind you're headed for Paris, or learns you're on your way there, he's bound to tell his SS handlers where agents like you can be found in the city."

"I think he already *has* told them," Marcel replied. "He knew your major and I had been to see Peter Churchill and Odette across the lake in St. Jorioz last spring. Those two were picked up right after that."

"No!" Viv exclaimed. "Odette and Peter? Both of them?"

Marcel nodded, continuing, "Peter had been back to London for consultations and had just been parachuted in above the lake. He and Odette were arrested at their hotel early the next morning."

"So you think Lucien betrayed them, too?"

"He might have been part of it. There's also an officer in the regular German Army who had been pretending he wanted to defect and then turned in agents to the SS. No one knows for sure." Marcel paused with a thoughtful expression. "And, like Peter and Major Merrick, I've also made a trip back to London since I saw you last."

"So Lucien, as Air Operations Officer, might have heard of your takeoffs and landings near Lyon and told Barbie's gang, even if he didn't supervise them?"

"Very possibly."

"So for God's sake, *why* won't you go to Switzerland with me?" she demanded.

"I don't answer to you or your SOE," he explained with measured patience. "I answer to—"

"The Almighty Charles de Gaulle."

She heard how petulant she sounded, but just then, the roar of airplane engines overhead interrupted their heated exchange. Viv and Marcel both cocked their heads as the reverberations grew even louder.

"Oh, no! The *Luftwaffe*! They're attacking!" Viv exclaimed, and ran to the back door.

Throwing it open, she gazed up at so many airplanes filling the sky, they looked like a swarm of vultures swooping down on a carcass.

"Ah, the *Luftwaffe*, come to call," noted Marcel. He'd managed to make his way on Viv's old crutches to stand in the doorway and stare at the masses of planes headed toward the plateau. "The *maquisard* up there is done for," he added quietly.

"Just as you and the major predicted," Viv murmured. "'Sitting ducks.' But they'll put up a fierce fight."

"Martyrs to the cause," Marcel replied, bitterly. "Just what London wants right now, I imagine. The tragic deaths of those young partisans are an effective way to rouse the French public and motivate them to rise up in fury to avenge the deaths of their friends and neighbors when the invasion finally comes."

Viv pulled her attention away from the planes to stare at Marcel.

"You honestly think that's been the plan all along?" she asked, a feeling of revulsion replacing her anger at Marcel's stubbornness about wanting to go to Paris.

"A plan among many to choose from," was Marcel's cynical reply.

Viv, Marcel, and so many others had risked their lives to get the message to London that the French patriots were begging for help.

She wondered whether she had merely been an unwitting party to an action bound to doom the people of the Haute-Savoie to martyrdom, but which would help the Allies in some sort of diabolical long game?

For the next half hour, the planes swept through the skies in waves. Soon, air artillery began brutally raining down on the plateau above the valley.

"We must leave here," Marcel declared, hobbling back into the main room.

"Well, at least we agree on something!" Viv replied.

Marcel's expression was hard and uncompromising.

"I'm going to Paris, Viv."

She stared at him, no longer her lover, but a soldier...a former *Légionnaire*, who answered to the chain-of-command—and certainly not to her. She went cold at the very thought of how she'd barely eluded Hans Kieffer's SS headquartered on Avenue Foch. Silently she watched Marcel struggling into his boots, his face grimacing with the effort.

Viv threw up her hands in frustration.

"All right! You win. Wherever we're going, we're going together. If it has to be Paris, *fine*. We'll go to Paris."

Marcel looked up from tying his shoelace.

"There is absolutely no reason for you to go to Paris. And besides, you've been ordered to leave France, and you should obey Major Merrick."

"I *do* have a reason to go to Paris," she countered, searching for a way to convince Marcel they must stick together. "My American passport is buried in the vegetable garden outside the nurses' quarters at the American Hospital."

Marcel looked at her skeptically. "You certainly know that having that in your possession could get you executed as a spy if the Germans stop you and find it on you. And besides, what do you need it for? You're supposed to be passing as French."

"I'll need it after liberation to prove to officious French authorities like Charles de Gaulle that I'm one of the good guys."

"He already knows you're one of the 'good guys,'" Marcel replied in accented English. At Viv's look of astonishment, he added, "Because I've told him about some of your exploits on behalf of us paltry Free French fighters. It made for amusing dinner table conversation."

Ignoring his curious compliment, Viv searched for more reasons to justify traveling north with him. "And besides, there's my mother who's been interred at a camp for enemy aliens at Vittel. Even though I'd be the first to say that she's a total pain in the *derrière, if* the war is coming to an end as you say, I should try to be ready to get her out of there as soon as Paris is liberated. Until then, you and I can wait it out in her flat on rue des Canettes. My friend Adrienne will help us stay incognito. She'll bring us food—"

Marcel gruffly interrupted her. "How do you know the place hasn't been requisitioned by the Nazis, just like practically every other decent living space in Paris?"

Ah ha! she thought. Even Marcel knew a good possibility for a safe house when he heard one.

Viv shrugged. "The flat is a very modest third-floor walk-up *pièd de terre*. I'm betting it's too small to be of much interest to those who work at Number 84 Avenue Foch. I left Adrienne the keys, so who knows if she's living there herself?"

She felt a chill. Pamela Bradford had told her SS captors that she had a daughter working at the American Hospital who should be instructed to respond immediately and demand her release. This had put Viv herself in the crosshairs for arrest. She wondered if her mother's experience in the war had in any way mollified the woman's innate selfishness. Or had Pamela's loose tongue ultimately exposed Adrienne or Dr. and Mrs. Jackson to danger? And what of the rest of her hospital colleagues? She'd been gone from Paris so long without communications from anyone she knew there, anything could have happened these last few years.

"Please, Marcel," she pleaded, making one last effort, "let Clément get us to Switzerland."

"That is what's best for *you*," he repeated with a familiar stubborn look in his eye. "Now that Fingers sent a message that I'm alive, the General is counting on me."

"Goddamn it, Marcel! It's even more dangerous for *you* in Paris than it is for *me*!"

"I'm to meet him there," he declared as if the matter were settled.

Viv's mouth fell open. "You mean meet de Gaulle *himself*? Soon?"

Marcel looked as if he'd instantly regretted his revealing words. "Whenever it's to be, I must be there…if only to help prepare the way."

"Well then, that's decided," she declared. "If you're to rendezvous with the Great Charles de Gaulle, you will never make it to Paris on your own in your condition. My cover story will work just as well if we're traveling north as it would if we were heading east. With you on crutches and me accompanying you as your equally tall, solicitous and dutiful 'sister,' you'll have at least a *slim* chance of surviving the trip without being arrested en route. On your own, you'll be picked up the first day!"

"I got this far, didn't I?" he shot back.

She pointed at his leg. "Don't be a fool! That wound of yours is an infected mess. Without me, *you're* the sitting duck!" she declared, adding for good measure, "and you will never be able to find a better place to be under-the-radar and wait for liberation than rue des Canettes." She silently prayed no German was now living there.

"You have just one problem," Marcel informed her. "The minute France is freed, de Gaulle wants all foreign secret agents like you to leave the country immediately."

"*What*?" Viv replied, dumbfounded. "But it was 'foreign secret agents'—namely the SOE's French Section—that have done the lion's share of rallying your countrymen to help the Allies drive out the Goddamned enemy!" she protested.

Marcel's face was a mask. "De Gaulle's Free French have done their share," he replied stiffly. "But those are the General's demands," he said. "Fingers told me that London has agreed to allow de Gaulle to order all of you to leave once Paris is secured."

"Well, *that's* gratitude for you," Viv exploded. She slapped her hands on her hips, her temper boiling over. "So that's what it's all been about! The leader of the Free French wants to be seen getting all the credit for liberating the country that surrendered itself to the Nazis. De Gaulle will march down the Champs Elysée in triumph with every single two-timing Parisian claiming to have supported the Resistance. Your countrymen are to be told that the Great God de Gaulle, *alone*, led the return to freedom for his loyal people under the despised German yoke. There *was* no Vichy regime, I suppose? No barbaric French *milice*? No anti-Semites in French ranks? Is that how the post-war story goes?"

"Does it matter who gets the credit…if France *is* free at last?" Marcel asked quietly.

Viv stared at him. "The question is for me: does it matter to *you*, or were my British and American compatriots merely pawns to be pushed around on the great chessboard of occupied France?"

The silence between them was deafening.

Finally, Marcel replied, his voice weary, "It matters very much to me." He tried to smile with his cracked lips. "I'm aware that a man with missing fingernails and a hole in his thigh isn't the most romantic of suitors, but I *love* you, Viv. I want you to know that, especially in case I don't make it through to the end. Most of all, I want you safe, so I'm begging you: go to Switzerland." He shook his head, his own frustration obvious. "Don't you *see*? You and I don't count for much in the great scheme of things."

"Then what was all this *for*?" she whispered, still stunned to learn that de Gaulle had ordered all Allied secret agents to be forced out of France. "Was this war just a chance for people like my stepfather to make millions selling supplies to an insane monster like Adolf Hitler?" She had a flash in her mind's eye of the star-shaped pattern of blood spattered on the white ski suit of the man she'd killed earlier this day. "Was all the pain and suffering and sacrifice and *death* merely so de Gaulle could one day parade through the streets of Paris like some victorious peacock? Don't you and I count for *anything*?"

Marcel didn't offer a response.

"Well, then… *damn them all*!" she shouted.

Before Marcel could reply, she spun on her heels, stormed toward the chalet's front door, yanking her knapsack off the nearby hook. When she turned back, she was brought up short by Marcel's pale, strained expression and the furrow between his eyes. She saw, instantly, that he was in serious pain. Suddenly, all the steam went out of her righteous protests and she rushed to his side.

"Elevate your leg on the chair," she directed, chastened by the thought of how much physical agony he must be in. "And no more arguing. I'll start packing for Paris. And by the way," she said, a feeling of anticipated sorrow flooding her chest as she heard her voice crack. "I love you, too. Remember that, Marcel, if I don't make it either."

"Ah, my Miss America," he said softly, leaning back and closing his eyes. The tenderness of his tone told her she'd won the battle of accompanying him to Paris. "Your pure heart puts the rest of us to shame. You are truly a daughter of France, *chérie.*"

She offered him a sad smile as plane engines flying low still roared overhead. "It would seem that you and I are bonded forever by this pesky love we have of a free France…and amazingly enough, for each other."

The glance they exchanged was tinged with sadness and regret at the sorry world as they'd both come to know it.

CHAPTER 58

For hours outside the chalet, the ear-splitting sounds of war continued to reverberate off the sheer walls of the Plateau des Glières only a few miles distant as the crow flew. What alpine men on the ground the *Luftwaffe* didn't annihilate in that large stretch of open meadow, German troops and heavy armament would finish off, as the *maquisards* attempted to flee down the few trails to the valley below.

Viv fought sudden tears. She was so weary of it all. She tried to blot out the images of what must be happening at that very moment to the likes of young Jacques La Salle and his comrades, Yves and Gaspard, along with their leader Julien Paquet and the other young men she'd seen dutifully drilling with their makeshift weapons in the freezing cold all those months. She could already visualize that theirs would be the names listed on the memorial plaques erected in the years to come. Beside them would also be the names of the innocent civilians killed in German reprisals for the damage Viv and the Boom-Boom Boys had wrought at the ball-bearing plant and in the Annecy rail yard. Viv's physical fatigue and mental exhaustion felt overwhelming, and she yearned to climb the ladder to her bed and simply fall sleep.

Just then, yet another enormous reverberation shook the chalet's small windows.

I can't think of any of that now...we just have to get out of here...

Marcel remained slumped in the chair, eyes closed, while she began to throw her few articles into her knapsack. Meanwhile, her mind raced to come up with an additional scheme to outfox and outmaneuver their way north through territory controlled by the enemy. The irony was not lost on her that she was returning to the place she had fled in fear for her life. If any German officials she encountered traveling north found out she'd been an Allied secret agent since escaping the City of Light, she wouldn't just be arrested—they'd simply put a bullet through her head.

Even more insane than *her* returning to Paris was Marcel doing the same. Glancing at his bruised and battered body, the stubborn, wounded Resistance fighter Viv loved had pledged his life to a general who'd mostly fought this war from London. Now that the Gestapo had killed Jean Moulin, de Gaulle's other deputy in France, in July of 1943, the capturing of Marcel Delonge would be a top priority for the SS. Like the wanted leaflets with her description on them that Fingers reported were plastered all over Annecy, there were probably posters demanding Marcel's arrest in every major town and rail station they would travel through to Paris.

What a macabre twist of fate that she and Marcel would both end up in Paris. Even if they made it there, would they survive long enough to witness the city's liberation?

Viv seized her pistol from where she'd left it on the kitchen table and stuffed it into a hidden compartment at the bottom of her knapsack. She then began to consider what clothing she could wear to pose as a harried French woman traveling with her ill brother to seek medical help from their sibling, a doctor in Paris.

With the sound and fury of the German assault on the plateau echoing loudly down the valley, she crossed the room to stand beside Marcel.

"I'm glad you have my scarf tied around your leg like that," she said to him while he gazed at her from his chair. She pointed to the silk square with the letters 'Hermès' discreetly printed in one corner. "No one will see it beneath your trousers, but it's bound to bring us luck, right?"

"Let us pray it's the good kind, for once," he murmured with a wince.

———◇———

It was a surprise to both Viv and Marcel that his posing as an injured factory worker seeking medical help in Paris from his brother, a doctor in the capital, turned out to be the perfect cover story. Marcel was in constant pain as he hobbled on crutches past the guards at checkpoints throughout their train trip north. Amazingly, the authorities regularly waved them past, clearly taking note of the physical discomfort Marcel was feeling that was etched deeply on his face. Viv's head was swathed in a woolen scarf to disguise her hair, and her own expression reflected genuine worry that her companion's infected leg might cause his death before they could safely arrive at their destination.

Gare de Lyon, their final stop in Paris, was nearly empty on this last day of March 1944. The German newspapers that hung in neat rows on the walls of the train station's news kiosk screamed triumphantly in big black letters about the massacre of "terrorists" on the alpine Plateau des Glières. Heartsick, Viv turned her back on the display and kept pace with Marcel as he hobbled on the crutches that were too short for his height.

"Let me see if I can find a taxi to take us to rue des Canettes," she said. She patted her knapsack. "Yes, we can afford it. The major was kind enough to leave a wad of francs in the hiding place we had in the chalet."

"No doubt he thought you'd need it for your journey to Switzerland," Marcel said pointedly as he slowly maneuvered his crutches toward the exit.

It had been a terrible, nerve-wracking trip, and neither of them was in good spirits. Outside on this cold, windy day, there were no taxis to be had.

"I'm afraid we'll have to take the Metro," Viv said, trying to keep her tone casual.

"If it's even running today," was Marcel's glum rejoinder. "Half the time the electricity is out."

As they walked along, they could see Paris had become a virtual wasteland compared to the beautiful, gay city of Viv's school years. Pedestrians with pale, pinched faces gave witness to the terrible food shortages. Hedges weren't clipped. The parks and boulevards were dirty and bedraggled. The cafés served ersatz coffee and little else.

Nazi soldiers were everywhere, on nearly every street corner, crowding the bistros, driving down otherwise empty streets in their sinister black Citroëns. After painfully negotiating a series of staircases into the bowels of the Metro, Viv and Marcel emerged from the stop at Mabillion in the Sixth Arrondissment and hobbled along the few blocks to rue des Canettes, a tiny side street only steps from the Church of St. Sulpice. A German soldier walked toward them as they drew near to a door embedded in a wooden wall at Number 20. On the other side of the entrance would be the courtyard fronting a series of small flats where Viv hoped to find Adrienne at home.

The soldier stared at the two of them with mild curiosity but passed by without stopping them. Viv lifted the latch and breathed a sigh of relief that the gate wasn't locked. She guided Marcel and his crutches over the raised lintel and swiftly shut out the street noises. Once they'd crossed the cobbled courtyard, Viv set down her knapsack near the entry to a staircase that led to her mother's flat.

"No point in your navigating three flights if we can't stay here," Viv said. She led him into the hallway and pointed to a niche under the first flight of stairs. "Don't move."

"You don't even know who's up there," Marcel grumbled, leaning against the wall and propping his crutches beside him. "Some German sonofabitch could have taken it over by now, or it's empty and we have no key."

He closed his eyes, convincing Viv that he was near collapse.

"Just let me see what's what," she replied with forced cheerfulness, wondering how soon she could find some medical help for his infected leg. "I won't be long, but if anyone comes, just go through that door." She pointed to his right. "But be very careful on the steps to the cellar."

At the top of the third flight of stairs, Viv tiptoed to the door and pressed her ear to the wood. A jolt of anxiety rippled through her chest as she wondered who might be behind it. When she heard the sound of female voices, she was awash with relief. Maybe the Hermès scarf *would* continue to bring Marcel and her even more luck. She gently rapped her knuckles on the door.

There was silence inside, and then the sound of low female voices once again. After a few more moments, the door opened a crack, and then it was flung wide.

Standing at the threshold was Adrienne Vaud dressed in the uniform that they'd both worn at the American Hospital. Behind her stood Viv's mother, Pamela Bradford, chic as ever, wearing a wool Chanel traveling ensemble. Surrounding the elegant woman, her blond mane upswept in a chignon without a hair out of place, was her steamer trunk, along with a scattering of hand luggage.

With an expression registering pure shock, Pamela blurted Viv's given name.

"*Constance*? What in God's name are *you* doing here?"

Viv's next moments in Paris felt as if she'd been hit by a torpedo from a German U-boat. Speechless, Viv could only stare at Pamela, who had turned in place to throw an accusing glance at Adrienne.

"You said my daughter had sashayed off to Switzerland two years ago." Her eyes narrowed as she returned her gaze to meet Viv's. "If you've been daft enough to come back to France, and now you've come here, expecting *me* to take you to Geneva with me, you are very much mistaken. I'm afraid—"

Viv cut her off. "You escaped the camp at Vittel?" she asked incredulously. "And now you think *you're* going to Switzerland?"

"I don't *think*," she said with a toss of her head. "I was granted *release* from Vittel, and, yes, I'm going to Switzerland! They're coming for my luggage any minute, now."

Fear gripped Viv as she pictured Marcel downstairs on the verge of collapse.

"Who's 'they?'" she demanded, praying he'd stay hidden behind the stairs or somehow manage to drag himself downstairs into the basement.

"The man who got me out of the camp," she said, her chin rising in the air defiantly. "Wilhelm Gerhardt."

"The SS officer who took over our place on Avenue Kléber? The member of the Gestapo that had you *arrested*?"

"*He* wasn't the one who had me arrested," her mother retorted. "Someone who had it in for him told the local commandant that he and I—"

Viv cut her off a second time.

"So some *other* Nazi managed your release?" she demanded.

"No, it was Colonel Gerhardt," Pamela countered. "The SS who had me arrested was later found profiteering off the black market, so Wilhelm was able to...well...have him court-martialed and then he arranged to bring me back to Paris."

Viv gestured toward the luggage surrounding her mother. "So, what did you have to trade your Nazi colonel *this* time to get him to agree to all this?" she asked, unable to curb the accusation that sounded venomous even to her own ears.

Their voices rising, Adrienne shushed them both and took a step toward Viv.

"At least just let me just shut the door, will you?"

Adrienne's swift move reminded Viv that it would be dangerous to allow their heated conversation to carry downstairs.

The truth was, she realized in a sudden flash, she was furious with herself for having wasted a moment's concern for her mother's welfare. Clearly, Pamela Bradford hadn't spared a single thought about her daughter's wellbeing these last years. In fact, given the scowl on Pamela's face, her mother seemed annoyed by Viv's sudden re-appearance.

"Wilhelm Gerhardt has been nothing but a gentleman," Pamela declared with an airy wave of her hand "He kept this flat in my name and was good enough to get in touch with Karl who, in turn, has been communicating with German business colleagues with whom he'd dealt in the Third Reich. Karl knew who best to contact in Berlin about the dreadful mistake sending me to an internment camp."

"Ah...the magic of Karl's almighty ball bearings came to your rescue," Viv commented sarcastically, her mind streaking back to her successful caper: blowing up the transformers at the ball-bearing factory in Annecy.

Pamela pursed her lips. "I'll have you know that because of the efforts of Wilhelm and Karl—along with my putting Wilhelm's name on the deed to the apartment on Avenue Kléber so it won't be confiscated by other Germans when we leave—I've been given safe passage out of France."

Viv's voice lowered an octave. "You gave your lover the flat my father bought for us?" she accused. "*My* name is also on the deed, you know."

Pamela studied her diamond watch on her wrist and offered a little shrug.

"I signed an affidavit that you had fled the country and thereby had deserted France. Wilhelm said doing that would suffice, and a new deed was drawn."

Viv felt enraged. The apartment had been her one solid link to her father and ultimately was to be bequeathed to her.

"Well, I haven't 'deserted France,'" Viv countered, her fists clenched, "and I'll be sure to inform your Nazi colonel of that fact."

Her mother took a step toward her, glaring. "You wouldn't *dare!*"

"Why wouldn't I? You gave away my property without my permission."

"*Half* your property! And if you do one thing to prevent me from finally getting out of this dreadful country, I'll have Wilhelm arrest you! I mean it!"

Viv could only stare at her mother. Would Pamela truly send her only child to a Nazi prison camp?

She was bluffing.

Viv feared what she might say if she responded to her mother's string of insults, so she turned to address Adrienne.

"Has it been awful for you?" she asked. "I see from your uniform, you must still work at the hospital. Are the Jacksons all right and—?"

Pamela interrupted. "I strongly suggest that neither of you two girls get too cozy with the likes of Toquette Jackson. And I'd certainly steer clear of the hospital if I were you."

"Why?" Viv demanded. She would need Dr. Jackson's help for Marcel who, by this time, could be half dead downstairs.

Pamela shook her forefinger at them, declaring, "Let's just say I'm giving you two a word to the wise." She glanced again at her watch and then at her Louis Vuitton trunk standing open nearby. "I have just a few more things to pack and then, don't worry, girls. I'll be gone."

Viv struggled to control her temper, asking, "But even if you and your colonel eventually do make it into Switzerland, how in the world will you manage to fly home from there to North Carolina? And what will Karl say of your *ménage à trois*?"

"Oh, there'll be no way I can fly anywhere any time soon," her mother assured Viv with a casualness that rang false. "I plan to stay in the city of Bern until…well…we know what is to happen in the future."

"Ah…the City of Spies. How appropriate for you and dear Wilhelm," Viv declared. She assumed the SS officer knew only too well how badly the war was going for Germany. Undoubtedly, he was looking for a new assignment, perhaps informing Western intelligence agencies what he knew about the territory-grabbing Russians?

Pamela smiled conspiratorially. "Wilhelm is my passport out of France, and I'm his out of Germany. Rather clever of us, don't you think? After that, we'll just have to see."

"But what about *Karl*?" Viv pressed, curious in spite of herself.

"Naturally, he assumes I'll be returning to North Carolina but, of course, it all depends on…well…the international situation."

"I see," Viv murmured, wondering silently if eventually there would be any reprisals for Americans who aided and abetted the Nazi war effort. And what of known Nazi SS officers themselves? Would they ever be held to account by the victors?

Staring at her mother for several long seconds, it dawned on Viv that this might be the last time she ever saw her. It might be the only time to ask her mother a question that had been on her mind since the day Toquette told her that Pamela had been apprehended by the SS.

"Didn't it occur to you, Mother, that telling the people who arrested you that your daughter would pull strings to get you released put me—an American and considered an enemy alien by the Germans—and the other Americans at the hospital directly in the crosshairs of the Paris Gestapo?"

"Well, you never even tried to get me out, so it's moot," she retorted.

Viv shook her head in frustration, adding, "Thanks to you, I had to flee for my life."

"Oh, don't pull that dramatic nonsense with *me,*" scoffed Pamela.

Viv fell silent, worn out from sparring with the woman whose presence she'd been in for less than ten minutes. She realized with some shock that she had absolutely nothing else to say to her own mother.

"Well, I guess that's it then," she murmured. "You and Colonel Gerhardt will be off, off and away."

Pamela paused and reached out to put a hand on Viv's arm.

"Don't spoil this for me, Constance."

Pamela's expression was a mixture of pleading and belligerence.

Viv inhaled a deep breath, then replied, "I won't, if you won't call me Constance."

"Oh, for goodness sakes! Is that all you care about?" her mother pouted.

"No, it's not all I care about," Viv replied carefully, "but please, from here on out, refer to me in or out of my presence as 'Viv' in honor of my father and the Vivier family. If you will just do that one thing for me, I promise I won't say a word to Karl about the deal you've struck with an enemy of both Britain and the United States."

Viv knew with a leaden heart that there was no use arguing with her mother anymore or trying to win out over behavior Pamela seemed incapable of changing. There truly was no more to say.

"I'll just let you finish your packing," Viv murmured, then turned to Adrienne. "Let's go into the kitchen, shall we? I need to talk to you about something."

CHAPTER 59

Viv was desperate to return to Marcel. When she heard Pamela click shut the fastenings on her trunk, Viv said from the kitchen doorway,

"I have to go pick up my own baggage and probably will miss your departure, Mother, so I'll say my goodbyes now. Safe travels," she added, surprised to realize she meant it.

Before her mother could respond, Viv told Adrienne, "I'll be back soon."

Turning to leave the flat, she calculated that Marcel and she could wait in the building's basement until Herr Gerhardt arrived in his big, black Citroën to fetch her mother and her ridiculous trunk. Once they were gone, she'd somehow transport Marcel upstairs to the blessed safety of the third floor flat.

And won't my neutral Swiss friend be surprised when she sees she's acquired a third flat mate...

Speeding down the first flight of stairs, the significant events of the past two-and-a-half years flashed before Viv in a millisecond. She remembered the day she had signed the Official Secrets Act that forbade her ever to reveal to Pamela her arduous weeks of training to be an SOE agent. She could never tell of her long odyssey with Clément Grenelle crossing France and then up and over the Pyrenees with Marcel. Her mother would never know of, or care about, Viv's near crash landing in France; the missions she had completed; the explosives she'd detonated; the soldier in the white camouflage suit she'd killed on the trail coming down from the Plateau des Glières. Nor would Pamela ever learn how Viv had managed to elude death several times as an Allied secret agent. Neither parent would be interested to learn of the work she had done with Jean-Paul to save Jewish children from the Nazis; nor the miles she had skied all over the Alps delivering crucial messages to the *maquis*.

As Viv reached the third and final flight of stairs, it occurred to her that Pamela Bradford would never even know her daughter had fallen in love.

Her mother could never imagine Viv choosing to do the things she had while she slowly evolved from a spoiled American teenager into someone so different.

A fool, perhaps? Or at least someone who could live with her own conscience.

———◇———

"Is he asleep?" Adrienne asked, looking up from chopping vegetables in the tiny kitchen when Viv closed the bedroom door.

"Either that, or unconscious," Viv fretted.

Viv and Adrienne had somehow managed to carry Marcel upstairs, an effort that was brutal for all concerned. Viv had offered her Swiss friend a sanitized version of the clandestine work she and Marcel had been engaged in since the last time the two women had been together. Both of them had been aware of Dr. Jackson's permitting downed airmen to seek safety pretending to be patients at the hospital, so Viv felt she could trust her friend with an abbreviated explanation of why Marcel had arrived wounded.

"I've got to get a doctor to tend to Marcel's wound. Do you think you could—"

"Ask Dr. Jackson to come here?" Adrienne shook her head no. "Viv, listen to me. Your mother's warning should be taken seriously. My embassy told me this week that I should quit working at the American Hospital. Too many people know that Dr. Jackson hides those downed flyers and Jews seeking escape there, and that Toquette... well, we both are aware of the kinds of things Toquette has been doing for the Resistance." Adrienne paused, her kitchen knife in the air. "Do you remember Gaston DuPuis?"

"Your embassy friend here in Paris?"

Adrienne nodded. "He's lined up a file clerk's position for me a few days a week. That's why I took you up on your offer of this flat and moved out of our quarters at the hospital. You can imagine your mother's surprise when she came here to pack up." She fell silent and then added, "I hope you don't mind or think poorly of me for—"

"Of course, I don't mind about anything!" Viv declared. "And as for leaving the hospital, I did the same, didn't I, when I was threatened with arrest?" Viv looked at her sharply. "But have you given your notice, yet?"

"I was going to at the end of this week, but now I think I'll do it today."

"Oh!" Viv exclaimed. "Let me do it *for* you. I'll need to borrow your hospital uniform, all right? It's actually a good cover for me in the interim."

"Just don't wear my nametag, all right?" Adrienne teased. Resuming slicing the vegetables, she nodded in the direction of a dark corner. "By the way, your Louis Vuitton cosmetic case is over there, waiting for you."

"You're joking!" Viv exclaimed. She walked across the room and seized its leather handle. "I can't believe you were able keep it with you, considering."

Adrienne said, "I kept thinking that if I held on to it, you'd come back someday, and here you are!" Continuing to dice a few carrots and parsnips for the vegetable broth that would have to suffice as their dinner, she added, "As you probably saw, things are getting pretty desperate in Paris. Food shortages. No one trusting anyone. The Germans losing in North Africa, and now their disastrous Russian campaign. I've been thinking of trying to make my way back to Switzerland myself. My passport is still valid, and I'm—"

"Neutral," Viv supplied the end of her statement with a grin. "But please know that I welcome your company here. Stay in this flat as long as you wish. My mother paid three years' rent in advance. I just don't want to put you in danger because I'm back."

"Accompanied by a man whose face is on Wanted posters all over Paris?"

Stricken by Adrienne's words, Viv knew all too well her presence had thrust her friend into serious jeopardy.

"Believe me," Viv said, putting a hand on Adrienne's arm, "I wouldn't have come here if we'd had any other choice." Viv briefly recounted how Marcel and she had been both colleagues and later, lovers. "But who knows better than we two do that nothing is permanent in this crazy world we're living in," she said, with a sigh. "Marcel will simply disappear from here once he's back on his feet."

"You don't think you'll...well...be together once the war is over?"

Viv slowly shook her head. "I try not to think about the future at all...just about somehow staying alive while holding out hope that we're getting close to the end." She put her arm around Adrienne's shoulder, giving it a squeeze. "Whatever happens, I love having you here in this flat as long as you want or need to be."

"That's really kind of you," Adrienne replied, giving Viv's arm a reciprocal pat, "but I must warn you to steer clear of the concierge downstairs. She's new in the last year and she's a mean old crank. Some of us in the building think she makes money on the side reporting things to certain people."

"Just what we don't need at this juncture," Viv murmured, thinking how lucky they were the woman hadn't seen Marcel and her arrive. "Has she gotten anyone arrested?"

"Not as far as I know. A few of the tenants have been charged with infractions that earn them fines, a percentage of which we're all sure she gets as a cut. Your mother scared her to death, though," Adrienne said with a laugh. "When the old witch was rude to her, Pamela threatened to call the SS to haul *her* away for questioning!"

Viv's thoughts had begun to race with alarm. She *had* to find medical help for Marcel before someone like the concierge made serious trouble. Adrienne's warning also meant Marcel needed to find a better safe house than rue des Canettes.

A plan suddenly formed in her mind.

"Do you have a bicycle?" she asked.

"A rusty one. Downstairs in the basement."

Viv smiled. "Yes! Right! I saw it down there when I went to get Marcel. Okay if I borrow it?"

Adrienne threw her cut vegetables into a pot. "Of course." Then she added, her brow furrowed, "You're going to ride to Neuilly? To the American Hospital to get help?"

Viv nodded. "With a stop, first, at Number 11 Avenue Foch. If Dr. J is at home, I might not even have to go all the way out there. At least he might give me some medicine for Marcel's leg, and I'll tell the Jacksons you've got another job." She pointed to Adrienne's uniform. "I'll trade you some of my clothes for your uniform. Deal?"

"It's a deal, but you should know that Pamela told me that the SS are watching Toquette and Dr. Jackson night and day," Adrienne warned. "I think it's too dangerous for you to stop there since the Jacksons' apartment is literally a stone's throw from *Sturmbannführer* Han Kieffer on Avenue Foch. Everyone says that what the SS does to prisoners at Number 84 is horrible. Honestly, Viv, I wouldn't go *near* the Jacksons now."

Viv sighed. "You're right. I guess I'll just have to sneak in the back way at the hospital, then, and try to recruit a different doctor. If Marcel doesn't get better and make a certain rendezvous, trust me, we'll all likely be arrested before the invasion comes."

"*If* it comes," was Adrienne's gloomy reply. "And don't forget, there's still that SS unit in Neuilly that's based right across from the hospital."

CHAPTER 60

Adrienne's predictions held true. There were too many German soldiers marching along Avenue Foch when Viv rode by on Adrienne's decrepit bicycle for her to dare stop at Number 11. Her anxiety had increased even more by the time she wheeled onto the hospital property and leaned the bike against the wall of the nurses' quarters.

When she made her way to the ground floor hallway, the place was buzzing with activity, as usual. Clad in Adrienne's uniform, her friend's hat covering most of her telltale red hair, Viv reached Dr. Jackson's office without anyone stopping her.

"Oh, my God, Viv!" Head Nurse Elizabeth Comte jumped up from a desk in Dr. J's outer office and embraced her. "We've all been so worried since you left. I can't believe you're actually standing here right in front of me!" Her expression grew grave. "The SS came looking for you right after you'd gone. They're still across the street, you know. I hope that no one—"

"No one saw me," Viv finished her sentence for her. "And I won't stay long." She lowered her voice. "I'm with someone… uh…quite important who has a bullet wound in his leg. The bullet is out, but the area around it is infected. I was wondering if Dr. Jackson or someone on the staff could…well…come tend to him?" Before Elizabeth could demur, Viv added, "Tell Dr. J it's the same man he asked me to drive to Dunkirk."

Elizabeth slowly shook her head. "I'll tell him, but you should know that we cannot afford for any of our medical personnel to be arrested. Especially Dr. J," she emphasized. "But look, *you* know first aid. In case no one can be spared to come, let me give you some sulfa medicine to put on the wound and some clean dressing supplies."

Viv reached out and squeezed the nurse's arm. "That's tremendous of you. I'll do my best, but if there's any way you could send someone? It's very important to the Allies that this man recover," she emphasized. She gave her address on rue des Canettes and then asked with a nod in the direction of Jackson's inner office. "Is he here?"

"He's on rounds, of course," Elizabeth replied, "and it would be a shock if you could see him." She lowered her voice again. "Like everyone, this war has taken a huge toll. On Toquette, too. The stress on the two of them—"

She halted, mid-sentence.

"I know," Viv murmured, thinking it was a miracle the Jacksons hadn't been hauled in by the SS long before now. "Tell Dr. J that I've been involved in some of the same... ah...activities myself since I left here."

Elizabeth merely beckoned Viv to follow her. "Come with me and let me give you what you'll need. Then I think it's best for everyone if you left right away."

Clearly, there was no job for Viv at the hospital. She was tempted to reveal that she was also there to retrieve her American passport from the institution's vegetable garden. Instead, she expressed her thanks, explained Adrienne's resignation, and departed as directed. She'd have to return one moonless night to the carrot patch to see if her precious document was still there.

———◇———

The medicine that Viv applied to Marcel's wound began to work wonders; he was getting much-needed rest and administered bowls of broth that Viv was feeding him. One evening in late April, the three housemates were startled by a soft knock on the front door of the flat. Viv cautiously opened the door and nearly collapsed with relief. There, standing on the threshold, black doctor's bag in hand, was Sumner Jackson. As Nurse Elizabeth had warned, he was much changed, his lanky height stooped, his face gaunt.

"Hello, Viv," Dr. Jackson said with the trace of a weary smile.

"It's so good to see you again. I understand our mutual friend might be in need of a house call. Elizabeth told me of your visit, and I was pleased to hear she prescribed something for the patient. I'm sorry I could not come by before this."

At the sound of this exchange, Marcel rose to his feet and extended his hand.

"You needn't have risked coming here," he said with a pointed look in Viv's direction. "I'm actually nearly recovered, but I have to say, it's very good to see *you*, especially since you've managed to save my life twice."

Dr. Jackson inclined his head in Viv's direction.

"Don't you think this young woman had a hand in both rescues?"

Marcel nodded. "True enough." He pointed to the area where meals were served. "Come, take a seat. I wish we could offer you—"

Jackson interrupted. "I can only stay a few minutes, but I wanted to make sure you were being properly taken care of this time, too. We've been told that certain people in London have been extremely concerned since you were reported missing."

"The medicines truly were life-savers, so thank you." Marcel replied.

"May I have a look?" Jackson asked, and the two men retired to the back bedroom so he could inspect Marcel's wound.

A few minutes later, both emerged with Jackson looking pleased and relieved.

"So once again, Viv did a decent job of it?" Marcel asked in a teasing tone.

"An *excellent* job," Dr. Jackson confirmed, "and now I must go." He nodded toward the two women. "Toquette sends her very best to you all," he said with an air tinged with melancholy. "May we all meet one day, soon, when France is liberated."

And as quickly as the head of the American Hospital had arrived, he was gone. Viv didn't say anything to Marcel, but she was both awed and frightened that Dr. J had risked coming to see if he could help a man he knew was a key player in the Resistance. But like Jean-Paul, Sumner Jackson was a healer, and his first loyalty was to his patients, regardless of the danger to himself.

———◇———

By early May, Marcel was walking without the aid of crutches, and with only a slight limp. That week, Viv calculated that the moon would be absent from the night sky, rendering it a time when it might be safest to retrieve her passport from the hospital's vegetable garden. When Marcel was napping, she left before evening curfew began and rode Adrienne's rusty bicycle all the way to Neuilly.

She walked the two-wheeler onto the hospital grounds at dusk, hiding it in a gardener's shed. With a small shovel in hand that she'd found on the floor, she counted four rows of carrots from the edge of the vegetable bed, hoping spring planting hadn't revealed the presence of her passport to any gardener. Cringing at the sound, she burrowed into the soil, hoping each shovelful of dirt she tossed aside would reveal what she was looking for. About two feet down, she rooted around in the loam feeling for the packet with the precious document she'd buried that night so long ago.

Out of the corner of her eye, she saw light appear in a doorway to one of the hospital wings. Frantically, Viv scraped her hand back and forth until, at last, she felt the edges of the leather passport case and pulled it out of the hole.

"Who's out there?" a voice shouted into the black night.

Without answering, Viv abandoned the shovel in the hole and raced inside the shed where she'd parked Adrienne's bicycle. Praying the man calling out was merely the hospital night watchman, Viv stuffed her passport wrapped in its filthy oilcloth into the front of Adrienne's Red Cross uniform she'd donned as a precaution. Clambering aboard the bike, she raced toward the nearest back exit from the grounds. It was getting close to the nightly curfew, and if seen by an authority, she would be subject to immediate arrest.

Gasping for breath, she pedaled furiously down the side street toward a larger road that would take her across the bridge and back toward the heart of Paris. As the minutes ticked by, Viv realized she would never be able to reach rue des Canettes before the German patrols would start looking for curfew violators. On impulse, she took a turn toward Avenue Foch, not far from her current position. She swiftly calculated she might sneak down the back street parallel to Number 11 that let on to the Jacksons' back garden and hide there until dawn.

The narrow road was, in reality, just an alley, seldom frequented except by trash collectors. Once in the shadows, Viv dismounted the bicycle and crept toward the familiar back garden gate. She was about to lift the latch when she heard voices and saw pinpricks of flame dancing in the night air.

Smelling smoke, Viv realized several men were enjoying cigars on the Jacksons' back garden terrace. She rejoiced when she recognized Dr. Jackson's voice, but then froze in alarm. To her dismay, harsh, guttural French floated toward her as well as the equally discordant sound of the colloquial language spoken by a member of the unruly *milice.* A lantern sat on the garden table, and to her horror, Viv realized Dr. Jackson and his wife, Toquette, were being held at gunpoint.

"You will be allowed to sleep here tonight, under guard, Herr Doctor, while we continue the search of your house" said one of the men surrounding the Jacksons. "In the morning, you will be taken to Vichy for further questioning, do you understand?"

"Yes," Jackson's defeated voice floated toward Viv on the night air. "What of my—"

"Your wife and son will be taken to Vichy as well," was the stern reply.

Minutes later, she could see Dr. Jackson and Toquette being herded back into their house, leaving Viv to wonder if the concierge in her building was due for a bounty payment for having spotted Dr. J arriving at rue des Canettes on a mission of mercy? Would the woman also have ratted on the two recent arrivals in the apartment on the third floor? It was a definite possibility.

———◇———

Viv remained crouched near the gate next to a large rubbish bin for the rest of the night. As soon as the hour of curfew ended, her muscles felt barely able to move. She rose and wheeled her bike to the end of the alley. Suppressing a groan at her protesting hamstrings, she mounted the seat and was turning at the corner of Traktir and Avenue Foch when she saw that all three Jacksons were crammed into the back of a Citroën, a small Nazi flag on each front fender. Viv's knuckles turned white as she gripped the handlebars, watching the car speed away to a destination that could only spell disaster. Two of the bravest people she had ever known were now in the clutches of the Gestapo.

Viv's hold on the handlebars grew even tighter. Less than fifty feet from where she had paused to straddle her bicycle with both feet on the ground stood the all-too-familiar figure of Lucien Barteau— SOE code name, Gilbert. He had just closed the front door to Gestapo headquarters at Number 84 and was sauntering toward the wrought iron gate that led to the street. Viv could only stare, dumbfounded, as a kaleidoscope of images flashed before her eyes: the stunt pilot at the landing field in Manchester greeting her after her first and only parachute jump; the heart-pounding memory of Lucien grabbing her wrists in the kitchen of the safe house in Loyettes her first night back in France; Lucien nosing around Annecy, and now, here the bastard was in Paris, just as she was, a stone's throw from where the Jacksons had been taken. None of it could be a coincidence.

If agent Gilbert were leaving Number 84 under his own power and without an SS escort, clearly he had just met with the notorious Hans Kieffer whose methods of torture at the main Paris headquarters of the SS struck fear into every Resistance fighter, no matter how courageous. Kieffer had obviously ordered the Jacksons' every move followed and arrested them immediately after Dr. J's kindness led him to the flat on rue des Canettes. Clearly, Barteau had offered to help Kieffer hunt down Marcel—and her as well. The arrest of the Jacksons could only mean Marcel and Viv were probably next.

Every impulse in her body called out to attack Lucien Barteau with her bare hands. Instead, she stood frozen in Adrienne's uniform, straddling a borrowed bicycle and stared at his back while the double agent sauntered down Avenue Foch in the opposite direction.

Lucien has betrayed us all. Kieffer knows everything. None of us is safe in Paris for another second...

———◇———

Viv sat on the bed where Marcel had lain for weeks regaining both his strength and the full use of his left leg, now nearly healed of the bullet wound. She watched in silence as he swiftly threw his few belongings into his haversack, his face grim at the thoughts she imagined were whirling in his head—including the treachery of Lucien Barteau that she had witnessed with her own eyes. Per their SOE training, they had to split up, but where should they each go next? And how to convincingly inform SOE brass in London of the nefarious actions taken by the double agent who clearly had been the cause of an avalanche of SOE and Free French arrests in Paris and throughout France?

"But *why* is Barteau doing this?" Viv exclaimed suddenly. "This is *his* country!"

Without looking at her, Marcel spit back an answer.

"Greed. Recklessness. Narcissism. Loyalty only to himself. All the qualities that made him a foolhardy stunt pilot in a second-rate air circus before the war." Marcel threw Viv's pistol into the pouch with vehemence, his own weapon having been seized when he was arrested by Klaus Barbie's men in Lyon. "I warned them! I warned them all, both the Free French and the head of SOE's French Section. But no! The bastard could fly a plane and speak English and German, and that was all it took to land him in the crucial slot of Air Operations Officer! *Merde, merde MERDE!*"

"Where are you going to go?" Viv demanded.

"Anywhere they won't catch you and Adrienne in my company," he retorted, fastening the buckles on his canvas bag with a tug. "And you should immediately do the same for Adrienne's sake. Leave this flat *today*!"

"What if Dr. Jackson or Toquette have already been tortured and revealed that you and I are in Paris?"

"I wouldn't blame them if they gave us up, given the methods of the SS goons. Another reason for you to leave, *now*!"

"What if Barteau has told Kieffer about your special assignments for de Gaulle—"

Viv halted mid-sentence as Marcel gave her a warning look.

"I'm sure he has. But look, Viv, you and I have been trained what to do if the worst happens. If you're caught, try not to spill any information to the SS for at least forty-eight hours to give other agents the chance to blow Paris. If it gets really bad with Barteau's friends at Avenue Foch or anywhere else, you know the other remedy."

The L pill...

Viv's stomach turned over. Marcel slung the haversack's strap over his shoulder.

"So that's *it*?" Viv exclaimed, wondering how much of this conversation Adrienne was overhearing. "Roger, over-and-out?"

Marcel paused. "The sooner I leave, the safer you'll be. I can't stop to say the things I'd like to, Viv. This is *real* war, not a pretend spy school exercise. Try to stay safe until the invasion. Meanwhile, I'll be busy blowing up bridges and railway connectors to keep the Germans from heading where the invasion lands. And after," he added with a sardonic expression, "if we make it, we'll have to assess what's left of our world. At this moment, your safest bet is to try to persuade the hospital or the Red Cross to take you on as an ambulance driver or medical volunteer. Hide in plain sight."

Viv recalled Nurse Elizabeth asking Viv to make herself scarce at the American Hospital, but she couldn't tell Marcel that. What choices were left?

"And how long do you expect it to be before the invasion occurs?" Viv asked, her own emotions of fear, regret, and anger at the situation, along with Marcel's all-business attitude channeled into the lump in her throat.

Marcel took a step toward her.

"Soon..." He paused. "As in...early next month."

"June?" Viv said, shocked. "That's in *two* weeks!

The corner of his lips displayed a familiar twitch. "You didn't hear that."

"I've heard it all before," she retorted, "just not that specifically. *Where* is this supposed to happen? How near Paris?"

"Can't and won't tell you, and besides...who knows if my information is still operative?" He leaned forward, framed her face in his hands, and kissed her hard. "I've got to go. By this time, you know what wins between love and duty during a war."

Viv closed her eyes, her hands resting on his shoulders.

"I know and I hate it," she whispered.

"Then, don't say *adieu*," he urged, his forefinger pressed against her lips, his voice both gentle and gruff. "We'll just say *à bientôt*."

In contrast to his kiss, she brushed her lips lightly against his,

392 | CIJI WARE

consciously imprinting the feeling of Marcel's presence in her memory bank.

"*À bientôt mon amour,*" she murmured.

I'll see you soon, my love…

But would they, ever? She watched him turn and walk out of the bedroom. Viv's feet remained rooted to the floor as she listened to him say a hasty farewell to Adrienne, who was standing in a state of shock in the kitchen. It was all happening so fast. The front door to the flat opened and shut. She listened to Marcel's footsteps echoing down the stone steps. Running to the window overlooking the courtyard that led to rue des Canettes, she peered through the glass, but of course there'd be no last glimpse of the man she loved. He'd left through the basement and out the cellar door into an alleyway hidden from view.

Viv called to Adrienne as she pulled her knapsack from under the bed where she'd kept it stored. "I'm leaving too. No need for you to pay for our sins."

CHAPTER 61

Had the three men who were sent from 84 Avenue Foch arrived only ten minutes later the following morning, they would have found SOE agent "Violette Charbonnet" long gone.

Instead, a few minutes after 5 a.m., four sharp raps on the front door echoed through the flat. Viv was in the act of closing the Louis Vuitton cosmetic case that Adrienne had so carefully guarded for her return to Paris. She assumed immediately it was the SS.

Why *didn't I leave last night, right after Marcel?*

The answer, she knew, was that she'd been paralyzed with sadness and a sense of growing dread, to say nothing of the danger posed by leaving her building when the nighttime curfew was in full force. She was certain that Marcel's after-hours departure meant he faced almost certain peril on every Paris street corner.

She'd been awake nearly the entire night, convinced that Marcel's idea of her hiding in plain sight as an ambulance driver was a bad one—even if they gave her the job. The Jacksons had been apprehended by the very Paris Gestapo she was trying to avoid, and the hospital was probably under 24-hour surveillance.

Finally, as the spring sun rose and the bells of St. Sulpice rang out the early morning hour, Viv had decided her best move was to try and make her way back to Val d'Isère where she could wait out the invasion. The thought of sheltering with Jean-Paul and the Morand family in the clear, refreshing air of the Alps filled her with her first shred of hope after a long night of darkness and despair.

Now, the insistent pounding on the front door grew even louder. Viv walked across the main room sensing impending doom. The second she lifted the latch, three intruders pushed past, guns drawn.

Viv knew for a certainty, now, that the identity of two out of the three residents living on the third floor at rue des Canettes must have been confirmed by the concierge downstairs, thus matching Lucien Barteau's list of secret agents operating in France that he'd provided to Hans Kieffer. Thanks to Barteau's treachery, Kieffer's men had arrived at her door.

Two of the uniformed men barging into the flat were, indeed, SS. The third, who wore the black shirt of the dreaded French *milice,* jabbed his weapon into Viv's stomach.

"The tall redhead!" he declared triumphantly to his confederates. With a sneer at Viv he said, "They told us what to look for, and now we find you!"

Viv calculated that the French militia punk couldn't be more than twenty. Members of the *milice* like him were nothing more than a sadistic bunch of guttersnipes.

"You will come with us," ordered the SS officer who appeared to be in charge. His stocky build, ruddy complexion, and frontal baldness was set off by a pair of small, round eyes like marbles, giving him the look of a barnyard pig grunting out sentences in atrocious French.

Thinking quickly, Viv displayed a practiced, wide-eyed attitude of confusion and naiveté.

"Why are you arresting me?" she asked. She tried made her New York-ese more pronounced as she spoke to them in inferior French. "I'm just here in Paris visiting my friend. I've done nothing wrong, and neither has she!"

"That is not the information we have," he said gruffly, grabbing her arm while motioning to the punk to put his gun away. "You are an American *spy*. An enemy of the Third Reich!"

Viv forced her voice up a notch and offered a schoolgirl whine. "Yes, I am an American, but good Lord, I'm no *spy*! I came to Paris to try to find my mother, who was put into an internment camp for British aliens. I haven't seen her in three years and—"

"Shut up, bitch!" yelled the *milice*, slapping Viv hard across the face. In seconds, blood spurted from her nose and dribbled over her lips onto her chin.

Looking highly annoyed at the punk usurping his command, the SS officer with beady eyes pulled out a handkerchief and handed it to Viv. Then he nodded to his uniformed colleague. "Start your search of the flat." He ordered the *milice* to stand guard at the door "in case the women make a run for it," although Viv figured the officer was just trying to keep the kid from causing more of a scene. He pointed to Adrienne, who had come to the door of the bedroom in her nightclothes.

"You, too. Get dressed," he said. "Let's go!"

"She's *Swiss*!" Viv protested, her dismay genuine as she tilted back her head and pinched her nose with the cloth to try to stop her bleeding. "A former school friend. She merely let me stay in her flat until I could locate where my mother is."

The officer gripped Viv's arm even tighter.

"You can tell those lies to the gentlemen on Avenue Foch," he said, his look hard and uncompromising. "Where's Victor Fernique? Or should I say Marcel Delonge? Still asleep in your bed?"

"Who?" she exclaimed indignantly. "There's no *man* here! How dare you?"

Fighting her panic, Viv gestured with her other hand in the direction of her cosmetic case sitting on the bed in the bedroom. Her knapsack, already cleared of incriminating evidence, was hanging on the bedroom doorknob, positioned for her planned departure. Her interrogator roughly pushed her toward the front door.

"Please sir," she begged like a deprived teenager. "I have all my make-up in the case and some clothes. My American passport is in my pack. Can't I *please* take them with me? That way, I can explain everything to the authorities."

The other German soldier appeared to be the opposite of his SS colleague. Handsome, dark-haired, with a pale complexion, he was dressed in an immaculately tailored uniform. Viv gazed at him with pleading cow eyes.

"Oh, all right, get your things, then," he relented as evidence that her pose as a whining dimwit had been reasonably convincing. To his superior officer he said, "They'll both be searched at 84, and Kieffer's men will decide about all this."

The SS whose round head and close-set eyes made him *cochon comme*—pig like—merely grunted his assent.

Viv and Adrienne scurried into the bedroom. Viv whispered a desperate apology for involving her friend while trying to staunch the blood flowing from her nose.

"When they find out I work at the Swiss embassy, they'll let me go," Adrienne replied under her breath. "It's you I'm worried about."

While Adrienne dressed, Viv donned her warm *Canadienne*, the L pill now resting in the lining of her coat where she'd inserted it the previous evening. Her nose had stopped bleeding by the time she swung her knapsack over her shoulder and made a grab for her cosmetic case filled with the last lipstick and face powder she owned, along with a woolen scarf, sweater, and a blouse lining the bottom.

Recalling her trip from Athens in 1939 with the Louis Vuitton luggage in tow, her life had grimly come full circle.

———◇———

Viv would have given anything for Fingers Malloy to be able to wire London laying bare the terrible extent of Lucien Barteau's betrayal of the Special Operations Executive agents. Upon arrival at 84 Avenue Foch, Viv's knapsack and elaborate cosmetic case had promptly been taken away from her, and she was soon shut into a narrow room on the top floor, with Adrienne shoehorned into the chamber next door.

Viv leaned her back against the wall and gazed through a

window that generations of upstairs parlor maids housed in the formerly elegant townhouse had no doubt stared out of at the rooftops of Paris. Despite her warm coat, the bleak, gray sky gave her chills. Instinctively, she searched all her pockets for anything that might belie the story she was busy concocting of a naïve, rather dim-witted young woman, bent on escaping the internment that had been her mother's fate. She would maintain that she'd bolted from Paris in 1942 to wander about in various ski resorts in the Free Zone.

Her hand felt something in her right pocket. She withdrew a packet of matches from a café known for hosting meetings of *résistants* in its back rooms—a café she'd never been in. One of the SS had obviously slipped "evidence" into her coat to justify her arrest.

Merde!" she muttered, looking for a place to hide the matchbook that, if found, would incriminate her. Fortunately, there were only a few paper matches left, so, as they'd taught at spy school, she carefully chewed them, along with the paper cover case, and swallowed the lot, leaving a strong taste of sulphur on her tongue. Then...she waited.

———◇———

To her shock and dismay, Viv was left in this same small room for ten days. Her guards would shove a bowl of watery soup and a crust of bread through the half-opened door at night and undrinkable coffee and bread in the morning.

She spent her days of silence creating a narrative to account for her last years in wartime France and found herself reflecting on what a lonely life it had been. Now, suddenly, it had ended. No more looking over her shoulder or stopping to let people behind her pass by so she could get through a checkpoint hidden in a crowd. No more suddenly changing trains to avoid being followed or huddling in dirty waiting rooms so as not to be caught on the streets during curfew.

But now that she *was* caught, she felt desperately tired. Her eyelids grew heavy as she mulled over her cover story. Her one encouraging thought was that as long as Lucien Barteau didn't appear in person at Number 84 to confirm she was, indeed, an Allied secret agent sent behind enemy lines, she had a chance...

———◇———

"I didn't want to be interned like my mother!" Viv insisted shrilly to the two men in the interrogation room the first week in June. "When I heard she'd been arrested, I just took a train and left Paris, I swear!"

"Nonsense!" her bald-headed interrogator spat. "We know you are a spy! We found fake French documents and your American passport in your possessions."

"I had no French documents!" she protested. "*Just* my American passport."

Like the matchbook that had been slipped into her coat pocket, some SS flunky had planted forged documents in her knapsack. They were now displayed on a table in front of her near a young French woman at a small desk who was dutifully typing each word of her interview with Officer Piggy—as Viv had decided to call her SS 'minder.'

Behind a larger and far more impressive mahogany desk sat a well-dressed man in civilian clothes who sat listening but said nothing. This was presumably SS-man Hans Kieffer's 'persuader.'" He had the broad shoulders of a prizefighter dressed in a pinstriped suit. His silvery-blond hair was slicked back off his high forehead and parted on the right side. Viv kept up her whiny tone of voice, sticking to her story, and repeating its basic tenets so often that the man behind the desk and the typist both kept glancing at their watches. She could only hope Lucien Barteau was occupied with his role as SOE Air Operations Officer and was no longer in Paris to prove she was an audacious liar.

"You couldn't have just been wandering around France since 1942," scoffed her original captor.

"I was skiing, mostly," Viv said, buffing her nails on her jacket sleeve in a gesture she hoped appeared nonchalant. She smiled prettily. "Actually, I'm a crack skier, if you must know. If the war hadn't started, I was going to try out for the Olympics."

"*Skiing*? For three years during a war? *Where*?" he demanded.

Viv was loath to mention Dr. Jean-Paul Morand or Val d'Isère, lest they send someone to check out her story. Instead, she ticked off the names of all the ski resorts she'd frequented in the last ten years of living in Europe, describing each one with glowing enthusiasm.

"I stayed quite a lot of the time in Chamonix," she said with girlish gusto. "The ski instructors there are so...well...handsome, you know."

"And how did you pay for this endless holiday?" Piggy demanded skeptically.

Thinking of Jean-Paul and the children he'd saved, Viv answered the question with the first thing that popped into her head.

"One of them gave me a job teaching the little ones to ski," she lied. She looked down at her clasped hands as if embarrassed. "He even let me stay in his chalet for an entire year until he got called up to work in Germany."

That would account for one of the three years in question, she thought with a small sense of triumph, *with no masculine benefactor available for questioning.*

The well-dressed man behind the desk slammed his hand on its polished surface.

"This is getting us nowhere," he declared to Piggy in German, although Viv didn't let on she understood every word. "She's at least telling the truth about her mother," he added, pointing to a file on his desk. "I have the records of Pamela Vivier-Clarke—now Mrs. Karl Bradford—interned at Vittel." He shot his porky colleague a warning glance. "This woman's mother is a Brit with an American daughter, 'whereabouts unknown,' it says here. Most of what she says matches up. The Bradford woman was recently released earlier this spring on orders of some higher-ups in Berlin and is no longer in Paris, so if I were you," he warned, "I'd be careful about this one. She may have important connections." He waved his well-manicured hand in Viv's direction. "I'm due for lunch. Send her back to her cell. Either you get more information to prove the accusations she's a spy—or release her, do you hear me? We can't afford to feed and house every over-indulged waif that our source accuses of being a spy." He glared at Piggy. "Stop wasting my time with matters like these, do you understand?"

"But our double agent says—"

"I've never trusted the man," was the reply. "My bet is the bastard just wanted to get paid for bogus information. I deal with these shysters every day." He rose from the desk. "Meanwhile, let us not forget that *you* let de Gaulle's man slip through your fingers and spent all your valuable time on this nonsense. *This* woman and her Swiss friend are nobodies. Their cases obviously should have been handled by the regular army *Wehrmacht* staff, not ours. I have no time to sort all this out. Have you *any* idea what's going on in Normandy this morning? Thousands of Allied troops have landed, and they're headed toward Paris!"

And with that, he stomped out of the interrogation room.

Viv's ears rang with the wonderful news that the invasion had apparently occurred as Marcel had predicted on the beaches 285 kilometers to the north of Paris. A very out-of-sorts Piggy promptly ordered her to stand at attention in the interrogation room, now abandoned by his disgusted superior. The SS functionary had his fat fingers on the handle of her Louis Vuitton cosmetic case.

"Oh, please, can't I have it back?" Viv begged in French, her deliberate New York accent discordant to her own ears. Recalling the old trick she'd pulled in Marseille with the American embassy minion, Roger Gianakos, she whined, "The case has my sanitary napkins in it and I'm...ah...well, you know...about to get my monthly."

Piggy angrily slammed the case onto his desk, opened it, and ordered Viv to take out her "necessaries." She swiftly dumped the contents on the cardigan she'd packed and wrapped her woolen scarf around everything like a hobo with his pack. Officer Piggy slammed the case shut and instructed the secretary to make out a receipt stamped with a black swastika. The young woman did as she was told and gave the scrap of paper to Viv, who tucked it into the pocket of her *Canadienne*, feeling, as she habitually did, for the single L capsule snuggled deep inside the inner lining.

The arresting officer sounded spiteful. "You won't get your fancy case back until you're cleared of all charges, or served your time," adding with a truculent look. "But don't worry, we've made a record."

So German of you... Viv fumed, watching the case being stowed beneath the secretary's desk. *I have a worthless receipt and this slut will be rewarded with my cosmetic case!*

Within minutes, she was marched downstairs and shoved into a straw-filled room off the townhouse's back courtyard. There she found Adrienne talking to an overly made-up woman whom Viv assumed to be a prostitute. Propped against one wall nearby leaned an older couple in handcuffs. A few minutes later, the door opened and a woman, soaked to the skin and very pregnant, was roughly shoved in and fell to the floor, sobbing. Her teeth were chattering and she was trembling head-to-toe.

The prostitute bent over and held her hand. "Why are your clothes wet, dear? What did they do to you?"

"P-Pushed my h-head under the w-water," she stammered. "I had no idea what they want from me. I have no answers to give them!" She began to sob inconsolably. "They nearly drowned me! They took my husband away…but *where*?" She clutched her stomach and cried even harder. "I have no idea what they think he did. Our poor b-baby… What will happen to our *baby*?"

Viv looked at Adrienne and thought she'd be sick. The training and play-acting of German interrogation techniques learned in Scotland told Viv this was only the beginning. Within the hour, they were shoved into separate rooms once more. Then, as the days droned on, she heard screams and moans nearby, but no one came to her door.

CHAPTER 62

Viv surmised that it had to be late June by the time she and Adrienne were loaded into the back of a canvas covered truck parked at the rear of 84 Avenue Foch.

"Fresnes," croaked the prostitute they'd seen earlier, climbing in after them. "That's where they're taking us."

Viv and Adrienne exchanged looks. Fresnes was the notorious prison a few miles outside Paris where "undesirables" had been locked up ever since the 1880s. Viv tried to maintain her deadpan expression as more detainees climbed into the truck. Word had spread like wildfire that some sort of Allied operation had, indeed, occurred on French shores June the 6th, but no one seemed to know where, exactly, it had taken place and if it was a success.

Sitting near the canvas opening at the back of the truck, all Viv and Adrienne could see were SS soldiers scurrying around carrying stacks of file boxes out of Number 84 and either burning paper in a back-courtyard bonfire or loading the boxes into canvas-covered trucks like the one that was taking prisoners out of Paris.

"I think the invasion was in Normandy," Viv whispered to Adrienne, who'd finally been able to get word to the Swiss embassy requesting her release, but no reply as yet.

"Normandy is a long way from Paris," Adrienne whispered back glumly. "I, for one, don't want to be the last prisoner shipped out to God-knows-where in Germany if this damn thing is actually winding to a close."

Viv was awash with guilt, knowing that bringing Marcel to Adrienne's doorstep was the reason her friend was also going to prison. If only she had left when Marcel had, she agonized. If she hadn't wallowed in her own misery that night, things might have been different now. The prospects now looked bleaker that she'd be released any time soon. The Germans occupying Paris were now in a state of chaos preparing their departure, which made things even more dangerous for anyone under their control.

It was past five o'clock in the afternoon when they arrived at Fresnes, passing through huge iron gates set between high walls crowned with jagged glass. Viv was allowed to keep her coat and woolen sweater, but a female guard appropriated Viv's knapsack and snatched her Piaget watch off her wrist as soon as she walked into the reception area. Thanks to German efficiency, Piggy had apparently sent her cosmetic case along, for it was on a shelf behind the desk, and soon joined by Viv's most recently confiscated possessions.

"At least our friend in the truck told us there's running water," Viv said, trying to sound upbeat. "She said each cell has a straw mattress, a chair, and a slop pail with a spigot over it."

"That's probably why Fresnes has such a sterling reputation for being the most modern prison in France!" Adrienne replied snidely. With an air of embarrassment she added, "When I asked the admitting woman to please check with the Swiss embassy in Paris, she actually said she would and that I should be released in a day or two because I'm a neutral." She leaned closer to Viv's ear. "The Germans want to get rid of as many of us as possible before the Allies lay siege to Paris."

"Let us hope so, but how did you explain my presence with you on rue des Canettes?" asked Viv under her breath.

"I told them that you begged me to take you in with your latest boyfriend, and I did it because you were a friend" Adrienne explained. "I said the guy was also American who dumped you just before the SS boys showed up and that I knew nothing about anything."

"You were lucky they didn't decide to hold your head underwater for five minutes like that poor pregnant woman," Viv replied.

Adrienne shrugged. "And especially lucky for me that you and Marcel were like sphinxes. Thank God, you hardly told me anything."

Thank God, indeed, thought Viv. *We might have just saved your life. But what about ours…?*

———◇———

Viv had reason to remember the exchange with Adrienne when the prisoners in Fresnes whispered messages through the open spigot and pipes in the middle of the night. They confirmed that Allied forces had, indeed, landed some 156,000 troops on the beaches of Normandy. Each night more news filtered in that the Americans were battling their way toward Paris, with General Charles de Gaulle leading the way with the other generals.

"Liberation" was whispered each day, but time crawled and the food became scarcer. Often prisoners were given just a hunk of bread that had to last a day along with thin soup that had a tiny portion of vegetables and grease floating on the top. Inmates "on the pipeline" included political prisoners like Viv, along with black marketers, thieves, whores, and "imbeciles" talking to themselves.

The news whispered down the line was that the Russians were advancing westward. Viv and some of the other women prisoners considered low risk were allowed to promenade in the interior court a few times a week. One morning, the two tall entrance gates swung open to admit several trucks full of newcomers. Men shuffled out the back of one truck carrying parcels and battered suitcases with their belongings.

As with every batch of new arrivals, Viv scanned the bent, disheveled captives stumbling out of the canvas-covered trucks. On this day, her breath caught as she realized it was Marcel shuffling, head down, one hand holding up his beltless trousers, his battered haversack slung over his shoulder. He'd aged years in the few weeks since she'd last seen him. In shock, she halted her circular walk and the woman trailing behind bumped into her.

"Watch it, bitch!" the prisoner snarled, but Viv could only stumble forward. She wanted to reach out, to seize his hand, but realized she didn't dare for both their sakes. She wondered how long he'd been in Gestapo custody this time, for he was at least twenty pounds under weight with one eye blackened and completely shut.

Oh, God, Marcel...what horrible things have they done to you?

Another part of her brain whispered what felt like a potential betrayal of him.

No one must realize we know each other...

The knowledge that she knew—let alone loved—de Gaulle's deputy meant certain death if anyone at Fresnes learned she'd been a fellow Resistance fighter and companion of the arrested Marcel Delonge.

Just then, Marcel raised his head and their eyes met. He gave the tiniest negative shake of his head and limped into the reception area where Viv knew he'd be searched once again and shoved into a cell.

The rest of the day was anguish for Viv. She didn't dare to send a message to him through the pipeline communication system. The only way either of them had any chance of survival was to keep quiet "until liberation," as the prison mantra went.

"If only the Americans would get here!" a disembodied voice croaked in the dead of night.

"Amen to that," came the answer from an anonymous someone down the line.

Each day the prison cells with windows offered a view of the frantic efforts by their captors to remove all incriminating evidence from their prison files documenting the black arts they'd practiced on their captives. Bonfires of records were held in the courtyard, and more trucks began to cart away the paperwork for which German functionaries were so infamous.

And then began prisoners' nightly whispers of the names of those to be shot the following day.

Two nights after Marcel's arrival, Viv heard echoing softly down the spigot above her cell's slop pail, "Xavier Belmont... Antoine Albertville... Marcel Delonge... Louis Moreau..."

All to be shot at dawn.

Viv sank down on her straw mattress in the corner on the floor and covered her face with both hands. Her body began to tremble.

Not Marcel! Not tomorrow...not with liberation possibly so near...

That terrible night, the news echoed down the rusty iron pipe that "de Gaulle's man, too" was, indeed, to face a firing squad. Viv lay on her back, staring at the ceiling with its black mold clinging to each corner. Her thoughts turned to the L pill safely sewn into the lining of her *Canadienne* that she wore to bed each night for warmth. If Marcel was shot, she supposed it would be the noble thing to take it. It would put an end to this torture, to the memory of what the morning would bring that was bound to haunt her forever. Crushing it between her teeth would prove their bond was their love for each other and their mutual love of France. But in the next moment, her thoughts folded over on themselves. Surrendering her life while there was still a breath to be drawn would seem to give the Nazis a victory. At length, she admitted that she couldn't take the lethal dose unless it was to prevent her from spilling what she knew about others whom the SS would then kill.

As the morning light crept into her cell, Viv heard the guards shouting at one another the names of the four prisoners about to be escorted from their cells into the courtyard below. Viv rushed to peer out her minuscule window in time to see a quartet of human shadows, surrounded by their jailors, marched across the stone pavers, through the tall iron gates, and pushed roughly into the back of a ubiquitous dirty-green truck. Within seconds, it disappeared around the corner.

Viv knew that if she listened intently, she would hear the volley of shots that always rang out from the nearby wood where the convicted stood at the edge of an open pit, awaiting the firing squad to let loose its fuselage of bullets. Viv braced for the barrage she knew would come.

Rat-a-tat-tat-tat-tat-tat-tat...

The staccato killing sounds reverberated against her cell's solitary window. Viv wrapped the fingers of each hand around two of the rusted bars and sank her forehead against the edge of the sill, wails rising to her throat from the pit of her despair.

Suddenly, the water pipe above the slop pail began to vibrate with loud shouts instead of whispers. Numbed by the tide of grief that was sweeping over her, she stumbled the few steps across her cell and threw herself down on the straw mattress. A foot away, the sounds echoing out of the spigot soon became a thunderous roar streaming from the metal piping.

"Invasion! Invasion in *southern* France!"

Another voice cried, "Normandy and now—Antibes and Cannes, too! A *second* invasion!"

"*Ils ont débarqué en Normandie et Nice!*"

"They have finally landed, north and south," Viv whispered to her cell walls—but she felt no joy. From the marks she'd carved in the wall with her spoon, she knew it was August 18, 1944. Apparently, a second Allied invasion had landed that week on the beaches between Nice and Toulon.

"There's to be a final pincer push," disclosed an excited informant, the voice bellowing through the pipe. "The two forces will drive the Nazis east—out of France!"

Around Viv, all hell was breaking loose. Rising up from the men's block were shouts of triumph, female shrieks from her side. The beating of spoons on tin bowls began. It was deafening, and the guards could do nothing to stop it. Cascading off the prison's stonewalls was the pent-up emotion of four years of terror and repression, along with the opening strains of France's national anthem, the *Marseillaise,* ringing out, thin and uncertain at first. Within seconds it grew stronger and stronger, the musical notes being sung, now, full throated, bouncing off the walls in joyous, off-key splendor. The swelling tide of melody floated toward where the truck, just returning from its latest assignment, was now parked, its motor running, poised for another journey to the Gestapo killing fields in a forest close to Fresnes itself.

406 | CIJI WARE

Marcel... Marcel...you can't die on this day, Viv's heart cried out. *Not on this, of all days...*

But she could almost see his thin, lanky frame crumpled in an open pit, his body desecrated with bullet holes, his dark blue beret soaked with blood on the very day that everyone who was still alive in France would treasure forever.

Everyone but her.

PART VI
CHAPTER 63

August 1944

The end of the war for Viv arrived in a fashion she could never have predicted. For the week following Marcel's removal from the prison and his execution, she refused all food and stayed as far from the water spigot as she could. She felt incapable of listening to the joyous, jubilant whispers that the last of the Nazis were beginning to pack up and depart Paris ahead of the Allied liberating forces that reportedly were fast approaching the city. She fought waves of guilt every time she donned her coat, aware the L pill remained sewn in the lining. She wanted to die but didn't have the fortitude—or the will—to liberate the capsule and squeeze it between her back teeth.

A few days after Marcel was murdered, Viv's cell door banged open, and Officer Piggy filled the threshold.

"Interrogation!" he grunted, but he was strangely subdued. "Come! Now!"

Instead of a lumbering truck like the one that carted prisoners to their doom, a black Citroën was parked in the courtyard. The woman Viv knew who had been jailed practicing the oldest profession in the world was pushed into the back seat next to her.

"What are you being judged for?" the woman asked.

"Judged?" Viv repeated, confused. "Are we to be judged today?" A stab of fear made her catch her breath.

"I was caught pilfering a soldier's cigarettes who had slept with me and then giving him the wrong directions on the Metro." The woman smiled, a missing tooth undermining its effect. "I was always very clever at it, carefully explaining all the wrong train changes."

For the first time in months, Viv felt like laughing.

"Clever you!" she complimented her companion under her breath so Piggy in the front seat beside the driver wouldn't hear such blasphemy.

She gazed out the car window as familiar streets rolled by, expecting to be taken back to 84 Avenue Foch—or someplace worse. Instead, she saw that they had turned into the stately solitude of the rue Boissy d'Anglais in the Eighth Arrondissment. The car halted in front of a large public building flying a swastika and guarded by sentries. Across the street was the elegant Hotel Crillon. Viv sucked in a gulp of air. Nearby was the abandoned American Embassy.

As she and the prostitute were hustled past the sentries, Viv noticed that they weren't wearing the black-and-silver tabs of the SS. They were *Wehrmacht*—regular German Army soldiers. Officer Piggy appeared and ordered both his charges to take seats on a polished wooden bench. Raising his arm in the despised salute, he turned to face a chubby soldier hunched over a typewriter and declared, "Heil Hitler!" and departed.

"That's our guard?" giggled Viv's companion-in-crime whose name turned out to be Juliette. She inclined her head toward the male typist.

"It would seem so," Viv whispered back.

Viv appraised their otherwise deserted, grand marble surroundings. She began to wonder if she could simply bolt down the corridor and make an escape. Before she could come up with a plan, the phone rang on the soldier's desk, and soon she was being escorted through a door into an office furnished with a thick carpet on the floor, a glass-fronted bookcase, and two eighteenth century tapestry-upholstered armchairs positioned in front of a large walnut desk. Behind this sat an earnest-looking young man, an officer wearing the uniform of Germany's regular Army.

"So *you* are the American," he greeted her pleasantly.

There was no yelling. No barking orders. Viv was shocked speechless.

———◇———

Major Johann Ziegler, as his desk plate verified, was of medium stature with a thin face, conventional features, and the air of a soldier intent on doing a decent job conducting the unappetizing tasks to which he'd been assigned.

He continued to regard Viv with a curious gaze as he declared, "The Gestapo has turned you over to me. I'm a judge attached to the legal section of our army." He glanced down at a file. "Good heavens! What a rather amazing list of accusations they made against you." Reading from the papers in front of him, he recited, "*Résistant*... parachutist...spy...in possession of false identity." He looked up. "Are you Jewish?"

"No, Episcopalian," Viv managed to reply, dumbfounded by his polite demeanor.

He regarded her across the desk and smiled. "Well, I'm glad for that."

Viv deliberately slouched in her chair and summoned her practiced, slow-witted comportment that she hoped would dissuade anyone from believing that she was clever enough to be an SOE secret agent. An actual spy could be executed immediately, without a trial or messy paperwork.

She plastered a befuddled expression on her face and responded, "Why would anyone think I'd parachute into *this* country from England? If I'd been in London, believe me, sir, I'd have *stayed* there."

"Ah...quite sensible of you," he murmured, scanning the second page of her alleged sins against the Third Reich. "But why didn't you go to Vittel with your mother?" he asked, looking puzzled. "It was once a luxurious spa. No one ever complained about being sent there that *I've* heard."

Viv cast her eyes down to her hands folded in her lap.

"My mother and I...well...we didn't always get along, you know?" She looked up to meet his gaze. "And besides, the idea of being behind barbed wire, even at a nice spa, frightened me. I had money in those days, so I just decided to go visit the various ski resorts I remembered from my childhood in Europe."

The officer nodded, as if indicating that what she was saying matched the file. A flicker of a smile broke out on his scrubbed face.

"Did you know that a Red Cross ambulance driver vouched for you?" Viv shook her head in genuine astonishment. "A very charming lady, *Frau* Benedict of the Red Cross. She told me you're *incapable* of doing all the things you are accused of. She said… uh…how shall I put this? She found you a rather undisciplined American."

Viv could barely keep from laughing out loud. "They d-didn't let me drive for very long," she lied in a deliberate stammer, praying the Benedict connection wouldn't prompt Ziegler to investigate her time at the hospital.

It was lucky, Viv realized, that the disagreeable Nurse Beverly Benedict who had been her superior in the ambulance corps had judged Viv to be the "rather" self-centered young miss she actually was back then. Maintaining her familiar pose as a dumb-as-a-post expatriate, Viv nodded meekly. Her spirits were buoyed to think that the old epithet her mother and Karl had often flung at her—'spoiled brat!'—was the very thing that might save her now. Given the Official Secrets Act, none of her old acquaintances would ever know how totally her life—and her character—had changed in the years since joining SOE. She thought of Marcel and all he had taught her about what she was capable of…and the necessity, at times, of putting the needs of others ahead of her own.

Feeling the onset of familiar pangs of grief, she pushed the thought of Marcel to the far corners of her mind and concentrated on convincing this seemingly decent young soldier of a defeated German Army that she was innocent of the charges against her.

"You may eventually be sent from Fresnes to Vittel," Ziegler advised her. "You have only a few days more to serve on the charge of possessing a false French identity card."

"But that card was planted on me!" she countered. "You must have seen my valid American passport. The French ID was obviously a fake. Why would I think it would protect me?" she demanded.

He pointed to a medium-sized envelope. "Your passport is right here, but may I suggest, such an *insignificant* charge of a false identity card now allows me to… uh… order that you be released from imprisonment within two weeks." He paused, adding, "If the hostilities here in France come to an end before that, as they soon might, I'll recommend they release you forthwith." He smiled, as if waiting for her agreement that this was a better solution than staying stuck in Fresnes Prison for the duration.

"I see," Viv said, pouting a bit as if trying to fathom what he'd just said. "Tidy paperwork and all that. And what of my friend, Adrienne Vaud, who was arrested with me? I haven't seen her in ages. Do you know if she has to remain in Fresnes?"

"*Mein Gott*, absolutely not!" he exclaimed. "She's *Swiss* and therefore a neutral," he continued, as if imparting this news to Viv. "Someone from her embassy learned of her whereabouts. Once your claims of why you two were together in that flat on rue des Canettes checked out to our satisfaction, we released her weeks ago." He pointed to papers on his desk. "It says here that she was immediately repatriated to her country."

"Well, thank heaven for that," Viv murmured, wondering if Adrienne and she would ever cross paths again.

Out of the corner of her eye, Viv noticed stacks of legal file boxes on a long, polished wooden table that she assumed were being prepared for transport back to Germany. Her present conference clearly had interrupted the project. As if to confirm this, Ziegler rose from his chair, smiling, charming, benevolent—and extended his hand.

"I'm afraid I now must get back to my work. Goodbye, miss...and good luck," he said, smiling politely. "I'll have the proper documents sent to Fresnes this afternoon." With a wistful look he added, "I expect you'll be back in America, soon."

Viv seized his soft, pliant hand and shook it firmly.

Assuming the look of a true penitent, she replied, "You've been very kind, sir. I behaved stupidly after the war started." Eyeing his packing boxes, she added, "The best of luck to you, too," wondering what tales of tragedy were contained within the cardboard.

Officer Piggy was waiting at the curb outside to drive her back to Fresnes Prison. Juliette, the young prostitute who'd stolen a pack of cigarettes, apparently had been released, as Viv was now alone in the Citroën's roomy back seat.

As she exited the car in the prison courtyard, Piggy grunted, "Released soon, they tell me. *Gut!*" Then he added plaintively in his atrocious French, "Don't think too badly of us, will you?"

Viv's stomach turned over on itself as she remembered being viciously slapped across the face by the black-shirted *milice* the day Piggy arrested her. Without answering his outrageous plea for forgiveness, she marched toward the prison entrance and within minutes, was locked up once more in her cell.

Two days later, the Commandant—his office crowded with file boxes like the ones she'd seen in Major Ziegler's office—turned out to be the person tasked to bid her a final farewell.

"I've received a new order for you."

Viv's felt panicked. Were they overriding the judge advocate and sending her into the local woods to be shot, like Marcel?

"But—"

"The decision was made to release you now, here in Paris."

Viv couldn't believe her ears. The Commandant frowned. "The *Wehrmacht* recognizes that we can no longer supply food or expensive transport for minor criminals like you." He waved his hand dismissively. "Since your prison term is almost up anyway, you are free to go."

Months of privation and degradation, and poof! 'You're free to go'?

Viv tried to process the true meaning of the Commandant's words. So the Germans were departing Paris *post haste*, she marveled. That must mean that the Allies had already pushed their way southeast from Normandy! She could only stare at her jailor, his pale blue eyes gleaming at her through rimless glasses. To Viv, he almost looked as if he were petitioning *her* for a favor.

"It's not easy, you should know, administering a place as decrepit as this," he complained. "Compared to German prisons, this French one is a disgrace. But we can only do what we can do," he added.

Absorbing the stupefying hypocrisy of his comment, Viv was once again rendered incapable of speaking. Her captors had done absolutely nothing but starve and torture the inmates at Fresnes before either executing them, like Marcel, or shipping them east by cattle car to Germany to face further incarceration and horrors yet unknown.

Thinking of the battered condition Marcel was in when he'd first arrived in the courtyard, a stone's throw from where she now stood,

Viv suppressed a wave of boiling rage that nearly choked her. All she could see in her mind's eye was a vision of Charles de Gaulle's emaciated deputy who'd heroically overseen networks of French partisans, being marched out of this hellhole to his death by firing squad.

As Viv gripped the edge of the Commandant's desk to calm the fury churning in her chest, he handed her a sheaf of release papers, saying simply, "Please sign here and then you may leave." He smiled thinly. "Here is your American passport. I've even provided my driver to convey you wherever you wish to be taken in Paris."

Reaching for the treasured document, Viv struggled to maintain a measured tone. "Your receptionist assumed possession of my gold watch the day I arrived here. I'd like to have it back, please," she said, "along with my canvas knapsack and Louis Vuitton cosmetic case?" She dug into her coat pocket and produced the swastika-stamped receipt for the luggage. "I assume it was stowed here somewhere by the arresting officer."

"Of course."

Snapping his fingers, the Commandant barked an order for his secretary to retrieve the confiscated belongings.

After Viv signed her release papers, she didn't wait to be dismissed. She merely nodded, turned on her heel, and exited his office, waiting outside his door until one of his minions delivered her battered knapsack and cosmetic case…but no gold watch.

"I am so sorry, *m-mademoiselle*," stuttered the Commandant's underling. "I looked everywhere downstairs, but I couldn't find it. I realize you must be eager to leave, but if you provide me an address, we can try to—"

"Believe me, I *am* anxious to leave," she snapped, "but thanks to you Germans, I have nowhere to go."

She knew she would never see her Piaget again. She turned and marched out the prison's door and stood in the hot August sunshine. In the distance, she detected the first, faint rumbles of bombs and artillery exploding. By the sound of it, the Allies had to be close to the outskirts of Paris. Earlier in the week, whispers spoken through the pipes had predicted a partisan uprising was planned even before Allied troops entered the city, so perhaps that was what she was hearing.

Her eyes drifted to a line of simple wooden coffins neatly stacked against the courtyard wall. Whoever was lying inside—be they German casualties or partisan victims of the Nazi regime—the even rows of caskets were neatly labeled and readied for removal, along with the remaining vestiges of the German occupation of Paris.

So very efficient, those coffins. So very German, Viv thought bitterly as another wave of grief and indignation swept over her.

Without looking back, she strode past the prison's tall gates toward the waiting black Citroën. She had absolutely no idea where to go next.

CHAPTER 64

August 25, 1944

Viv sank into the back seat of the commandant's car, *sans* Officer Piggy. After a long pause, she finally instructed the uniformed driver to take her to the only destination she could think of—the American Hospital in Neuilly-sur-Seine. With war still raging throughout the countryside, and now in Paris itself, it would be far too dangerous to attempt to travel to Val d'Isère. Viv figured that there were bound to be casualties when the Allies arrived to liberate the French capital in the next day or two. Making herself useful at the hospital would offer her shelter and food while providing a way for her to keep occupied. She also held the faint hope that keeping busy would push the harrowing memories of Marcel and Fresnes Prison from her ever-revolving thoughts. Another reason to reconnect with former colleagues was her anxiety about the fate of Dr. Jackson and his wife, Toquette.

"Leave me outside the gates, please," she called to the driver as the grounds and buildings loomed into view. It wouldn't do to pull up to the hospital in a black Citroën with two miniature Nazi flags flapping on the front fenders. The local SS headquarters across from the hospital already appeared to have been abandoned by its occupants.

Once standing in the street, Viv hiked her knapsack over her shoulder and grabbed her cosmetic case off the back seat. Without a thank you or farewell, she slammed the passenger car door and walked onto the grounds whose hedges were burnt brown from neglect. Preoccupied staff were scurrying to and fro when she entered the main building and headed, unchallenged, for Dr. Jackson's office on the fourth floor. The elevator wasn't working, so she mounted the first of three flights of stairs.

As she planted her foot on the second step, a voice startled her, calling out, "*Viv?*"

Shocked to hear her name, she glanced up to take in the sight of a tall figure in a white doctor's coat standing on the landing above her.

"*Jean-Paul?*" she cried, her voice nearly a shriek.

The man who had healed her broken leg and whose family had shown her such kindness stood staring down at her, his expression as full of surprise and joy as her own.

"*D'accord, chèrie,*" he said. "I'm not a mirage. Are you one?"

"What in the world are *you* doing here?" she demanded, racing up the steps, dropping her luggage at her feet, and throwing her arms around his broad shoulders.

"I could certainly ask the same of you!" he said, his mouth wreathed in smiles. "Before Adrienne Vaud left for Switzerland, she told us you were locked up in Fresnes."

"Why they let me out takes too long to tell, but *you*! Why are you here and not in Val d'Isère?"

"That's also a story that takes time in the telling, but first let's go to my office. I'm not due for rounds for a half hour. You look as if you could use a cognac."

"Due for *rounds*?" she repeated, dumbfounded. "You're working here now? But what about all the children—"

Jean-Paul quickly interrupted, saying, "All right. I'll tell you the story quickly while we walk upstairs to my office." He seized her knapsack and cosmetic case, leading the way. "You remember that I took part of my training here? A month ago, they pleaded with me to come to fill in, as they're so shorthanded and anticipate many casualties soon."

"I did know that Doctor Jackson and Toquette were arrested," Viv disclosed, "so I'm not surprised they begged you to come help out." She met his glance. "Did you just hear the gunfire on the outskirts of Paris?"

He nodded. "The uprising is underway, and the Allied troops should be here soon. We're trying to prepare for the inevitable wounded as best we can."

By this time, they had reached the fourth floor. Jean-Paul guided her to a door that let out into the corridor where Dr. Jackson's office was located. As if sensing she wanted to stop there, Jean-Paul ushered her into a smaller office across the hall and set down her belongings. Viv took the seat he offered opposite what she assumed was his desk now.

"There's bad news," he began, sitting down across from her. "After Dr. Jackson, his wife, and son were arrested, we've learned that they were eventually sent east to Germany."

"Germany? Oh, God, no!" Viv cried, bracing one hand on the edge of his desk to steady herself.

"Adrienne told the staff here that you and she had both been arrested right after the Jacksons were." He reached for her hand. "You can't know how relieved I was just now to see you miraculously standing on those stairs."

Viv could only offer a wan smile. "It was the same with my seeing you, Jean-Paul, but I'm devastated to hear this news about the Jacksons being deported to Germany." Thinking of Marcel's execution, she said, "Once the SS has you...."

Her voice trailed off.

"But you!" he exclaimed, a smile of encouragement lighting up his face. "Here you are. You survived Fresnes. *Truly*, a miracle after what Adrienne told us."

"I think an Allied double agent betrayed us all," she said, adding, "and I think I know who it was."

Viv briefly described to Jean-Paul the suspected treachery of Air Officer Lucien Barteau that took place when she crash-landed in France—and afterwards in Annecy and Paris.

"*Mon Dieu,* Viv," he said, "you are the proverbial cat with nine lives."

She shrugged. "Maybe I am," she responded, launching into a recitation of the events that followed her leaving the Morands in Val d'Isère on crutches to return to her clandestine duties in Annecy, including blowing up the locomotives in the town's rail yard. Then she described her amazing encounter with the *Wehrmacht* officer who determined he would let her go, judging her too dim ever to be a spy.

Listening intently, Jean-Paul responded, "I must admit, I'd prepared myself for the worst, Viv, but I could never have imagined all you've been through."

"It almost *was* the worst for me, but here I am."

But Marcel isn't...

Too emotionally exhausted to tell Jean-Paul about seeing Marcel taken away and then hearing the volley of shots ring out, she wondered aloud, "Will we ever think life can be good again?"

Jean-Paul remained silent. Viv could sense he had more he wanted to say to her but was holding back. She felt so empty, now, after that first rush of joy seeing his kind, handsome face at the top of the stairs.

"I want to work here," she declared with sudden determination. "I want to be so busy that I can't think. I can't remember." She looked across the desk at him and pleaded, "Please help me make that happen."

Before he could answer, there was a sharp knock on the door. Someone Viv had never seen popped his head in.

"Dr. Morand, we've gotten word! The Allies are just entering Paris! We've been told to go to our stations and prepare for..."

"Yes, of course!" interrupted Jean-Paul, rising rapidly to his feet. "Miss Vivier-Clarke, here, has returned from being released from Fresnes Prison to take up her former duties as a first-aid worker and an ambulance driver, if needed. Can you please take her to the nurses' wing to store her possessions and assign her a cot?"

The orderly nodded and disappeared, closing the door.

Jean-Paul turned to Viv. "Are you sure you're ready to do this? It will be bloody and dangerous." He paused with a look of concern. "You've just been through hell. Are you completely—"

"Ready to drive?" she interrupted. "Absolutely! I'm ready to do anything you ask of me."

Despite her erstwhile weariness and despair, Viv felt a familiar rush of adrenalin. This was what she needed to fight the black clouds of her imprisonment and Marcel's death, she thought, turning to follow Jean-Paul out of his office, her battered luggage in hand. She had no doubt that her dark thoughts would still be lurking at the base of her brain for a long time to come, but Paris was about to be liberated, and she prayed the same was true for Annecy and the Haute-Savoie.

For some reason, her thoughts turned to Major Merrick; she wondered where he was at this very moment. Wouldn't he be surprised to learn that she'd never gone to Switzerland as he'd ordered. Instead, she would be a witness to the Allies' triumphant march down the Champs-Élysées!

———◇———

Viv was, indeed, a witness to the victorious entry of Charles de Gaulle, himself, as he led the first phalanx of soldiers parading down Paris' famed thoroughfare. For Viv, the moment was bittersweet. She watched the uniformed ranks, led by the tall, beribboned general, march by to the sound of triumphant band music filling the warm, August air.

Marcel should be marching by his side, with Jean Moulin and Tom Morel...

But all she could think of was an image of Marcel's body tumbling into an open pit in the woods near Fresnes Prison; of the innocent townspeople executed by the SS in the wake of her sabotage at the train shed; and of the blood and destruction that took place on the broad, open meadow atop the Plateau des Glières.

Jean-Paul had seen to it that, rather than driving an ambulance through streets where fighting flared as the last of the Germans were killed or were fleeing the city, Viv was assigned to the receiving station directing orderlies where to take the patients, depending on their wounds and overall condition.

Paris had been officially declared liberated on August 25, 1944, but pockets of fighting continued. Even more astounding, word filtered back that the townspeople and surviving *résistants* of Annecy had driven out the Germans on their own. "Apparently," Jean-Paul reported soberly, "Annecy liberated *itself* on the nineteenth of August in revenge for the massacre on the Plateau des Glières."

And as London intelligence had forecast, De Gaulle ordered all non-French secret agents to leave the country to ensure the credit would belong to him and his troops.

Viv ignored the general's directive she'd heard circulating around Paris. When the active fighting had died down, and with the help of a few "friends in high places" from the hospital, she managed to establish with the new French authorities her right to take possession of her family's flat on Avenue Kléber. Once she had her name restored on the deed and Wilhelm Gerhardt's removed, she moved into her former home while continuing to volunteer at the American Hospitals for as long as she was needed.

With a deepening sense of melancholy, she unpacked her few remaining possessions from her knapsack and her single piece of Louis Vuitton luggage and stowed them in the hall closet. As she re-entered the sitting room with its peach silk upholstery and yards of matching drapery framing the tall windows, it felt to Viv as if the many ghosts of her past lurked in every corner.

CHAPTER 65

One evening, as the tumultuous summer of 1944 was shifting to early fall, there was a knock at Viv's door. Opening it, she couldn't believe who was standing at the threshold. Dark-haired Vera Atkins, SOE's deputy of the French Section, spoke first.

"You're *here,* Viv! We knew you'd been sent to Fresnes, but this was the address you gave us when you enlisted in London. I thought I'd chance it and see if I could find out anything of your where-abouts."

"Oh, my goodness, Miss Atkins!" Viv responded, "I can't believe it! Come in, come in! It's so wonderful to see you! What are you doing in Paris?"

"Trying to find my lost agents, like you," she replied with a sad smile. "Colonel Buckmaster and I have established a temporary office at the Hotel Cecil on rue St. Didier, hoping to greet our personnel as they find their way in from the field."

And then tell them de Gaulle has ordered them to leave the country, Viv said to herself silently.

Meanwhile, she urged her guest to enter through the foyer into the front room. Crossing to her mother's wheeled drinks table, she poured them each a cognac.

"Do you mind if I take notes while we talk?" Atkins inquired. "I'm conducting as many agent debriefs as I can for my files. For starters, I want to hear about everything you've done since I bid you farewell at Tangmere Air Base. But first of all, how in the world did you manage to get yourself released from Fresnes?"

"That, and everything else that's happened since you saw me off at Tangmere, is a very long story," Viv replied, taking a seat opposite her visitor and raising her glass. "I'm glad the damned Germans left us a full bottle of Camus. We're going to need it."

———— ◇ ————

The two women sitting across from each other on the apartment's elegant Louis XVI furniture, sipping cognac, spoke far into the night. Viv answered Vera Atkins's detailed questions about being arrested and incarcerated in Fresnes Prison, along with lengthy descriptions of every phase of her duties on her assigned missions serving as Major Merrick's courier on skis, "as you came to be known in our office," Atkins joked.

"Did the Major make it back?" Viv asked, holding her breath.

"He certainly did. He's already taken a position as Headmaster of a posh school in Somerset."

"And what about Catherine Thornton, whom I got to know well in training? And Henri Leblanc?"

"Catherine came through beautifully, like you," Vera replied slowly. "But sadly, at this point, Henri has still not been heard from and feared missing. Catherine has set off to Germany to determine if he was one of our agents sent to a concentration camp."

"But there's still fighting in the east!" Viv protested. "How can she—"

Vera laughed. "You know Catherine...a woman not to be deterred. She's traveling just behind the Allied troops advancing deeper into Germany, hoping to find some clue about Leblanc's whereabouts."

"Yep, that sounds like Catherine," Viv agreed. "I liked her so much. Can you give me an address for her in D.C. where I can write?"

"Of course," Vera said with a nod.

Viv hesitated and then broached the subject that she knew might be a minefield.

"I'd like to tell you of my experiences with another SOE agent, code name Gilbert, but I first met him as Lucien Barteau during parachute training in Manchester."

Miss Atkins arched an eyebrow. "Yes? How did you find him as a colleague?"

"He not only tried to force me into his bed at one point, he also betrayed agents I knew to the SS...and probably ratted on me as well," Viv declared, her voice flat.

She immediately wondered if that might not have been her best answer. After all, Merrick said Lucien Barteau's skills as an Air Operations Officer were quite respected by the London brass. Would any British intelligence higher-ups believe her accusations?

For some reason, Vera Atkins didn't seem to Viv to be reacting with surprise.

"He 'tried' to coerce you, you say? I take it he wasn't successful?"

"I broke his nose. Thank God I knew a bit of jujitsu, plus our silent killing training up in Scotland probably helped."

Viv detected the merest trace of a smile on Miss Atkins' lips.

"Well, I know you didn't kill him," she revealed, "as he's about to have a hearing. He's accused of treason, actually."

"Well, that's something, at least!" Viv exclaimed. "That was the other thing I was going to tell you. I saw him with my own eyes, coming out alone from the front door at 84 Avenue Foch, right after Dr. and Mrs. Jackson from the American Hospital were arrested and driven away." She paused to inhale, then continued. "I also spotted him in a café in Annecy during the period when members of Merrick's Mountaineer network were getting apprehended right and left."

Viv sought Atkins' troubled glance.

"And...?" Buckmaster's deputy asked.

Viv swallowed hard, the mere memory of Marcel's words clogging her throat. "One of de Gaulle's Free French agents whom you met the night we flew out of Tangmere—"

"Marcel Delonge?"

"Yes, Marcel." Viv fought to keep her emotions in check. "He once told me he was *certain* Lucien Barteau was a double and had tipped off Klaus Barbie that Marcel was operating in and around Lyon. Marcel was arrested, escaped, and then was arrested again and ultimately taken from Fresnes and executed." She waited, but Vera Atkins remained silent. Viv demanded, "So do you think Barteau will be convicted?"

Vera Atkins paused before answering.

"Well, I certainly never liked him or trusted him," she said, "but he got on well with fellow pilots, and I'm sure he'll have several respected flyers speaking on his behalf. As for myself? There were too many suspicious arrests of our agents here in France that were linked to agent Gilbert in one way or the other to just be coincidence. But I'm afraid we'll just have to wait to see what the Tribunal does."

"I hope they nail the bastard!" Viv muttered, her tone almost a hiss. "I think he was the one who betrayed all those agents working in the Haute-Savoie—including me."

Vera Atkins gave a small, affirmative nod. Then she said, "There's been one thing that truly cheered me up this week in Paris. You'll be pleased to know your wireless operator, Fingers Malloy, as you called him, arrived at the Hotel Cecil just the other day."

Viv clapped her hands. "Oh, what wonderful news!"

"We were quickly able to find him transport back to America." Miss Atkins cast Viv a searching look. "We can do the same for you, if you wish."

Viv lowered her eyes to stare at her glass of spirits without answering, uncertain what she would do once her duties wound up at the hospital.

Vera quickly added, "But feel free to take your time deciding. We can arrange your passage at whatever date you wish, my dear. Just say the word." She paused, and then added, "As a matter of fact, we've had some final intelligence about Marcel Delonge." Atkins' dark eyes radiated a sense of deep sympathy. "We just received the physical proof that he was executed by the SS. I won't go into the details of the forensics, but…we can confirm he was shot and—"

Viv held up one hand as if to seek permission to speak, yet she struggled to find words as the finality of what Atkins had just said sank in.

Finally, she murmured, "From my cell window I saw them take him out before dawn. I heard the shots from the woods nearby."

But a secret part of you kept hoping against hope that somehow Marcel could have escaped one more time…but now you know for sure he didn't…

Vera Atkins took up her pen and began writing in her notebook again.

"So his death is official?" Viv said softly. She couldn't bear to think about the means by which this had been confirmed. Yet she had to ask one more question. "You're saying there was evidence in the wood that it *was* Marcel among the four shot that day?

Vera Atkins hesitated a split second and then replied, "The Germans burned the bodies, but dental records were matched from when Marcel Delonge underwent facial plastic surgery in London." She sought Viv's hand. "A memorial will be placed at the site to honor those who died there. I thought you'd want to know."

Viv stared at her glass filled with amber cognac, aware of the slight bump under the lining of her shoe—Marcel's parachute patch with embroidered wings and canopy that he gave her the day she flew back into France. It was her last tangible connection to the man whose fate would be so hard to accept. He was truly gone.

"You probably know this, Miss Atkins, but Marcel Delonge was from a vintner's family in Perpignan on the border with Spain. He was one of de Gaulle's most trusted deputies…yet he won't even have a grave there to mark his passing."

Atkins smiled sadly. "As I said, there will be memorials built, of course…but yes, Delonge and Jean Moulin—both tortured horribly, killed by the Nazis, their bodies desecrated. So many losses. So much grief." With another faint shake of her head, she added with some vehemence, "To date, we've confirmed that a least fifteen of our young women secret agents won't be coming back. I've sworn to myself I won't stop until I learn the fate of each and every one of sixty-two women we sent into the field."

Miss Atkins lit a cigarette, inhaled deeply, smoke streaming out of the corner of her lips. "Did you know they call you Churchill's Angels?"

"Yes, Marcel told me just before I came for my interview with you in '42."

A vision of the bloodied white ski suit of the soldier Viv had killed flashed in her mind's eye. "But trust me, Miss Atkins," Viv murmured, "given the things we had to do, we women were hardly angels."

Atkins gave her a wry look of agreement and scribbled down the Washington, D.C. address of Viv's spy sister, Catherine Thornton, handing it to her. Then she rose to depart.

"Please know, my dear, if we don't chance to meet again, how deeply grateful the British government and our King are for the wonderful, selfless contributions you made to the Allies in winning the war."

Viv was stunned to hear such a full-throated compliment, but before she could reply, Atkins seized her handbag off the chair, adding, "We *will* win, you know. The Germans are beaten, and I'm convinced the Japanese surrender will come soon."

"Let's hope you're right," Viv replied with a nod.

Turning to exit the room, Atkins looked back and declared, "You have dual British and American citizenship, Viv, and you own this flat in Paris. I can well understand why you'd need time to sort out what your future holds." Viv was startled when Miss Atkins pushed the strap of her handbag up her arm, seized both Viv's hands, and urged warmly, "Take all the time you need. I will be ready to help whenever I hear from you."

Deeply touched by her kindness and concern, Viv replied softly, "Thank you so much for that, Miss Atkins, and thank you for troubling to find me." She blinked hard and then managed to add, "And it's true. I'll need time."

Chapter 66

Viv remained at Avenue Kléber as war waged on across Europe for another eight months when the unconditional surrender of German forces to the Allies took place on May 7, 1945. Victory in Europe was proclaimed the next day, and four months later, after two atomic bombs were dropped on Japan, the Japanese Emperor signed their surrender.

Earlier in June, when the pressure on staff at the American Hospital had begun to ease up, Jean-Paul announced to Viv that he was preparing to return to his medical practice in Val d'Isère at the beginning of July. To her surprise, she felt dismayed to be losing the companionship of such a dear friend so soon. She scolded herself for not celebrating the fact that he probably was eager to return to his home and the company of his family.

One evening, soon after she'd learned he would be leaving, Jean-Paul invited her to dinner at a small bistro near her flat. Following several glasses of excellent burgundy, she'd confided to him for the first time about her relationship with Marcel, telling him the story of their climb over the Pyrenees when she'd had a serious case of the mumps. She described the way in which Marcel secured her the interview with Colonel Buckmaster at SOE and disclosed that Marcel and she ultimately had disobeyed the cardinal rule of undercover work and become lovers.

"We both ended up in Fresnes, but two months apart," she revealed slowly. "A day after he got there, I saw them load him in a truck and then I heard shots ring out from a nearby wood. His death has been officially confirmed through dental records."

Jean-Paul regarded her with compassion, saying, "I can only imagine the horror of witnessing him taken away like that." He paused, then said, "I could tell there was someone in your life before we met." He gazed at her steadily over the rim of his wine glass. "I'm glad if he made you happy. You deserve that. If he had lived, do you think you would have married, once the war was over?"

His question caused her to sit up straighter in her chair, her thoughts drifting back to the day Marcel had told her the sad tale about returning from the Great War as a twenty-year-old soldier to discover his young wife had betrayed him with a friend. They'd been divorced, quickly followed by his enlistment in the French Foreign Legion. Viv would never forget the way Marcel had looked at her with hooded eyes and said, "No, I never married again and don't *ever* intend to!"

That reply had always lingered in the back of her mind.

"Would we have married?" Viv repeated Jean-Paul's question. "I guess I'll never know." Wanting to shift the onus onto him, she asked, "But what about *you*? Why haven't you ever married? Or have you?"

Jean-Paul took on a rather sheepish expression.

"Oh, no… I've never been married. I was always so preoccupied with getting my training as a doctor and establishing my practice while my friends developed the ski resort—and then the war came. There hadn't seemed the time or opportunity to get close enough to a woman to marry her. Once I came to Val d'Isère, though, I had girl friends of course. One in particular that…" Viv waited, but his sentence remained incomplete. He offered a Gallic shrug along with a wry smile. "Now the war is over, though, I have all the time in the world."

Not knowing what reply to make to a man who would be leaving Paris soon, Viv refilled her glass sitting on their bistro table and took a generous sip.

If I'd never met Marcel…if we'd never been in love…if he hadn't asked me to be with him at his vineyard…if we both had managed to survive the war…

The "ifs" were numerous, but only she had survived. Marcel may not have formally asked her to marry him, but in time, he might have.

Or not.

She had no answers to give anyone, living or dead.

Viv tried to smile at Jean-Paul but succeeded only in tilting her glass in a kind of salute to their friendship and drank down the last of her wine.

————◇————

Two days after their dinner together and Jean-Paul's announcement he would be leaving Paris at the end of the month, the young doctor appeared at the door of her reclaimed apartment.

His expression drawn, he greeted her with a formal, "May I come in?"

With a sense of foreboding, Viv led him into the front room filled with her mother's pale, upholstered furniture and the silken drapes that puddled on the parquet floor. If she remained in Paris, she thought absently, she was definitely going to change the décor. Except for the dust coating everything when she'd first moved back in, Colonel Wilhelm Gerhardt had left her family's residence remarkably intact.

With full awareness that Jean-Paul had something important to say, Viv indicated he should take a seat on the silk divan. She sank into the adjacent matching chair.

Leaning towards him she urged, "Tell me. What's happened?"

"It's… Doctor Jackson."

A heavy silence bloomed between them.

"He's dead?" Viv said quietly as if making an announcement.

"Yes."

"When?" she asked, fighting tears that had immediately welled in her eyes. The war in Europe had been over more than a month, yet here was more horrible news.

"That's what makes this even harder," Jean-Paul said, his voice catching. "We've just learned that our brave American doctor—who refused all compromise with the Nazis from the day they occupied Paris five years ago—died on May 2, two days after Hitler killed himself in Berlin."

"And five days before Germany *surrendered*?" Viv interrupted, choking on the words. "That's criminal! Where did he die? And how?"

Jean-Paul gazed down at his slender surgeon's hands clasped in his lap.

"After his arrest, he was taken east to Germany, as we'd feared, to some prison there. About a month ago, he and son Phillip were loaded into a cattle car and were transported even deeper into Germany...to Lübeck, to the harbor there."

"Oh, God...those terrible, closed-up wooden cattle cars they used," Viv murmured.

"Since D-Day, the Germans were frantic dealing with the onslaught of Allied troops pursuing them across France and then eastward. When Dr. Jackson's train arrived at Lübeck, the Germans loaded scores of their prisoners onto a cargo vessel, including Dr. J and his son." Jean-Paul fell silent, as if mustering the strength to continue. Finally, he said, "British warplanes mistook the ship for one with German soldiers fleeing the Allied advance and bombarded it with rockets."

"Oh...*no*..." Viv moaned. "Our *own side* killed him?

"A mistake, obviously," Jean-Paul hastened to make clear. "Young Phillip was up on deck. He looked for his father as the projectiles were crashing down but couldn't see him. In the end, he managed to jump into the water and swam to safety."

"But Doctor J?"

"He was below deck, taking care of some sick prisoners." Jean-Paul paused once more for a moment to collect himself, then finished, "He was never seen again. His body was not recovered."

"And Toquette?" Viv whispered, fearing the worst.

Jean-Paul seized her hand and held it next to his heart. His chest felt warm against her skin, and his gaze was filled with sympathy.

"Toquette had been separated from the men soon after their arrest in Paris, but miraculously survived the ghastly women's prison camp at Ravensbrück. She told our Nurse Elizabeth this week that there was terrible starvation there. Many female inmates were literally worked to death, and she saw others being tossed into gas chambers."

"Have *you* seen her?" Viv demanded, wondering silently how people who'd witnessed such atrocities could ever erase such horrifying memories.

Jean-Paul nodded. "Yes, she came to me for an examination so we could determine her future treatment. She's not at all in good health, I'm afraid, but I think, given time, she has a chance of a decent physical recovery, at least."

"So she's back in Paris?" Viv asked, her voice choked with unshed tears.

"Yes. She and Phillip have just been reunited."

"But not Dr. J," Viv mourned, unable to repress her emotions any longer. "Killed by our own side…" she repeated, wondering how poor Toquette could survive a loss like this. She buried her face in both hands, and for the first time since she'd left Fresnes Prison, began to cry.

Viv didn't protest when Jean-Paul reached out and pulled her into his arms. She cried for Sumner Jackson and Tom Morel and for Marcel. She cried for the Swiss partisan, Kurt, whose real name she never knew—and for all the brave men she'd met who had so recently died on the Plateau des Glières.

And she cried for herself. After everything she'd been through, what was left to her except an empty apartment with peach drapery, a few blocks from the former SS?

"Ah…my poor Viv," soothed Jean-Paul. "You *should* cry… you've been so brave for so long…"

She burrowed more deeply into Jean-Paul's embrace. He stroked her back, and she felt his lips gently kissing the top of her head as if she were a child. Like a drowning swimmer, Viv reached for the comfort of his touch, the affirmation she could still feel something, anything that wasn't death, anything that wasn't about human beings torturing each other. She leaned into him, his solidness confirming she, at least, was *alive* and not yet a dead person merely going through the motions of daily living.

Jean-Paul laced his fingers through her hair, kissing each eyelid and her forehead in a kind of benediction. His compassionate response reminded Viv of Kurt kissing her sweetly like that, wishing her Godspeed at the Swiss border as she crept back into France.

"Love me," she blurted, raising her head to gaze into his eyes filled with concern and…something else she guessed might be there. "Love me!" she repeated her demand and wondered at how desperate she sounded.

He held her gaze, his hand continuing to stroke her back.

"Are you sure?" he asked.

In answer, she fiercely kissed him on the mouth, her tongue seeking his. She felt one of his hands drift gently around her torso to cup her breast.

"Viv...ah... Viv," he whispered, "have you any idea how long I've wanted to touch you? To know your body in the way I feel I know your mind? Your giving heart?"

An image of Marcel's hands in her hair and his lips seeking hers rose up, and she squeezed her eyes tightly shut.

I'm alive, Marcel...and I am so lost...so lonely without you to love me.

As Jean-Paul gently pushed her down on her mother's peach satin settee, Viv concentrated solely on the sensations of his warm, roving hands and the weight of his long, lean body pressing down on hers.

Her last conscious thought was that she'd deal with her guilty sense of betrayal of Marcel sometime later. But for now, Jean-Paul's touch was electrifying, calling her back to the land of the living, and the sweet oblivion she craved would overtake her soon.

———◇———

The afternoon summer sun slanted through the floor-to-ceiling windows of Viv's flat. She kept her eyes closed and waited until Jean-Paul padded to her bathroom down the hallway. Rising from the sofa, she quickly tidied herself and went into the kitchen to fill two glasses with water and brought them back just as Jean-Paul returned.

"Viv, I hope—"

"Jean-Paul, I'm fine. It was lovely," she insisted. And it had been, but she simply was not prepared to discuss anything more about what had just happened between them.

"Really, what I'm concerned with right now is what you've told me about Toquette. I want to go see her. Today."

He paused a moment, and then, as if agreeing not to press her on the subject of their making love minutes before, he said, "I'll go with you, then." He pointed to his black doctor's bag he had left on the floor when he'd entered her front room. "I had planned to call on her this afternoon to see how she was doing."

Viv nodded her thanks and changed to go out. On their walk over to the Jacksons' home, Jean-Paul filled their initial, awkward silence by telling her of the plans to re-open the village of Val d'Isère for skiers in the coming winter.

"And in summer, the resort already has a few ambitious schemes to repair and extend trails for alpine hikers who we hope will start to come. Once that happens," he joked as they approached the Arc de Triomphe, "there are bound to be enough broken bones and other maladies for me to re-establish a private medical practice. At least I hope so."

"It will be good for you to do that," Viv assured him, subdued, once again, by the thought he'd be leaving Paris so soon.

Jean-Paul sought her gaze, saying, "I also plan to help with the resettlement of people displaced by the war. My friends reopening the resort are enthusiastically supporting my idea of establishing a small youth hostel where orphans can come to recover their health and spirits while waiting for placement. Meanwhile, they can learn to ski in winter, and in summer, walk the beautiful mountain trails."

He has plans for a life after the war, Viv thought bleakly.

Just then, they rounded the corner on Avenue Foch. Taking in the length of the graceful esplanade, Viv halted in her tracks as an avalanche of memories assaulted her. She'd been avoiding the street for months and had put it out of her mind what an elegant block it was. Yet there it stretched—impressive, cream-colored four- and five-story townhouses embellished with wrought-iron balconies and molded plaster framing the windows. On several buildings, Corinthian entablature soared in stately columns up their front facades.

Viv realized as they resumed walking that only a rare group of survivors of SS interrogations could even imagine the terrible methods of torture that had taken place behind the stately walls of Number 84. She speculated that most French citizens preferred not to think that such horrors had ever happened.

"Time to move on...put the past behind us" were phrases she'd heard often since the end of the war in Europe had been officially declared, and France, like some Gallic Humpty-Dumpty, was struggling to put herself back together again. Viv knew, however, that if the blatant inhumanity that took place in this city and throughout the country was forgotten and ignored, people like her and Jean-Paul and Toquette could never "move on" and make life better than it was during the fighting.

Jean-Paul reached for her hand as if he sensed such a notorious street would bring back recollections she'd rather forget—but could not.

"Here we are," he declared, guiding her through the iron gate toward the front entrance of the Jackson home at Number 11. "Toquette will be so glad to see you."

Viv kept her eyes glued to the Jacksons' graceful brass doorknocker that Jean-Paul lifted to signal to the occupants that visitors had arrived.

Standing side-by-side on the stoop, Viv tried not to think of making love with him earlier, or even of the night she'd hidden in the Jacksons' back garden while the SS held the family at bay. Instead, she told herself to rally her compassion and support in response to the painful rendezvous with Toquette that most likely lay ahead.

And then another thought intruded.

What if she got *pregnant* from the totally spontaneous event that had just occurred between Jean-Paul and her? Before she could even begin to calculate the odds of that complicating possibility, the door opened, and a housemaid bid them enter.

"Ah… Viv," Toquette greeted her warmly. "How wonderful it is to see you! Jean-Paul has been telling me of the amazing things you did to help France win this war."

Viv's hostess was thin as a rail and wore a silk scarf wrapped around her head with little wisps of her hair poking out, evidence that her head had been shaved at some point during her captivity.

"Oh, Toquette! I'm so glad—"

"Come in! Come in!" Toquette interrupted, turning to instruct her maid to bring a tray of coffee into the back garden.

Viv's stomach clenched at the memories that going into the garden would bring up. In an effort to push aside such thoughts, she said brightly, "You can buy coffee now?"

Food shortages in Paris were still nearly as bad as when war raged throughout the country. Toquette smiled fondly at Jean-Paul.

"I suspect our friend, here, raided the hospital kitchen. He brought me some."

Toquette walked them through the first level of the flat and out the back door with its cream-colored linen awning partially shading the sandstone pavers of a small terrace. A cluster of outdoor wooden furniture beckoned. Beyond it, a large rectangle of lawn recovering its greenness stretched to a clipped hedge. Viv was glad it obscured the alley where she had hidden near the dust bin the night Toquette, her husband, and son were held hostage by Hans Kieffer's counter-intelligence SS.

Their hostess directed them to take seats on the canvas cushions where she plied Viv with questions to fill in the gaps since they'd last seen each other.

For several minutes, Viv described her witnessing the SS taking the Jackson family away, and as one clandestine operator to another, briefly sketched for Toquette what her past as a secret agent had entailed and how she'd come to know Jean-Paul.

Toquette remarked somberly, "You've both had quite an amazing few years."

"Years you've gone through as well," Viv replied starkly.

"So many losses…" murmured Toquette, "but still, so much *good* still to be done in this sorry world of ours."

Viv gazed at her in awe. Here, the woman had lost the husband she had dearly loved and with whom she had shared a long life of service to the Paris medical community. Yet Toquette felt there remained a desire for her to do more. She didn't sound bitter about the fact Dr. J had been killed by "friendly fire," only resolved that she had a teenage son to mother and nursing skills that would be useful as Paris struggled to heal the sick and soothe the wounded in soul and spirit.

"And what are *your* plans, now, my dear?" Toquette asked Viv.

"I wish I could tell you," she replied, her eyes briefly sliding toward Jean-Paul who was looking at her intently as if asking the same question.

Given Toquette's query about Viv's future possibilities, she realized with a start that she *had* none. Her hostess leaned closer and patted her on her arm.

"You're a clever, talented, courageous young woman, my dear. I'm sure you'll find the right path for yourself. We've all been through…well…some very difficult experiences. We should be kind to ourselves and allow time to heal, both our physical ills and the ones up here," she said, pointing to her forehead.

"How are you so wise?" Viv asked, wondering what it would have been like to have had a mother like Toquette?

"Life itself brings one wisdom, don't you think?" she answered. "That, and, in my own case, having had the extraordinarily good luck to have lived so many years with a wonderful man like my Sumner."

Viv was alarmed to see the tears gathering in Toquette's eyes.

"I'm so sorry," Viv apologized. "I know it must be so hard to speak of—"

"No!" Toquette said emphatically, reaching for a linen napkin and dabbing her cheeks. "I need to say his *name*. I need to remember Sumner Jackson each and every day and be grateful for our long years together. In a strange way, it's a blessing to know he died quickly from a rocket hitting the ship's hull while tending those needing his care."

Humbled by the aura of serenity Toquette exuded, Viv could only nod and take another sip of her coffee.

"He always helped people in whatever he did," Viv agreed, remembering how he'd showed faith in her as an ambulance driver, trusting her to drive Marcel to Dunkirk.

For the first time in weeks, Viv could feel herself relaxing in the warmth of Toquette's calm presence. Drinking the excellent cup of coffee with its luxurious splash of fresh milk, she began to enjoy the banter back and forth between Jean-Paul and their hostess, who was reminiscing about the year she'd invited him to lodge with them during his training at the hospital. Viv could tell by the warmth they exhibited toward each other that Toquette almost considered him a second son. As they rose to make their farewells, Toquette seized Viv's hand.

"Please keep in touch, will you? Let me know what unfolds for you in the future, Viv. Those of us who know what it was to fight for the cause that freed France have an unbreakable bond, you know."

Thinking suddenly of Catherine Thornton, who became an instant friend during SOE training in Scotland, Viv murmured, "Sister spies? Yes, we do."

She found herself wondering about the bond with those who had died for the cause. Would they, too, remain links over time, or rather chains of sad remembrance?

Chapter 67

Jean-Paul casually placed his right arm around Viv's shoulders as they walked side-by-side back to Viv's flat. Without warning, he stopped and turned toward her.

"Why don't you come with me to Val d'Isère?" he proposed, his golden hair gleaming and his profile startlingly handsome in the late afternoon sun. "You were wonderful with the children you helped escape to Switzerland, and you'd be sensational as a ski instructor for little ones." He tilted his head and gave her a sidewise glance, his lips curving at the corners. "It's not just your delightful companionship I would cherish. I definitely need someone like you as a full partner in the refugee organization and holiday camp I want to start."

Taken aback by this unexpected proposal, Viv played for time. She knew that his feelings for her were much more intense than she felt ready for—or could handle—in her current state of numbness and grief over the brutal loss of Marcel.

"Oh… Jean-Paul…what a lovely idea," she temporized. "But as I said to Toquette, I have no idea what is next for me." At his disappointed expression, she added, "Can you let me have some time to sort myself out before I give you an answer?"

"Of course, chèrie," he replied, but he dropped his arm from around her shoulder.

In recalling all the clandestine work they'd done together, she realized with a start that in a hidden corner of her mind she'd always known Jean-Paul had been attracted to her. Hadn't he even said the word "love" the day she'd set off in the sleigh? And given their weeks working together at the hospital as the war wound down—to say nothing of their afternoon's tryst—his feelings obviously were as strong as ever. Maybe even stronger now. Considering all these factors, she'd have to admit that his suggestion that she move to Val d'Isère with him wasn't such a surprise.

Viv knew, now, having made love with Jean-Paul this day, that as wonderful a man as he was, *she* was in no fit condition to do anything other than lick her wounds for the moment.

The truth was grief had become her constant companion since Marcel's execution. The vision she'd witnessed through her prison cell window played over and over in her mind, blocking out most everything else. Perhaps Jean-Paul was ready to make a lifelong commitment, but *she* definitely was not. Certainly Toquette Jackson had endured the years of this war that were much more harrowing than Viv's. Even so, Viv was certain that it would take a lot more time for her to make peace with it all, including the disturbing roles that her mother and stepfather had played with the Enemy.

———◇———

Viv waited until she was certain that her unprotected lovemaking with Jean-Paul hadn't resulted in pregnancy before she told him that she was considering a visit back to the United States. Ten days after seeing Toquette, Viv had received her first letter from Pamela Bradford since the war ended. In it, her mother, writing since abruptly returning to New York City, revealed that she had been diagnosed with "heart trouble." Viv couldn't help but notice she made nary a mention of Colonel Wilhelm Gerhardt.

> *Now that I am finally back in America, it seems Karl has to remain in North Carolina running the factory.*
> *Given my condition, I could certainly use some company and a little help here in New York.*

Viv could almost hear the manipulative, beseeching tone in her voice. She stared at her mother's bright blue ink with its schoolgirl scrawl stretching across elegant stationery embossed 5050 Fifth Avenue, Penthouse, New York, NY.

By the way, if you're reading this letter sent to Avenue Kléber, please describe the condition of the apartment as you found it after the war ended. I have no doubt you fought tooth-and-nail to get your name back on the deed. I hope all my chinaware wasn't stolen by the damn Krauts! And if you're using it yourself, do be very careful. It's Meissen.

Karl bought it in Dresden in Saxon Germany and it cost a bloody fortune!

Oh yes! Viv thought with a grimace. She'd had to fight tooth-and-nail—and then some—to get her name restored as co-owner of the flat, obtaining affidavits from neighbors that swore she'd lived there before the war and who'd also witnessed Colonel Gerhardt taking forceful possession of the place.

Soon after receiving Pamela's plea to come to New York—or was it a demand?—Viv and Jean-Paul met on the eve of his departure for Val d'Isère at a café facing the church of St. Sulpice, less than fifty yards from the flat she'd briefly shared with Adrienne and Marcel on rue des Canettes.

"So, you're leaving Paris just as I am?" Jean-Paul asked, his tone a study in neutrality after she'd told him of her mother's letter.

"Honestly," Viv replied, "I have no idea if my mother is being overly dramatic, or if she has something serious going on medically." She frowned. "She tends to over-dramatize the situation if she's in pursuit of something she wants. Without her husband Karl in New York very often, I think she needs a more reliable nursemaid."

"Well, she knows you learned first-aid," he joked. Then his expression grew serious. "But 'heart trouble' could be anything. Did she describe her symptoms?"

Viv shook her head. "No, and that's why I'm suspicious. She seemed more worried about the condition of her German chinaware than her health. Still…"

"Why don't you just go and see what's going on?" he suggested. "If nothing is seriously wrong with her, you could come right back."

"Well, maybe…" Viv replied, her tone revealing her indecision.

Jean-Paul reached for her hand. "It could prove to be a chance to…reconnect with her in new ways. You've given me some notion what a difficult relationship that's been. Her having been interned—even at Vittel—can't have been very pleasant. And then her time in Bern may also have been difficult. She might have changed some of her views. Maybe she wants to forge something better with you."

Viv thrust the letter across the table as annoyance crept into her voice.

"After all I've told you about her, and the contents of this letter, do you really imagine she's 'changed' much?" Viv realized that she sounded as if Jean-Paul had somehow betrayed her by urging her to confront her past devils involving a woman who'd always gotten the better of her emotionally.

"It's just a thought," he replied mildly. "But you've told me lately that you feel like a person without a country. Perhaps you miss your former home more than you realize."

I miss Marcel! she protested silently. *I miss knowing there's a man in my life who will always have my back! Who understands what the war was really like, always having to keep secrets. Who will always...*

Oh, what was the use! Viv said to herself forlornly. She sat up straighter in the spindly bistro chair facing the tiny round table that held two cups of dark, strong espresso that she and Jean-Paul had been drinking. She stared across the short space that separated them. He was leaving for the Alps in the morning, and she realized she was acting like a petulant, abandoned child. Wasn't it time she bestirred herself and did *something*?

They exchanged glances, and Viv said brightly, "You know, I think you're right. I'm going to take your suggestion and head for the good old U. S. of A. Who knows? Maybe Pamela and Karl will greet me like their long, lost daughter, returned from the war."

But a voice in Viv's head said, "*Good luck with that, kiddo. The truth is you could be in for the biggest pitched battle since the Nazi invasion.*

———◇———

Jean-Paul left the next day. Viv spent the next weeks of summer changing her mind a dozen times about returning to the States. Finally, in early September after the Japanese signed the surrender document on the second of that month, she contacted Vera Atkins in

London and made the request for transport to America that the SOE deputy had promised she'd gladly arrange.

"I can't get you on any air-transport at the moment, but I've booked you passage on a U.S. troop ship departing from Southampton to New York October fifteenth. Does that suit you? The captain has been alerted you'll be on board, and I think if you keep to your cabin, except for meals," she warned in her letter, "you'll find it all right, despite all those returning soldiers."

Viv was grateful for Atkins' efforts, as no commercial ocean liners were back in service yet. She'd learned from soldiers recuperating at the hospital that a spot on a U.S. military plane as a female was virtually impossible to come by unless you were a high-ranking military nurse, still in uniform. At least a sea voyage could give her time to prepare for interacting with a mother and stepfather who'd consorted with the enemy responsible for killing so many people whom Viv had loved.

PART VII
CHAPTER 68

October 1945

The autumn seas were rough, but Viv was a good sailor from her school days on Lake Geneva and fared well, remaining mostly in her cabin to avoid "terminal ogling," as one nurse she'd met onboard had put it. She slept, mostly, and read second-hand books she'd bought at a stand along the Seine before she'd sailed. At night, after dinner, Viv and Captain Anderson or one of his aides escorted her around the top deck to take the air before they delivered her to her small stateroom.

Viv rose early on the day of their arrival in New York. For the first time on the trip, her stomach was in turmoil as the huge ship glided by the Statue of Liberty. The captain had arranged for her to disembark among the first of the few civilian passengers on board, hours ahead of the thousands of soldiers chomping at the bit to get off the ship after their years at war. Viv walked down the gangway, searching for signs of her mother, although in a corner of her mind she prepared herself to be disappointed.

And disappointed she was.

A chauffeur in a black suit and cap held up a sign with her name and then ushered her into Karl's sleek, burgundy red Cadillac, an exact match to the color of her hair. The driver was silent as he wheeled his way through the streets of New York City. In the roomy leather back seat, Viv gazed out the windows at skyscrapers she hadn't seen in years. Pulling up to 5050 Fifth Avenue near the Metropolitan Museum, Viv marveled that the scene stretching before her showed no evidence there had ever been a war—or perhaps America had better things to think about. Smartly dressed matrons pushing baby carriages and men in expensive suits carrying leather briefcases crowded the sidewalks. To Viv, it spoke of life swiftly "getting back to normal," a far cry from the scenes she'd left in Paris.

The doorman at 5050 was new and insisted she be announced over the intercom.

"Yes, Mr. Bradford," he said into the receiver. "I'll send her right up."

Viv felt her breath catch. So Karl was back from North Carolina. She calculated that her trip to see her mother was likelier to be even shorter than she'd anticipated.

The elevator to the Bradford penthouse let out directly into the apartment's black-and-white checkered tile foyer. The brass doors clanked open, and Viv could see at once that the entire apartment was in a state of massive disarray. Packing boxes were on one side of the living room and furniture pushed against the walls. Karl stood in the middle, consulting a man in overalls, his bib stamped with the name of a transport company.

Her stepfather looked up. "So you made it. Hold on until I finish here."

"Where's Mother?"

Ignoring her question, he returned to his conversation. Viv set her two pieces of luggage down on the black-and-white tiles and began to fume.

Finally, Karl hiked his thumb over his shoulder indicating she should follow him into the study. Already infuriated by the chaos that had greeted her, she entered the richly paneled room with matching, forest-green leather settees that faced each other with a coffee table between. An enormous partner's desk took up most of the far wall, flanked by glass-fronted bookcases with shelves full of expensive art objects—but no reading material.

Exasperated, Viv asked again, "For heavens sakes, where's *Mother*?"

"Your mother died five days ago," Karl announced without emotion. "I buried her yesterday."

Viv wilted into a chair opposite his desk.

"*What?*"

"I figured it wasn't likely a cable would reach you on that army troop ship you told us you were coming over on," he said with a shrug, "so I figured bad news was bad news, whenever you ended up hearing it."

Viv stared at the man she'd known since she was twelve who'd sent his chauffeur to fetch her from the docks like an arriving shipment of iron ore. Obviously, he figured he'd "deal with it" when she walked into the apartment for the first time in a decade.

"Mother's *dead*?" Stunned, she asked, "What *happened*?"

"Her heart. The doc said it'd been weakened by eating such rotten food—and not enough of it—when she was in that internment camp."

"So she wasn't exaggerating when she said she had 'heart trouble' in her letter," Viv murmured.

"Well, it was news to *me*," Karl bristled. "She never let on anything was wrong! I was in North Carolina when Sadie, our cook, called saying Pamela suddenly clutched her chest and keeled over. Boom. Gone! 'Sudden death heart failure' the doc said."

"Sudden death heart failure?" she echoed faintly. A knot of anger had begun to tighten in the pit of her stomach. She gestured to a pile of boxes filled with items being packed for shipment to North Carolina. "Maybe it wasn't just the stress of the war, but this sudden decision to sell the place she'd lived in for years. She never said a *word* to me about putting it on the market. How long have you been planning to do this?"

As with the Paris flat on Avenue Kléber, the New York apartment had belonged to her mother and Viv's father.

Her stepfather shot her a look of defiance, declaring, "It didn't make any sense to keep both places anymore, so when your mother *finally* came back from Switzerland," he emphasized with a nasty ring to his words, "we decided to sell this place and live in the North Carolina house near the factory."

"'*We*' was it?" Viv said sarcastically, only too aware of the way in which all major decisions were made—always by Karl.

Under Viv's unwavering gaze, her stepfather replied with a defensive air, "Sure, it was probably a little stressful on Pamela, packing up and everything." He paused. "She wasn't getting any younger, that's for sure."

"None of us are," Viv countered with a pointed stare at his protruding belly.

Karl had the grace to look mildly embarrassed as he'd grown a major paunch and had lost a considerable amount of hair since she'd last seen him.

"She seemed just fine when I left for North Carolina," he declared. "She even mentioned she was looking forward to your arrival," he offered as an apparent defense.

"She *said* that?" Viv asked doubtfully. "Looked forward to my coming?"

"Yeah, yeah," he said with a wave of his hand as if batting away a fly. "So I have no idea what *stress* could cause her to just up and die. Her heart was defective, is all," an opinion he pronounced with an air that his wife's death had been a major inconvenience.

Viv could only continue to stare at him, the impact of her mother's passing starting to penetrate in small bursts of bittersweet revelation. It was impossible to think Pamela was actually *gone*. Gone, too, apparently, was the relationship her mother had had with the German colonel. Viv began to sense that the random thoughts whirling in her mind were only beginning to process what all this might mean.

To be sure, Viv was startled to hear that Pamela actually said that she was "looking forward" to her daughter's visit. Perhaps Jean-Paul had been right. Their spending some time together might have offered a chance to discover whether the two of them—after the upheaval of living through a war—could have forged a more loving mother-daughter relationship. Or at least a less tumultuous one. As with so many things the war had wrought in her life...now she'd never know.

Viv struggled against an unexpected well of emotion. It struck her that, like the orphans she and Jean-Paul had tried to help in Val d'Isère, Constance "Viv" Vivier-Clarke did not have a solitary blood relative left in the world.

Chapter 69

Pamela Bradford's New York lawyer took a seat behind the big desk in the study and addressed the daughter of his client.

"Your mother's will bequeaths to you full ownership of the apartment in Paris and a healthy financial portfolio of stocks and bonds put in trust for you by your grandparents," he announced. "This apartment at 5050 Fifth Avenue—"

Karl interrupted the attorney before he could finish his sentence, his tone bullying as if he were in a negotiation over the price of his ball bearings.

"I'm having my lawyers look into challenging my wife's gift of all the profits from the sale of this apartment going to *her,*" Karl declared with a reptilian look in Viv's direction. "I put plenty of money into this place over the years. My wife should have given it to *me*—or at least I should get *half!*"

The lawyer gazed at him steadily. "As I believe you're well aware, Mr. Bradford, this apartment has always been designated in your wife's will—revised after the death of her first husband and put into a trust—as her separate property." He glanced down at the document. "The deed designates 5050 Fifth Avenue as belonging to 'Pamela Vivier-Clarke Bradford, a married woman, sole and separate property.' Did she ever agree to put your name on the deed or write a codicil regarding this matter?"

"No, but—"

The lawyer's tone sharpened. "Well, then, I'm afraid what you have done all these years was to make generous contributions to the residence in which you've been living, rent free. Now if I can just proceed."

He then described a bequest to Sadie, the household's cook and housekeeper, that had been added recently, as well as listed the dispersal of several pieces of jewelry and furs to friends. Pamela's attorney wrapped up his remarks by addressing Karl directly.

"One final thing. Mrs. Bradford did, in fact, write an additional codicil a few weeks ago offering her daughter the choice of the art on the walls of this apartment that had come to her through inheritance. Remaining items are Mr. Bradford's to keep or sell."

Ignoring Karl's indignant snort upon hearing this, the lawyer handed Viv a large manila envelope.

"Inside you'll find the original copy of your mother's will, along with the codicils and other documents pertaining to her estate."

Without further remarks, he pulled from his jacket pocket a piece of Pamela's 5050 Fifth Avenue embossed stationery and handed it to Viv. On it was written in Pamela's distinctive penmanship:

*Combination to the Safe in the study
located behind the small, gold-framed
painting by Renoir: L22- R42- L75- R47*

The attorney gathered his own papers from the desktop, stowed them in his leather briefcase, and pushed back the desk chair, rising to his feet.

"I am very sorry for your loss, Miss Vivier-Clarke. If anything comes up regarding your mother's estate, don't hesitate to call me. My card is enclosed." To both of them he inclined his head and said, "Good-day. I'll show myself out."

Clearly, the man had dealt with Karl Bradford before and couldn't leave fast enough. Viv followed him out of the study, but after bidding him farewell once the elevator arrived, she turned toward a hallway to escape to the kitchen.

Sadie Abrams took one look at Viv's tense expression and said, "Now, you just sit down here at my counter, dearie, and I'll brew us a nice pot of tea made just the way Mrs. B always insisted."

Viv nodded her thanks and wearily sunk down on a stool. She watched while the woman, who looked to be in her sixties, made the tea strong and dark, piping hot, and served in porcelain cups with milk—no sugar.

"Thank you so much," Viv murmured, accepting her cup, wondering that her mother had been thoughtful enough to remember her house servant in her will.

"Sadie?" she asked, "Did you have any idea how ill my mother was?"

The cook-cum-housekeeper was attired in a starched black uniform and white apron. She stared down at her own cup of tea and slowly poured in a splash of milk from a small pitcher that matched the cups. Finally, she met Viv's gaze.

"I was only with her when the mister and missus stayed here in New York, of course, but I could tell her time in that prison camp had taken its toll. Not in her looks, mind you," she added. "I was amazed how well she seemed when she first came back, considering where she'd been and all." Sadie hesitated and then continued, "But she did seem very tired. Under strain, you know? Weary, I think, is a better word."

"Weary?" Viv echoed. "Do you have any idea of what?"

"She mentioned to me once that her time in Switzerland felt just like when she was in North Carolina. She mentioned that...well... she was sick and tired of having to do what other people told her to do because they were 'pig-headed men'—is how she said it."

Ah-ha! mused Viv. The Nazi colonel sounded as if he turned out to be just as dictatorial as Karl Bradford. That wasn't particularly surprising, since both were of German stock and sympathetic to Adolf Hitler.

Viv asked Sadie, "Did Mother agree that selling this apartment made sense?"

"No!" exclaimed the cook, and then seemed to think better of her vehement response. "She and Mr. B...*discussed* it for quite some time, but in the end, the decision was made to put it on the market and the packers arrived about three weeks ago. As things began to be dismantled, Mrs. B seemed... well...very upset about it all. She refused to participate in the packing and told me not to lift a finger to help. In fact, the move seemed to knock all the stuffing out of her. She certainly didn't seem to have the energy she had before."

"Mother? Not energetic? That certainly was a warning sign her health was declining."

Sadie nodded. "It surely was, but I didn't realize it, more's the pity." She took a deep drink of tea, set down her cup, and declared, "She offered me a job if I wanted to move south, but I have my grandkids in Brooklyn and all, so I thanked her and said no. It was very kind of her to remember me in her will," she added softly. "I didn't expect to be even *mentioned* in it, let alone given twenty thousand dollars."

"Well, I'm very glad you were," Viv said, taking a sip from her own cup. "You've obviously been very supportive of her, and I want you to know I'm relieved to hear she had someone in her corner."

Hearing this, Sadie reached for a linen napkin and wiped a few drops of moisture sliding down her cheeks.

Why can't I cry for her? Viv asked herself as a familiar sense of bleakness settled in her chest. This view of Pamela as a thoughtful employer seemed so out of kilter with most everything Viv had experienced concerning her mother. Maybe the life Pamela thought she might have with Wilhelm Gerhardt had turned disastrous and finally made her want something else—but whatever that was, Viv could not even imagine. The years spent living with the bullying Karl Bradford, followed by the war, and then embarking on an affair with a Nazi officer in order to keep her possessions and later, to escape incarceration from Vittel had to have been a cumulative "strain" as Sadie said. Her mother's letter requesting Viv come to New York was written in her usual push-pull fashion. It certainly hadn't revealed how truly sick she must have been. Perhaps its flippant tone was simply all Pamela knew how to express when it came to her daughter.

With an inward sigh, Viv lifted her cup and declared, "Well, here's to Pamela Bradford...and please accept my gratitude for all you did for her."

Meanwhile, her mind was beginning to revolve with plans as to how she could counter Karl's inevitable attempt to grab ownership of the penthouse at 5050 Fifth Avenue. Her mother's will *appeared* iron-clad, but Viv knew only too well that would not stop her stepfather from hiring lawyers as bullying as he was to file a long, drawn out and expensive lawsuit to make her life so miserable, he figured he'd get his way.

———◇———

From Sadie's kitchen quarters, Viv heard Karl slam out of the apartment, apparently heading for his office downtown. She slipped back into the study and took down a small, gold-framed Renoir her father had purchased in Paris as a young man just before he starting to fly for the French during the Great War.

"I'll just slip this right into my suitcase," she murmured to herself, smiling as she laid the painting on the seat of the leather desk chair. Spinning the tumblers of the safe hidden behind the painting, she followed the numbers prescribed on the slip of paper her mother's lawyer had given her and easily opened the door. There, close to the edge of the felt-lined box embedded in the wall was her British passport, still valid.

Squinting, she saw there was a pile of documents toward the back of the safe. She extended her arm and retrieved what turned out to be a collection of Bradford Ball Bearing Company invoices and tax records. Viv couldn't help but wonder why Pamela had concerned herself with documents like these. Or did Karl also know the combination, and he'd put them there?

Curious, she laid the packets of papers stacked in separate files on top of the desk. Flipping through them, she realized they were records that chronicled the company's transactions with Nazi Germany in the years leading up to the outbreak of the war in the fall of 1939, through early1945. As she delved deeper into the files, it dawned on Viv that at some point *after* her mother had returned from Switzerland, she'd decided to accumulate records that confirmed her husband's extensive dealings with a declared enemy of the United States and Britain. The safe had been installed by Viv's father, Charles, so it made sense that only Pamela might know the combination and feel secure storing important items in it.

Was this stash of incriminating documents intended to serve as a little "insurance" for her mother's later years, in case of divorce? It was more than possible that Colonel Gerhardt had turned out to be no more of a knight in shining armor than Karl had been. Viv could only wonder if Pamela had ultimately realized she'd jumped out of the proverbial frying pan and into the fire. According to Sadie, they'd not parted friends.

And then the thought struck her: Perhaps Gerhardt knew from his SS boss, Kieffer, via that rat, Lucien Barteau, that Viv had been an

SOE secret agent during the years after she'd escaped from Paris! What if Wilhelm had revealed that to her mother when the two were living together in Bern? In the end, had Pamela been both shocked and proud that her wayward daughter had finally done something *useful?*

Viv settled into the desk chair and began to read each document in turn. The more she absorbed their import, the more she understood that Pamela had finally comprehended how criminally dangerous it was that Karl had surreptitiously done business with Hitler's brutal regime. Pamela, herself, had signed numerous documents at Karl's behest and traveled to countries in which he'd sold his wares. Perhaps it had dawned on her mother that she could *also* be held to account if the U.S. or British authorities ever learned of the company's business dealings before and perhaps even during the war.

Viv could only conclude that Pamela Vivier-Clarke Bradford had made moves to protect her own hide. But maybe she'd done something else as well. In her mother's hand was written on the file marked 1939-1943: "Blood money. Save for Viv in case I die," along with a date Viv guessed was around the time of Pamela's diagnosis of a serious heart condition.

At the very bottom of the pile of the papers was a group of invoices listing thousands of items Karl shipped to Germany indexed as "Bradford Baker's Rolling Pins, a subsidiary of Bradford Industries."

"What the—?" Viv said aloud.

A diagram showed how marble-sized steel ball bearings had been inserted into hollow metal cylinders made to look like ordinary pastry rolling pins with handles on each end. They appeared innocent kitchen implements that a chef or home cook might use to roll out dough. Viv noted that hundreds of shipments of "rolling pins" were documented in these papers, every one of them passing first through Switzerland.

Viv re-assembled the files in a pile next to the Renoir and was about to close up the safe when a glint of metal caught her eyes. At the very back of the felt-lined box was a petite, lady's pearl handled revolver and a box of bullets.

Viv laughed aloud. Instead of bullets in a gun, her mother had

450 | CIJI WARE

given her a different kind of ammunition. Leaving the shells in the safe, she slipped the little weapon into the pocket of her slacks. Next, she scooped up the evidence she'd need to become as big a bully as the pugnacious Karl J. Bradford, closing the safe and spinning the tumblers.

After stowing the Bradford company papers in the hidden compartment at the bottom of her battered knapsack, Viv's next action was to call the airline office of Pan Am to secure a seat on the inaugural January1946 flight on its DC-4 from New York to London. She planned to spend the rest of her stay through the Christmas season sorting through a lifetime of her mother's possessions, as well as preparing to beat back any of Karl's attempts to steal more of her family legacy.

That same afternoon, she sent a cable to Vera Atkins asking her to join her in the New Year as her guest for lunch at London's Hotel Savoy on the day she arrived.

———◇———

Viv's inevitable confrontation with Karl wasn't nearly as difficult as she'd anticipated. Just as she'd figured he would, he met her the next morning at breakfast with a raft of lawyer's papers of his own.

"Unless you sign this agreement giving me the profits from the sale of the penthouse, my lawsuit will tie you up so I guarantee there won't be any money left in Pam's estate."

"And if you don't stop this nonsense *now* and honor my mother's wishes in that will," Viv spat back, "I will inform the Feds how you illegally did business selling vital war materials to Hitler's Nazis from 1935, all through the war."

"Prove it!" he scoffed, but his expression told her he was shocked by this threat.

"*Pastry rolling pins!*"

While he'd been out, Viv had her mother's lawyer make copies of the files Pamela had left her. She reached down next to her dining chair, grabbed the copied documents and flung them onto the highly polished breakfast table, including the schematic of how metal bakery rolling pins could disguise shipments of contraband ball bearings.

By this time, Karl's face had drained of color like a red thermometer plunging to subzero degrees.

"Where did you get these?" he demanded.

Viv shrugged. "They're only copies. The originals that Mother must have taken from your files are now in a safe at her lawyer's office."

"Why, you thieving bitch!"

Karl jumped up from his side of the table and lunged toward Viv, his fist upraised. In response, she leapt to her feet and pulled Pamela's empty, pearl-handled revolver from her pocket.

"Stay right there, you big oaf!"

Karl made a grab for the gun, but Viv's SOE weapons training kicked in. She whipped him hard across the face with the side of her fist holding the gun, smashing the bridge of his nose as the gun barrel scrapped across his forehead for good measure.

"Ow! Shit! My nose!"

I've killed a man for less than this pig's sorry efforts...

A vision of the soldier in a white mountain brigade's ski suit with blood spattered down its front rose before her eyes. Karl's own blood began to pour down his cheeks and chin and onto his shirt. Viv waved the gun in her hand.

"With or without a pistol, I seem to be an expert at breaking nasty men's noses."

Her overweight stepfather stumbled back into his dining room chair and collapsed. Viv made a show of tidying up the files and pushing them to his side of the table.

"So what's it to be, Karl? Are you going to head down to North Carolina like a good ol' Southern boy and leave me to close up this apartment and collect the money when the sale goes through, or...expose yourself to something else far less pleasant?"

"*Bitch!*" repeated Karl in a hiss. He slammed a beefy fist on the table. "You're just like your mother, you little money grubber. She only married me for the dough *I* made."

Viv nodded with a feigned show of sympathy.

"Actually, I expect that's true, but I guess—for her—blood, in the end, was thicker than water." She made a sweeping gesture around the breakfast room with its molded window frames and chintz curtains grazing the floor. "I suppose once she escaped from being interned in the war and dumped that Nazi Colonel Gerhardt after she made it into Switzerland, she just didn't want to be bullied any more. Not by the Nazis and not by *you*. I think she was plotting her escape from your vile little world, and if she wasn't going to succeed in that, she was going to be damn sure *I* did—which, frankly, is quite amazing, don't you think?"

Karl struggled to his feet. Viv pointed the empty gun barrel toward open door that led to the central foyer.

"I want you to leave here before noon today," she ordered. "And if you keep your part of the bargain and never contact me again, those papers in the attorney's office will never see the light of day, and the U.S. government or the Brits probably won't come after you."

"How do I know you won't double cross me and turn me in anyway?"

Viv smiled sweetly.

"Because I'm not *you*. These days, if I say I'm going to do something, I do it."

"Well, *that's* a change," he retorted sarcastically.

"You know," Viv nodded in agreement, "you're absolutely right. It is."

Karl's blood-spattered face reflected a combination of shock, pain, and fury.

"I see you've snatched the Renoir. I suppose you'll take *all* the good stuff?"

"No," she answered as an amazing sense of calm settled in her chest, "just the Renoir. Everything else in this place will be sent to North Carolina as you planned."

"How nice of you," he said acidly.

"Isn't it?" she agreed. "But if it makes you feel better, why not just consider the Renoir painting a bribe from *you* to *me* to keep my mouth shut—just like my Louis Vuitton cosmetic case and all your other bribes over the years?" She pointed at boxes labeled Wedgwood and Waterford stacked in the dining room. "Meanwhile, I'll make sure your crew finishes the packing and have everything in the apartment sent to you by the end of the week." She took a deep breath and added, "Now, just get the hell out."

Karl stared at her a long moment before lowering his eyes and stumbling out of the room. Viv remained where she was, the pearl-handled revolver now placed beside the plate of eggs, bacon, toast, and marmalade that Sadie had prepared for breakfast. She put her fork in the cook's creamy scrambled eggs and chewed slowly, savoring each morsel, remembering a time when a single egg or a splash of fresh milk was the most precious thing in the world. She heard Karl slamming about the apartment, first in his office and then in his bedroom. Sadie emerged from the kitchen and stood in the open doorway with a questioning expression.

"He's leaving?" she asked, amazement lacing her words.

"Yes, and as soon as he does, will you help me push that large French armoire out in the foyer up against the front door?"

"You mean like a barricade?" Sadie asked, awestruck.

"*Vive Le France!*" Viv smiled and nodded. Then she added, "Well, just until the locksmith arrives this afternoon and gives us new keys."

CHAPTER 70

The next morning, Viv sat down at the desk in the study and wrote a long letter to Catherine Thornton, her 'spy sister' from SOE training. She briefly sketched out the main events in her life during the three years since they'd met in Scotland, adding that she had much more to tell her when they met in person someday. Viv also mentioned that she'd come to New York because her mother had recently died and was in the process of determining what was next for herself.

> *Maybe an unauthorized autobiography*
> *about my adventures in the war—*
> *for your eyes only, of course, my friend...*

She ended her missive, sent to the address in D.C. that Vera Atkins had given her, adding the hope that they could meet either in the U.S. or in France.

Viv thought about writing to Jean-Paul, but thus far, she'd heard nothing from him, so she decided to leave things as they were. She'd said in Paris that she "needed time," so she really couldn't blame him for his silence. As soon as the apartment sale concluded, she planned to send an anonymous contribution to the charitable foundation he'd told her he'd set up to provide for displaced war orphans at his holiday camp in Val d'Isère.

The next days were filled with the painful process of sorting through her mother's many possessions. As the myriad tasks of closing up things in the city drew to an end, she found herself in her mother's bedroom, fingering one of Pamela's many silk scarves.

Pulling the creamy fabric through her hand, the scent of her mother's perfume still embedded in the threads, Viv wondered what it might have been like if Pamela hadn't died before she'd arrived? Would they have found any common ground, given they had each gone through the war in France, but in such vastly different ways? Had her mother been changed at all by her experience at Vittel, or would the reality have been that Viv would have faced the same old disappointments?

"Another thing I'll never know," she murmured aloud, sighing as she tossed a collection of Pamela's expensive make-up into a trash bin sitting in a corner. There had always been, first and foremost, the question of what would be best for Pamela.

Viv's hand clutched an empty perfume bottle she was about to toss when she was struck by a thought that brought her up short.

Isn't it pretty pointless to wish for a better past?

After all, she mused, the past was *past!* It couldn't be altered. No one knew that better than she did. Marcel had been killed despite her Hermès scarf. She had been spared.

"It *is* what it *was*," she declared out loud.

Acknowledging the truth of that might be the only key to truly "moving on." All she really had was what came next—and that was solely up to her. Her mother had, in the end, not utterly forgotten, slighted, or abandoned her. Her will was proof of that.

It was definitely time, Viv concluded with a new awareness that caused chills to slide down her spine, simply to accept the reality of the good, the bad, and the ugly concerning both her mother's behavior—and her own.

Viv remembered with chagrin the times when she had deeply disappointed Pamela; her failure to apply herself at the expensive boarding schools; her series of ne'er-do-well boyfriends; her flippancy, bordering on rudeness when she felt hurt or shunned; her utter lack of discipline the time she'd hired the pricey Olympic ski coach.

Oh yes, Viv could certainly claim her own fair share of bad behavior. Wasn't it time to give up being the wounded child and—as her British-born parent had been wont to say in her posh, upper-class accent—*just get on with it?*

In Pamela's role as a mother, Viv could only conclude that "push-pull" was apparently the best the woman could do. Her lapses of empathy were most likely embedded in her own childhood, Viv concluded, and for reasons that had little to do with Viv, herself. At least Pamela Bradford had made sure that Karl couldn't bully either one of them anymore. In the end, Viv realized with some surprise, just the fact that Pamela, even if as only an aside, had looked out for her daughter's welfare offered significant solace in the wake of her sudden death. Still, a question remained.

Where did Constance Vivier-Clarke—herself—truly belong?

Musing on this thorny subject, Viv entered the oak-paneled study to pick up her British passport still sitting on the desk that she'd decided to leave for the new owners. She smiled as she slipped the document into her handbag. Now that she'd inherited a serious chunk of money from her parent and grandparents, surely she could devise ways to be genuinely useful that would have totally amazed the late Pamela Bradford.

———◇———

Vera Atkins met Viv for lunch at the Savoy on the January day Pan Am's first flight across the Atlantic since the war touched down uneventfully in London.

The Deputy Director of SOE's French Section walked into the hotel restaurant dressed in her trim WAAF squadron uniform, sporting a solitary line of military ribbons worn above her left pocket. Her dark hair was stylishly short and her make-up understated, creating an image of an impeccably groomed female officer that no one of lower rank would dare disrespect.

They took their seats at a table covered with snowy linen laden with heavy silver cutlery and exchanged the customary pleasantries. Viv was anxious to ask Miss Atkins what had happened at a recent hearing that she'd been told had taken up the case of suspected double agent, Lucien Barteau.

"Acquitted," Miss Atkins reported glumly.

"You're *kidding*?" Viv replied, aghast.

"He had persuasive people testify in his favor, and there were too many who weren't present to take the witness box."

"I feel terrible that I wasn't able—" Viv began.

"No need," Miss Atkins intervened. "The most important people who couldn't be there to testify were the ones who'd been killed, thanks to his treachery."

There was no mistaking the bitterness in her tone, for Viv was aware that Colonel Buckmaster had not taken seriously the allegations leveled against a variety of suspected double agents, Barteau included.

"So the bastard just walked out of the tribunal?" Viv protested.

"Unfortunately, yes," Atkins replied, her bright red lips pursed. "Last I heard, Barteau was back flying as a stunt pilot at air shows all over Europe while trying to sign on as a commercial captain with one of the airlines just starting up again."

Viv shook her head in disgust and then moved on to the other subject that had been troubling her for months.

"How goes your effort to discover what happened to all the missing SOE agents?"

"Slow, but thus far, we've learned the fates of six more of the women."

"And?" Viv asked, hoping for good news.

"Executed as spies."

Viv felt Vera's statement like a physical blow.

One of those women easily could have been me. It could have been any one of us...

Finally she murmured, "Oh, God...how terrible."

"I'm still seeking information about another six or seven."

"Could you use my help?" Viv asked, hearing the fierceness in her tone. "I can pay my own way, if that's an issue."

Atkins appeared startled by this offer. She smiled, but shook her head 'no.'

"That's extremely kind of you, but even my solitary efforts are getting severe push-back from the higher ups in both the British and French intelligence communities. It would seem everyone would just like to forget the truth that Churchill, rather illegally, you'll recall, sent women into combat and some were killed, just like the male agents. Given this reality, I've dubbed my on-going efforts my 'private enterprise.' I'll continue to seek answers, but just not officially. It wouldn't do to make you an accomplice."

"I understand," murmured Viv, disappointed, and now determined to send a second of her anonymous donations, this one to help Vera Atkins in her noble endeavor.

Viv watched as her luncheon companion pulled out a folded piece of ornate vellum.

"Goodness!" exclaimed Viv. "What's *that* official-looking thing?"

"Something far more pleasant than speaking of Lucien Barteau or our missing colleagues, I assure you. Look what I have for you."

"What?" Viv asked curiously as she was handed the paper.

"An announcement that you're being given an MBE and two French medals...the *Croix de Guerre*—which is a French military medal recognizing those who fought with Allied forces against the Axis—and also the Legion of Honor award."

"No!" gasped Viv. "You can't be serious! The *Légion d'Honneur?*"

Miss Atkins smiled benevolently.

"Not only that, Charles de Gaulle, himself, is to bestow both French medals on a number of SOE and Free French agents in Paris next week. You literally returned to our shores in the nick of time to be celebrated for your stellar service in the war."

Viv shook her head. "I can, sort of, understand my being given the Member of the British Empire because, after all, I have British citizenship as well as American. But the *Croix?* And the *Médaille de la Légion d'Honneur?*" Moisture rose to the rim of her eyes. "My father was given the *Croix*...posthumousl*y.*"

Miss Atkins reached across the table and offered Viv's hand a maternal pat.

"I imagine if he'd lived, he would have been very proud of you, my dear. And of *course* you deserve all three! I've seen the paperwork. You were nominated for the Legion of Honor and the *Croix de Guerre* medals over a year ago by Marcel Delonge. It was noted in your file that he'd put in the forms to de Gaulle on his last clandestine trip to London. Non-French citizens like you can be honored with such military decorations, although only French citizens can be actual members of the Legion."

Viv's throat was tight with unshed tears. She almost felt Marcel's physical presence. With it came memories of the ways in which he had always goaded and challenged her, while in the end, loved her for who she was—flaws and all. Even so, she felt a few twinges of guilt for all her negative feelings about the "Almighty de Gaulle" wanting to take total credit for freeing France. Maybe, like her mother, the General had gained a little humility as a result of the war and begun to recognize the efforts of others.

My mother and Charles de Gaulle. Two peas in a pod?

Viv was laughing to herself when Miss Atkins handed her another sheet of instructions detailing where the ceremony was to be held—and what to wear.

"*You* should be awarded the medals," Viv said to her luncheon companion.

Vera Atkins, whom Viv now considered a friend, smiled faintly.

"Perhaps one day I'll be in the lists," replied the older woman. "But I fought the war from my desk in London. You were in the thick of it in France." Looking down at her menu as if the subject of her receiving accolades was of no import, she asked, "Now, what do you think would be lovely for an entrée?"

While Viv perused the menu, she found herself wondering if there still could be a life for her in Paris. Doing *what*, however, was the question.

CHAPTER 71

February 1946

Viv was thankful she'd brought something decent to wear at such an august occasion when she'd packed her suitcase in New York. As the taxi sped along the Quai Anatole-France toward the Palace of the Legion of Honor, she smoothed the skirt and adjusted the woolen jacket of her forest green suit. The vibrant tone of her ensemble set off the dark red of her hair quite attractively, even if she did say it herself. She smiled over the driver's shoulder at her reflection in his rearview mirror, aware of the sensation beneath her right heel of Marcel's parachute patch under the lining of her shoe.

From her handbag, she pulled out the gold compact that Vera Atkins had given her the night Viv had flown into France in the Lysander, and checked her make-up. Snapping it shut, she studied the engraving on its lid: *À ma chérie Violette... Maman.* Viv thought of her own mother in her chic Chanel suits and gold jewelry and smiled at the thought of her reaction if she could see her daughter on this amazing day.

The cab glided to a halt in front of the Palace's grand arched entrance flanked by pale stone colonnades on both sides. As Viv shut the vehicle's door, she spotted small clusters of people walking through the central courtyard that led to the entrance of the Grand Chancellors' stateroom—the location she'd been informed was to be the site of the awards ceremony scheduled to start in the next half hour.

She hurried to catch up with the group when the tallest man

among them let the others go ahead and turned around to face her, waiting for her to reach his side.

"Viv!" he exclaimed. "Or should I say, '*Bonjour Mademoiselle* Violette Charbonnet?'"

"Fingers!" she exclaimed and threw her arms around her former comrade.

"I *thought* I saw a stunning red-headed woman I once knew emerge from that taxi! No one thought you were even in Europe, let alone would be in Paris for this shindig."

"You're getting one of these things, too?" she marveled happily.

"We're the only two Americans I know of this time around," he said, enveloping her in another bear hug, "but I expect there'll be plenty of Brits and Frogs getting the top honors today."

"Frogs? Now, Fingers," Viv scolded him with a grin, "we're in high clover these days. We Yanks both better behave." She glanced over at the building's elegant front entrance. "C'mon, we're going to be late!"

In all Viv's years in Paris, she had never been inside the Legion's Grand Chancellors' Hall. Its ornate cream and gilded domed ceiling and Wedgwood blue and white walls hung with large, gilt-framed portraits of Worthies impressed upon her that this was no mere "shindig." The invited guests were decked out in their finest, and a phalanx of French press and photographers lined a far wall. The American Ambassador to France, Jefferson Caffery, stood in a circle of his aides. Viv could only stare in bone-tingling amazement at a familiar figure with thick, black-rimmed glasses too large for his thin, pinched face. None other than her nemesis, Roger Gianakos, was hovering next to the ambassador, the underling appearing obsequious and anxious by turns.

Won't old Roger be aghast to watch me receive my medals today, and this time he can't screw it up for me! thought Viv, feeling a bubble of laughter rise in her chest.

Meanwhile, the voices of the ceremony attendees speaking in hushed, respectful tones echoed among the several knots of people clustered around the room. Viv was about to launch into the story for Fingers of ultimately outfoxing the creep who'd put the kibosh on her working for Allen Dulles as a secret agent when she felt a tap on her shoulder.

"I was so happy and pleased for you when I saw your name on the list."

Viv whirled on her brand-new high heels just as Fingers hailed someone he knew and left her side.

"Jean-Paul!" she exclaimed, shocked to see him and excited, despite mildly injured feelings that he'd never gotten in touch in all these months. Then she reminded herself once again that had been *her* call. She kissed him on both cheeks, European style. "No one told me you'd be here! I've only just arrived in Paris this morning."

He thrust the event's program into her hands.

"Then that must be why you didn't see my name as a recipient. I cabled you my congratulations when I heard you were being honored—but I take it you never received it?" He held her gaze. "I was…a little disappointed when I didn't hear back from you."

Viv put her hands on her hips. "Well, let's lay it all out here. Because I hadn't heard from you at *all*, I've acted like a stupid child and never got in touch. After all, I was the one who left France." For some reason, it felt good just to admit she'd been the cause of their breach in communication. She could tell immediately that Jean-Paul had felt he'd suffered a slight. "But just so you know, I never received your cable. I must have left New York by then, I suppose. I would have been thrilled to hear from you."

"I didn't contact you before as you made it rather clear that you were…well… you were struggling like so many of us with the loss of people you cared deeply about." After a pause, he added pointedly, "And still mourning the man you'd loved."

Viv inhaled a deep breath and confirmed Jean-Paul's evaluation of her emotional state following the liberation of Paris.

"You're right. I *was* in mourning," she replied. "And complicating things even more, my mother died of heart failure last year before I could reach New York, so I've been dealing with the aftermath."

Jean-Paul's expression was one of immediate contrition. He sought her hands, tightly clasping them both in his.

"Oh, Viv, I am so sorry. No wonder I didn't hear from you. I think my feelings and my pride were hurt when you left France.

You'd mentioned her heart condition. I should have reached out long before now, but my life soon became complicated as well."

He let go of her hands and allowed his own to drop by his sides. Viv wondered if he were about to tell her he'd fallen madly in love. Perhaps he was even married by now.

"Complicated?" she repeated, willing her heart to stop thumping in her chest.

"Things in our village were in a terrible state after the war ended," he said. "Those first months I was back, it was almost impossible to accomplish any of the efforts I'd planned to help displaced orphans. I barely could afford to reopen my doctor's practice."

"And now?" Viv asked, her breath caught in her throat.

"The most miraculous thing happened recently," he said, a broad smile lighting up his handsome face. "An anonymous donor recently gave us a generous bequest that is allowing us to launch our first summer program in a few months!"

Jean-Paul's voice had taken on the warm, enthusiastic timbre of times past. Viv couldn't help beaming at the knowledge that her gift had made such a difference.

"That's truly wonderful!" she exclaimed. "And congratulations to you, too! Whatever medals they're giving you today, Jean-Paul, are hugely deserved."

"That's what I said to *you* in the cable I sent," he replied, holding her gaze. "Look, Viv, I can't tell you how wonderful it is to see you. I—" He glanced to one side as if assessing whether he could say what he'd held back expressing for months. "I missed you. Very much."

Viv was astounded to realize in that moment how much she'd missed *him*.

"It was the same for me," she acknowledged, "and I could only understand how much I missed you after I'd come to terms with the boulders that stood in my way."

"Well, I *more* than just missed you," he whispered hoarsely. "I told you once before: I *love* you, dammit...boulders and all! Ever since I put that cast on your leg, I've wanted us to make a life together, but only if you could love me half as much as you cared for Marcel."

Just then, Dominique Morand and Toquette Jackson rushed up to greet Viv. Behind them stood Marian Moraski Bardet, the Jewish teen Viv had escorted down the mountain and served as her *passeur* for her escape to Switzerland.

"You're here!" Dominique exclaimed, but Marian was the first to throw her arms around Viv, prompting tears mixed with joyful laughter at their unexpected reunion.

"I'm to help Jean-Paul with the kids at our summer camp," Marian said proudly.

Meanwhile, Dominique gave her brother the scolding look of a big sister and declared, "Jean-Paul, I hope you've told Viv how you were good for absolutely *nothing* when she went back to America." Addressing them both, she added, "Will you two just please sort yourselves out and get on with it?"

Get on with it...

Shades of Pamela Bradford! Just get on with it. Wasn't that what Jean-Paul and all who had survived this terrible war must do, including Viv herself?

Toquette then greeted Viv with more subdued pecks on each cheek. "I came to cheer on Jean-Paul, and I am so delighted I can do the same for you, my dear." She turned to Dominique. "Now let's let these two catch up while we have a glass of champagne."

Marian and the two older women moved off as Viv reached out for Jean-Paul's hand. She could see that they both would have to rebuild from the wreckage of war and try to make life good again for themselves—and with the same spirit of people like Toquette Jackson who had suffered even more than they had.

Just then, an announcement cut through the burble of voices echoing throughout the elegant chamber. A man taller, even, than Marcel and Jean-Paul strode into the room in full military regalia, his dress uniform embellished with a red satin sash worn from shoulder to waist, along with a chest full of medals that dazzled the eye.

The Almighty Charles de Gaulle had entered the Grand Chancellors' Hall and the awards ceremony was about to begin.

EPILOGUE

December 29, 1946

"Is this the spot where you threatened the mountain troops with a grenade?"

Jean-Paul halted with his ski tips extending a few inches beyond the ridge that overlooked the village of Val d'Isère nestled in the valley below. Gamboling at his side was his enormous Swiss Mountain Dog spraying flurries in all directions.

"Good boy, Alphonse," he murmured, patting the furry beast on its broad head.

Viv's skis pulled up less than a foot from the only doctor within twenty miles practicing medicine in these towering, snow-covered Alps. She thrust her ski poles into the side of the hill and inhaled deeply, memories of one of the most frightening moments in the war coming back with a rush.

"In fact," she replied, pointing at Jean-Paul's skis, "you're practically standing where I was on this day *exactly* three years ago."

She pointed downhill. This sunny winter afternoon, the sky directly overhead was as blue as the Mediterranean with only a few clouds clustered around the soaring peaks. The glare reflecting on the slopes was almost blinding. How different from the biting cold and billowing mists in the lower valley that other day in late December in 1943 when she'd confronted two members of a German mountain division on this very trail.

"Did you spot them first?" he asked.

"I *heard* them, first. They were hiking uphill carrying their skis and their rifles on their shoulders," Viv related. "We all were wearing army-issue white camouflage ski suits, which was a dead give-away the three of us were combatants—on opposite sides."

"Two against one, and they had long guns, just like the commendation de Gaulle read at the awards ceremony." Jean-Paul's voice was full of admiration. "But you outfoxed them, as you're always saying, and got away with no one killed."

"*And* I broke my leg on the downhill run, skiing toward your safe house as if the devil were chasing me," she reminded him with a rueful smile.

Jean-Paul's skis were near enough Viv's to allow him to put his arm around her shoulders and kiss her soundly. Alphonse whined at their feet.

"And Alf saved you," he murmured against her cool lips.

"You both saved me, and in more ways than you'll ever know."

It had been nearly a year since the day they'd both been given medals by Charles de Gaulle at the Legion of Honor in Paris. By the end of the ceremony, Viv had decided to return to Val d'Isère with Jean-Paul and his sister, Dominique.

At first, she and the village's sole physician agreed to proceed cautiously regarding their relationship. Viv had had a difficult time believing that J-P, as she'd come to call him, could completely accept that a part of her would always love Marcel.

On his side, Jean-Paul insisted he understood that well, as he disclosed one evening in front of their roaring fire that he'd once cared for a young woman who had died in an avalanche his first year at the resort.

"You never told me that!" protested Viv.

"You never asked if I'd loved and lost someone. Only if I'd been married. The shock of knowing you'll never see the person again lasts a long time…maybe forever."

Viv recalled the morning a few days later when he'd nuzzled the base of her neck and declared, "My question for you today, my darling Viv, is—do you have room in that defended heart of yours for the love of *two* men? Especially the one in your bed?"

Viv had reached for him, pulling him close, Alphonse curled up at the foot of their four-poster.

"I do...now," she'd whispered against his ear. "And I will say that in front of the magistrate in the village, or the priest in church—if only you will ask me."

They were married on a summer's day, surrounded by a gaggle of children who had been living in a new chalet the Val d'Isère Foundation had built nearby that featured a floor for young girls under sixteen, as well as another chalet nearby for the boys. Viv had ultimately revealed to Jean-Paul that she had been the original anonymous donor to his Foundation. She had also sold her apartment on Avenue Kléber in Paris and put eighty percent of the profits from that sale into the Val d'Isère Trust for Displaced Children.

Jean-Paul had initially protested that he was beginning to feel like a "kept man."

Viv replied somberly, "You forget. I was 'kept' for years by the profits from Karl Bradford's damn ball bearings that he sold to Hitler's war machine. Don't you agree it's only justice that blood money that prolonged the war in your and my father's beloved Alsace should end up helping Jewish orphans?"

Jean-Paul shook his head helplessly.

"I'm no match for such Anglo-Saxon logic. Come here, *mon amour...*"

Jean-Paul used the funds to hire several teachers in the village to provide classroom studies for the orphaned children until they could be placed in families throughout Western Europe and in America.

"I was never much of a student," Viv had been quick to disclose. "I'll leave the academics to people like you who know what you're doing. Let me run the ski school for these kids and the summer camp for them from June through August." She laughed, adding, "And when all the children have found homes in a couple of years, we can convert the Foundation funds into a non-profit partnership with your childhood friends and fellow skiers from Alsace and create the best damn summer resort and winter ski school in France that caters to young families—and not just wealthy, entitled little brats like I was!"

Balanced on her skis this sparkling late December day, Jean-Paul's new bride roused herself from her reverie. She pointed to a lower cornice where sudden clouds had begun to boil up from below and the mists surrounding the peaks had grown dark.

"It looks like the weather's changing," noted Jean-Paul.

"Maybe a winter storm brewing?" Viv suggested.

"Race you downhill," he challenged, and pushed off before she could grab her ski poles that were still dug into the side of the hill.

Above her, Viv heard the sounds of a lone skier schussing down a nearby trail, most likely anxious to outrun the weather. She turned and caught sight of a tall figure wearing a dark beret. Her breath caught as memories of Marcel flooded her thoughts.

"Hello, my love," she whispered to the wind, amazed to think it would soon be 1947. She was achingly aware of Marcel's embroidered parachute patch under the lining of her right ski boot, its permanent resting place now.

Alphonse, not having moved a canine muscle, emitted a long, pitiful moan, urging Viv to follow his master. "Good boy," she murmured absently, scratching his velvet ear.

Viv turned to look just as Jean-Paul skillfully paralleled his skis along a bend in the downhill trail. As the mountain's stillness settled over her again, it came to her that the single regret she harbored was that she couldn't tell Marcel she had survived Fresnes Prison and was safe at last. In the back of her mind, she fretted that she'd had no signs of pregnancy in the year she and Jean-Paul had been together. She worried that this might be due to the severe case of mumps she'd had when she and Marcel had climbed the Pyrenees fleeing the Nazi net. Jean-Paul had gently agreed that was a possibility.

Mumps might explain it, chérie, but at least you have plenty of children to care for...

His words had left her musing how strange and mysterious life could be.

Viv reached for her ski poles and prepared to take off down the hill, thinking that even her late mother might admit her daughter could be considered doing something "useful," thanks to her new life with Dr. Jean-Paul Morand. For certain, Viv thought, her father would have been proud of her.

And if she could have, Viv would have told Marcel that she finally had room in her heart to love again.

But perhaps he knew?

AUTHOR'S NOTE

Weaving fact and fiction is a tricky business and at times requires a kind of 3-D thinking to blend a story that is, at its essence, the invention of the author's imagination, with known historical facts and physical documents.

Novels like *A Spy Above the Clouds*, set in a specific time period such as World War II, not only must be tethered to historical records and first-hand accounts, but often involve historical figures that actually walked upon the earth. As a consequence, there exists a heavy weight that sits on an author's shoulders during this fact/fiction process of creating a wholly imagined story. A single mistake of fact or an important omission can prompt World War II buffs, especially, to throw the book across the room in disgust. As a result, I've made it my guiding principle in every work of historical fiction I've written never to include something I *know* to be untrue. In realms where it's impossible to pin down all the facts, I employ intelligent supposition, *based* on the facts that are known.

However, in the telling of an entertaining tale, especially in the military thriller genre, in a very few occasions it becomes necessary to faintly blur a timeline (as with which month in 1942 Allen Dulles set up his spy shop in Bern. I have him arriving a few months early). I also felt free to put words in an historical character's mouth (based on the record, of course) *as long as* what I created on the page didn't distort the figure's character or substantially change the meaning or general timing of an event or the actions of participants in it.

As with *Landing by Moonlight* (Book 1 of my American Spy Sisters series), I was required to grapple with these same issues of fact-versus-fiction in this second book—a fictional account based on the life of one of the few American women who joined the British intelligence services in the 1940s.

So, with the caveat that *A Spy Above the Clouds* is, indeed, a work of *fiction*, and with appreciation for the Herculean achievements of professional historians and writers of well-researched nonfiction that informed my narrative, I have tried to navigate this literary and ethical minefield by adhering to those guidelines mentioned above. If there are mistakes, they're my own.

I would probably never have been pulled from the "comfort zone" of the 18th century historical settings of many of my previous novels and *into* the 20th century if not for several factors that collided in a most serendipitous fashion.

For some thirty years, I have been visiting Talloires, a small alpine village on the banks of Lake Annecy in France's Haute-Savoie where my husband, Tony Cook, was once a twelve-year-old summer camper. The MacJannet camp was founded in 1925 on the banks of Lake Annecy by an amazing couple, Donald and Charlotte MacJannet. He was an American schoolmaster teaching in France after WW I; she, his German-born wife whose anti-Nazi sentiments estranged her from her family. After WW II, they provided temporary refuge for war orphans there. Young Americans continued to come for a summer of learning French, swimming, hiking the Alps, and "learning by doing" in a culture dedicated to fostering world understanding. After the deaths of the MacJannets, the MacJannet Foundation was established to support these goals, and does to this day.

For as long as we've been going to Lake Annecy to attend the annual MacJannet Foundation board meeting, we've passed by statues and plaques to which, I'm embarrassed to say, I paid little attention. That is, until one of our French friends, Claire Majola LeBlond from the town of Annecy at the head of the lake, insisted one year that I would find the local French Resistance museum "*très intéressant.*" She had become aware over the years of our friendship that much of my writing has been based on the question, "What were the *women* doing?" in the telling of human history.

The pocket museum Claire recommended visiting was situated deep in a valley surrounded by alpine mountain peaks on one side and the towering Plateau des Glières on the other. The building housing the impressively named *Departmental Museum of the Resistance in Haute-Savoie* looked more like a miniature ski chalet than a repository of images and information that would spark my writing life for the next five years!

Tacked casually onto the rough, wooden walls were photos of women as well as men who, as secret agents, parachuted into France to help local Resistance fighters prepare for the hoped-for Allied invasions that eventually arrived. Outside the peak-roofed building were rows of pristinely kept graves marking the final resting place of 129 local *Glières Maquisards* killed at the battle of the Plateau des Glières in late March of 1944. Nearly a thousand of these local Resistance fighters were outnumbered by 4000 German troops, and many were annihilated as the *Luftwaffe* picked them off "like sitting ducks" in the open field fourteen months before WWII finally ended in Europe.

As I dug deeper into these subjects, I discovered that a handful of American women were inserted into France among some 60 female agents recruited by the SOE (Britain's Special Operations Executive) intelligence agency, a pet project of Prime Minister Winston Churchill. A few of these American "Churchill's Angels," as they came to be known, enlisted in the organization *prior* to the United States joining the European war. *Why* was my question—and thus was born the American Spy Sisters Series.

In novels based on historical events, readers are always curious to know "What is real? What's made up?" In *A Spy Above the Clouds,* the plot and characters are drawn from many of the heroic and tragic events in the lives of real-life Allied secret agents. "Viv's" beginnings are based on the wartime adventures of Devereaux Rochester Reynolds, an American SOE secret agent hailing from the U.S. Eastern seaboard but raised for much of her life in Europe. Her autobiography, *Full Moon to France,* reads like a fast-paced novel itself, centering on, as the book jacket says, "a pampered American girl—rich, headstrong, idle…caught in Europe at the outbreak of World War II."

"Dev," as she preferred to be called, became my prototype for "Viv." In Dev's book, published in 1977 thirty years after WW II (but still under the restrictions of Britain's Official Secrets Act) she describes how she fell in love with a fellow agent (which happened often); was arrested and incarcerated by the Gestapo; and managed to bluff her way to freedom from the notorious Fresnes Prison outside Paris. She supervised and participated in explosive sabotage missions and memorized long messages that she delivered to partisans all over the Alps. What especially riveted me was how she was transformed from a devil-may-care spoiled brat into a devoted, brave, and daring clandestine underground fighter determined to free France from its oppressors.

That she was also a superb and apparently fearless skier and the only female Allied secret agent "courier-on-skis" I had ever encountered in my research—and yet she had a morbid fear of parachuting into space—ultimately convinced me there was a reason to write a second novel about an American woman secret agent in WW II. Dev's story became my jumping-off spot for creating "Constance 'Viv' Vivier-Clarke's" adventures behind enemy lines in occupied France. Viv's tale developed into a wonderfully absorbing project during the Covid Year of 2020 that found me inventing a "Yank" who embodied both a complicated family history—as did the real-life Dev—and the heroic attributes of all the women who risked their lives in Churchill's "secret war."

To be clear, Viv and the other fictional characters in the novel are *composites*. In other words, they are imagined figures based on the historical records of a *variety* of real-life women and men who, at great personal peril, served on the Allied side.

Until I delved into the specifics of these agents' day-to-day lives, I had no idea, for instance, that the train station in Annecy that my husband and I have passed through countless times over the years was adjacent to the scene where several locomotives were blown up in January of 1944. On a pre-Covid trip to that same town, my husband and I stumbled upon a modest memorial located a hundred or so yards from the rebuilt station. A plaque testified to the fact that the former rail yard was attacked, thanks to explosives prepared and brought to the scene by local Resistance fighters. In Devereaux Rochester's autobiography, she explains *she* was the one who led that mission! That marked the day I realized that I was totally committed to the effort that became *A Spy Above the Clouds*.

The character of Viv's great love, Marcel Delonge, was created from the records that exist of General de Gaulle's Free French deputies who were charged with preparing various—and extremely fractious—local Resistance groups in France to rise up and fight before and during the 1944 Allied invasions in Normandy and the South of France. In France, we followed in the footsteps of heroic Jean Moulin, de Gaulle's deputy, who was eventually arrested, tortured by the Nazis, and died of his injuries.

The character of Dr. Jean-Paul Morand, on the other hand, was rooted in research that has come to light fairly recently. A friend sent me a clipping in 2019 about a "ski doctor" named Frédérick Pétri in the alpine resort of Val d'Isère. The brave physician hid Jews in his attic despite a Gestapo headquarters located directly across the street from his clinic. However, events surrounding the two men whom our fictional heroine loved are a total creation of *my* imagination, based on accounts of relationships that developed among secret agents fighting the Nazi terror while they also battled merely to survive.

The nefarious double agent, "Lucien Barteau," is partly based on the mysterious machinations of Henri Déricourt, a French air-circus pilot commissioned in the RAF. The SOE/French Section brass gave Déricourt the sensitive position of receiving and dispatching British aircraft that inserted secret agents during the German occupation of France. Evidence later proved he was in direct communication with German intelligence agents, and after the war, he was accused of treason. Déricourt was acquitted due to confusing and conflicting testimony and—perhaps—"friends in high places." For more on this enigmatic figure, read Jean Overton Fuller's *Déricourt: The Chequered Spy.*

In my selected bibliography, I list additional nonfiction works that helped inform the novel's entire cast of fictional and historical characters, the setting and time period, as well as daring operations successfully accomplished by these silent warriors.

As with *Landing by Moonlight*, I found that my twenty-three years as a print and broadcast journalist uniquely equipped me with a useful skill set to chase a story that occurred some seven-plus decades ago. Both heroines "Catherine" (in Book 1) and "Viv" (in Book 2) were sent to SOE's "Spy School." Imagine my excitement when Netflix released the five-part series "Churchill's Secret Agents: The New Recruits" in 2018 that accurately depicts their training in the UK and is vastly entertaining to watch.

My husband, a former financial journalist, and I spent an entire summer tracking down locations where many dramatic moments involving the French Resistance took place. One lovely summer's day, we and our friends Sandraline Cederwall and Steve Barrager tramped across the broad expanse of the Plateau des Glières, imagining as we walked through the knee-high grass what it must have been like to have the German Air Force raining down hell from the crystalline skies above our heads.

We also learned that St. Eustache, a tiny village that we'd often driven by on the west side of Lake Annecy, was the tragic spot where the Nazis executed innocent inhabitants and deported the surviving men in reprisal for Resistance operations in the area. That same day, we found the boarded-up hotel in nearby St. Jorioz where Peter Churchill and Odette Samson were arrested due to a double agent's perfidy.

In Paris, my research included a private tour, "The Nazi-occupied City of Light," with close attention given to Number 84 Avenue Foch, where Hans Josef Kieffer ruled over life and death in a beautiful *Beaux Arts* building that held terrible secrets of brutal torture behind its elegant walls. Prisons at Fresnes and in Annecy were also chilling fortresses to see. More enjoyable was the third-floor flat on rue des Canettes—the description of which is based on one we rented for a week, courtesy of Airbnb.

As Bogart said to Bergman in the classic film *Casablanca,* not only will my husband and I "always have Paris," we will forever have and love Lake Annecy and the Haute-Savoie—and remember those who gave their lives to regain France's freedom.

And now, Dear Reader, so will you.

Ciji Ware
Sausalito, California

ACKNOWLEDGEMENTS

None of the European research activities that underpin *A Spy Above the Clouds* would have been possible without the encouragement, moral support, and assistance of many friends and acquaintances on and beyond America's shores.

In London, among various research forays concerning Britain's Special Operations Executive, my husband, Tony Cook, and I spent a day in Churchill's War Rooms beneath the city's streets, located the former SOE headquarters on Baker Street, and discovered the apartment building on Orchard Court where secret agent recruits were vetted—all due to the expert guidance and warm hospitality of Susanna Jennens, Bill and Fiona Orde, and Tony's cousin, Christopher Cousins—all British friends of longstanding.

My warmest thanks for information and confirmation regarding all things French to Sylvie Toinard, Claire Majola LeBlond and Jacques LeBlond, Jean-Marie and Pauline Hervé, Winship Cook, Leslie and Geoffrey de Galbert, Gabrielle Goldstein, Steve Barrager, Sandraline Cederwall, and the various proprietors over the years of the Hotel Beau Site in the lakeside village of Talloires.

I am grateful, too, for the hospitality in past summers of Stéphane and Carole Deloulme in our most loved Talloires. Their wonderful home became a base of operations several years in a row as I followed the trails of the American women secret agents battling to stay alive during a war raging across France. We hope to return *bientôt*!

In the U.S., I am indebted to my two "Plotholes" partners (Yes, that's our critique group), novelists Kimberly Cates and Cynthia Wright who, as they always have, provided encouragement, important editorial insights, and friendship during drafts of this work.

Huge thanks must also go to my beta readers Steve Barrager, Angie Espich Bearden, Sandraline Cederwall, novelist Diana Dempsey, Naomi Fliflet, and Maria Paterno. Cheryl Popp, owner of Sausalito Books by the Bay, read *two* versions of this novel and offered crucial feedback on both. Various members of the Sausalito Women's Club (you know who you are!), along with my fellow hillside dog walkers played supportive roles in every novel I've written since moving to Sausalito in 2001—including this one—so blessings on your heads!

As with Book 1 - *Landing by Moonlight* in my American Spy Sisters Series, special kudos for Book 2 - *A Spy Above the Clouds* go to the Lion's Paw Publishing production team. I extend heartfelt appreciation to Peter O'Conner at BespokeBookCovers.com for the second stunning cover design for the series. Deepest thanks, also, to interior book designer/formatter Amy Atwell for her excellent work, Tamara Kaupp for her top-notch proofreading skills, and to Paul Hirst, keeper of my cijiware.com. Meetings of BAIPA (the Bay Area Independent Publishers Association) were enhanced by ride sharing and shop-talking with travel-writer, Janet Faulkner Chapman,

I'm happy to report that Viscount Dashwood, a.k.a. "Dash," (named in honor of Queen Victoria's beloved Cavalier King Charles Spaniel), is a puppy that has immediately taken to snoozing companionably beneath my desk just like my other two late, great Cavaliers. His Lordship has become the perfect writer's pal, and each day of this Covid Year I was—and continue to be—profoundly grateful for his company.

Hank, our king-sized neighborhood Swiss Mountain Dog, greeted then-tiny Dash with a wildly wagging tail on the day he was hand-delivered to us from Indiana by breeder Rhona Carroll. Hank became "Alphonse," Viv's rescuing angel when she broke her leg skiing in Val d'Isère. My thanks to this big boy's human companions, Russ Zink and Sean Calloway, for letting me borrow their canine's loving and loyal personality.

And finally—as always—eternal gratitude is due Tony Cook, my talented and understanding husband of 45 years and my partner in virtually everything I do. This is most especially true regarding this project, having introduced me to the Haute-Savoie early in our marriage and since then, provided handholding, cheerleading, and perceptive editorial advice over three decades of writing novels. *Merci, merci, merci, mon amour.*

Ciji Ware
Sausalito, California

Research photos on Pinterest.com: https://pin.it/6UJJSGX
Website: www.cijiware.com
Facebook: www.facebook.com/cijiwarenovelist

PARTIAL BIBLIOGRAPHY & RESEARCH PHOTOS

For more information on WWII and the real lives that inspired the characters and settings of this novel, here is a partial bibliography of my research.

Devereaux Rochester, *Full Moon to France*

Richard Heslop, *Xavier: A British Secret Agent with the French Resistance*

Hal Vaughan, *Doctor to the Resistance: The heroic true story of an American surgeon and his family in occupied Paris*

Charles Glass, *The American Hospital of Paris: Brave Volunteers & Heroes of the Resistance*

Charles Glass, *Americans in Paris: Life and Death Under Nazi Occupation*

Alan Riding, *And the Show Went On: Cultural Life in Nazi-Occupied Paris*

Alex Kershaw, *Avenue of Spies: The true story of terror, espionage, and one American family's heroic resistance in Nazi-occupied Paris*

Scott Miller, *Agent 110: An American Spymaster and the German Resistance in WWII*

David Talbot, *The Devil's Chessboard: Allen Dulles, the CIA, and the Rise of America's Secret Government*

Hugh Verity, *We Landed by Moonlight: Secret RAF landings in France 1940-1944*

Mary S. Lovell, *Cast No Shadow* [Betty Pack a.k.a. "Cynthia"]

Howard Blum, *The Last Goodnight: A World War II Story of Espionage, Adventure, and Betrayal,* [Betty Pack a.k.a. "Cynthia"]

H. Montgomery Hyde, *Cynthia, The Amazing, True Story of the Seductive American Who Spied for the Allies in World War II* [Betty Pack a.k.a. "Cynthia"]

Sarah Helm, *A Life in Secrets: The Story of Vera Atkins and the Lost Agents of SOE*

Sarah Helm, *Ravensbrück: Life and Death in Hitler's Concentration Camp for Women*

Jerrard Tickell, *Odette: The Story of a British Agent,* [Odette Samson Churchill a.k.a. "Lise"]

Larry Loftis, *Code Name: Lise, The True Story of the Woman Who Became WWII's Most Highly Decorated Spy* [Odette Samson Churchill]

Peter Churchill, *Duel of Wits*

Sonia Purnell, *A Woman of No Importance: The story of the American Spy Who Helped Win World War* II [Virginia Hall a.k.a. "Marie"]

Judith L. Pearson, *The Wolves at the Door: The True Story of America's Greatest Female Spy,* [Virginia Hall a.k.a. "Marie"]

Marcus Binney, *The Women Who Lived for Danger: Behind Enemy Lines During WW II*

Kathryn J. Atwood, *Women Heroes of World War II: 26 Stories of Espionage, Sabotage, Resistance, and Rescue*

Elizabeth P. McIntosh, *Women of the OSS - Sisterhood of Spies*

Gordon Thomas & Greg Lewis, *Shadow Warriors of World War II: The Daring Women of the OSS and SOE*

Major Robert Bourne-Paterson, *SOE in France 1941-1945*

Giles Milton, *Churchill's Ministry of Ungentlemanly Warfare*

Bernard O'Conner, *Churchill's Angels*

Maurice Buckmaster, *They Fought Alone, The True Story of SOE Agents in Wartime France*

Jean Overton Fuller, *Déricourt: The Chequered Spy*

Ray Jenkins, *A Pacifist at War* [Francis Cammaerts, a.k.a. "Roger"]

George G. Kundahl, *Riviera at War: World War II on the Côte d'Azur*

Robert Kanigel, *High Season in Nice*

Andrew Stewart, Ed., *Operation Dragoon: The Invasion of the South of France, 15 August 1944*

Jean-Louis Perquin, *Clandestine Parachute and Pick-Up Operations, Vol. 1*

Sarah Kaminsky, *Aldolfo Kaminsky: A Forger's Life*

Guy Sanglerat, *A Student and Resistance Fighter in the French Alps During World War II,* translated by Gayle A. Levy

Michele German, *La Libération de la Haute-Savoie, 70e anniversaire: 1944-2014*

Véronique Olivares Salou & Michel Reynaud, *Le Roman des Glières: La Résistance Des Républicains Espagnols au Plateau des Glières 1941-1944*

ABOUT THE AUTHOR

Ciji Ware is a *New York Times* and *USA Today* bestselling author of thirteen works of historical and contemporary fiction and two of nonfiction. Among many accolades, she was bestowed the Dorothy Parker Award of Excellence for Fiction and short-listed for the 2012 Willa [Cather] Literary Award for Historical Fiction. For her novels set in Scotland she was granted the designation of FSA-Scot (Fellow of the Society of Antiquaries of Scotland), an honor she cherishes. A graduate of Harvard University in History and recipient of its Alumni Award, she was the first woman graduate of the University to serve as President of the Harvard Alumni Association, Worldwide. Ware is an Emmy-award winning television producer, a DuPont awardee for investigative journalism, and an American Bar Association winner of a Silver Gavel for her magazine work. For eighteen years, she was a broadcaster and commentator for KABC Radio/TV in Los Angeles and now lives in the San Francisco Bay Area.

www.cijiware.com

More World War II intrigue and danger in
AMERICAN SPY SISTERS

And look for her popular FOUR SEASONS QUARTET books, available in ebook and print at your favorite online book retailer.